I0639546

Lottie's Lot

Nancy O'Connor

La Mariposa Press

Nancy O'Connor

La Mariposa Press
1990 E Campbell Terrace
Tucson, Arizona 85718-5952
www.lamariposapress.com

Cover designed by Zorodesigns.com

Manufactured in the United States of America

First Trade Edition July 2014

10- 9- 8- 7- 6- 5- 4- 3- 2- 1

ISBN 97809830642-1-3

4

"Lottie's Lot is a thorough and engaging exploration of a family matriarch during a pivotal time in women's history. The changing role of women is first revealed when a young girl defies her father and follows her heart to marry the man she loves. She would later defy social convention in a small prairie town to defend her daughter's reputation. Despite having to struggle constantly with poverty, terrible family tragedies, and being frequently uprooted, Lottie's lot in life turns her into an admirable survivor who never loses her resolve to support and defend her large family.

Nancy Buchannan, Librarian

"Lottie's Lot is an emotionally jarring--page turning drama portraying the hard facts of child bearing and rearing as it relates to family challenges and the role of women's rights or lack of them, in the late 1800's and through American History to date.
This journey would be a good choice for reading by modern young women to educate themselves in a person to person understanding of the reality of how good life is today in this country. Lottie life is a perfect example of "tragedy and hope" for five generations of one family's women, their suffering, grieving, dreams, hopes and the nightmares of real life. I personally feel enriched by this knowledge. It's an inspiring read.

Diana Rey-McGrew

The author has done extensive research unraveling the details of her family and in particular, the life of her grandmother, Lottie, and has added dialog and details to make this a fascinating and engrossing work of historical fiction. Lottie's Lot is not just the story of one American woman and her family; it is the story of a typical American family through the decades that marked America's transition from a rural way of life to a more complex, urbanized, and industrialized America. Learning of Lottie's struggles with a lack of contraception, homesteading, and irresponsible sons-in law and seeing how she and her family adjust to the right to vote, war, the temperance movement, and women's rights remind us that this is not just Lottie's story; this is America's story.

Hedley Bond. Ph. D.

Nancy O'Connor

Other books by Nancy O'Connor

Letting Go With Love: The Grieving Process

How to Grow Up When You're Grown Up:
Achieving Balance in Adulthood

How To Talk To Your Doctor

The Psychology of Aging: A Manual

Dedication

To Lottie, Hazel, Winnie, Georgina
and all the mothers, grandmothers
and great grand mothers
upon whose shoulders we stand
and benefit from their dedication,
sacrifices and advocacy
to make life better for subsequent generations.

Forward

Lottie's Lot is a Historical novel spanning five generations and 85 years in the lives of the women in an American family from 1870's to the 1950's.

Lottie Walker-Hastings was a strong willed bright young woman who had been raised in a strict Southern Baptist family in Cresco Iowa. In 1888 she meets Charlie Hastings who works for the railroad. At 17 she chooses to marry him revolting against her father's disapproval and fury. In spite of her rebellion she has firmly entrenched values and beliefs about right and wrong. She dreams of a perfect life and family. She strives with all her might to meet that goal.

She married for love. Together in 23 years of marriage Lottie and Charlie had eight children. One died in infancy. They raised six daughters and one son. Lottie suffered two toxic eclampsic pregnancies as did mother talking a toll on her health. While Lottie wanted a large family she wanted more control of planning when and how many children she would have.

The family moved often and along the way she encounters situations and crises that forced Lottie to reevaluate and change her positions on multiple unplanned pregnancies, illegitimate pregnancy, birth control and abortion. By the time the family moved to a homestead in North Dakota in 1904 she had four daughters. She was ready to quit but had no idea when she was fertile. Consequently, at 33 she got pregnant three more times, the last one another eclampsic toxic pregnancy. She was exasperated, exhausted and fed up with getting pregnant. She tried to find out how to space her children but had to rely on old wives tales, or indifferent physicians for information and guidance.

While living on the homestead one of her daughters Hazel is raped and gets pregnant. Lottie and Charlie decide to stand by Hazel and are shunned by the small farming community and forced to leave. Charlie is a farmer at heart and begins drinking to cope with his disappointment in leaving his beloved farm and moving to Minneapolis.

Lottie runs a boarding house to support the family while Charlie looks for a job on the railroad. The catch is that he is over the hiring age limit and several problems ensue.

Charlie's drinking becomes an insurmountable problem for Lottie. Early in 1911 she has an opportunity to relocate to the newly opened western frontier in Canada and moves her entire family to Edmonton, Alberta. Meanwhile Charlie has found a job with a railroad and she asks him to stay and work in Superior Wisconsin. They separate.

In September 1911 she receives a telegram telling her the Charlie was killed falling off a railroad car. Four months later her oldest daughter, Lillian who recently married, delivered a baby who died. Then three months later Lillian dies from peritonitis following a ruptured appendix.

Lottie goes into an emotional melt down forced to face all her previous losses as she grieves for Charlie and Lillian and ponders her fate.
At 40 she is widowed with six children to raise on her own with no income, a fourth grade education and sewing as her only

bankable skill. She faced challenges of supporting her children and transforming her values as they grew against the backdrop of radically changing social times including two World Wars, Woman's Suffrage, Temperance and prohibition, and loosening values of the jazz age including drinking and smoking.

Two of her daughter had abortions, one self-inflicted resulting in her death, leaving four small children behind. Hazel died young of ovarian cancer from syphilis transmitted by one of her four husbands. Another husband was a pedophile and when Lottie discovered him in bed with a little girl she did her best to expose him and get him arrested.

Lottie faced these and other challenges with the same stoicism and inner strength she exhibited when she defied her father, but she learned to bend enough to maintain a loving and fruitful relationship with her children to the end. She died at 85 after burying four of her eight children. All the survivors celebrated her life.

Lottie's Lot is a family saga that reveals what little control women had over their own reproduction, spacing and planning their families. The absence of information to support their option to make personal choices made their lives unbearable at times.

Most of the facts in this story are true and based on extensive genealogy research by her great-granddaughter. Some names have been changed to not disturb the living and some personality traits are imaginary. I met Lottie twice once as a child and once a few months before she died when she was very frail. She left 14 grandchildren and 26 great grandchildren.

There is a Time Line of Lottie's life at the back of the book.

CHAPTER 1

Lottie's hands trembled as she brushed her long auburn hair in front of the full-length mirror.

"Father, I won't be staying.... Father, I'm going out.... Father, I met a new friend...." She rehearsed what she might say until she got the words right, then and inhaled deeply to regain her composure. The more she thought about Charlie the more determined she was to confront him and make him see her as a grown-up capable of making sound decisions. She knew he wouldn't agree, but what she wanted was worth the risk of openly defying her father for the first time. If she could hold her own at supper, everything would be fine.

Her oval full length mirror reflected a pretty girl with cocoa brown wide-set eyes with natural long lashes, a narrow nose, full rosy lips, high cheekbones, and flushed cheeks.

She was a confident young woman of 17. She was such a good seamstress people from all over Cresco, Iowa, asked her to make clothes for them.

She turned from side to side and examined the new yellow gingham dress she had finished yesterday. It had bouffant sleeves, and a billowing floor-length skirt. She had added a lace collar, the latest 1888 fashion as a finishing touch. She smiled approvingly at her reflection as she tied her hair back with a matching lace trimmed yellow ribbon.

Smoothing her dress, she stood tall and proud. As she started downstairs she could hear her sisters, 10-year-old Carrie and 14-year-old Stella, laughing and teasing 2-year-old Robert Lee as they helped put the food on the table. A door slammed and the sudden silence let Lottie know her father had just entered the house from his carpentry workshop. Taking her usual seat at the dining table she met her mother's nervous eyes.

Lottie had told her mother yesterday about meeting this interesting young man and his invitation for a stroll after dinner this evening. Abbie had warned her, "You'll have to ask your father, Lottie. You'll have to deal with him."

As they finished eating, Lottie gathered her nerve. She cleared her throat and calmed herself until she was sure her voice wouldn't shake. She began: "Father, I won't be joining the family this evening for the Bible reading."

Lottie watched James Walker's face redden. His mouth tightened and his eyes narrowed. Without looking up, he shoveled another forkfull of potatoes into his mouth and said, "Of course, you'll be here, Girl. Why would you say such a foolish thing?" She didn't flinch. She was prepared for his reaction.

"I have a new acquaintance, and he invited me to go for a walk." She examined his face carefully, trying to read his mind.

James slowly and deliberately put down his fork and glared directly into her eyes his black pupils dilating, "You are *not* excused."

Abbie reached over and gently patted his hand, a gesture he knew meant, "Hold your tongue and let this alone." He didn't always heed Abbie's signals to restrain his temper, but tonight he sputtered like a

10

firecracker, sparking, then fizzling. For all of his 61 years, James' reaction to being usurped had been to intimidate with threatening looks and a raised thundering voice. If that didn't work he would stew and make everyone miserable with his gruffness.

After a minute's silence, James, still looking Lottie directly in the eyes growled, "Who is this man? Do I know him?"

"His name is Charles Hastings. I don't think you know him."

"What does he do? Who are his parents?"

"Well," Lottie, gaining confidence, dabbed her mouth with her napkin. "His parents live out of state, and he works for the Milwaukee St. Paul line."

His eyes flashed. "You mean he's a railroad man!"

"Yes, Father. He works for the railroad."

James shook his head and closed his eyes for a moment as if in silent prayer.

"Lottie, I know things about railroad men that a young girl like you wouldn't know. They drink. Many of them have wives and children in other towns, but they present themselves to foolish girls like you as unmarried. This man may be deceitful and even dangerous. I won't let you see him."

"You haven't even met him," she argued. "How can you know what kind of man he is?"

Abbie tapped his hand and James knew she meant, "Let it go."

"Humph. I *know*," was his response, along with a scowl. He stood up abruptly and left the table. He had been dreading the day his daughters would want to court and he knew it was inevitable that they would find a young man who interested them. Lottie was the second oldest daughter of his five children with his second wife Abbie, and the most head strong.

As soon as he was out of the room, Lottie kissed her mother on the cheek. "Thanks, Ma," she whispered, and ran upstairs.

James was adamant about the evening Bible reading. Every night after supper the family would gather in the parlor and a different daughter would recite her assigned Bible passage. James would then interpret the scripture in his best preacher voice and demeanor.

After about 15 minutes, Abbie would touch his hand and quietly say, "Dear, the children need to do their school lessons." After another five minutes, she'd say, "The baby's getting restless. I need to put him to bed," and James, glowing with righteousness, would wrap up his message.

James was a deacon at the First Southern Baptist Church. He was dedicated to seeing that a fundamentalist doctrine was preached correctly, for it and was the foundation of his family's conduct. His church interpreted the Bible literally, especially the threatening parts that warned against sin and eternal damnation. Their black-and-white lessons provided James with a firm structure for his life and for the rigid rules he set for himself and his family. The Walker girls were forbidden to dance, wear make-up, play cards, drink alcohol or sodas, or go to parties.

Abbie had been raised by Methodist parents and followed their less judgmental ways. When she married James Walker she took a vow to obey her husband, but in her heart she remained true to her personal values. In her own quiet way she was able to impart some of her more charitable beliefs to her children.

Preparing for the evening, Lottie recalled how Charlie had come into her life just yesterday.

She had taken her sister Carrie to Johnny's Ice Cream Parlor for a birthday treat. Carrie ordered a strawberry ice cream soda, and Lottie had a hot fudge sundae. A young man walked in, someone she had never seen before, carrying two rucksacks and looking a bit grimy and dusty. He sat beside Carrie at the counter.

"I'll have what she's having," he told Johnny, pointing to Lottie's hot fudge sundae.

Lottie barely noticed him speaking to Carrie. She was in ecstasy, savoring each tiny bite of the sundae and unaware of the small spot of chocolate on her chin. Carrie turned to ask her, "Do you know where Mrs. Ramsey's boarding house is?"

"Yes, it's on Fifth Street," she answered. "Why?" She saw Charlie out of the corner of her eye but busied herself with her ice cream. It wasn't proper to appear too forward.

"This gentleman wants to know."

As if on cue Charlie offered his hand to Lottie and smiled.

"Hi, I'm Charlie Hastings. Pleased to meet you!" His hand was strong but gentle, and she met his eyes, which she noticed were a clear deep blue, like the irises blooming in front of their house. His face was friendly and his light brown hair was thinning a bit in front, making him look wise and mature.

He quickly added, "I work for the railroad and Cresco is my new home base. I'll be staying at Mrs. Ramsey's when I'm in town. Do you know how to get there?"

"Yes, of course," Lottie said. "If you want to leave when we do, I'll show you."

Carrie motioned to Lottie's chin. She understood and delicately moistened the corner of her paper napkin and rubbed the spot away. Sitting up straighter, she smoothed her dress and ran her eyes down the front, but found no other embarrassing chocolate spots.

"I'd be obliged," Charlie said with a grin. "I'll be glad to settle in and get cleaned up. By the way, your name is --?"

"Oh, forgive my bad manners. I'm Lottie Walker, and this is my sister Carrie. Today is her birthday."

"Nice to meet you, Carrie," he said, offering his hand to shake. Carrie liked the attention, and felt very grown up shaking hands. "Happy birthday Carrie! How old are you?"

Carrie proudly beamed, "Ten."

"Goodness!" Charlie said, "You're a big girl." Carrie grinned and finished the last of the liquid in her soda with a noisy slurp. She giggled.

They walked the five blocks to Fifth Street, the lovely April evening graced them with a spectacular setting sun of purples, oranges, roses, and pinks doing a slow kaleidoscopic dance against a fading blue background – ever-changing, breathtakingly beautiful.

"What a beautiful sunset!" Lottie exclaimed.

"Gorgeous," Charlie said, staring at her in a way that made her blush.

Carrie skipped ahead and Lottie and Charlie chatted as they walked by block after block of white-painted wood-frame houses, shaded by tall maple and oak trees. Lottie told Charlie she was 17 years old, and he told her he was 21.

He asked if she would like to go for a walk the following evening.

"Well, I don't really know you," she said, though she wanted to shout Yes! "I'd have to ask my parents first."

"You can assure them I'm a gentleman, Miss Walker," Charlie said. The twinkle in his eye belied his seriousness. "I promise to be on my best behavior."

Lottie turned her face away trying to resist his contagious smile. I mustn't appear too eager, she thought. Then a voice in her head asked,

14

Lottie's Lot

"Why?" and she gave him her address on Third Street. "Come by about 6 o'clock tomorrow evening," she said as they turned the corner, pointing to Mrs. Ramsey's house.

She crossed the street very slowly, turning her head just enough to watch as he walked up the porch steps. He was strong, self-assured and confident. She noticed his muscular, compact body. She liked what she saw. He was so different from any young man she knew in Cresco. A smile crossed her face. She wanted to get to know him better. From this short acquaintance, she was willing to defy her father to see him again. Her stomach did strange somersaults when she thought of him. Her reverie was interrupted when she heard a knock on the door.

Her father opened the door and she heard Charlie's friendly voice as he introduced himself. From the top of the stairs, she saw him curtly shake Charlie's hand, look him up and down, and without a word turn and walk out of the room.

His cold disdain was embarrassing, but Abbie graciously welcomed Charlie and invited him into the parlor. Lottie waited another couple of minutes to make her entrance. She barely recognized Charlie with his clean face, neatly combed hair, and fresh clothes. It was clear that he had taken great care with his appearance. She approved.

Lottie on the other hand, took Charlie's breath away as she made her entrance slowly descending the stairs one step at a time. He stood and his eyes opened wide. "Oh! You look … err… *swell*." The skirt of her new yellow dress swirled around her ankles. She carried an ivory shawl to protect her shoulders against the evening chill. Standing straight and poised she was almost as tall as his 5 foot 8 inches.

Charlie's eyes followed her graceful hands as she pulled the shawl around her shoulders. He loved her long, tapering fingers, satin smooth and pink, with neat rounded fingernails. He longed to touch those hands. But he knew he must go slowly and follow the protocols of courtship, especially with that stern old father and the quiet-spoken mother. He knew this, but every cell in his body wanted to hold Lottie's hands, put his arms around her, and kiss that lovely mouth. He took a deep breath to control himself. Then another.

Abbie followed the couple onto the porch.

"Have a nice time, and be home by 9 o'clock."

"We will," Lottie said, as they walked toward the west, catching the last fading streaks of color from tonight's dazzling spring sunset.

Abbie was tired. She was getting over another kidney infection. She had them often now, a result of two difficult pregnancies that had left her with a poison in her blood, weak kidneys and dangerously high blood pressure. She hated the frequent urinary tract infections, teeth-chattering chills followed by raging high fevers, and the never-ending weakness. Lately she couldn't take care of her family the way she wanted to.

Slowly she lowered herself into the big white rocking chair on the porch and watched the two vibrant young people sauntering down the street. Lottie's face had glowed when she saw Charlie. Her wish for her daughter was that Lottie would be lucky and marry for love as she had once.

She closed her eyes and smiled as she remembered Orlando Woodworth. She was just 16 years old when they married. Orlando was 24 and had his own farm in McGregor, Iowa. He wasn't handsome, but he was tall and as strong as a sycamore tree -- a gentle soul who worshiped and respected his bride. They soon had a son, Delbert, and Orlando adored him.

Another boy was born prematurely and died soon after birth. This difficult pregnancy left Abbie weak. Her doctor called it eclampsia,

16

commonly known as a "toxic pregnancy." Her doctor warned her that another pregnancy could put her life in jeopardy.

Only six months later, Orlando died suddenly when his plow turned over and he hit his head on a large rock. She was widowed before she was 20. Devastated and numb with grief, she couldn't function for months or care for herself or her Delbert. She moved in with her parents, Charlotte and who nursed and cared for both of them.

Two years later, Abbie reluctantly agreed to marry James Walker, a widower 14 years her senior with two teenage children. She didn't like the lanky foul smelling carpenter but knew that she needed a husband to support her and Del. In 1864 all of the eligible young men were away fighting in the War Between the States often returning wounded and unsound.

James proposed several times before she accepted. She had a few conditions and wanted him to agree to them before she married him. One had to do with his teenaged children who didn't accept her as their "new" mother, especially his daughter, Mary. Secondly she didn't want to be forced to convert to his Baptist religion. Finally, she told him, "James, I've been warned by the doctor not have any more children. I almost died with my last pregnancy." He agreed to respect her wishes even though secretly he thought she was being irrational.

He took her delicate hands in his cold rough ones and with all the sincerity he could muster said, "Abbie, you have to trust me. I work hard, and I'll be a good husband to you. I'm sure if there are any problems, I'll find a solution." She wasn't convinced but with no other evident options she agreed to marry him. It wasn't long before she regretted her decision.

After moving into James' house, Del was afraid and insecure. James gruffly ordered Abbie to "make him behave," and told Del, with a scowl, to "Stop being a crybaby." She told her mother, that she felt like a failure as a mother.

Charlotte offered, "Why not just let me keep him until you get settled in with James' family?" Abbie let him go and he never came back. In time he came to think of her as an aunt, not his mother. Letting Del live her parents was one of the greatest regrets of her life.

After the wedding James demanded sex almost nightly and impregnated her five more times. When Abbie protested he replied indifferently, "It's God's will."

Lottie was their second daughter, after Cora, followed by Estella, Carrie and finally another son. Robert Lee, Abbie's last child was another toxic eclampsic pregnancy. Her blood pressure soared, her ankles swelled and her damaged kidneys left her weak and sick. He was born premature but survived.

There was no way to remember Orlando and Del without reliving her losses. She pulled her handkerchief from her apron pocket, wiped her tears, and blew her nose. Now Lottie Jane, her second daughter, was courting. If Charlie Hastings was the man Lottie wanted, Abbie would support her until her last dying breath.

Abbie's train of thought was interrupted by the squeak of the opening door. "What are you doing out here?" James demanded. "It's getting chilly you will catch your death. Come inside right now," he ordered.

She stood up and did as she was told.

CHAPTER 2

From the first day they met, Lottie and Charlie spent all their free time together. The more they got to know each other, the more they liked each other. She was smart and serious; he was witty and made her laugh. She was open and direct; he was friendly and liked people. She was loving and kind to her mother and sisters and little brother. He was thoughtful and romantic, bringing her little gifts of candy, flowers, a handkerchief and a new hair bow.

They went for long walks and talked and talked and talked, sharing their life stories.

"I had just gotten off the train when I looked up and saw you and Carrie walking down the street," Charlie told her. "You were so beautiful. I just had to follow you."

"Really?" Lottie asked.

"Prettiest girl I ever saw. Tall and proud. Long wavy hair. Right away I could see you were someone special."

She blushed, and quickly changed the subject. "How long will you stay in Cresco?"

"Several months at least. The railroad is important here. Without the Milwaukee-St. Paul line, this town wouldn't have all these businesses and nice houses."

"Yes, it's grown a lot since the train station opened five years ago."

They talked about their hopes and dreams. Charlie confessed that he wanted to be a farmer, like his father. But his father had quit

19

farming after having a stroke. After Charlie graduated from high school he got a job on the railroad with the help of his brother, Elmer.

"But someday, I'm going to have a farm. What about you, Lottie? What kind of life do you want? You want to marry a rich man and travel the world?"

"Oh, no, no. Not that. I just want to have a good life. I …" She hesitated. She'd never discussed her ideas with anyone other than her sisters.

"What?"

She was a little embarrassed, but she felt she could trust Charlie. She looked up at the trees as she spoke. "Well, I've learned all the lessons that school and my parents could teach me about right and wrong, and I've tried to develop good habits – you know, speaking well, and dressing nicely, and always looking and behaving my best."

"Yes, I can see that."

"So, I want to have a family, of course, and teach them the same things. And I want everyone in my family to be … well, perfect." She glanced at him and thought she saw a twinkle in his eye.
Charlie started to laugh but realized she was serious. He cleared his throat and nodded. "That's a great ambition, Lottie. I bet if anyone can do it, you can."

"Oh, my sisters laugh at me when I talk about it, but I don't see why not. All you have to do is follow the rules and do your best all the time. I like it when people compliment me and tell me I have high standards. I'm … I'm proud of that. I want my family to be that way, too."

Charlie led them to a bench in a small park near the school and they sat close together shoulders touching.

"And what kind of a husband do you see in your perfect world?"

Lottie felt the blood rush to her face and with it came a surprising thrill.

"I want someone I love, of course, and who loves me." She glanced away.

Charlie nodded and smiled. "Go on."

"And he would have to listen to me and consider my opinions...." She felt a rush now and talked faster. "Not like my parents' marriage. My father makes all the decisions and ignores my mother's feelings. I don't know why a husband and wife can't make decisions together."

"I think you're right, Lottie. Making decisions together is important."

Charlie reached for her hand. It was the first time he had touched her since their initial handshake. When he took her hand in his, she didn't pull it away, just smiled and lightly squeezed his hand back. She felt a surprising thrill through her entire body.

Abbie often invited Charlie to Sunday dinner. He charmed Lottie's sisters and brother – everyone except James. One late fall evening, after they had helped clean up and put away the dishes, he and Lottie found themselves alone in the parlor.

She stood at the window looking out at the first snowfall. Charlie stood behind her and, without a word; he turned her around and kissed her.

It happened so fast. "Oh my!" she gasped. Her face turned cherry pink. "Oh my!"

"I hope I wasn't being too bold." Charlie was flushed too.

"No...I... I...liked it!" she exclaimed. "In fact I will treasure it forever. It was my first kiss." She looked away from him and whispered, "Did I do it right?"

"Let's see." And he kissed her again. "Perfect!" he declared, beaming like he'd caught the gold ring. "But I think we need to practice it more," he grinned. She giggled but pulled away as her sister Stella came into the room to get warm in front of the fire.

Lottie felt another unexpected thrill engulf her body every time she relived that precious kiss. She couldn't sleep at all that night, remembering him. She wanted to be with Charlie always, to get more and more kisses.

On Christmas Eve when they were alone in the parlor again, he shyly gave her a poem he had written.

"Oh, Charlie. Please read it to me."

Embarrassed, he began:

The reasons I love you

Are too many to say.

Your smile and your bright eyes

Your proud and thoughtful ways.

Your confidence and your beauty

Make my heart race fast

My only wish is

This will always last.

It brought tears to her eyes. He kissed them away. Then he got down on one knee and said, "Lottie, please be my wife." She nodded, yes, through her tears. He gave her an engagement ring of sterling silver with lovely detailed filigree work highlighting the quarter-karat diamond.

After supper, he nervously asked to speak to James privately. They went into a small downstairs room, and James closed the door and sat behind a small desk cluttered with papers.

Lottie's Lot

Charlie cleared his throat and said, "Sir, I would like to marry Lottie … and I would like your consent and blessing."

James didn't respond.

Charlie nervously cleared his throat again. He went on, "Sir, I love her and will take good care of her. I have a steady job and make good money. I have some saved and can support her."

James didn't invite Charlie to sit, so he continued to stand, feeling increasingly uncomfortable and invisible. His arms and hands hung powerless at his side. James enjoyed watching Charlie squirm and stretched the silence into minutes.

Finally, without looking up, he said, "You work for the railroad, and that means you must travel and be away from home much of the time. Isn't that so?" He went on, without giving Charlie a chance to answer. "Who will take care of my Lottie if she gets sick and you are far from home?"

Charlie shifted his feet. He opened his mouth to answer, but James continued talking.

"What is your church affiliation, Young Man?"

"I was raised Methodist, Sir," Charlie said.

James replied, "We are Baptists, as you know, and I will only allow my daughters to marry another Baptist. Are you willing to join our church?"

Charlie was ready for this one. "I would need time to consider what such a change would mean to me."

Smugly, James quoted the Bible: "*And every daughter that possesseth an inheritance in any tribe of the children of Israel shall be wife unto one of the family of the tribe of her father.*" He stood

23

abruptly and looked at Charlie with narrowed flashing black eyes. "We have nothing more to discuss until you make up your mind. So, Sir, I bid you a good evening."

He bent close to Charlie's ear, and in a surly, threatening whisper he said, "Take back that ring until you're ready to agree to my terms." He escorted Charlie to the front door.

Lottie had been pacing in the hall throughout the closed-door conversation. With one glimpse at James's face when he opened the door, she knew it had gone badly. Charlie glanced sideways at her, and in a second, he was gone. James smugly opened the front door for him to exit.

Exasperated Lottie ran outside after him, calling, "Charlie! Charlie!"

He stopped and waited until she caught up with him. She collapsed in his arms panting, "I want to marry you anyway. I don't care what my father said."

"Are you sure? I want you to be sure."

"I'm sure!" she said emphatically. "I've watched him ruin my mother's life and I won't let him ruin mine."

They kissed, right there on the sidewalk, in public. If Charlie's kisses foretold their married life, Lottie would defy her father a thousand times to stay with him.

That evening after her sisters and mother went to bed, she asked James to go into the parlor. He remained standing and she did too. Charlie stood at her side. This time, quietly but firmly, Lottie did the talking.

"Father, I want to marry Charlie. I love him. Please give us your blessing."

James shook his head emphatically. "No. I forbid it."

"If you don't approve I will marry him anyway as soon as I'm 18. It's only a few months." Charlie shifted his feet.

Lottie's Lot

James could feel his blood beginning to boil. He bared his teeth, his eyes blazed, and his face grew shockingly red, as he unconsciously clenched his fists.

Fuming, he moved his face closer to hers and hissed, "I will never accept his man as your husband. I forbid you to marry him. I've been told that he drinks alcohol. You know what that can lead to."

"Charlie may have an occasional drink with his railroad friends but he never gets drunk."

The madder James got, the calmer Lottie stayed. "Father," she pleaded, "I love him. Doesn't that count for something?" To reassure her Charlie moved closer to her side and reached for her hand.

James shouted. "No! You are still a child. I am your father and I know what is best for you! This man is not good for you. Mark my words. He'll break your heart, Missy."

She began to protest again and James held up his hand to gesture silence. He took a deep breath, then another. "Let him go," James said slowly, in a quiet, measured voice. "LET … HIM …GO." He glared at Charlie.

Lottie hesitated for a moment. She had rehearsed this speech so many times she could almost say it without fear engulfing her. Calmly, she said, "Father, I have never defied you until now, although there were times I wanted to. I have always been an obedient daughter and honored your decisions. But on this I have made up my mind. I *am* going to marry Charlie Hastings with or without your blessing."

James knew he was defeated. Backing down, his voice barely audible, he whispered, "Lottie …. I beg you. Don't do this."

Defiantly, she stood taller and closer to Charlie, her hand in his. She looked her father straight in the eye for a full minute. Neither of them blinked.

She repeated quietly, "I've made up my mind."

James looked at the floor, then murmured, "So be it," and quickly left the room. He recognized the sinking feeling in the pit of his stomach. It was the same feeling he had the night Zioedia, his first wife, had died in childbirth. He was again overwhelmed by the same feeling of terrible, irreversible loss. He went out to his cabinet shop, locked the door, sat on his work stool, and cried for the first time in over 30 years.

Charlie and Lottie held their breath for a moment. Then he gently took her in his arms. "You were so brave."

Lottie collapsed into a chair. Suddenly she felt tired and drained, yet victorious.

Abbie gave the couple written permission for a marriage license since Lottie was still 17. James refused to allow the wedding to be held at home so they planned to marry in Milwaukee on March 17, 1889, at the invitation of Charlie's brother, Elmer, and his wife, Fanny.

Lottie spent the next several weeks sewing her wedding dress, making new clothes for herself and Charlie, and finishing up a few sewing jobs she had promised the neighbors.

One afternoon when Lottie was working at the old treadle machine, Abbie came into the parlor with two cups of tea, a sugar bowl, and a plate of cookies. She carefully placed the tray on the side table.

"Ready for a cup of tea, Sweetheart?"

"Sure Ma. Thanks."

Abbie began hesitantly. "Lottie dear there are some things you need to know about being married."

Lottie nodded and waited. "Okay ..what?"

Lottie's Lot

"Well, you will have certain duties and responsibilities when you are a wife. You are a fine cook and housekeeper and seamstress, and you have taken care of your younger brother and sisters, so you'll be excellent at those duties." Abbie paused.

"And, you must respect your husband, and be at his beck and call. If you disagree, bury the hatchet as soon as possible. The longer a problem goes on the harder it is to fix it."

"That's all right. Charlie and I always agree."

Lottie picked up her teacup and, after adding two teaspoons of sugar, moved to sit directly across from Abbie.

"Well, Daughter, no matter how much you love each other, there will be disagreements. Just watch your step and tell your husband what you think. He may not agree to your wishes, but it makes your life easier if you keep the air clear."

Abbie picked up a cookie and handed one to Lottie. Her voice low and hesitant, she cleared her throat and went on.

"Lottie, do you know what husbands and wives do in bed?"

"Sleep, I guess."

"Sleep, yes, but there is something else."

"What else?"

"Love. Int-intercourse. I mean physical love within marriage, with bodies connecting. Do you understand?"

Lottie shook her head no.

Abbie wiped her forehead with the hem of her apron. She ate two more cookies, stalling for time and waiting for inspiration on how to tell Lottie without frightening her.

"Lottie," she took a deep breath and started over. "Boys and men are made different from women. You have seen Robert Lee's pee-pee. It sticks out, and that's what makes him a boy."

"Ma, what does Robert Lee's pee-pee have to do with me?"

"Well, all men have a pee-pee, Charlie has one too."

That was something Lottie had never thought about, but she supposed it was true.

Abbie swallowed and quickly went on. "Men are more physical than us, and they like to put their pee-pee into their wife's err … hole."

"Oh my! Oh MY! Why would they want to do that?" Lottie was aghast.

"They say it feels good and they like to do it and do it often. Charlie will want to do it as soon as you're married."

Silence.

"I just want you to be prepared to know what to expect."

More silence followed as Lottie tried to comprehend this very strange information.

"That's how babies are made," Abbie said.

"What?" Lottie looked up.

"A woman has eggs inside of her and the man has sperms. When they come out of him and connect with an egg, a baby can start. It takes both a man and a woman to start a baby."

"Why didn't you tell me this sooner?" Lottie was shaking and felt like she might cry.

"Only married people have babies. You had no reason to know sooner."

"And one more thing," Abbie continued, relieved that she was almost finished with THE TALK. "You may learn to like it, some

28

women do. But the first time could hurt and you will probably bleed. Don't be scared, Lottie. This is normal."

Abbie stood up took the tray and asked, "Do you have any questions, dear?"

"Not right now." Lottie, sat stunned, let her head drop back and stared at the ceiling.

Two months later Lottie and Charlie left Cresco on a cold March morning.

Carrie woke up from the bed they had shared for over 10 years as. Lottie was dressing.

"I'm going to miss you," Carrie said sleepily, but I'll have my own room now."

"Yes, and your own chamber pot to empty."

"You look beautiful Sis," Lottie kissed her rumpled hair.

"I'm going to miss you too. Promise to write to me often and tell me everything, and I will do the same. We'll always be close. Goodbye for now and promise to write soon."

For the train trip to Milwaukee, Lottie had made a pink taffeta dress trimmed with maroon ribbons and a bonnet to match. She had bought some lip color from the mercantile store – something that would have turned her father beet red if he knew -- and coated her lips, making them a pale pink. She rubbed her lips together and smiled at her reflection.

Lottie went down the stairs slowly, looking over her shoulder as she realized that she would never leave her bedroom again as a single girl. Her life was changing. She set her suitcase down near the front door and went into the kitchen. Abbie had breakfast ready and Lottie sat down to eat a bite. Abbie's eyes were red. She turned her head and wiped them on her apron hem. "Ma have you been crying?"

"No...yes," Abbie blurted out." I'm going to miss you so sweetheart."

"Ma, don't worry – I'll be fine. Charlie will take good care of me. He is sweet and he loves me."

"I know that. I'm just being selfish. I want to be at your wedding."

Abbie sat next to her daughter with a cup of coffee.

"I know you'll be fine. You can take care of yourself. I'm just missing you already. I wish you were getting married here."

"Me too, Mama, but you know that's impossible. I tried. God knows I tried but that stubborn fool you married wouldn't bury the hatchet," Lottie said sadly.

"It may surprise you to know that you two are very much alike."

"Ha!"

"Neither of you would give in -- so here we are."

Abbie reached for Lottie's hand. "My sweet daughter, I have something special for you."

Abbie handed her a box tied with a red ribbon. When Lottie opened the box and saw what was inside she gasped, "Oh, Ma. This is one of your treasures."

"Yes it is. And now it's yours."

Lottie was speechless. Her eyes glistened. Abbie took her hands and said, "My mother gave me this cameo when I married Orlando. Her mother gave it to her. So now I give it to you. It needs to go to a woman in our family who marries for love, not duty. Do you understand?"

Lottie nodded, struggling to hold back tears. She squeezed her mother's hand back. "Thank you, Mama. I will treasure it forever."

Lottie's Lot

"I know you will. And I hope you'll have a chance to pass it on to your daughter someday."

"You've been such a great mother to me. No daughter could ask for more. Thank you!" She put Abbie's hand to her lips and kissed her fingers. They sat there for several moments, silently and tearfully stroking each other's hands. Touching or hugging was uncommon for this family. She was comfortable being affectionate with Charlie but it was unusual among the Walkers. Today was an exception and Lottie felt a strong surge of love for her mother. She stood up to leave and embraced her. Both held on tight knowing that their lives were about to be changed forever.

Abbie gave Lottie a box of food for the train, "Be happy, my sweetheart, and write me often."

"I will. Ma, please take care of you," Lottie whispered.

As she opened the front door to leave, Lottie turned and looked at the closed door of her father's office. She took a step toward the shop in back where James worked as a carpenter, then stopped. Yes, her mother was right, she reflected. She was as stubborn as he was. She picked up her suitcase and walked to the train station.

Charlie was waiting for her. When he saw Lottie, he held his breath for a moment, and then held her at arm's length, looking her up and down. He hugged her and kissed her cheek.

"I am the luckiest man on earth," he whispered in her ear, "and you are the most beautiful woman in the world."

She grinned, "I'm lucky too. I love you so much." She let him take her arm and help her up the steps into the Pullman car.

When they were settled into their seats, Charlie took Lottie's hand and said, "Did you hear about the man who was mad because his train came in three hours late?"

"No, I haven't heard that. Please tell me."

"He says to the porter, 'What's the use of you having a timetable if your rotten trains never stick to it?"

"The porter says, 'Well, Sir, how would you even *know* they were running late if *not* for the timetable?'"

They laughed, cuddled, and glowed with happiness all the way to Milwaukee. Elmer and Fanny met the train and welcomed them warmly. Fanny and Lottie became instant friends as they arranged wedding details.

On March 17th, they were married at the neighborhood Methodist church. Lottie's grandparents, Simon and Charlotte, and her half-brother, Del, came from McGregor to attend the wedding. Simon proudly gave the bride away. It was a beautiful wedding.

Elmer and Fanny had reserved the bridal suite in a downtown hotel for the couple's wedding night, complete with champagne and roses. When Charlie and Lottie arrived at the hotel they were escorted to their room and told to contact the desk if they needed anything.

When they were finally alone as husband and wife, Charlie opened the champagne, poured two glasses, and offered one to Lottie. She started to shake her head no, but thought, "Oh! It's the most special day in my life. I can have a sip."

He held up his glass and gestured to her to do the same. With his glass touching hers, he said, "I propose a toast. *To life. Our life. Our wonderful new life together!*"

Lottie added, "Our new life and our love. I love you, Charlie Hastings." She took a sip and made a face. "Ugh! That tastes awful!"

Charlie took a sip and smiled at her. "Honey, you take the cake."

Lottie's Lot

After taking a bath–her first time in a real bathtub. She added bubbles and delighted in playing with them. Then she toweled dry in a luxurious fluffy towel and sprayed herself with Eu de Toilet by Channel following instructions by Frannie.

Then she put on a delicate pink satin nightgown. She looked in the mirror for a long time wondering if she would look different tomorrow. When she went back into the bedroom, she found Charlie sprawled across the bed asleep. She felt guilty for taking so long in the tub.

Ever so gently she lay next to him and began ever so gently to twirl his hair with her finger. He opened his eyes and took her in his arms. "I've been waiting so long for this moment," he whispered in her ear.

He was tender and slow. She was astonished that her body could have so many delightful feelings, and his touches made her want more. She forgot time and felt only her pleasure in his caresses and kisses. Then she was overwhelmed by the strongest sensation she had ever felt -- so intense that she cried out in pleasure. Charlie cuddled her, and then inserted his penis inside of her. After a few pumping movements he too cried out. They fell asleep in each other's arms.

The next morning after a delicious breakfast they took the train to Fort Jackson, New York to visit Charlie's parents. Ira and Rebecca met them at the train station. Rebecca cried and hugged Charlie so tight he lost his breath.

At their home, friends dropped in, bringing food and gifts to help the new family set up their household. Soon the house was overflowing with Rebecca's family, the Converses, and Ira's Hastings's relatives, neighbors, and friends. Lottie glowed with all the attention.

They stayed for a week. Charlie showed her his favorite places from childhood. As he walked around his grandfather's farm, his face lit up like a child surveying his Christmas gifts. She understood then that working on the railroad was Charlie's job, but farming was his passion.

They left for Perry, Iowa, where Charlie would be working. It was only an hour's train ride from Cresco. Charlie had rented a one-bedroom railroad cottage close to town.

All the workers on the train to Perry knew Charlie and stopped by to congratulate him. While he visited with his friends Lottie caught her breath and enjoyed a few minutes to herself. She leaned back against the seat and closed her eyes. The Hastings family seemed so relaxed and accepting of new people, she thought. What a contrast to the Walkers! She wondered if it was religion that made the great difference between the comfortable and nonjudgmental way Charlie's family lived and James' dogmatic dictates and mistrust of all outsiders.

She wanted to be more like his family, but deep inside she feared that God might punish her. James' threatening Bible passages were deeply ingrained in her.

Charlie and Lottie arrived in Perry in late March. When she opened the door to her new home, she was greeted by an exuberant yelp from a curly-haired, coffee colored cocker spaniel puppy-a house warming surprise from her beloved, thoughtful Charlie. She named the puppy Curly. She'd be protection and have a companion when Charlie was away.

Their neat, one-bedroom bungalow had a small fenced front and back yard where they could have a garden and the puppy could romp. Within a week Lottie had washed, scrubbed, and cleaned everything thoroughly -- windows, floors, walls, their cooking and heating stoves.

She ordered new wallpaper from the Sears & Roebuck catalogue. As a finishing touch, she placed two special personal things in the kitchen cabinet: a cookie jar for the money she would earn by sewing and a hand-carved wooden box Del had made her to house her Bible.

Two weeks after they got to Perry, on Lottie's 18th birthday, Charlie surprised her with the latest model treadle Singer sewing machine. She was thrilled. He took her to dinner at the elegant Perry Hotel. It was her best birthday ever.

Life for Lottie was better than in her wildest imagination. She sewed sunny yellow curtains for the kitchen and living room. She made and embroidered percale sheets and matching pillowcases for their lumpy bed, and muslin towels with crocheted edges for the kitchen.

As a brakeman, Charlie was assigned overnight trips four days a week they spent three days at home. Most Sundays he was home. On many of Charlie's workdays, Lottie rode the train for an hour and visited her family in Cresco. Railroad workers and their families traveled for free.

When Charlie was away Lottie deeply missed having him close to her in bed. She found sex with Charlie delightful. He was a slow and thoughtful lover, and from her wedding night on she looked forward to more nights of warm cuddling and private pleasure with her husband. Sometimes on his days off they spent all day and night in bed, making love, eating snacks and dozing in each other's arms.

CHAPTER 3

Lottie's and Charlie's life settled into a happy routine. He planted a vegetable garden, berries and grapes. Soon they had fresh vegetables and fruit and a few chickens for fresh eggs.

Lottie stayed as busy, meticulously keeping her home neat and tending to the garden and chickens when Charlie was gone. She got to know several of the other wives who lived in the railroad cottages, and they chatted across the fence as they hung out the laundry or swept the back steps. The neighbors were impressed by her sewing skills.

"This is as nice as anything in the Sears & Roebuck Catalogue," her next door neighbor, Hattie, said, examining the crocheted trim on a pale pink blouse. "Lottie, you're a real artist."

Before long, several neighbors asked her to sew something for them. She got requests for baby clothes, little girls' fancy dresses, a lot of aprons, and a couple of wedding dresses. She made each item special, charging only the cost of the fabric and just a little more for herself. The coins quickly piled up in her cookie jar.

When she visited her neighbors' homes, she couldn't stop herself from glancing around their homes and noticing that none matched her housekeeping standards. She saw unmade beds, toys and sometimes clothes on the floor, and even yesterday's mud on the floor. Why can't these women keep their houses clean? She wondered, and then heard her mother's voice admonishing her: "Now, Lottie, don't judge people. Many of these women have several children or they're taking care of elderly relatives. You don't know what goes on in their lives. I'm sure they're doing the best they can."

Lottie's Lot

Almost a year after they moved to Perry, Lottie missed her menstrual period. When she was nauseated in the mornings she knew that she was pregnant. She wanted to give Charlie the good news in a special way. The thought of surprising her husband thrilled her to her toes.

His birthday on May 16th and she had just enough money from her sewing to order a special railroad watch from the Sears & Roebuck catalogue.

She made a long, flowing infant dress out of white percale. She embroidered tiny yellow flowers with green trim around the collar, sleeves and hem, and then made a bonnet to match. It would be appropriate for either a boy or a girl.

He came home a little early on his birthday. Lottie had prepared his favorite dinner of pot roast with onions, potatoes, parsnips, and carrots, and a devil's food cake with white cream frosting. She sang "Happy Birthday" while he blew out the 23 candles in one big breath.

She brought out the first gift and held it behind her, making him guess which hand it was in. After a few tries she gave him the box. He opened it slowly, dragging out the fun.

"Now, don't tell me, Lottie. I bet it's a jack in the box. It's going to jump out at me."

She giggled with excitement and shook her head no.

"Well, I know it's not a pair of shoes because it's much too little. I know – it's another puppy!" Curly was thumping her tail on the floor after her dinner of pot roast scraps.

Finally, he quit teasing and opened the box. When he saw the watch, his jaw dropped.

"Lottie, Sweetheart. How did you do this?" He examined it, and with a catch in his voice said, "I… I love it." He was truly surprised. She smiled ear to ear.

The fob was in the box and he began to fasten it to his pocket.

"Wait. Look inside," she said. He opened it and read: "*Charles I. Hastings, May 16, 1890. With love, from Lottie.*" He was flabbergasted.

"Oh Lottie, dear, dear sweet wife of mine you bought this for me with your sewing money, didn't you?" He turned it over and over in his callused hands. She locked her arms around his neck and kissed his cheeks. He said, "This is the best gift anyone has ever given me."

Then she brought out another wrapped box decorated with pink and blue ribbons.

"What's this for?" he asked.

"Just because I love you," she said, flashing her special smile.

He eyed her suspiciously. "Mmmm," he mused.

He opened the box and when he saw the baby dress, he immediately understood the message. He jumped up and twirled her around until they were both dizzy.

"When?"

"About the middle of December."

"Oh wonderful news! I hope she's as beautiful as her mother."

"What if *she is* a *he*?" She wanted to know.

"Well, then I hope *he* is as handsome as his mother. Either way: As long as he or she is healthy, I don't care."

He gave her a long, thrilling kiss.

"Darlin', I didn't think I could ever be happier than I was on our wedding day, but I think today has topped it. You are the perfect wife."

Lottie's Lot

The first week in December 1890, just before the baby was due, they went to stay with Abbie in Cresco. Lottie hadn't been able to share her wedding with her own family, but she wasn't going to have her first baby without them around.

The gray-haired midwife who had delivered all of Abbie's children in Cresco was there to help, along with all of the Walker women. Charlie and James paced outside the bedroom door, nervously exchanging scowls and grimaces, equally concerned for Lottie.

When the baby cried, Charlie thrust the bedroom door open and asked, "Can I come in?"

"In a minute," Abbie called out, pulled the door closed and wiped his brow and pacing the floor again until she opened the door swaying gently holding the infant wrapped in a receiving blanket. She handed the baby to Charlie with a loving smile. "Congratulations, Son-in-law, you have a beautiful daughter."

"Are all of her fingers and all of her toes there?"

"Yes they are. She's perfect." She motioned him into the bedroom and placed the infant in his arms.

He held her gingerly, then kissed her on the forehead and said, "Welcome to the world, sweet Lillian." He and Lottie had agreed they loved that name.

He studied the baby's tiny face. She looked like her mother. She had dark hair, brown eyes, and the slightest hint of a pointed nose. When she began to cry he handed her back to Abbie. He went into the bedside, knelt next to Lottie and stroked her forehead. Her hair was soaked with sweat, and even though she was smiling she looked exhausted.

"She's beautiful. She looks just like you," Charlie whispered in her ear.

When they returned to Perry two weeks later, a package was waiting for them from Fort Jackson with Christmas presents and a beautiful baby book for little Lillian. Rebecca's note to Lottie explained that she hoped Lottie would write down details about the baby's birth and her first years of life. It would be a lovely gift to pass on to her daughter when she was grown.

Lottie loved the book and meticulously recorded all of Lillian's firsts -- her first smile, tooth, words, and steps. Rebecca sent another baby book after the birth of each of Lottie's and Charlie's children.

Lillian was a happy baby. She rarely cried and was not demanding. Lottie took to motherhood naturally. Once they got the hang of breast-feeding, the next months were easy.

Charlie was a hands-on papa. He bathed the baby, sang to her, and rocked her to sleep, even changed diapers. The little family thrived. Lottie made baby Lillian pinafores, flounced fancy dresses, and warm flannel snuggles with matching bonnets for cold winter nights.

She proudly showed the baby off to the neighbors, but stayed inside most of the time to protect Lillian from the blustery Iowa winter. Looking out the window one day shortly after New Year's, she saw several of the women gathering at the house across the street. Many of them were crying. She wrapped Lillian in a warm blanket and hurried over.

"What's happened?" she asked Hattie.

"It's Russell, Dorothy's husband. He was crushed."

"Crushed?"

"By a train in the switching yard. His foot caught in the track and he couldn't get out of the way."

Lottie was shocked, and for the first time realized how dangerous Charlie's job was. Russell's funeral was the first of many she would attend for a railroad worker. Each time, she secretly thanked God that it wasn't Charlie, and she added to her nightly prayers a passionate petition to God to keep him safe.

In the fall, Lottie was pregnant again. This time she thought she had a tornado inside her. On March 31, 1892, Iris Hazel stomped her way onto this earth. She literally gave a final big kick, Lottie's water broke, and the baby made her dramatic entrance. She was named for the beautiful spring irises coming up all over their yard, but they called her Hazel.

She was the opposite of Lillian: fitful, demanding, and always hungry. While Lillian looked like the Walker side of the family, Iris Hazel was clearly a Hastings. She had a round chubby face, blue eyes, and a circle of blond hair, just enough to twist into a top curl.

When Lottie told Abbie about this restless, impatient baby she laughed and said, "That sounds like you."

With two children, Lottie had to work harder to maintain perfection. Her house was always spotless. She never went to bed at night until her kitchen was clean: the food put away; the dinner dishes from dinner dried, and stored in their proper places; stove, table, and counter wiped clean; and the floor swept.

She made Charlie take off his shoes before he came inside, and wash and change into clean clothes when he got home from work. She was equally fussy with the children. If they played outside and got dirty she scolded them and briskly cleaned them off.

Hazel was fearless and daring, never considering the consequences before she acted. She walked before she was 10 months old, and by the time she was 18 months old she was stringing words together. She ran everywhere and her favorite word was "Why?" Lillian, shy and obedient, hated to be on the receiving end of her mother's scolding,

41

whereas Hazel had a mind of her own and wasn't bothered by Lottie's anger, much to her frustration.

In 1893 the railroad offered Charlie a promotion as yardmaster in Iron Mountain, Michigan, with a significant pay raise. Lottie encouraged him to move up the work ladder and to earn more money for his growing family. He would work more hours but no longer have to travel. The only drawback was that she would be farther away from Cresco.

Their friends in Perry gave them a going-away party. Neighbors brought food and a keg of beer. Lottie drank iced tea and Charlie enjoyed the beer along with the other men. As the evening went on Lottie noticed that Charlie seemed to get louder and tell more jokes.

The next morning, Lottie asked, "Charlie, did you get drunk last night?"

"No. Why?"

She treaded lightly. "You were talking louder than usual and your face was awfully red."

"I had a few beers, that is all."

"You know I don't like drinking."

He answered, "Lottie, almost everyone has a drink now and then to celebrate, to relax, to be social. I know you don't like to drink yourself, but you can't dictate your beliefs to others."

"Well, I never saw you behave that way before, all that loud laughing and slapping everyone on the back. I do think you were drunk."

"I was just having fun. Don't worry. I'm still the handsome, perfect man you married," he said, and tried to hug her.

"All right," she said, stiffening to his touch.

She tried to be open-minded and accepting like the Methodists. But she believed some things were just wrong. Drinking too much alcohol

42

was one of these wrongs. James Walker's rants against drinking were seared into her brain. She kept an eagle eye on Charlie and every time he drank she winced, but held her tongue.

In 1893 Charlie was offered the yard master position in Iron River Mountain, Michigan with a substantial raise and a lot more responsibility. He would be in charge of the roundhouse where steam engines turned around to head in the opposite direction for the next trip.

In June, they moved to railroad housing in Iron Mountain close enough for Charlie to walk to work. The girls were three and one. They had a bigger two-story home, surrounded by woods –and lakes. Beautiful until winter set in.

Lottie told the girls Bible stories at bedtime, about the Good Samaritan and young Jesus in the temple, and at Christmas the birth of baby Jesus. In Iron Mountain she took them to church and Sunday school. She wanted her children to become churchgoers, but without Charlie's support the kids didn't take it seriously.

One fall day while Lottie was baking with the windows open to cool the kitchen, she heard a child's cry and ran outdoors to look for Hazel. Lillian was at school. She searched the yard and peered down the street but couldn't see her child. All the while, the screams grew louder and more desperate – the most frightening sound Lottie had ever heard.

When she couldn't find Hazel in front or back of the house, she ran inside and leapt up the stairs to Hazel's room. The little girl was sleeping soundly in her bed where Lottie had put her down for her nap.

She wondered what child was crying and why it was wailing so loudly. She heard the sounds again a few days later and again the next week. They must have come from several blocks away, but they pierced the daylight as if the poor child were calling out to the whole world for help.

The next Monday afternoon, Lottie took some loaves of bread to her nearest neighbor.

When the woman opened the door, Lottie said, "Hello, Florence. I made too much bread and thought you might be able to use a couple of loaves." Florence had six children and couldn't always keep up with her baking.

"Lottie, you're a life saver. This is so wonderful," she replied, inviting Lottie in.

After Florence brought a tea tray into the parlor, Lottie said, "Florence, I've been hearing something very disturbing. It sounds like a child crying in pain and fear. I can't figure out where it's coming from."

"I've heard it too," her neighbor replied, looking out the window.

"Well, it's very upsetting. Do you know where it comes from?"

"I have an idea. But it's really none of my business." She sipped her tea.

"I can't help thinking that if a child is in pain, we should help," Lottie said, leaning closer. "Who do you think it is?"

Florence dabbed her mouth nervously. "Oh Lottie, just stay out of it. It would be too embarrassing."

"Embarrassing?" Lottie felt the back of her neck growing warm. How could anyone be concerned about embarrassment if a child was being hurt? "Just tell me who you think it is. I won't mention your name."

"You can't tell anyone." Florence looked frightened.

"No, no, I just want to know."

Lottie's Lot

"It's the Campbell's. Jack Campbell hits Ann and he beats the child too."

"Oh my God!" Lottie blanched in astonishment. "I know them. And their baby is only two. How could ...why does he do it?"

Florence shrugged. "I don't know. Some men just do that."

As Lottie got up to leave, Florence grabbed her arm. "Now, Lottie, you promised you wouldn't say anything."

"Right. I won't," Lottie said. She felt no guilt about lying.

That night, after the children were asleep, she told Charlie about her conversation with Florence.

"Jack Campbell?" he replied. "You mean the guy who has the night shift at the station? I don't believe it."

"I can hardly believe it either. He's so nice and he looks so normal. And their baby is so cute. I've never seen a bruise on her."

"It's probably just a rumor started by somebody who doesn't like him," Charlie said, untying his shoes and placing them under the bed.

"Maybe so. But there is a child being hurt. You heard her crying too. We have to do something."

"Like what?"

"I don't know. But I want to do something. It's horrible."

Charlie was in bed by now and Lottie heard his light snoring begin as she brushed her hair. She stared at herself in the mirror. She had to figure out what to do.

The next day she spoke to Lillian's teacher, careful not to mention Florence's names or the Campbell's.

45

"No, I'm not aware of anything like that in our town," the teacher said.

She asked a few other neighbors if they'd heard the loud cries, but none of them said they had.

The next night she told Charlie about her inquiries. "Charlie, you've got to say something to Campbell's supervisor."

"Oh, no, I can't do that."

"Why not?"

He heard the determination in her voice and explained carefully. "First of all, it's only a rumor. Second, it's not related to work. Third, I just don't feel right doing it. I'm sorry, Lottie. This is not our business."

She wasn't satisfied but she knew she couldn't ask Charlie to do anything. Finally, she stopped by the church on a Tuesday and asked to speak to the pastor.

She told him about the cries and added, "I heard something that might tell us which family it is."

"Well, Lottie, you're a caring Christian woman, but this is out of our hands. We can't go around accusing people of something awful, and of course it would be wrong to spread such gossip. All you can do it pray that, if this terrible thing is happening, God will touch their hearts and they'll stop."

For the first time, Lottie felt disappointed with her church. Was there nothing more she could do? She'd already been praying for the child and she continued to do so. Soon her attention was occupied with troubles of her own.

With her third pregnancy in 1896, Lottie felt tired all the time and by evening her hands and feet were so swollen she couldn't get her shoes on. Her midwife recommended that she see a medical doctor, the first time Lottie ever visited a physician.

Lottie's Lot

"Mrs. Hastings, your blood pressure is seriously elevated," the doctor told her. "You have a condition called pre-eclampsia, and you must go to bed and stay there until the baby is delivered." To her great shock, he said she was in danger of having convulsions, even dying, if she did not take care of herself. For the first time she was afraid about having a baby.

Charlie took over as much responsibility for the children and the house as he could after work and on his days off, but it wasn't enough. She wrote to Carrie, who came to her rescue. For four months, Carrie, now 18 came from Cresco and stayed to take care of Lottie and the girls.

In August, 1896, Lottie delivered a baby boy, two months early. He weighed less than three pounds and was so tiny they put him in a shoebox for a cradle and in a dresser drawer for protection. He couldn't nurse and had to be fed a special formula with an eyedropper. He survived for two weeks.

Lottie and Charlie were saddened at the loss of their son. She fretted about the toll the toxic pregnancy had taken on her body and wondered if she would end up like Abbie. Carrie visited again to check on Lottie.

"Carrie, I am worried," Lottie said to her sister one day. "You may not remember, but these are the kind of symptoms Mama had with Robert Lee. And her second baby, Del's little brother, died. What if this is passed on in the family? What if I get as sick as Mama?"

"What does the doctor say?"

"He says every pregnancy is different and I may never have a problem again."

"Good," Carrie said. "And Cora and Stella haven't had any trouble with their babies."

"But he also says I have a higher risk than most women of having trouble again."

"Well, what can you do?"

"He says the best way is not to have any more children, not to get pregnant again."

"How in the world are you supposed to do that?" Carrie asked with wide-open eyes.

"I have no idea."

While Lottie was getting better, Abbie's health was failing. Lottie missed her mother. She wrote often, and she put all her love into making Abbie a lovely bed jacket of fine, rose-colored satin lined with flannel for warmth.

In May, 1898, Lottie got a telegram saying that her mother had died. She arranged for neighbors to care for her children and took the first train to Cresco.

Abbie was only 56 years old. James, now 70, looked much older, and leaned on Robert Lee as they walked from the church to the graveyard. He was devastated by Abbie's death.

"She was an angel," he kept muttering. "An angel sent from God."

Lottie bit her tongue to stop from asking James why he had never treated Abbie like an angel.

In the eulogy the minister said, "Abbie Young Walker was well loved for her gentle ways and her willingness to help others." He called her a "woman who at all times through her acts, deeds and words showed her truly possessed of all attributes and qualities that mark the abiding place of a Christian spirit and character."

Yes, Lottie thought. Abbie was the truest Christian she had ever known.

CHAPTER 4

In the summer of 1898 Lottie become pregnant again. She and Charlie had tried to have relations only when they thought it was safe and she couldn't get pregnant, but it was very hard to figure out.

Back in Perry, one woman had said, "You get pregnant during your period." But others disagreed and said that was the safest time to have sex and not get pregnant. It was very confusing Lottie suspected they were all guessing.

Charlotte was born on March 13, 1899. They had a break between babies for a few years, until Bethany joined the family in February 1903. After Bethany's birth, Lottie sadly told Charlie, "I'm sorry I haven't given you a son." The common belief was that the woman was responsible for the gender of her child. He tenderly touched her cheek. "It doesn't matter, Lottie. I'm just happy that this beautiful baby girl is healthy."

The family enjoyed life in Michigan for the first few years. In August they made blackberry pies and jams picked from the wild blackberries that grew everywhere. Lottie taught the older girls to make jams, jellies, and preserves from seasonal fruit, including peaches, apricots, plums, pears, and apples.

The girls loved playing and swimming in the summer and playing in the autumn leaves. Just after her fifth birthday, Hazel climbed a big oak tree to save a kitten. She couldn't get back down holding the

49

kitten, and Lottie had to rescue both of them. She scolded Hazel but it didn't faze her – she believed she had done the right thing.

As a railroad yardmaster, Charlie was responsible for the roundhouse. It housed huge mechanical turntabouts to rotate an engine and head it toward its next destination. The roundhouse also was used for making repairs. He hired and supervised several men, scheduled train arrivals and departures, and handled mountains of paperwork.

At first they loved having Charlie home every night, even though he was often called out for problems and emergencies. He often got home so late that the children were already in bed, or he was so tired that he would fall asleep in the middle of a conversation. Sex dwindled to almost none because both he and Lottie were too worn out. Their expectation of more family time together turned out to be disappointing.

Charlie was a good boss and showed appreciation to employees who worked hard. William Goode was a gangly young man with cornflower blond hair, who always looked like he was about to trip over his own feet when he walked. Like Charlie, he had grown up on a farm, but he preferred working with machinery. He could fix anything and build mechanical parts.

Charlie often invited the overgrown boy to Sunday dinner, and the family grew fond of him. Lottie noticed that Charlie was treating this young man like the son she could not give him.

In 1902 three days before Thanksgiving a messenger came to the house and told Lottie that Charlie was at Dr. Mellon's office. William had been seriously injured when a locomotive had entered the roundhouse too fast and jumped the track, pinning William under it. He died, and from that moment on , Charlie lost all enthusiasm for his job.

Shortly after Lillian's 13th birthday, Lottie found her crying and asked, "What's wrong?"

"I don't know. I'm bleeding and I have a stomach ache."

Lottie's Lot

"Oh, Lillian," Lottie said. "I should have told you before. This is part of being a woman. All women have a period of bleeding every month except when they are expecting a baby."

"Uggggh."

"Let's get you cleaned up. We use rags to collect the blood so it isn't so messy. I tear them from old towels or sheets or flour sacks."

She took Lillian into her bedroom and closed the door. "Take off your clothes."

Shyly the girl took off her house dress and stained panties. Lottie dipped a towel into the basin and handed it to Lillian. "Clean yourself." Lillian timidly obeyed, shamed by the red stain left on the towel. She folded it to hide the blood.

"Don't fret." Lottie patted her shoulder. "It washes out with cold water." She pulled several long, narrow strips of clean cloth from her bureau drawer and a few safety pins. She sat on the edge of the bed and made a circle with one rag, then laid another perpendicular to it.

"This one goes around your waist and you pin it to hold it on. Then the other one goes between your legs and you fold it over the waist one and pin it in place back and front." She watched as Lillian took the two cloths and tried to put them in place.

"It's best to pin the two of them together, like this." Patiently Lottie showed her. "Now, slide it around to the back, reach through your legs, and pull it through and pin it in front."

Lillian said, "Oh Ma, I can't do this."

"Of course you can. All women do this. It's nothing to fear. You'll get used to it." Lillian struggled but finally got the apparatus in place. She calmed down a bit.

51

"When it is full of blood you put on a clean one," Lottie explained. "The soiled one is soaked in a bucket in your room. You'll wash it every morning and hang it out to dry."

"I wondered why you always washed all those rags. Ma, how long do I have to do this?"

Lottie put an arm around Lillian's shoulder and pulled her close. "Every month until you're about 50, except when you are with child. It only lasts for a few days, maybe a week each month."

She looked at the girl's confused face. "Are you all right now?"

"Well, my belly hurts."

"Right. I have some aspirins." She opened a bottle and handed two to Lillian. "Take these and lie down and rest for now and I'll bring you a hot water bottle to hold on your tummy."

In their third winter in Iron Mountain, the temperature reached 10 degrees below zero for weeks at a time. The three older girls came down with chicken pox, and Lottie was careful to keep them away from the baby, who was more vulnerable if she got too. The house was quarantined and a notice was placed on the front door by the health department. Except for Charlie going to work, the family couldn't go out, and no one could visit.

After being locked in the house with three sick children and a baby, Lottie was worn out and frazzled. Between the harsh Michigan winters and Charlie's long hours, Lottie felt she was raising her children alone. When Charlie was at home he spent most of his time catching up on his sleep.

Lottie no longer thought about making her life perfect. Even doing her best, it wasn't humanly possible to keep up with all her duties. In winter, scrubbed diapers were hung throughout the house to dry, and other clothes didn't get washed for days. Sometimes she only cleaned enough dishes for the next meal, and swept the parlor once a week instead of every day. She told herself she would do better when the girls were over the chicken pox. But even then, she was always tired and never got caught up.

One March evening, with the ground still frozen, Charlie came home excited with news. He told her the government was opening up free land for farming in the West. She hadn't seen him so enthusiastic in many months.

He asked Lottie, "What do you think about me quitting the railroad? We could get our own farm, grow our own food, be together, and have a healthy place to raise the girls. It's called homesteading." His eyes lit up as he talked.

Lottie sat down to nurse Bethany and listen to him. Charlotte padded out in her sleepers and crawled up into her Papa's lap. Charlie snuggled with the four-year-old, blowing air at the nape of her neck, which made her squeal with delight. Lottie smiled.

"They need their Pa around more. They miss you, and so do I."

Charlie held Charlotte tight and rubbed his beard on her cheek. She laughed and tried to push him away, giggling, "Don't, Papa," while holding her cheek up to his face for more. Finally, he gave her an Eskimo kiss, then a big noisy kiss on the cheek, and let her down.

With a gentle push, he said, "Good night, honey. Sleep tight."

"Don't let a bedbug bite," she giggled. Lottie brushed her cheek and she ran off to bed.

Charlie opened his mouth to speak, but just then Lillian brought a crying Bethany to Lottie. She slipped down the top of her dress to nurse the hungry infant.

She looked at Charlie and sighed, "Homesteading? How does it work?"

"Well, we have to put in an application and we could be granted 160 acres of undeveloped land. We would have to move there and we would be required to make a certain number of improvements. Every year the government checks on it."

"What kind of improvements?" she asked.

"Buildings, a house, crops, things like that. Things that can be measured and evaluated. Things worth money."

"We would have to build a house? That kind of scares me. We've never done that." Lottie hesitated.

"I have," Charlie said eagerly. "When my father retired from farming, he built the house in Fort Jackson and I helped him. I was just a teenager, but I remember a lot."

He continued, "Most people buy farm houses from the Sears catalogue. You just pick out the floor plan you like and they send all the parts. Then you just need to put it all together."

"That sounds too simple," she sighed. "I can't imagine it would be that easy."

"No, sweetie it won't be simple or easy. Nothing is, is it?"

She nodded with a small smile. "That's the God's truth."

"Lottie, let's look into it. It doesn't cost anything to get information."

"Where would we go? I don't want to live this far north again. I hate these long winters."

Bethany had fallen asleep and Lottie took a slow breath and slid her to the sofa while she put herself back together.

"I don't know if we can request a location or if we have to take what they offer us. I'll find out," he said. "Honey, can't you see me as Farmer Charlie?" He stuck one end of a pencil in his mouth and pretended it was a straw.

54

Lottie's Lot

She smiled and nodded cautiously. The thought of leaving Iron Mountain and of getting Charlie out of the railroad business with all its dangers was appealing.

As Charlie gathered more information about homesteading, his enthusiasm grew. Practical Lottie tried to think of all the pros and cons and weigh them carefully. Meanwhile, they put in their application for a homestead in North Dakota.

One evening after the girls were in bed, Lottie said, "Charlie, do you think just you and I and the girls can manage a farm? It would be easier with boys, wouldn't it?"

He had obviously thought about taking on farm life without a son to help. "We'll hire men when we need them. Besides, with the Grange, farmers help each other to plant, harvest, and do other work. I'll join the Grange right away."

"What's a Grange?" Lottie asked. His answer was encouraging.

"It's a group of farmers, like a union. To save money they buy seeds in bulk, and they harvest and sell their crops together. Sometimes they buy farm equipment that everyone can use. They have activities for women and families, too. It's kind of the center of farm life"

After several weeks, their application was accepted and they were given 160 acres about 8 miles from Denbeigh, North Dakota, and 15 miles from Towner, the seat of McHenry County. Early in May 1903, Charlie and Lottie got a neighbor to look after the children and went to look at the property they had been granted. They took the train to Denbeigh, a bustling town with a bank, a brick factory, a school, three bars, a general store, a land office, and a Grange building used as a church on Sundays.

They rented a horse and buggy and rode 8 miles along the county road which ran through their property. Excited and curious, they examined the site from every direction. They saw expansive openness with gently rolling hills. Very few trees obstructed the view where the sky met the land in a distant horizon.

Charlie paced in all directions, grinning more broadly at every turn. "Honey, isn't this the most beautiful place you've ever seen? We can have a great life here. It'll be wonderful!"

She allowed herself a big grin. "Yes, I can see it, too."

Charlie paced off about 40 feet from the bigger of two tall sycamore trees.

"How about here for the house? We would have shade in summer and shelter in winter."

Standing next to him, Lottie imagined the house. She was catching his excitement. "It's perfect."

They walked off the imaginary foundation of the house and decided where the well and the pump would go, and where to put each door to the house and the outhouse. By that time, the sun was setting and a dusky maze of colors glistened in the sky. A light breeze rustled their hair and brushed their cheeks. Sycamore leaves danced a tango.

They stood on a slight rise of land and watched the luminous sunset and its afterglow of bright oranges, roses, and purples. White fluffy clouds faded and blended into blues and slowly disappeared over hills – there was beauty as far as their eyes could see.

It was the most perfect moment Lottie could remember in her life so far. She reached for Charlie's hand, and he squeezed hers. They felt so close, so much in love, so hopeful.

Charlie got the carriage blanket out of the buggy. He stood behind Lottie and pulled her back to him, nibbling on her earlobe. He kissed the back of her neck. She turned and kissed his mouth, and he spread the blanket on the ground. Slowly they lowered themselves to the ground and made love on the spot that would be their new home.

CHAPTER 5

Charlie signed the homesteading contract in May and gave notice to the railroad that he would leave at the end of the month. Lottie had carefully saved money from his salary, and after long discussions they picked out a house and ordered it from the Sears and Roebuck catalogue.

Charlie left first with their furniture and other possessions. He slept overnight in the same railroad car to protect his belongings. In Denbeigh he bought a buckboard and two horses and hired two young men to help him unload his things, pile them on the buckboard and drive them out to his new land.

As he had instructed on their first trip to the property, the well had been dug and the pump installed. The three men made cups with their hands and drank deeply of the cool water from the well as they unloaded the furniture. At sunset Charlie walked over his land, as happy as a boy with a new toy he had wanted for a long time.

They had a lot to do in the next two weeks. They cleared land and set a lumber foundation for the tent the family would occupy while the house was being built. After they put up the tent, he arranged the furniture and boxes inside and set up cots and a small wood stove with a chimney for heating water. Then they built an outhouse.

Two weeks later Lottie and the girls boarded the train with the rest of the family possessions and left Iron Mountain behind. They knew all the railroad workers and got a hardy send-off. When they changed trains in Detroit a Negro porter helped them transfer their things. Lottie thanked him with a big smile. She didn't believe in tipping.

Lottie's Lot

It was late afternoon when the train pulled into the Denbeigh station. Charlie happily gave Lottie a big kiss on the cheek and hugged his four daughters. They unloaded the suitcases, boxes, and bedrolls, including a cradle for Beth. Then they headed "home."

Charlie rubbed Lottie's hand and said, "Dear, how I've missed you. It's going to be a wonderful life for all of us. Just you wait and see."

She smiled back and replied, "I hope so."

"How did the change of trains go? I was worried about you doing it all alone."

"It was fine. I got the porter to help with the suitcases. He was such a nice Negro, the nicest I ever met."

"Is that so?" Charlie smiled. "And how many Negroes have you met, My Dear?"

"Don't tease me, Charlie Hastings." She pinched his arm. "You know this was the first one I met personally."

"My, my. You are becoming so worldly."

"Never mind! What did you get done at the farm?"

"A lot. I've been working day and night. The tent is up and the cots are ready for the feather bedrolls. The outhouse is finished."

He added, "By the way, Girls, meet Beau and Belle. They're important members of our family now." The girls looked at the two sturdy brown horses pulling the wagon – the biggest animals they'd ever seen.

When they got to the property, Charlie unloaded their belongings and Lottie settled Beth into her cradle before she looked around.

59

"It looks different from the last time I saw it."

"Better, I hope." Charlie beamed.

The girls explored the tent and the land around it. Lottie peeked into the outhouse.

"We need toilet paper," she told Charlie. "I don't use corn cobs."

He laughed, "There's an old Sears catalogue. Will that do?"

"For now, but I'd like something softer. You have a lot of girls here and we wipe a lot."

"All right. All right!" He grinned, happy just to hear her voice again.

Lottie approved of the delicious well water. While she was directing the men to rearrange the furniture in the tent, the girls descended on Charlie, all hugging him at the same time.

"Papa, we love it." Charlotte said, "Is that tire swing for us?"

"You bet it is."

"Yeah!" She ran and jumped into the swing. "Hazel, come and give me a push!"

They settled in. Lottie went to work becoming the perfect farmer's wife. First she set up a makeshift kitchen outside the tent under a canvas tarpaulin held up by four posts, each about 7 feet tall and dug into the ground. They set iron rods in the ground to support a heavy cross rod to hold big pots of beans or vegetables and to be used as a spit to roast rabbits, pheasants, and grouse. The big coffee pot was always brewing hot coffee for Charlie and the other men.

A table made of an old door set on wooden barrels served for eating, cleaning, washing, and food preparation. Seats were sawed-off tree stumps. They had a fire pit for outdoor cooking, heating water, and providing warmth in the evenings.

"Living outdoors is fun!" Charlotte exclaimed.

Lottie's Lot

Lottie put as much of their food as possible in jars and airtight cans, but at night animals regularly raided the kitchen for scraps. Often the family was awakened by the sound of a raccoon or skunk rattling a pan or knocking over a box. One night, a bear found the kitchen and made such a racket that Charlie fired his shotgun into the air to scare it off, while Lottie and the girls huddled together trembling.

The men set a cinder block foundation for the farmhouse, which arrived in August. It cost $149 for a two-story, four-bedroom frame house, complete with blueprints, framing, lath and plaster, windows, wood flooring, nails, and more. Grange members gathered and helped them quickly set up the walls and raise the roof. Charlie and the hired men worked fast to get the windows and doors installed before winter set in, which could be as soon as late September. Lottie and the girls kept them fueled with coffee and food.

Monday was usually washday. Under Lottie's direction, Lillian and Hazel heated water in a big bucket over the fire pit, and then poured it into two galvanized washtubs, adding a little cold water. They scrubbed each item, using homemade soap on a washboard, until it was clean, then wrung it out by hand and put it in the other tub to rinse out the soap. One of the girls would dunk the garment up and down several times, and then wring out the water again and again until the entire soap residue was gone. Then the clothes were hung on the clothesline, a rope strung from a tree to a post in the ground.

Lottie taught them a song to sing while they worked.

"This is the way we wash our clothes,

Wash our clothes, wash our clothes.

This is the way we wash our clothes

So early in the morning."

The women at the Grange taught Lottie to make her own soap, which was much cheaper than ordering it from Sears or Mr. Gee's general store in town. She saved the ashes from cooking and fires and piled them on top of a layer of straw. When she had a barrel full she poured water through the ashes and straw to catch in a bucket below. When an egg could float on top of the solution – called lye water – it was strong enough to mix with lard or fat saved from cooking and form blocks of soap. The soap was harsh and could cause chafing if not rinsed out of the fabric. It was cruel to the hands, leaving them red and raw.

The Grange became the center of their social life. Easygoing and likable, Charlie soon gained respect from other grange members for his knowledge of farming. Through the Grange, farmers had a strong voice in local, state, and national politics. As a group, they were able to persuade the banks to give them better interest rates for loans and more relaxed terms if there was a bad weather year. Besides buying seeds in bulk, the Grange members built several storage chutes for corn and wheat right on the railroad line to get their crops to market by train.

The women socialized, exchanging recipes and talk about their children. They welcomed Lottie and offered to show her how to use a butter churn and a cream separator and other things that were new to her. They invited her to their next quilting bee.

After dinner, Lottie would cheerfully say, "Girls, Pa's getting Beau ready; put on your boots and come on. Let's see how much land we can clear before dark." Charlie would rig up one horse to pull a hand plow and he walked behind guiding the plow to bust sod. Lottie and the older girls followed Charlie and turned the soil over again and again by hand to shake out the grass and weeds and prepare it for a fertile garden bed. By the end of July they had a garden space 18 by 30 feet.

When Bethany started to crawl, Lottie rigged up a homemade harness with a long rope, then put her on a blanket and tied the end of the rope to the sycamore tree. More than once Lottie looked over and saw that Beth had crawled to the edge of the blanket and was sampling the grass or dirt. She ate a bushel of dirt long before she was a year old.

To make the work more fun Lillian would start to sing and soon they all joined in. She knew the newest Stephen Collins Foster songs, and the others quickly learned "Oh! Susanna," "Swanee River," and "Beautiful Dreamer." When Charlie led off "Camp Town Races," he made funny faces on the "Doo-dahs" and his daughters giggled at his silliness.

They planted winter crops that were well under way by the time they moved into the new house early in October 1903, just before the first snowfall. It was still a shell with bare walls, wooden floors, no insulation, and little furniture, but it provided the shelter they needed, and they were all proud of their work.

They celebrated with homemade donuts and apple cider. Charlie and Lottie spent most of the first winter finishing the inside of the house, putting up interior walls and insulating outer walls with newspaper. Lottie ordered some pretty Victorian floral wallpaper. By spring they had the parlor and dining room finished.

Lottie soon grew to love the life they were creating. She was with Charlie all the time, and the girls were old enough to help. She had learned so many new things and felt very close to the land they worked. She loved watching the tomatoes and beans and other vegetables grow from seeds, holding them in her hands and smelling them when they were ripe. She was proud to see the dinner table completely laden with food they had grown themselves.

The hard work felt good because each chore they did made their lives better. In the second year, Charlie built a barn and bought a couple of cows for milking, chickens for eggs, ducks, and a few cranky geese. The following spring they added two wiener pigs and a goat. The third year, they got five sheep and another milk cow.

They didn't milk one of the cows. Charlie took her to spend a few days at another farm with a healthy bull and the next spring she had a calf. As soon as it was weaned, Charlie sold it to a neighboring farmer. As he led it away, Charlotte and Bethany tearfully waved goodbye to their "baby cow."

A few days before Thanksgiving in 1904, Lottie sent Hazel into the newly dug root cellar to get some potatoes, carrots, and apples to prepare for Thanksgiving dinner. The tin doors were covered with snow from a storm a few days earlier. Hazel swept off the snow and pulled the handle of the door, which leaned against the side of the house when open. She climbed down the ladder, and just as she reached the bottom, a big rat jumped out of one of the bushel baskets, heading toward her in its attempt to escape. Hazel screamed, and the rat dashed up the ladder.

Hazel scrambled back up the ladder and ran into the house, yelling, "I'm *never* going down to that root cellar again."

"Oh! Don't be such a sissy," Charlie teased her. "You're much bigger than that little old rat. I'll bet he was more scared of you than you were of him."

Hands on her hips she declared, "I don't care. I'm *not* going back."

Lottie went to get the food, taking a broom to scare any other vermin away before she descended the ladder and tapping all the baskets with a broom handle before reaching into them.

At the table before the Thanksgiving meal they held hands, and Lottie asked everyone to say a special blessing and thanks. She began: "Hem your blessings with thankfulness so they don't unravel."

Lillian was next. She said, "Thank you, Lord, for this wonderful family and the food we share. I love you all."

Lottie's Lot

Hazel followed: "I am thankful for our home, except for the root cellar, and the love and care we all have for each other — and, oh yes, the great food!" They all laughed.

Charlie ended, saying, "Gratitude is appreciating what you have and not fretting over what you don't have. I am grateful for my beautiful wife and children. Thank you, Lord."

When the schoolteacher in Denbeigh resigned that summer to get married and move away, the School Board, many of whom were also Grange members, recommended Lillian for the job. She had just finished the tenth grade and was a standout student. She was hired for $15 per week.

Lillian taught children from the first through the sixth grades in one room – 10 students including Hazel and Charlotte. The White Oak School building had a few windows to open for a breeze when it was hot outside, and a big potbelly stove for warmth during the winter. Boys cut and brought in wood for the stove and cleaned up the schoolyard. Girls swept, dusted, and cleaned the room at the end of each school day.

Hazel quit school after completing the fifth grade. At 12, she was needed at home more than ever, with Lillian gone most of the day, and she didn't care much for reading and schoolwork. Her day began at 5:30 am and ended after 6 pm. She milked the cows twice a day, fed the other animals, and gathered the eggs. She cooked, washed clothes, sewed, helped look after the babies, and tended the kitchen garden. When her father needed her, she worked in the fields.

Christmas was festive the second year in their new farmhouse. After Thanksgiving, secrets abounded as the sisters made presents for each other from bits of paper, ribbon, and scraps of fabric. They worked together on a bed jacket for Lottie. Hazel embroidered a trellis of rosebuds and tiny green leaves around the edges of the

65

sleeves. For Charlie they made a muslin nightshirt with a matching cap to keep his balding head warm at night, with "We Love Pa" embroidered on the front.

Lottie's Christmas gift from Charlie was a mineral oil back rub followed by an hour of slow lovemaking. They were as passionate as ever when they could make time for each other. While Lottie enjoyed their intimacy, she dreaded the possibility of another pregnancy. It was still a mystery why she would get pregnant one time and not another. In February, 1904, when she missed her period, she knew she was expecting again. Bethany was just a year old. One night after they went to bed, she matter-of-factly told Charlie her news. "Are you positive?" he whispered.

"Yes. I missed my period and my breasts are sore, and I am nauseated in the mornings. All the usual signs."

"Oh God! Bad timing, huh!"

"Worse than that. I don't want any more kids. Not now!"

"I know," he replied. "It will be fine. We can always use an extra farmhand." He feigned a little laugh.

"Not funny! It will probably be another girl," she said sarcastically. "I'm still nursing Beth. It's your fault. You are always pressuring me." He was silent for a minute. "I thought it couldn't happen when you were nursing."

"Apparently that is not true," she said coldly.

"What do you want me to say?" he pleaded.

"There's not much you can say now. It's too late. The damage is done."

"Lottie, you enjoy making love as much as I do." He tried to cuddle next to her. He hated it when she was unhappy. "Lottie, I'm sorry, but it takes two to make a baby. I will do everything I can to make it as easy as possible for you." He went on stroking her. "We will get through this together."

Lottie's Lot

Her back was to him and she didn't answer or turn around; he felt her body heaving and knew she was crying.

The next week, Charlie went to see a doctor in Towner. He asked for a prescription for condoms. After grilling him to make sure this would satisfy a real need, the doctor gave him one.

Charlie had heard of the new latex rubber condoms, but the Comstock Law of 1873 prohibited advertising any form of birth control or sending contraceptive devices through the mail. Men on the railroad had said a doctor could give you a prescription, but you had to go to a pharmacy that sold them to get it filled. Fargo was the nearest place that had them, but it was 250 miles away -- too far to go.

Early in her pregnancy, Lottie became crabbier and more impatient. She had tried refusing to have sex with Charlie, but their intimacy was important to both of them, and it was often a needed release from their enormous responsibilities. She knew in her heart it wasn't all Charlie's fault.

She took catnaps when she could in the winter months, and the older girls took over some of her chores. As spring emerged she felt better, and planted the kitchen garden, cooked, sewed clothes, and went to the general store once a month as usual.

On a hot night in August 1904, Ruby Ellen made her way into their life. Lottie's resentment of the pregnancy grew with her disappointment at having yet another girl. She saw Ruby as a burden and decided not to nurse her. She ordered glass nursing bottles and nipples from the Sears catalogue, and they were boiled, sterilized, and waiting to be filled with cow's milk before baby Ruby arrived.

The new baby's cries to be fed or changed were often ignored. Everyone had so much work to do that her needs sometimes went unmet, except by five-year-old Charlotte. She loved this baby and treated her like her own living doll.

Lottie missed the company of other women. She had grown up with her mother and sisters always around, and families in Cresco had shared potluck suppers and celebrations.

Here she felt alone. The nearest farmhouse was three miles away too far to walk. She was often too tired to take the horse and buggy to meetings at the Grange, but she did enjoy her once-a-month quilting party with other farmers' wives. She usually took Lillian and Hazel along, even though the women were all older. She wanted them to learn quilting.

At one meeting, old Mrs. Burton, who was alleged to be 83, but didn't have a birth certificate to prove it and had lost count some years earlier, kept passing gas. Everyone ignored the obtrusive noises, from little toots to long whines. But Hazel and Lillian started to laugh and couldn't stop.

Lottie shot them a "Stop it *now*!" look from across the table They tried to stop but just as they were getting themselves under control, out came another burst of noisy gas. The girls snickered, then giggled, and then laughed out loud. Lillian asked to be excused and went outside, with Hazel following. The group could hear them laughing for another 10 minutes. On the ride home Lottie chastised them for being rude.

"Shame on both of you. You embarrassed me and that poor old lady."

"Sorry Mama. Hazel made me keep laughing," Lillian said.
Hazel followed. "It was so funny. The way nobody even noticed. It was *so loud*!"

"Old people can't always control themselves. It just slips out," Lottie said.

Lottie's Lot

"Well, she could have said, 'Excuse me,' or 'I'm sorry,' or 'Oops!'" Hazel said, and they began to laugh again, and soon Lottie was laughing along with them.

Lottie went to Denbeigh once a month with Charlie to buy supplies at the general store. Before the first year ended, they had used up their credit limit with the store. They still needed supplies of flour, lard, sugar, baking powder, oatmeal, beans, cornmeal, and other basics.

She struck a deal with Mr. Gee, the store owner. She would make aprons and potholders for him to sell in the store. He supplied her with the fabrics and she returned with the finished products. She got 50 percent of the sales price, and it was applied to her food account.

One day after school, while Charlotte helped Lillian dust and get the schoolhouse ready to lock up, Lillian asked, "How do you think we can surprise Ma for her birthday next week?"

"Let's get her something special. And pretty!"

Closing the shutters, Lillian said, "I saw a lovely cameo brooch for sale at Mr. Gee's. It costs $4. I only have about $1.85, but I think she would love it."

Charlotte added, "I have about 55 cents. That makes it, um, over $2?"

Lillian, never one to miss a teaching opportunity, asked, "*Exactly* how much?"

Charlotte got a piece of chalk and added $1.85 and .55. She said, "$2.40."

"Good. Now how much more do we need to buy the brooch?"

Charlotte figured again, and after a few minutes she said, "We just need $1.60 more."

"Let's talk to Hazel and Pa tonight. But let's keep it a secret so we can surprise Mama."

"Right." Charlotte Jumped up and down and clapped her hands she loved being part of a happy conspiracy to please her mother.

Hazel had $1 and Charlie added the rest. He picked up the brooch on his next trip to town.

Together the girls made a big birthday card, decorated with red construction paper hearts, and everyone signed it. Hazel made a flannel drawstring bag to keep the brooch from getting scratched, and they wrapped it in a tea tin. Hazel baked a two-layer birthday cake and decorated it with yellow confectionery sugar frosting. The placed a big paper three and four on top.

After dinner they brought in the cake and sang "Happy Birthday." Then Charlotte came in with the present, holding it behind her back, and said, "All right, Mama, guess which hand."

Going along with the game, Lottie said, "Let me see, maybe I will choose this one." She paused. "No" -- she pulled back her hand -- "I think I will choose this one," tapping Charlotte's other elbow. Charlotte giggled, shifted the gift to her other hand, and brought out an empty hand.

"Oh my!" Lottie said, "I guessed wrong."

"Try again, Mama." Charlotte was delighted to see her mother so playful.

"How about this one?" Lottie smiled, touching Charlotte's other elbow.

Charlotte hesitated, and then brought out the tea box, wrapped in bright red paper, with a white bow made from one of her hair ribbons on the top.

"Open it, Mama," Charlotte said, jumping up and down in her excitement.

Lottie's Lot

Very slowly, to drag out the fun, Lottie opened the paper, then the lid of the tea box, and pulled out the flannel bag. When she pulled the drawstring and saw the brooch she was stunned.

"My goodness! This is beautiful. I've never had anything so lovely." She held back tears.

"It's from all of us," Charlotte said with a grin.

The brooch was oval and 2 inches long. It was framed in decorative gold filigree, encasing a shiny black onyx, and mounted on top was a pink carved shell cameo of a woman's head with long hair. It was exquisite. When Lottie turned it over, she saw that the clasp said 14k.

She hugged and kissed each of them. They cherished her rare embraces; the children knew they had awakened a part of Lottie that she usually kept buried inside.

Lottie put the brooch in a small box on her dresser, right next to the cameo her mother had given her the day she left Cresco. Whenever she felt tired or discouraged, she opened the box and saw the two brooches side by side. They reminded her that her life was full of love.

CHAPTER 6

Charlie hired two men to help him cultivate 40 acres in 1905. Every year he added more acreage until most of his 600 acres were planted in alfalfa, wheat, corn, and other grains. A year with sufficient rain produced a bumper crop – bigger than expected – resulting in a profit. In dry years they would sink into a financial hole, borrowing a little more from the bank for next year's seeds and equipment. Every year he planted his spring crops with a prayer, "Don't fail me now, Mother Nature."

At times when money was scarce there was always an abundance of food from the kitchen garden, eggs from the chickens, milk and animals hunted by Charlie. Pheasants, ducks, rabbits and deer were welcomed when added to the menu. By the second summer there were plenty of vegetables to harvest as well as berries to preserve, to feed the family all year. Lottie and the older girls put up just over 200 jars of fruit, pickles, vegetables, jams, chutney, applesauce, relishes, even sauerkraut, from the food they grew, and traded with other farm families.

After they moved into the house they settled into a routine. Everyone had jobs to do. Complaining wasn't tolerated. Lottie also made time for family fun to celebrate birthdays, holidays, and sometimes a spontaneous surprise party with a sing-a-long, games, and always a sweet treat of cake or pie or cookies.

In Towner, the McHenry County seat, there was a barn dance every other Friday evening from May to October – Hazel's favorite event. Charlie rigged the horses to the cart and drove Hazel and

Lottie's Lot

Lillian to attend as often as possible. He enjoyed a few drinks with the men in the local tavern while the young people danced.

On Decoration Day in May, 1905 the family dressed in their Sunday best for the all-day picnic in Towner. Lottie mixed up a big batch of her famous potato salad. Lillian made lemon meringue pies. Hazel baked dozens of oatmeal cookies. The three younger children were excited to have a day of fun and no work.

Hazel and Lillian fixed box suppers and decorated the boxes. About 5 p.m. all the teenagers gathered in one tent and the boxes made by the girls were auctioned to the boys, accompanied by the auctioneer's jokes about finding out if a girl was a good cook before you proposed. The highest bidder won the box and went off with the girl who brought it, and they ate together. The proceeds of the auction went to a fund to help orphaned children of farmers.

Jeb Graham, determined to spend time alone with Lillian, bid a whopping $4.25 for her box supper. Martin Jones was smitten by Hazel and won hers. She considered him a boring suitor but was polite and spoke kindly to him. Everyone had a good time.

After a bumper crop in 1905 Charlie had a little extra money and decided to buy his first car. A traveling photographer at the Decoration Day party took a photo of the family seated in Charlie's pride and joy.

He had to borrow a little more money from the bank in Denbigh to buy the Ford Model F. Lottie objected to the increased debt, but was partially won over when Charlie pointed out the time they'd save time getting back and forth to town.

"Let me teach you to drive, Lottie," Charlie offered.

"No, thank you," Lottie refused haughtily. Since she had been opposed to buying the car she wouldn't soften her stance by driving it.

But Hazel and Lillian were willing students and little by little they learned by driving around on the farm.

Life was good until Lottie got pregnant again. This child would be number six, and Ruby was only 10 months old. Dear God! Why?! This was bad timing. At first, Lottie was so despondent that some mornings she had to force herself to get out of bed.

Once again, her fertility had overpowered their efforts to prevent pregnancy. One of the women at the Grange had suggested putting half of a scooped-out lemon or orange rind inside her with the open side facing down to prevent the sperm from reaching her egg – the idea gave Lottie a good laugh. Getting it in would be trouble enough, but how would you get it out again? Another possible solution was for Charlie to withdraw his penis just before he ejaculated. They tried this but it obviously wasn't foolproof.

The early months of each pregnancy brought predictable nausea and sleeplessness. After her round-the-clock summer canning effort she was exhausted. By fall, she was behind on everything – mending, making school clothes, gardening, cleaning, cooking, washing, ironing, sewing and shopping. Frustration gnawed at her. It seemed she would never catch up. She'd managed all right with four girls but each new baby made life harder.

She yearned for a little time for herself to do her hair properly, relax, read her Bible. She was tired of wearing the same dowdy, plain dresses day in and day out. She longed for time to brush her hair and bathe and put some cream on her face to protect it from the chapping wind. She dreamed of spending hours making pretty clothes for herself and the girls. At times, she fantasized about leaving this lonely, demanding life and moving to Minneapolis to live closer to Carrie and enjoy the conveniences of a city life. Carrie had married a banker and she and Bill now had two children. They had a nice home there. Carrie could buy things in stores to make her life easier and the schools were well equipped with modern books and playgrounds.

When Lottie was despondent and feeling sorry for herself, she blamed the farm and frontier life for her unhappiness. She was torn between wanting to support Charlie and finding an easier way of life. Her negative thoughts and feelings built up until she couldn't keep them inside any longer.

One October evening after dinner, she asked Charlie to sit on the porch swing with her. She wanted to talk to him privately while the girls did the dishes and cleaned up. They put on jackets because a chill was setting in. They sat in silence for five minutes, collecting their thoughts.

Finally, looking at the floor, Lottie said, "I want to leave here and move to Minneapolis."

Charlie was blind-sided. "Why?"

She held her breath for a minute, and then started talking fast. "I'm exhausted. I can't go on here. I'm pregnant again. I just can't keep up! The laundry is piling up. We're wearing dirty clothes, and I haven't mended anything or darned any socks for months. I work from dawn to dusk and don't see any progress. No matter how hard I try, I get farther behind, and now we're in debt. We may lose everything anyway if we have another drought next year."

She stopped abruptly, lips pursed, fighting back tears. Charlie reached for her hand and gently squeezed it. He hoped that if she let it all out it would release her pent up feelings

She continued, "I can hardly get out of bed in the morning, I'm so tired." Tears crept into her voice, "Charlie, I didn't expect this life to be so hard. Can't we move away?"

He hesitated and then said firmly, "No. Not now."

"Why not?" Did he really understand how difficult life was for her now? Did he care, she wondered.

He wanted to understand but everything he loved and worked so hard to achieve was on the line. He took a deep breath to keep from losing his temper.

"For one thing, I can't go back to the railroad. I'm 38 years old and the maximum age for hiring is 35. How can I support us if I can't get a job? I don't know anything except railroading and farming. At least here we can grow our own food, and we have a nice house. Despite everything, don't you think it's a good life?"

"It's not good for me. It's too hard, too much work," she sobbed.

"More important," he went on, "if we leave now we will lose everything we've worked for – everything!" After a pause he asked, "Is this about being pregnant again?"

"That's just the last straw. I thought you got a prescription for condoms. Where are they?" Lottie challenged.

He shifted in his seat and tried not to sound defensive. "I did get the prescription, but the drugstores in Towner and Denbeigh didn't have them. They told me I would have to go to Fargo to get them, and I never had time to go all the way there." He added impatiently, "I've already told you all this."

She knew she was equally responsible for conceiving this baby, but he didn't have to carry and deliver it or nurse it and keep an eye on it all day. Resentfully, she said, "This *better* be the last one."

"All right. I'll think of something."

"Promise me!" she demanded

"I promise." He had no idea how to prevent a pregnancy other than to give up sex. He hoped he could think of something else.

Relieved to change the subject, he said, "Now, about the farm and the debt. I can't control the weather; occasional droughts are just one of the risks that go along with farming. We have to bear up under the unpredictable weather. We can just hope and pray that next year will be better and we'll have a bumper crop to pay off the loan."

Lottie's Lot

"Maybe, but there's no guarantee."

"Life has no guarantees, Lottie. We all just do the best we can." Sometimes it seemed to him that Lottie was still a 17-year-old bride in her expectations. He knew the homestead would mean hard work and thought she understood that too.

"You know I'm doing my best — I work around the clock too, doing the work of three men." Charlie continued, "We made a commitment to stay for five years to get our land deeded to us. If we leave now, we'll lose everything we've done so far."

She nodded. "I know how hard you work, Charlie. But can't we sell our house?"

"No. It's built on land we don't own yet. We need to stick it out for the full five years or we can't recover anything we've done to this place. We have to stay for another two and a half years, at least."

He patted her hand, then put it to his lips and kissed it. They sat in silence, watching the fireflies darting here and there. She was glad she had gotten her thoughts off her chest. She remembered Abbie's advice to clear the air and not let resentment build. Charlie went off to bed and Lottie sat alone for another 45 minutes and felt the first movement of the new baby. She loved Charlie, and she liked many things about their life here. But she missed her sisters, and she was so tired she couldn't think straight. All she could foresee was more problems – more bad crops, more work, more debt, more pregnancies.

But what choice did she have? She was responsible for her children, and she had made a promise to Charlie. For his sake, she would keep going -- come hell or high water.

The next morning, Charlie spoke to the girls and asked them to help their mother more and see that she had time to rest and take a nap sometimes. They nodded their heads solemnly.

77

Lottie resumed her duties in a better mood. Talking to Charlie always helped. But she was constantly aware that Charlie smelled of sweat and dirt from his long days of toil and she did too. She allowed herself the luxury of washing her hair and a long soak in a warm tub on Saturday nights. It wasn't much, but it helped.

In the middle of a late winter blizzard, Lois Kermett Hastings was born on March 9, 1906. The baby was amicable and easy to care for. Within a few weeks Lottie pulled herself out of her depression. Glad to be back to her old self again, she vowed to stay strong no matter what.

"It's just mind over matter," she told herself over and over until she believed it with her whole heart.

The older girls once again took over the mothering role, except for feedings. Lottie nursed this baby. Nursing gave Lottie a few moments of quiet and a chance to rest and relax. Little Lois charmed her mother when she opened her baby eyes and smiled. Lottie bonded better with Lois than she had with Ruby.

By the time Bethany was three she wanted to spend all her time with Charlie. Even as she got older, she hurried through her daily chores and went to find her Pa.

When he harnessed the horses to the wagon she was at his side and she sat on his lap while he drove them. She followed him around as much as she could. When she was with him she felt special. He talked to her, teased her, and took time to play silly games with her. She was a daddy's girl.

One day when he was feeding the horses, Bethany, now five, sat on a hay bale beside the stalls and said seriously, "Papa, I want to marry you when I grow up."

Charlie was surprised. "Well, I would like to marry you too, but I already have a wife. Your mama is my wife. I can't have two wives. I guess you will have to find another husband."

She quietly pondered what he had said.

Lottie's Lot

"I want to live on a farm," she said.

"Then we'll find a farmer for you to marry. I'll help you get a good one."

"Good, Papa, promise me."

"I promise." He raised her over his head and spun her around. "I promise, Sweet Pea."

The summer of 1906 was fruitful. Lottie was her old strong, and determined self, working hard and encouraging the girls to do their best. She set a good example for them. She taught the girls to sew on her machine and to do handwork, including embroidery, knitting, and crocheting. Hazel and Beth took to sewing like their mother. They became expert at mending clothes with pieces of cloth from flour and sugar sacks. Clothes were passed down from sister to sister until they were completely worn out.

The weather was good, and the crops productive. In July, Carrie and her family came from Minneapolis for a long visit. Lillian was honored as McHenry County's best teacher of the year and rewarded with a bonus check of $25 and her picture in the weekly newspaper. She blushed at the honor. Still shy at 17, she preferred to stay out of the limelight.

Hazel was the opposite. She craved being the center of attention. She was outgoing, friendly, social, savvy, and smart. At 15 what she wanted most was a boyfriend. She didn't like being out on the homestead, so far away from other young people.

On New Year's Eve, Lottie and Charlie celebrated with homemade wine and toasted their good luck and their wonderful children at midnight. Lottie took her usual single celebratory sip.

After the girls went to bed Charlie put his arms around Lottie and whispered in her ear, "Come on, darlin,' let's go for a walk. There's a beautiful full moon and it's clear and crisp outside." He nuzzled her ear and the back of her neck.

Lottie felt a deep stirring and teased, "You romantic old fool." She kissed his cheek.

They put on boots and jackets and took a long walk, holding hands and enjoying a few precious moments alone together. Back home they went to bed and made love like they hadn't done for a long time, and fell asleep in each other's arms.

The reawakening of their sex life had consequences. Within a month Lottie knew that she was pregnant again. She was almost 36, and this was her eighth pregnancy. She felt the familiar sadness and exhaustion coming back. She tried to put on a brave face, but a few times Charlie found her crying for no apparent reason.

By the end of May, her ankles and feet were badly swollen. She got pounding headaches -- symptoms like those in her previous toxic pregnancy. Charlie took her to a doctor in Towner, who said her blood pressure was too high. When she told him about her previous eclampsic pregnancy and her mother's experiences, he ordered her home to bed.

"Mrs. Hastings, it seems that you are having another pre-eclampsia pregnancy Your health -- even your life – may be at risk," the doctor said. "You could experience convulsions, or need surgery to remove the baby and save your own life. You *must* go to a bigger city. Our little town is not equipped to provide this kind of specialized care."

In despair she went home and tried to stay in bed. The girls did double duty, frightened of losing their mother. She did what she could from a chair -- shelled peas, scrubbed clothes on a scrub board, and even scooted around on an old board to weed the garden. She went to the doctor twice a month to check her blood pressure and listen to the baby's heartbeat.

Lottie's Lot

By the end of July, the doctor firmly ordered her to go to Minneapolis and stay with her sister until the baby was born. He made an appointment for her with a doctor he knew there, and told Charlie that if he wanted to keep his wife alive, he must take her there immediately.

Lottie packed a bag and spent a sleepless night worrying about the trip and leaving her family for so long. Early the next morning, she and Charlie left driving in the automobile to Carrie's house. It was a long, two-day trip on a dusty two-lane dirt road.

Charlie stayed for a few days and went to the new doctor with her. He asked for a moment alone with the doctor and requested a prescription for condoms. "I can't get into town very often, so I'll need a lot of them," he explained. He visited a large drugstore and bought a gross of condoms. Lottie laughed when he told her, but she was relieved: "Maybe this really *will* be our last baby!"

With Lottie's promise to telegraph him if her condition changed, Charlie reluctantly returned to the homestead.

Lottie was happy to see her sister again. Carrie was still pretty with her dimples and turned-up nose. She had grown into a warm and approachable woman. Carrie remained Lottie's most trusted friend and confidante. She gave wise and practical advice.

Carrie was overjoyed to have her sister to herself again. Her spare room had a comfortable bed and cheerful pictures on the walls and a big window to let in light and a cooling breeze. She tiptoed into the guest room each morning with Lottie's breakfast.

"Oh, Carrie, you're spoiling me," Lottie said.

"You deserve to be spoiled," Carrie laughed.

81

"You used to spoil me. Mama always said so. Remember that birthday when you made me a dress just like yours, and you took me to Johnny's Ice Cream Parlor?"

"Of course I remember. That's the day I met Charlie."

"You and Charlie have been through some tough times, haven't you? He's a good man. He can't take his eyes off you, Lottie. He's still in love with you, after almost 20 years."

Carrie sat in a chair beside the bed while Lottie drank her orange juice and ate scrambled eggs and toast with strawberry jam. She had brought Carrie several jars of homemade relishes, pickles, and jams from the farm.

"I love him, too, Carrie. We're lucky to have each other." Carrie saw a frown develop on Lottie's face.

"What's that frown about then?"

"I just keep getting pregnant, and I'm so tired."

"Well, when you're married to a man you love, it's not surprising you get pregnant so much," Carrie replied with a sparkle in her blue eyes.

"That's kind of what Charlie says. I mean, there's nothing better than having his arms around me. And we are married, and we like to…. Oh Carrie, you know what I mean!" They laughed away their embarrassment.

"But work on the farm is *so* hard – it's all day, every day -- so many things to do. I'm up at dawn and not in bed till after midnight and I still can't keep up. I don't have time to enjoy my children or even take care of all of them properly. If I could stop having babies, I might be able to manage my life a lot better."

Carrie nodded her head. "Babies are a mystery. We know what causes them, but we don't know how to stop it from happening. I guess Pa would say babies are a gift from the Lord and we shouldn't question."

Lottie's Lot

"I'd like to see Father work like Charlie and I do, and go through these pregnancies and have all those kids underfoot," Lottie said as she chewed a bite of toast. "He never really understood what Ma went through. She wasn't even supposed to have any more children when she married him. It's a miracle that all of us lived, and that she lived to see us grow up."

"No one knows what it's like to be a mother, except other mothers. You can't explain it to anybody." Carrie's children were now six and eight.

"How did you manage to stop at two, Carrie?"

"Who says we've stopped? I don't know why I haven't gotten pregnant again since Amy was born. It still could happen."

"I wish I knew your secret," Lottie said, wiping the crumbs from her mouth. "After this one, I really won't have another. But that's what I said after Ruby and after Lois...." She told Carrie about Charlie's condom purchase. One hundred and forty four. "They should last awhile."

They laughed so hard Lottie almost peed her nightgown. She jumped up and headed for the bathroom.

Carrie clapped her hands and laughed. "Praise the Lord! I hope they work -- for your sake."

As she picked up the breakfast tray and left the room she said, "You're the strongest woman I know, Lottie. If anyone can deal with all of this, it's you. For now, let's just focus on keeping you rested and having a healthy baby number seven. Get some rest now."

With no chores to do, she slept long hours, luxuriating in the much needed rest. On September 22, 1907, she went into labor. Charles

Junior was born premature, puny, and frail. Lottie beamed victoriously when she was told she had a boy. Finally!

Carrie sent Charlie a telegram announcing the joyous event.

Lottie told herself, "you are a strong woman. You're rested and healthy, and you can take care of your family. Many women have six or seven or even 10 or 12 babies, and they manage."

She prayed. "Thank you, Lord, for giving us a son at last. Thank you for keeping me safe and my family safe. Thank you for each one of my precious children. Please help me to be a good wife and mother, and give me the strength to do your will."

Charlie drove to get her the second week in October. He hoped the weather would stay mild until they got home in time for Thanksgiving -- their best ever with Lottie and the baby back at the homestead.

When the car pulled up to the house, jubilation reigned. The girls were delighted to see their mother again, and the new baby was welcomed as the king of the castle, doted on by six big sisters.

Lottie was surprised and pleased that Charlie and the girls had managed to run the farm without her, and did a good job to boot.

"I taught them well," she congratulated herself. The girls' competence meant that if she planned her time a little better she might be able to squeeze in a few hours a week to sew again and maybe even take an occasional nap.

Charlie was so proud of his son. The first time he held him in his arms, he said, "Hey, Buddy, you and I are going to be pals." The name stuck and he was called Buddy all of his life. He was spoiled from the beginning. At his first peep, one of his sisters was there to meet his needs. To Lottie, he was her heart's fulfillment. She nursed and cuddled and constantly kissed and petted him as she had never done with any of her daughters.

In May, 1908, the family celebrated the end of their five years on the homestead and received the deed to their farm. But they weren't out of debt yet. When Charlie had borrowed from the bank to buy his car, he had put the farm up for collateral on the car and his other loans. Altogether, they owed about $500. Even with the deed, they wouldn't own the farm until the loan was paid in full. Charlie prayed for a bumper crop in 1908.

Lottie came home rested and feeling healthy and energetic. In the mirror, she saw a transformed woman – one happier and more content than the Lottie of last year. Finally, things were falling into place. They had their farm, and they had a son, and they had condoms.

CHAPTER 7

At a Christmas dance in Towner Hazel thought she was in teenager heaven. She had taken extra time to fix her hair and wore a pale blue dress with ruffles and a slightly lower-than-proper neckline and her flouncy skirt was just ankle length. Most of the local boys couldn't keep their eyes off her and followed her around like sick puppies. She was a natural dancer, at ease with her body, clearly enjoying herself, and she especially liked being the center of attention. She danced every dance.

While waiting for one of the boys to bring her a glass of punch, she noticed an attractive couple dancing. The man was younger than her father and his wife was clearly pregnant. Soon they approached her and started to chat. They were Gus and Libby Stover. He was a manager at the bank in Denbeigh.

Libby said, "Miss Hastings, you look radiant this evening, and that blue dress is so pretty. Did you make it?

"Yes I did. In fact I just finished it this afternoon."

Gus looked at her admiringly, "Well, Young Lady, you are indeed the belle of the ball."

"Thank you, Sir."

They sipped their punch and Libby said, "I've got three children at home, and number four will be here in the spring. I don't know what I'm going to do if we can't find a good nanny to help with the children."

"We'll find one, Dear," her husband said and turned a big smile on Hazel. "Maybe Miss Hastings would be interested in the position."

Hazel was surprised but as soon as she heard the idea she found it exciting. On the way home with Lillian driving, she jabbered on. "I'd be in town, and I could see my friends, and I could make some money, and maybe meet some of Gus's friends. Oh, I can't wait." Charlie allowed the girls to drive to the dances on their own now that they were older.

At home she was glowing as she told her parents, "Gus Stover offered me a job helping his wife and taking care of their three children. His wife is really nice. Her name is Libby and she's pregnant again." Lottie, who was knitting a sweater for Charlotte, was flabbergasted that her flighty, fun-loving daughter wanted the job.

Lottie said, "Such a long way!" Denbeigh was about 8 miles from their farm.

"Not that far, now that Pa has the car."

Charlie looked up from the fireplace he was stoking and asked, "He wants you to live with them all week?"

"I could come home on weekends."

"And how do you plan to get back and forth?" Lottie asked, sitting back in her chair and putting down her needlework. She folded her hands and looked Hazel directly in her eyes, probing for a hidden motive.

Nervously ignoring Lottie, Hazel gave her father a hug and a *pleeeeease* look. "Pa, could you take me and pick me up?"

"How much are they going to pay you?" Lottie, always practical, asked.

"Gus, I mean, Mr. Stover, said $25 a month, and they will feed me and I'll have a bed in their daughter's room."

"When will you come home?" Lottie asked.

"I could come home Friday evening or Saturday morning and go back Sunday night. I have to be there on Monday morning to get the children ready for school. Libby likes to sleep late in the mornings, especially when she's pregnant," Hazel explained.

The money would be welcomed and would just about make the car payment, Lottie thought.

"Are you willing to drive her back and forth, Charlie?"

Hazel went over and hugged him again. "Please, Papa, I want to do this."

Charlie said, "Well, we can give it a try for a month or two and see how it works out."

Hazel squealed and jumped up and down. She hugged him again, harder this time.

"Thanks, Pa." He smiled to see her so happy.

Lottie cleared her throat and nodded her tentative agreement, still doubtful.

It was agreed that Hazel would contribute $20 to the family coffers each month and keep $5 for herself to buy whatever she wanted. Charlie would pick her up on Saturday mornings when he went into town to get supplies. He would take her back on Sunday evening.

Hazel and Lottie had similar personalities in some ways and often were on the same side of issues and decisions. Charlie allowed this daughter to manipulate him, and loved her for the same reasons he loved his wife. Both were quick-thinking, bright, hard-working, independent, and fiercely loyal to their family. On the other hand, both could be bossy, domineering, and impatient. They liked to be in control -- once they had made up their minds they would push until they got their way. Lottie had learned about the need to compromise, at 15 Hazel would do no such thing.

Hazel was the first to leave the nest and it was a difficult change for her parents. Lottie believed that she still needed guidance to make sensible decisions. She had always been her own person, and now that she was nearly an adult, her will was even stronger.

Lottie's Lot

She had Charlie's family features -- a round face surrounded with naturally curly blond hair. Her sea foam blue eyes sparkled when she was excited. Her full lips and blossoming body added to her appeal, although she wasn't fully aware of this. At this age – no longer a little girl but not yet a woman – she was innocent and vulnerable.

With her outgoing personality she made friends easily. She had a sense of humor that found fun in silly situations and she laughed easily. She was confident that she would blend into the Stover family with no problems. She was excited to be starting her first real job.

Hazel's experience with her own siblings had prepared her for taking care of the Stover children. Lowell was eight years old, Sybil six, and Adolph three. Each day Hazel got up early, dressed the two older children, fixed their breakfast, and made them lunches to take to school.

After they left, she cleaned up the kitchen and played games with 'Dolph or took him for walks and read to him. When the older children came home from school and changed into their play clothes, she supervised the few chores assigned to them by their father and then helped them with homework. Mrs. Stover cooked the mid-day meal and supper. Sometimes Hazel assisted her with meal preparation and she ate with the family. Then she cleaned up the dishes and kitchen after supper while Libby put the children to bed.

Hazel had her own bed in Sybil's room. In the evenings she had a little free time after the children went to bed. Sometimes she would go for a walk, or sit on the swing on the porch, or visit a girlfriend from school that lived a block away.

Libby was pleased with Hazel's services. The children loved her. One month stretched into three.

Gus Stover was 29, slim, short, and good-looking, with a quirky sense of humor. His father owned the bank in Denbeigh, and he was the assistant manager responsible for small loans and operations. He was friendly and affable with everyone. Occasionally he would come out in the evening and sit next to Hazel on the swing. He began to smile at her more frequently during meals and sit closer to her on the swing. She thought he was handsome and was flattered by his attention. She had little experience with the opposite sex, and thought he was just being friendly when he paid more attention to her.

One night in the middle of March, when the moon was rising, Gus put his hand on her knee and gently squeezed. Her heart raced; she blushed and felt terribly confused. She thought she should remove his hand or get up and leave, even slap his face. But he was her boss. She didn't want to make him angry and perhaps lose her job. So she did nothing, just sat frozen and confused. Her heart was pounding, her flushed face hidden in the dark.

His touch was warm and penetrating. Somewhere deep inside of her she liked the feeling. After a few minutes, he leaned over and brushed her cheek with his lips. Then without a word, he got up and went inside. She sat paralyzed and confused.

She avoided him for the next week. Then, on her 16th birthday, he waited until Libby went to bed and said, "Hazel, I have a special birthday present for you. Come with me." She hesitated, but he led her to the storage shed behind the house. He smiled wickedly as he pushed open the door.

Inside she saw a tarpaulin with a blanket and pillow on the floor. He stepped inside with her, and then closed the door. He pulled her toward him, pressing her body against the door and pushing himself against her. His mouth was on hers and he kissed her, hard at first, then slowly and gently. Her body craved more, but she heard herself pleading out loud, "No! No! Stop!" In her mind she knew this was wrong, but her body took over and won the battle. When he put his hand under her blouse and caressed her breasts, she let him, and when he reached up under her skirt she let him, and when he lowered her to the ground she let him. She started breathing faster, panting.

She was shocked as he continued. It hurt when he pushed his penis inside her, and pumped back and forth until he made a strange sound and pulled it out. Afterward when he helped her up, she was surprised and embarrassed to notice a bloody discharge. After the initial touching, she didn't feel anything pleasurable, just shame and fear.

She didn't know what was going to happen, what men and women did together. Although she had seen animals on the farm mating, it didn't occur to her that people might do something similar. Her short-lived arousal surprised and shamed her. Her body had betrayed her and so did Gus Stover.

He walked her back to the house and told her, "Honey, let's just keep this a little secret between us." She pulled her head away when he tried to kiss her cheek.

After washing herself, she went to bed and cried herself to sleep. The following day, a Friday, she went through her duties like a sleepwalker. Libby noticed how quiet she was and asked, "Are you ill, Hazel? You seem sick or something."

"No, I'm fine," Hazel answered. "Just got the curse."

Libby said, "Well, if you want to rest or take a nap, go ahead."

Hazel thanked her, happy to get a few minutes to herself. When she was alone in her room, the tears started to flow again. She struggled to keep them under control, not wanting Libby to ask why her eyes were red. After calming down a bit, she returned to the kitchen.

"Mrs. Stover," she began. Libby stopped and looked at her, a question in her eyes.

"Umm, I have to leave."

"Well, I know your father is picking you up tomorrow morning."

"Umm. I won't be back. I can't stay."

Libby was dumbfounded. Everything had seemed to be fine. "Why? What's wrong?"

Hazel, tight-lipped and fighting back tears, just shook her head.

The next morning, she ran to the car as soon as Charlie pulled into the driveway. He saw that Hazel's face was pale, her eyes red and bloodshot. She whispered that she wanted to go home with him and not come back. Puzzled, Charlie loaded her belongings into the roadster. On the drive home he probed to find out what was wrong, but Hazel just shook her head, tears falling all the while.

By the middle of May Hazel was throwing up in the mornings and had missed two menstrual periods. She knew this was what had happened whenever her mother was going to have a baby and realized that she was in the same boat. Lottie noticed her behavior and told Charlie, "I think Hazel is pregnant. We need to have a talk with her."

They sent the other children outside and sat Hazel down at the kitchen table.

Charlie looked her in the eye and said, "Your mother tells me that you're going to have a child. Is this true?"

Hazel looked at Lottie for support and got none. "Yes, I think so." She bowed her head and spoke so softly it was hard to hear her.

"How did this happen?" Charlie was unusually stern and angry. "You're only 16 years old – you're still a child yourself."

Reluctantly, she told them what Gus had done. She didn't tell them about her secret attraction to Gus and her failure to stop his advances, but her guilt nagged at her. Whenever she overheard stories about young girls getting pregnant, the girl was always to blame. People would say, "She asked for it." Hazel wondered if she had "asked for it."

Lottie's Lot

Lottie's worst fears were confirmed. The women at the quilting bee often gossiped about girls who became pregnant before they were properly wed and made jokes about shotgun weddings. She'd worried that something bad might happen when Hazel left home. Pregnancy outside of marriage was the most terrible disgrace a family could face.

Lottie blamed herself a little. She had intended to talk to Hazel about sex, intercourse, and pregnancy but the time never seemed right. She thought she had plenty of time before Hazel would be ready to get married.

Charlie couldn't contain his rage. Early the next day he drove to Denbeigh marched into the bank and straight up to the desk of Andrew Stover, the bank manager and Gus's father. Charlie didn't mince words: "Your son forced himself on my daughter. He took advantage of her and now she's pregnant. That son-of-a-bitch!"

Charlie stood above Andrew and glared at Gus, who had his face buried in paperwork.

"Hold on now, Charlie," Andrew replied. He gestured toward a chair but Charlie remained standing. He raised his voice, wanting other customers to overhear.

"He got my daughter pregnant. She's only 16. What are you going to do about this?"

Andrew whispered through his teeth, "I'm sure that if Gus had anything to do with your girl it was because she was parading around and flirting with him. She got what she asked for."

Charlie turned white as the blood drained from his face. "How dare you say that!" He grabbed a glass paperweight from the desk and slammed it down so hard it shattered into a hundred pieces. Andrew started to stand up, but Charlie held up a fist. Seeing his eyes full of pure rage, the banker slowly sat back down.

Charlie stopped in his tracks, realizing he was on the verge of hitting Andrew or Gus. Being arrested for assault would just make matters worse. As Charlie stood glowering at Stover, he realized he didn't know what he wanted. The damage couldn't be undone. The Stover's had heard what he had to say, and so had a number of his neighbors. Gus Stover had a wife and family, so they couldn't demand that he marry Hazel. What else could he do? He had never felt such rage and at the same time such impotence.

"You'd better make this right," he yelled to Gus on the other side of the bank. He didn't trust himself to get any closer to Gus. He wanted to beat him up so badly. With the blood pumping in his temples, he glared at Gus, then without another word, turned around and left.

Gus glanced up from his desk and smirked as Charlie stormed out the front door. Andrew signaled him to go outside. They went out the back door.

Andrew asked Gus, "What the hell did you do to that girl?"

Gus grinned, "What do you think! I gave her a birthday present …one she won't forget."

"You're a damn fool. You have disgraced this family and shamed your wife and children."

"Now, Pa," Gus began but his father cut him off.

"You keep your pants closed, or else! How would you like to move to Bismarck or maybe Milwaukee and find a job on your own to support your family?"

"Please, Pa, don't get mad at me," Gus said, a little fear trickling into his voice.

"I have never been so serious in my life, Augustus. You straighten up or I will disown you. I mean it!" Andrew glared at Gus, then turned abruptly and went back inside.

Lottie's Lot

The juicy story spread like a prairie fire and by evening everyone in the Denbeigh community knew about the confrontation at the bank and about Hazel's pregnancy.

As the news sank in, over the next several days, Lottie was angry at herself for not having told her daughter what she needed to know and angry at Hazel for being so foolish. She didn't know if Hazel had flirted and brought this on herself or if Gus Stover had simply taken advantage of her.

Yet in spite of her shock, disappointment, and anger a great sense of tenderness and protectiveness filled her heart. Whenever she looked at her daughter she saw a vulnerable, wounded child obliged to grow up too soon. At barely 16, Hazel was about to be saddled with responsibilities beyond her tender years in birthing and raising a child.

Members of the Grange were split in their loyalties. They liked Charlie and Lottie and thought Lillian was the best teacher they had ever had, but many were long-time residents and some were even related to the Stover's.

Sides began to form. Small-town loyalties to long-term friends and relatives took precedence over siding with newcomers. The Stover's had been in the area for three generations, the Hastings for just a few years. To protect their own interests, the farm families needed to stay on the bankers' good side, even those who liked the Hastings family and believed they had been wronged sided with the Stover's.

Families with pregnant daughters usually tried to escape humiliation by sending the girl away to a grandmother, an aunt, or a "foundling home," where the girl could stay until the delivery. Most often, the baby was given up for adoption, and the girl returned home from her "vacation" as though nothing had happened.

Lottie struggled between her shame at Hazel's condition and her maternal instinct to protect her child. This was a major sin, one that went against everything Lottie believed. But she knew that Hazel had not committed the sin willingly.

"What that man did was wrong, sinful," Lottie said whenever the family discussed the subject. Her face reddened and her throat tightened every time she thought of Gus Stover. She was shocked at her fierce hatred of him. Sometimes, while working in the house, she mentally plotted ways to get even with him. She wanted to hit him, to beat him up and make him pay for what he did to her daughter.

In her frustration, she unconsciously banged the dishes against the sink and broke a few bowls. Then she remembered that the Lord had said, "Vengeance is mine," and backed off. Gus would pay for his sin in some horrible way meted out by a just God.

Lottie's shame faded as the powerful, protective mother lioness in her emerged. She was going to shield her daughter no matter what happened. She knew in her heart that Hazel wasn't to blame, that she had been violated against her will.

For her part, Hazel wanted to hide from the talk and stares of people in the community. She went into isolation, staying at home day and night, even looking out the windows for signs of passersby before she did her outdoor chores. Feeling responsible for the ordeal her family was going through, she offered to move to Minneapolis and stay with Aunt Carrie. But the last thing Lottie could imagine was letting Hazel leave home again.

"Ma, let me go. It will be easier for all of you here."

"No." Lottie stood tall and squared her shoulders. "You are my daughter. We are all in this together and we will see it through to the birth of that baby."

Lottie had made up her mind, and Charlie and Lillian agreed that they would support, take care of, and protect Hazel. And the new baby would be welcomed into their family. The crisis brought them all closer. They were a family – and that was more important than being part of the Denbigh and Towner community.

Their decision had consequences. One day when Lottie was shopping at Mr. Gee's store Mary Rose Green walked in.

Lottie greeted her, "Hello, you're just the person I want to see."

Mary Rose, the friend and midwife who had helped deliver two of her daughters, was cool, avoiding eye contact. "Hello, Lottie. Are you well today?"

"I'm fine. Thank you for asking. I do have something I would like to talk to you about." She hurried on. "My daughter, Hazel, is going to have a child in December and I would like you to look after her during the pregnancy and to deliver her baby when the time comes."

Her friend stiffened and lowered her eyes. "I'm sorry but I can't help you out this time. I do hope you understand." And she quickly walked out of the store.

Lottie was stunned. This was just the beginning.

The school board informed Lillian that she wasn't qualified to continue teaching because she hadn't finished high school. Never mind that they'd hired her at the end of her tenth grade, knowing full well this would prevent her from graduating.

The younger Hastings children were called names at school. The first Sunday night in August, mean-spirited neighbors dumped garbage on their porch.

On September 5, Andrew Stover drove out to the farm and, remaining seated in his car with the engine running, told Charlie that he was two months behind in his payments. If the balance wasn't paid in full by November 15, the bank intended to foreclose and take the farm.

When Stover left, Charlie took the medicinal whiskey out of the cupboard, sat at the kitchen table, and drank until the bottle was empty. Lottie knew this was a time to hold her tongue. When she tried to put her arms around him to comfort him, he broke down and cried.

"I feel like a snowball rolling down a big hill, Lottie," he sobbed. "I just keep gathering dirt and rocks and ice, and I can't stop. I don't know what to do. Things just keep going wrong and I keep rolling faster and faster. Like a snowball to hell."

Hazel had never seen her father cry before. She watched with a heavy heart, feeling guilty and responsible for the bank's unreasonable demands. But mostly she felt sorry for herself. She was going to become a mother, because some jerk forced himself on her. It wasn't fair! This wasn't the way she had dreamed her life would be.

Their loans totaled almost $400 – an out-of-reach sum for the Hastings family. Charlie telegraphed his mother in desperation and Rebecca wired the money he needed.

On December 19, 1908, Abigail Charlotte was born. Lottie helped to deliver her first grandchild -- just 14 months younger than her own last child. Though they welcomed the baby with love, it was an unhappy Christmas for the Hastings family.

Charlie had hoped to live out his life on their farm, and Lottie, despite her doubts, wanted his dream to come true. Now she felt it was impossible to stay. In May, their five-year commitment to the homestead land grant had been completed, and they were free to sell it all and leave.

Buddy was frequently sick with ear infections and colds. At 14 months he still wasn't walking. Lottie worried about him and wanted to be closer to better medical care. Reluctantly Charlie listened to her arguments for moving to Minneapolis, where she thought Charlie had a chance of finding a job. Charlie didn't want to leave his farm. He felt at home here and had worked so hard to provide a good living for his family and build the life he wanted. Lottie's dissatisfaction bothered him.

Lottie's Lot

"Lottie, this is just another storm we have to weather. In time it will blow over," he said, but she wouldn't hear him. She shook her head vehemently.

"No, Charlie. This is too hard to bear. Everyone is suffering. The town, the people we thought were our friends, has all turned against us. The Stovers will find some other way to hurt us through the bank. No one wants us here."

"Please, Lottie," Charlie begged. "It will all be forgotten in a year or two."

But she was adamant and wouldn't give an inch. "No! All the children are suffering. What is it going to be like for little Abby to grow up here? We have to leave. The sooner the better!"

She wore him down. In February he gave in to her and agreed to leave. Besides Andrew and Gus Stover's threats to ruin them and all they had worked so hard for, Hazel feared Gus might try to hurt her or the baby.

In March 1909, Old Man Winter kissed Mother Earth with a freezing blizzard. The car couldn't navigate the icy roads. Lottie and Hazel took Lois, Ruby, and Bethany, Buddy, and Abby to Minneapolis by train.

They stayed with Carrie for a few weeks, until Lottie found a furnished boarding house with eight bedrooms. Lottie also saw an income opportunity, and asked the landlord for permission to use four bedrooms for her family and sub-let out the remaining four rooms, to help to pay the rent and buy some food.

The rest of the family would move in the spring, when the roads were passable. Charlie would make several trips in the car to bring Lillian and Charlotte and the family belongings after the farm was sold. He arranged for an auction of all their equipment and possessions.

At the end of April, Hazel took the train back to Denbeigh with Abby to help her father get things ready to sell and to help her sisters pack up their things for the move. At the auction in May, Charlie watched, heartbroken, as all they had worked so hard for over the past six years was practically given away. He was glad Lottie wasn't there to see her furniture sold for so little. He used the proceeds to repay Rebecca, and had just enough left to pay the moving expenses.

The one thing he didn't sell was Lottie's sewing machine, his first birthday gift to her after their marriage. Those giddily happy days seemed a century ago.

The day after the auction, Hazel borrowed Charlie's car, tucked baby Abby into a basket, and drove into Denbeigh. Her first stop was Gus Stover's house. Emboldened by the strong support of her family and empowered by her anger at the way their community had treated them, Hazel pulled up in front, gathered Abby into her arms, and knocked on the door.

When Libby, looking tired and harassed, answered her knock, she said, "Hi, Libby. I'll be leaving North Dakota soon so I came to say goodbye." Hazel smiled slightly at the shock on Libby's face. Libby had heard the rumors and wasn't sure what to believe. For the survival of her family, she had decided to blame Hazel.

Hazel went on, "Libby, this is Abby. I wanted you and her half-brothers and half-sisters to see her before we go."

Libby opened her mouth to speak, eyes widening. "What?"

"I want you to know the truth. On my 16th birthday, Gus forced himself on me in the shed. Abby is his daughter."

Libby stepped back from the door, put her hand to her mouth, and burst into tears.

Hazel spoke more gently. "I am sorry. I would never hurt you, but you have a right to know the truth about the man you married."

Abby started to fuss and Hazel said, "We have to go. Take care of yourself, Libby."

Libby's face paled. She backed further into the house, then quietly closed the door.

Hazel put Abby back into her basket and drove to the bank. She walked straight to Gus Stover's desk.

She said, "Take a look at your daughter, Gus. It will be the first and last time you'll ever see her."

Abby smiled sweetly at her father.

Gus was dumbfounded and embarrassed. Hazel watched his face redden.

She continued, deliberately raising her voice. "I stopped by your house to introduce Abby to her half-brothers and sisters -- and to Libby, of course. You should have an interesting evening when you get home tonight."

Gus found his voice. He growled through gritted teeth, "Get out of here." His father and all the bank employees and customers were watching with great interest.

"Of course -- we were just leaving." Hazel raised her voice so everyone could hear, "Say good-bye to your daddy, Abby."

She turned toward the door, took a few steps, then slowly turned back and spit in Gus Stover's face.

"In the future, leave young girls alone." Her voice was controlled, but loud enough for everyone to hear. Then, to the sound of nervous laughter, with head held high she and Abby marched out of the bank, out of Gus Stovers life, and out of North Dakota for good.

CHAPTER 8

A few months after they moved into the boarding house in Minneapolis, Charlie found a buyer for the homestead, including the house, the outbuildings, and the 160 acres. The money would be a cushion until he found a job. He sold it all for $600.

Lottie rented the entire boarding house. It had eight bedrooms, a large kitchen, a dining room, and parlor. She sublet four rooms to boarders who paid extra for meals. The rent from those rooms covered the Hastings family's rent for the rooms they needed. Lottie and Charlie took one bedroom and Lottie insisted that Buddy sleep in the same room. Lillian and Charlotte shared a room, and Beth, Ruby, and Lois had another room. Hazel and Abby had a room to themselves.

Lottie stayed busy as usual. She shopped for food, cooked meals for the boarders and the family, and supervised the older children who kept the house clean, did the laundry, and looked after the younger ones while Charlie looked for a job. She always found time to give Buddy special attention. Nursing him gave her a few moments of privacy and relaxation. As he approached three, Charlie questioned her about nursing the boy for so long. She shushed him and said, "He's just a baby," as Buddy smiled angelically into his mother's eyes.

She couldn't get enough of holding and caressing her son, she found emotional gratification in nursing him. As tension grew between her and Charlie, Buddy became the primary focus of her affection. Charlie felt more and more shut out of their relationship.

The older girls got jobs and contributed to the family coffers. Lillian worked as a clerk at a department store, while Hazel waitressed at a lunch counter. Charlotte and Beth helped take care of the younger ones. Ruby and Lois were assigned to set and clear the table, sweep the floors, dust the furniture, and fold clean clothes and put them away.

Whining or complaining wasn't tolerated. One look from Lottie stifled any talk of missing the farm, or any dissension over chores. She expected the children to fulfill their duties perfectly. She showed them how to do each chore once, and after that they had to do it right or answer to her. The girls hated her meticulous scrutiny and dreading a confrontation. She tested cleanliness with a white glove -- and pity the child who left a speck of dirt behind.

Charlie, painfully aware of his responsibility to support ten people, found looking for a job daunting. He was depressed about losing the farm and realized that he was over the age limit to work for the railroad. He applied for several other jobs with no luck. He came home one evening discouraged after being brusquely turned down for two jobs in the same day.

He watched Lottie dip pieces of chicken in flour and drop them into hot lard. She was doing much better than he was with this drastic change in their lives. She was busy caring for the children and running the boarding house. He knew she had private moments of regret and missed their old life, but he admired her strength to keep going, to do whatever was necessary. He had always thought he had that strength, too, but since arriving in Minneapolis he was beginning to doubt it.

"I know you're discouraged," she said without looking up. Lottie usually understood how he felt even when he didn't tell her. "Why not at least try the railroad? You have a good record of many years of loyal work with them." She smiled and gently pinched his cheek, leaving a trace of flour.

"You know the maximum age to get hired by the railroad is 35 ... and I'm 42."

"I know, but maybe they'll consider your past service and make an exception."

"I asked the line manager about that last week, Lottie, and he said the age limit is strictly enforced."

"Then you must talk to Elmer." She dabbed at the fried chicken with a cloth, soaking up some of the excess grease.

He groaned. "I hate to take advantage of him."

"You mean you're too proud to ask for his help. But if the situation were reversed, you'd help him."

"The situation would never be reversed," Charlie muttered. "My brother would never get himself into such a mess."

"Charlie!" she spoke sharply. "I know that you've lost your dream. So have the children and me. Our family has suffered terribly, and none of it was fair. But what choice do we have? We must go on and make a new life. Now you need to shake off this self-pity and do what you have to do."

Charlie knew she was right. The next day he jumped on a freight car on a train that was heading west, and got off in Green Bay, Wisconsin, where Elmer and Franny lived. Elmer was a Division Superintendent for the Chicago, Milwaukee, and St. Paul Railroad and knew many supervisors and powerful people in the railroad business. Charlie knocked on Elmer's door and his surprised when his brother saw him he engulfed him in a big hug. It felt good. "To what do I owe this nice surprise?" Elmer asked as they walked into the parlor.

Charlie quickly swallowed his pride and said, "Elmer, I need your help." They talked about the situation, and Elmer made a few phone calls.

Lottie's Lot

"Charlie, I think your best bet is the Northern Pacific. Based on what a friend told me, if you give your age on the application as 41 it will be overlooked."

Gratefully, he followed Elmer's advice, and got a job. In July, 1910, he started work as a brakeman for the Northern Pacific Railroad Company, with his home base in Minneapolis. His spirits rose; at last he would be able to support his family again.

Six weeks later there was a disastrous accident in the yard. The brakes failed on one car and 20 railroad cars crashed into each other. Charlie was blamed. He and his supervisor were suspended from work for 10 days while the incident was investigated.

Charlie knew he would be blamed even though it wasn't his fault. He'd had a few slugs of whiskey from his flask before the collision, which witnesses would confirm. He quit before they could fire him. With a discharge for causing an accident on his personnel record he would never get another job with any railroad.

His usual working shift was from 4 pm. to midnight. When he walked in the door at 8 pm. Lottie was surprised, and she knew something bad had happened. She was playing with Buddy before she nursed him for the night and put him to bed.

He told her about the accident.

"It made a hell of a noise," he said.

She could smell alcohol on his breath. "Was anyone hurt?"

"No."

"Whose fault was it?"

"I don't know what happened. They claimed that I didn't set all the brakes right, but I know I did. I think someone up the line made a mistake before the cars got to me."

He told her, "I'm suspended for 10 days while they *investigate*. That almost always means they fire someone in the end. Somebody is going to pay for this, responsible or not!"

Lottie watched him for a moment. "Charlie, have you been drinking?" she asked quietly.

"Just a few," he confessed sheepishly.

"All right," she persisted. "Did you have a few drinks *before* or *after* the collision?"

He started up the stairs. "I'm tired. I want to go to bed now."

She raised her voice. "Answer me!"

"What?" he muttered, continuing up the stairs. She followed him to the bottom of the steps and repeated her question in the slow, no-nonsense voice she used with an unruly child.

"*Answer me!*"

He was caught and ashamed. He paused on the stairs, his back still turned.

"Charlie Hastings, did you have 'a few' drinks *before* or *after* the collision?"

Without turning around he answered, "Before."

"And after," he whispered as he went into the bedroom and closed the door.

Buddy started to cry. He didn't like it when Lottie raised her voice. She took out her breast and let him suckle while she fumed. He was getting heavy for her to carry around.

After the children had been put to bed, Lottie found Charlie snoring in bed. She shook him awake roughly. "Charlie, we need to talk."

106

Lottie's Lot

He rolled over and muttered, "Tomorrow."

"No. Now," Lottie insisted. He reluctantly turned over to face her and opened his eyes, his arm bracing his head.
"What is it?"

"Why were you drinking on the job? You know that is strictly forbidden and you can be fired for it. How could you put your job and the livelihood of your family at risk?" She started out whispering but the volume rose as her anger surfaced.

He had no defense. "It was Roger's birthday, and we all had a drink to celebrate. I just had a short slug."

"Really! Charlie, don't lie to me. I saw you when you came home. You had more than a short slug."

"Lottie, let's not argue tonight. I'm worried."

"You should be. It took so much effort to get this job, and now what? What are you going to do if you get fired?" she demanded.

He turned and faced the wall, refusing to look at her or answer. She took the blanket and her pillow and went downstairs. That night she slept on the parlor sofa.

The next day, when Charlie told her he had quit his job to avoid having the results of an investigation show up on his record, Lottie wouldn't talk to him. She was fed up with his drinking. They'd had dozens of discussions of possible consequences, which he had obviously ignored. He didn't think he had a problem, but it was becoming apparent to everyone else that he drank too much and too often.

Hazel's unplanned motherhood had made her somewhat more mature, and she wanted to take responsibility for herself and her child, rather than depend entirely on her parents. She got a job waitressing from 10 am to 3 pm at a lunch counter a few blocks from their boarding house.

Lottie agreed to take care of Abby when Hazel was working in exchange for $5 a week and help with supper.

Although Abby and Buddy were 14 months apart, they grew up like siblings. Abby was younger but she was more competitive and aggressive. She never learned to share. If Buddy was playing with a toy she would grab it, glaring at him with narrowed eyes as if daring him to defend himself. If he tried to take his toy back she would hide it behind her or hit him and run away.

He would let her take the toy, then run crying to his mother, who scooped him up and comforted him with kisses and murmured words of affection. On occasion Abby was scolded, but most of the time she got away with it and gloated. She learned early to get her own way no matter what it took.

At 17, Hazel often thought about the fun she had missed, laughing and gossiping at parties and dances with her friends, wearing pretty dresses, and flirting with boys her age. She supposed all that was behind her now.

One of her regular customers at the diner, a telephone line installer, went out of his way to tease her every time he stopped in for lunch – always a bowl of vegetable soup or a cheese and tomato sandwich: "Watch out, Hazel. You're going to drop those plates! Don't drop them! Oops, there they go."

Hazel never dropped a plate, and she sometimes wrinkled her nose and made a face at him when he was ribbing her. She liked his easy friendly smile and quick sense of humor.

Trim and handsome at 30, George Frederick Hopf was 13 years older than she. He was just 4 inches taller than her 5-foot-2. His gray-blue eyes were welcoming, yet they had a hint of sadness. He was losing a little of his light brown hair in the front, raising his forehead and giving him an intelligent look.

Lottie's Lot

After eating at her lunch counter for a few weeks and exchanging laughs, he invited her out to supper. She had never been on a real date and didn't know what to say so she turned him down. He asked her again the following day and every day after that until she gave in.

George picked her up at the boarding house, wearing a clean white shirt and dark blue necktie. He met Lottie, her sisters, and Abby. He took her to a nice but comfortable restaurant; Hazel appreciated his good manners and found him easy to talk with. She was tempted to order a steak, but settled for a bowl of beef stew. He had a fish dinner. She felt safe with him. He was kind and thoughtful.

After they had gone out a few times, she knew she had to be honest with him. He thought she was a "normal" young woman. But she wasn't. She was flawed, with an illegitimate child.

At the beginning of their next date, after they had ordered their meal, she took the plunge. "There's something you should know about me, George."

"What?" he asked curiously.

She swallowed, head bowed as she twisted her napkin in her lap. Getting up her courage, she looked him directly in the eyes and blurted out, "I have a child… a little girl. Her name is Abby. You've seen her at our house. "

He didn't react. Time seemed to stand still as he watched her twist her napkin beyond recognition. Finally he asked, "How old are you, Hazel?"

"I'll be 18 next month," she answered.

"How old is your daughter?" he asked calmly, stalling for time to understand.

"She's 15 months old," she answered.

"Then you were just 16 when you had her. Right?" He tried to hide his surprise. "Who is her father and where is he?"

She lowered her face and mumbled, "I don't like to talk about it."

"Please tell me. You can trust me, Hazel. I'm your friend."

She explained how her employer had forced himself on her. Tears of nervousness and shame fell down her rosy cheeks and her nose began to run. He handed her a handkerchief and she gratefully accepted it. He reached across the table to take her hand. Feeling she could trust this gentle man, she told him about her family's humiliation in the small North Dakota town and her feelings of guilt and responsibility.

Hazel had never told her story to anyone outside the family. She found herself gulping down sobs as she relived the feelings that had been buried until now. She was surprised at her own reaction. When the food came she couldn't eat a bite.

George moved across the booth and sat next to her, holding her while she cried. She was embarrassed to be crying in public or even to be crying at all; it was not something she did very often. She tried to stifle her tears but they just kept coming. She felt safe cradled in his arms.

When Hazel felt better, George paid the bill and they walked for hours, talking, crying, and laughing. He said, "Hazel, I don't mind you having a child. I like children and want some myself."

His smile and the tender squeeze of his hand made her feel much better. Her shame was gone.

George told her that he had been raised in Pittsburgh, Pennsylvania, the son of an emigrant from Germany. His father was a butcher and George worked in his shop after school and summers.

"I hate meat!" he said. "I hate the smell, the blood, the carcasses hanging in the cold box. I hate everything about it. I never eat it now."

Lottie's Lot

When he was 15 his father died of tuberculosis. George quit school and got a job as a telephone clerk to help his mother support his seven brothers and sisters. A few years later he was offered a better job stringing new telephone wires in Minneapolis for a lot more money. He took the job, and sent money back this mother every week.

When George came to pick up Hazel, he brought Abby some chocolates and teased her, saying he owned a chocolate factory and there was more where that came from. The delighted toddler dug into the bag, rewarding this nice man with a big smile full of chocolate-covered teeth.

George was a practicing Seventh Day Adventist and went to church on Saturdays. He invited Hazel to go with him, but she found their practices a little too strict for her liking. He was disappointed, but she was happy to let him follow his religion on his own. That had worked for her parents.

The Seventh Day Adventists believed in healthy living and preventive measures to keep from getting sick, which included eating no meat, few dairy products, and eggs only from clean chickens. They forbade the use of coffee, tea, tobacco, alcoholic beverages, hot spices, pepper, and rich desserts. Sugar was a special culprit, so the chocolates George had brought Abby were a rarity for him. George said he had first been attracted to the church because of its opposition to meat, but had found its other healthy and moral guidelines good ones to live by.

On their first few dates, he squeezed Hazel's hand when he brought her home or occasionally lifted it to his lips. George was gentle and respectful because of her history of rape, but he was also a lonely, virile man who found this young girl irresistible. In February he gave her a beautiful lace-trimmed Valentine card as they sat alone in the parlor of her boarding house. After she opened the card and smiled her thanks, he kissed her on the mouth.

"Oh," she said, surprised. She instinctively drew back. He held her hand. "Hazel, you are so beautiful."

"No. I'm not. I'm just an ordinary waitress."

"My dear, you are so much more than that. You don't know how special you are. I find you incredibly beautiful. When I'm with you I feel so happy and hopeful."

A few months later George proposed.

She hesitated. "I would like a few days to think about it."

The next day when Lottie sat down for a cup of tea in the kitchen, Hazel slid into a chair across the table from her.

As she poured a cup for herself she said, without looking up at her mother, "Ma, I have something to tell you. Last night George asked me to marry him."

Lottie's first question was, "Well, do you love George? He seems like a good man."

"Yes, he is a good man, I suppose," she agreed in a quiet voice.

"But you don't love him." Lottie knew the answer by Hazel's demeanor. She sighed. Her usually headstrong girl was uncharacteristically subdued.

"Hazel, I hoped that you would find someone you truly loved. But I think George will treat you well. He has a steady job, he's sober, and he follows the Bible. If a man is that devoted to his church, he must be a good man. And little Abby needs a father."

Hazel realized that as a single woman with a child, she could not support herself for long. She thought she could do worse than George. They were married in July 1910 at City Hall in Minneapolis. Lillian was her bridesmaid and witness.

Lottie's Lot

She got pregnant immediately and on April 5, 1911, she gave birth to George Kenneth Hopf, a healthy baby boy. Little George looked just like his father, and George Sr. couldn't stop bragging about him. Hazel nursed the hungry baby and he flourished.

Abby, at 2½, hated this interloper. The more George loved the baby the more she hated George, too. He was supposed to be her papa and now he had betrayed her and put her in second place.

After the railroad yard accident Charlie consoled himself with whiskey for a few days, but he knew he had to get sober and get a job. After cleaning himself up, he went to see Elmer again. Knowing that "Charlie Hastings" wouldn't be hired by any railroad now, the brothers brainstormed, and came up with a risky plan.

In September, Charles *Harkin, 33,* applied for a switchman's job with the Great Northern Railroad Company in Spokane, Washington. Two weeks after he began his new job he was called into the personnel office and confronted with lying about his name and age and was fired on the spot.

Her returned to Minneapolis so despondent and depressed he hated to face Lottie. He called Elmer first and Elmer got him a job as a brakeman with the Great Northern. He started work on November 11, 1910 and was assigned to Superior, Wisconsin.

Superior was a big railroad town at the tip of Lake Superior, right next to Duluth, Minnesota. This was a major switching area where trains loaded their contents, like coal, steel, and lumber, onto freighter ships, to be delivered to world ports. They also loaded freight cars with imported goods from all over the world to be distributed across the United States and Canada by train or truck.

Charlie asked Lottie to go to Superior with him, but she refused, saying that she didn't want to disrupt the family again so soon. The truth was that she was happy to have him out from under her feet for a while, especially when he was drinking so much. He left and rented a room in Superior. To fight his loneliness and depression, he often spent his evenings at a bar.

The night he left, as Lottie climbed into bed she thought about how many nights she had spent alone this year. How many more would there be? Every time she tried to figure out a solution to Charlie's drinking, she ran into complications in every direction. It was one of the rare times in her life when she didn't know what to do.

The next morning, she called Carrie and said, "Can you meet me at Daphne's Tearoom this afternoon?"

"What is it, Lottie? What's wrong?"

"I don't want to talk about it on the phone, but I really need a good chat with my sister."

"Of course. I'll meet you at 2."

"Thank you so much, Carrie. I can't wait."

Lottie took a streetcar to Daphne's, a place she seldom had a chance to go, and where she didn't expect to see anyone she knew. After they ordered, Carrie waited while Lottie arranged and rearranged the forks, spoons, knife, and cup around her plate. Finally, she looked up into her sister's familiar, comforting eyes.

"It's Charlie. Well, its Charlie's drinking. You know we've been through so much, and we have remained happy through it all. But lately he's changed. He drinks all the time."

"All the time, Lottie?"

"Well, a lot. Every day! He sneaks into the bathroom every hour or so with a flask. I think he drinks when he's working. There was a big crash in the yard when he had that job with Northern Pacific and he said he'd had 'just a few' before it happened. He quit the job so he wouldn't have to face the investigation."

114

Lottie's Lot

Lottie looked into Carrie's eyes. Carrie had never seen her sister so helpless, so distraught. She answered carefully. "Well, Lottie, he has been through a lot … with Hazel, and the farm, and …"

Lottie interrupted with a deep sigh, "I've been through the same things, Carrie, all of them, and I don't drink. He was strong when he was defending Hazel and selling the property and getting us ready to leave. But once we got here, he just turned into someone else. He just crumpled."

Carrie took a sip of tea and a bite of her cranberry muffin. "Men have so much pride, Lottie. Maybe this is the only way he knows to handle his pain. I expect it will stop when everything settles down again."

"I've tried to talk to him about it, and he just tells me he likes the taste and it helps him forget his problems. He says the drinking isn't a problem."

"And what do you say?"

Lottie poured herself another cup of tea and stirred milk into it.

"I tell him what Father taught us. That drinking alcohol is a terrible sin and leads to evil. The other night he told me that Father was the meanest, most hard-hardhearted man he had ever met and that I was just like him! Is that any way for a man to talk to his wife?"

Carrie placed her hand over Lottie's. "Do you really believe that, what Father said?"

"Yes, I believe most of it. It helps me figure out right from wrong. But I've learned a lot since those days, and I've tried to look at Charlie's drinking differently, I really have. I didn't make a fuss when he only had one drink sometimes and worked so hard. But this is different. Oh I don't know, Carrie. Sometimes I think I'm too hard on him but I know his drinking is causing his work problems. And it's the only real problem we have ever had in all these years."

Lottie glanced at the grandfather clock in the corner of the restaurant. "My goodness. It's almost 4 o'clock. I have to go home and make dinner. Carrie, I need to talk some more. Can you stay for dinner and maybe after?"

"Of course, Lottie. I know you're troubled. I only hope I can help." At the boarding house, Lottie headed for the kitchen, while Carrie called her husband to say she wouldn't be home. After dinner, the sisters went to the parlor on the first floor, closed the door, and talked quietly until dawn.

"What do you think you'll do?" Carrie asked.

Lottie walked around the room and looked out the front window at the dark sky for a minute before answering. "I don't know. I am so torn. I have never felt so mixed up, Carrie."

She sat next to her sister on the settee. "Part of me says I must be a good wife and stand by him, no matter what he does. But another part says it's not good for the children to see him this way. And that I should take them and leave."

"That's a really big step," Carrie said. "How will you live?"

Lottie just shook her head over and over.

"What do you think Mama would have done?" Carrie asked.

"She would have stood by Father. She stood by him through all his meanness and cruelty. But I swore I would never stay with a man who treated me badly."

"Is he treating you badly? Or hurting the children? Or is he only harming himself?" Carrie asked.

"Well, he can't hold a job," Lottie stifled a sob. "The house is full of tension when he's here. He ignores the children and avoids me – he never did that before. I don't want Bud growing up to think Charlie is the kind of man he should be. I never dreamed I would say that,

116

because I have always admired Charlie so much, but it has come to that point."

Lottie looked up and noticed, to her surprise, that the sky had grown lighter.

"Look, Carrie," she said. They watched silently as pink and pale yellow streaks erased the darkness and the sun peeked above the horizon.

"This has been a long talk," Lottie said, smiling. "I'm worn out. How about you?"

"I don't know if I've helped you."

"Oh you have. It helps to talk about it. I can't let the children know how upset I am and I don't know anyone else here."

"I think Lillian and Hazel already know something is wrong."

"Of course they do. They overhear everything and they're adults. But I still can't discuss it with them. You're the only one I can talk to."

"Lottie, you know that *you* have to decide. I can't tell you what to do."

Lottie nodded. "He's working in Superior, Wisconsin, right now and has taken a room there. He's s coming home for Christmas. That gives me a few weeks to think about it."

Carrie washed her face, and helped Lottie get breakfast on the table. They hugged each other tightly before she returned home.

Lillian liked her job in one of the city's largest department stores. And she found herself attracted to a man who stayed at the boarding house whenever he was in Minneapolis. Robert Hall was a truck driver from Alberta, Canada. She found charming, in his

English accent that he told Lillian that he had grown up on a family farm in Leicestershire, the third son of ten children with no chance of inheriting anything. He had immigrated to Canada when he couldn't find work in England. Robert loved the country life and was driving a truck to save enough money to build a cabin and establish his own farm once he received his homestead in western Canada.

At 27, he was tall and handsome in a rugged way, with a full head of wiry black hair and a beard to match. Robert was smitten with sweet, gentle Lillian from the day he first saw her. He liked to read poetry to her. At meals he entertained the Hastings family with tales of his adventures on the road and in Edmonton. He amused even no-nonsense Lottie, who looked forward to his dinnertime stories.

Lillian developed into a lovely young woman. At 19 she looked like her mother had at that same age. She had long, dark auburn hair that she twisted into a bun and pinned neatly with little combs and hairpins. Her brown eyes were soft and curious. Her demeanor was quiet and accepting. She never complained and always pitched in to help her mother and sisters. Robert was coming to spend Christmas with the family in 1910.

After six weeks in Superior, Charlie was able to get back to Minneapolis two days before Christmas. He was sober and subdued.

On Christmas Eve, Lillian glided into the parlor where her mother was placing Christmas gifts under the tree. She blushed as she held out her left hand and showed her mother a new ring with a small diamond. "Ma, Robert just asked me to marry him, and I said yes."

Lottie examined the ring, and then smiled at her oldest daughter. She held her at arm's length and asked, "Do you love him, Honey?" Despite her practicality, Lottie still felt a marriage should begin in love.

"I do, Ma.... with all my heart."

"Then I love him too. He's a good man. I think he will be a good husband to you."

"Robert," she called to him. "Come here."

Charlie and Robert came into the parlor from the porch where Robert had been sharing the news with Charlie, and Lottie said, "Welcome to our family." She grinned and embraced him. "You have good taste in women."

Charlie shook his hand and clapped him on the back. "Welcome, Son."

"Thank you, sir. I wanted to ask for your blessing before I proposed, but I couldn't wait."

"What are your plans?" Charlie asked.

Robert pulled Lillian next to him as she told her parents, "Robert wants me to move to Canada with him."

"Yep!" Robert grinned and replied.

"When?" Lottie asked. A feeling of dread set in at the thought of letting her firstborn move so far away … and to another country.

"We aren't sure yet," Lillian said. "But I was thinking, why don't we all move to Alberta? Pa could apply for another homestead."

Charlie perked up. "Great idea. That's just what we need, Lottie." He put his arm around Lottie's waist and squeezed her to him.

"When will you marry and where?" Lottie slowly slipped away from Charlie's arm.

"We haven't made any plans yet, Ma, but not for some months."

She smiled at Lottie. "Think about moving with us, Ma. It could be a clean start." She winked at Charlie. Everyone in the family knew that he'd never gotten over losing the farm, and that's when his drinking had started. Though Lottie simply nagged at him, Lillian was

119

more sympathetic. A new farm might be the only thing that would make him happy.

The thought of another big move overwhelmed Lottie. But the idea of a new start was appealing. Lottie knew Charlie wanted a new homestead more than anything, but she could not make a decision about moving until his drinking problem was resolved. He had been good so far this visit, but she had come to see him as undependable, and she didn't trust that he stayed sober when he was away from her.

On Christmas morning the children jumped out of bed early and rushed to the parlor to see their presents. Charlie, Lottie, and the older girls enjoyed watching them discover their new toys and shoes, which had been purchased with money earned by the hard work of Lillian, Hazel, and George. It was happy a Christmas.

Lottie set out a beautiful Christmas dinner of turkey stuffed with cornbread, mashed potatoes, scalloped corn, fruit salad, homemade bread, and a huge Christmas pudding for dessert.

As they sat down at the table, Robert brought out two bottles of champagne.
"This is the time for a toast," he said and announced to everyone that he and Lillian were engaged. Robert poured a glass for each adult and a tiny sip for each child. Lottie watched as Charlie placed a hand over his glass.

"None for me," he said quietly.

"Come on, Charlie. It's Christmas!" Robert urged, but Charlie continued to shake his head.

Lottie was pleased. This was a good sign. After the first toast and the first course, Robert poured each of the adults a second glass.

Even George Hopf, normally a teetotaler, had some champagne. "Charlie, please join us. Half a glass never hurt anyone."

Charlie couldn't think of a way to explain why he didn't want a drink. He moved his hand away and Robert poured the bubbly liquid. Charlie drank it all down quickly and everyone except Lottie cheered.

Lottie's Lot

After dinner the kids took their new toys upstairs and played in the bedrooms while the women cleared the table and cleaned the dishes. The men retreated to the parlor, as was their habit after a big Sunday or holiday dinner. Charlie gave each a cigar.

Robert had another surprise – a quart of Canadian Club whiskey. He took a swig and passed the bottle around.

"Take the chill off, Boys," he said. He was full of Christmas cheer and of being in love. He handed the bottle to George.

"No thanks. I've had my limit."

"One glass of champagne is your limit?" Robert asked.

"Yes. You see I'm a Seventh Day Adventist, and we don't believe in drinking alcohol. One sip of champagne at the holidays is the only spirits I touch."
He handed the bottle to Charlie.

Charlie admired the way George could stand up for his beliefs. But George didn't feel the mouth-watering desire he had for the whiskey. He could practically feel its heat through the glass of the bottle in his hand.

He thrust the bottle toward Robert. "I'll say no. Lottie, you know, she doesn't like it."

However, his desire for a drink overcame his wish to please Lottie. When Robert offered the bottle again, he rubbed the mouth of it with his sleeve and gulped down a large swig. "Cheers to moving to Canada! A fresh start!" he said. His cheers grew a little louder with each round.

Suddenly, little Buddy came galloping into the parlor. "I heard you, Papa," he said and jumped on Charlie's lap. Charlie stood up and held little Buddy around the waist and swung him around in the air.

"Stop, Papa, stop!" the child screeched between giggles. Charlie put his son on the floor and said, "Show me your new toys, Bud."

Buddy ran upstairs and scrambled back down with a bright red and green wooden toy truck with extra-large rubber wheels that Charlie had brought from Wisconsin. Charlie began rolling the truck on the floor. Then he ran it over Buddy's legs and Buddy lay flat down.

"Drive on me, Daddy. I'm the road." Charlie continued rolling the wooden truck over Buddy's legs and tummy, then around him on the floor, making loud motor noises. He stopped and tickled the child, giving him a few pinches on his round cheeks and chubby legs.

"That's my boy!" he shouted. "You are my little man, Buddy. My one and only son." He pinched a little harder each time, and Buddy said, "Papa, too hard! Stop!"

Lottie appeared in the doorway, having heard her youngest child's voice in distress.

"Hey, calm down. It's OK," he said, as Lottie stepped over the Christmas litter and pulled Buddy close to her.

She picked him up and comforted him. "Now what happened, Buddy? Where do you hurt? It's all right, Son. I won't let anyone hurt you." Charlie stood beside her and tried to put an arm around the boy.

"Papa!" he said and the tears started. "See?" He pulled the waist of his pants down to show her a bright pink spot on his side. He turned his face away from his father.

"I'm sorry, Buddy. I didn't realize I was hurting you," he said, patting his son's head.

Lottie lightly rubbed Buddy's leg as the boy clung to her and she murmured words of comfort. She gave Charlie a hard stare, and he couldn't meet her glance. In that moment, she knew Charlie had been drinking right here in their home, and her decision was made.

Lottie's Lot

That night, Charlie slept in one of the boarders' rooms. He started to plan his strategy for making up to Lottie, but he fell asleep before he could come up with an answer.

After breakfast the next morning, Lottie called Charlie aside.

"I'd like to take a walk with you, please."

"Sure," Charlie said, smiling. Maybe she wasn't so mad. It was a cold but sunny day, good for a brisk walk. They bundled up in their coats, gloves, and scarves, and headed for the park a few blocks away. She had her hands deep in her pockets so Charlie couldn't hold her hand as they walked. She was silent so he began.

"I am really excited about this move to Canada, Lottie. This is exactly what we need. A new farm, a new homestead. This is our chance to start over."

"Is it?" Her voice was low.

"Yes, yes, of course it is. Do you like living in Minneapolis?"

"No, not particularly. But I don't think a homestead is going to solve all our problems."

"Well, it would sure be a good start."

They watched the skaters on the pond as they continued to walk.

"Charlie," Lottie said. "How many drinks did you have yesterday?"

"Oh, not that again. Look, you saw me drink one small glass of champagne."

She waited.

"And the fellows had a bottle in the parlor. I took a couple of swigs. I didn't drink as much as Robert did."

123

"You didn't drink at all the first couple of days you were here. What happened?"

"It was Christmas. I was just enjoying myself. What is the big deal?"

"You hurt your son," she said, her voice rising. "You made that little boy cry."

"Oh, it was nothing. He overreacted. And I think you baby that child too much."

"He is a baby."

"All right, I'm sorry. I'll be more careful."

"I think you mean that right now. But I don't think you will do it."

"What are you talking about? I would never hurt the children." They had reached an empty bench and she sat down. He joined her.

"You have to face your drinking problem, Charlie." Her calm voice frightened Charlie even more than her angry yelling did.

"I don't have a drinking problem. Yes, maybe I shouldn't have had that last swig of whiskey with the kids in the house."

"You can't control how much you drink. You drink before you think about the consequences."

"I will stop drinking if it means that much to you, Lottie. I don't see why I should, but I'll stop just because you want me to."

"That won't work."

"When we get to the homestead, I'll be too busy to drink. It will be like it was before, in the good days. Remember?"

"I remember, Charlie. My happiest memories" (her throat choked on the words) "are of our years on the farm, until it all fell apart."

"Those are my best memories, too. And my worst."

Her worst doubts were confirmed: Charlie didn't understand the problem. She waited, hoping he would show her a glimpse of the old

124

Lottie's Lot

Charlie with all his energy, humor, and character, the Charlie who understood her doubts and questions. The Charlie who had helped her get through their hard times. He said nothing.

Finally, she spoke the hardest words she had ever had to say. "Charlie. We're going to Canada. But I don't want you to come with us."

He turned pale and said in a strangled voice, "Lottie, you can't mean that."

"I do. Your drinking is making this family unhappy."

"I can stop Lottie, but I need your help. I can't do it without you." He paused, "Lottie, don't you love me anymore?"

"I have never loved anyone as much as I love you and I know I never will." She began to cry and held her hands over her face. He put a hand on one of her shaking shoulders. "I will always love you but I don't see how I can live with you. Not with you drinking all the time. I can't stand it. You won't listen to me anymore."

"Lottie, I'm so sorry I hurt you. We've always been able to solve our problems, because we love each other. Can't we fix this together?"

Lottie took a handkerchief from her pocket and wiped her eyes. She took a deep breath.

"Love isn't enough, Charlie. We always trusted each other, too. But I can't trust you anymore. I can't even depend on you to hold down a job or to keep your word."

"You mean you could trust me if I stop drinking?"

"I don't know, Charlie. I hope so. But you have to really stop and you have to find the strength in yourself to do it." Her tears started again. "I think you have to be away from us and take care of yourself."

She looked up at him. She wanted to throw herself against him and hold him tightly and never let him go. Instead, she stood and took a step toward the house and continued walking. He watched her go. Her shoulders were shaking but she didn't look back.

Charlie stood, dumbfounded. He had never dreamed she would ask him to leave. He could see now how much his behavior had hurt her; he had never realized it before. He still had an urge to tell her she was overreacting. But she had made up her mind. He was in a sprung trap that he feared was closed for good.

Lottie cried all the way home and went directly to her bedroom. She was crying into her pillow when she heard him come in about 10 minutes later. He went to the room where he had been sleeping and in a few minutes he shut the door. After a moment of silence she heard him walk down the stairs, open the front door, and close it behind him.

CHAPTER 9

After Charlie left for Superior Lottie got the children together and told them, "We're moving to Canada when school is out. Papa won't be going with us, at least not yet."

"Why not?" Charlotte asked.

"He can't leave his job on the railroad now, so he'll be staying in Superior for a while."

"He didn't tell us goodbye when he left," Ruby said, puzzled.

"How long 'til he moves to Canada with us?" Bethany asked.

"I don't know. It depends."

"When will we see him again?" Beth asked, close to tears.

"I don't know," Lottie said. She couldn't bear any more questions, so she changed the subject. "Now, I want each of you to make a list of all the things you want to take to Canada with you. Then I'll go over them with you. We can't take everything, so just pick your favorite things. Charlotte, help Lois and Buddy with their lists."

"When is Lillian going?" Ruby asked.

"In a few weeks. She'll find a boarding house big enough for all of us to be together. Now scoot and do your homework. I want good grades from all of you."

Lillian and Hazel looked at each other. They knew something terrible had happened. They found Lottie sniffling in the pantry several times. In afternoons, they frequently heard her behind her bedroom door, crying into her pillow. When they asked what was wrong she just said, "It's your father. He's gone and I miss him."

Lillian said, "He'll be back, won't he?"

Lottie shook her head no and cried harder.

"Ma, did you have a fight or something?"

Gulping down sobs she told them, "There's nothing for you girls to worry about. Now get back to your work. We have a lot to do. I'll be fine."

Lillian and Hazel talked about their concerns. "I'll bet she threw him out," Hazel said.

"No, she would never do that. She loves him too much."

"Oh, Lillian, you're so much in love you can't see the truth."

"Don't say that. I know how much they love each other. That counts for a lot." Yes but they had a lot of arguments about his drinking. I bet that was it.

"Maybe," Lillian pondered, "but I hope not."

Over the next few months Lottie stayed close-mouthed, but blubbered at the drop of a hat. She kept herself busy running the boarding house and preparing for the move. When her thoughts strayed to Charlie, she would find her sewing basket, sit in her favorite rocking chair, and work on a scarf or sweater for one of the kids. Working with her hands always soothed her and calmed her strongest emotions.

Or she would grab Buddy and hold him close, smoothing his hair as she cried against his cheeks. He tried pulling away but she only held him tighter. Soon he found his mouth on her breast, and both relaxed into their familiar roles.

Lottie's Lot

Hazel was pregnant and helped with cooking for the boarders and took care of the little children. Buddy and Abby were only a year apart and Lois and Ruby were 4 and 5, still at home all day and full of energy. Hazel's job was to channel their energy by playing games and quiet times. Ring-around-the-rosy was a favorite.

Robert came to fetch Lillian in March, 1911 and they went to Edmonton ahead of the others. She rented a room at the Young Women's Christian Association and soon found a large boarding house, big enough for the entire family. The couple planned their wedding for July.

Lillian wrote to Charlie and asked him to come to Edmonton and to give her away in the ceremony.

"I wouldn't miss my first daughter's special day for anything," he wrote back. "I'll be in Edmonton with a heart full of love and bells on."

Lillian's letter brought on the only genuine smile Charlie had smiled in a long time. He went through his workdays with a stunned mind and with a wounded heart. When he wasn't working he sat in his lonely, sparse rented room and wept. Lottie's words were seared into his heart and mind: "I don't want you to come with us … I don't see how I can live with you … I can't trust you anymore."

He had lost everything. How had that happened? He searched his soul for some understanding. He missed the farm almost as much as he missed his family. He was in his element there and he had been successful by any farmer's standards. He still believed that if they had stuck it out the incident with Hazel would have blown over in time, but Lottie insisted that they move and sell the farm. Charlie couldn't change her mind, and he couldn't ask her and the children to stay in a place where everyone disrespected them.

129

When his thoughts started going in circles, whiskey and beer helped him to numb his aching heart.

After several weeks of soul searching, self-pity, and drinking, Charlie knew he had to get out of the hole he was digging. Lottie wouldn't talk to him and it wasn't right to discuss his marriage with Lillian and Hazel. He called Elmer, who sympathized but didn't offer any helpful suggestions. The only other person Charlie could think of to talk to was Carrie.

He dialed her number and was glad to hear her voice.

"Carrie. This is Charlie. Do you have a few minutes to talk to me?"

"Of course, Charlie. It's good to hear from you. How are you?"

"Carrie, Lottie has asked me to leave her and not move to Canada with the family. I'm desperate and I feel just awful. I can't believe she would send me away."

"She told me, Charlie. I'm so sorry to see this happen." He could hear the concern and tenderness in Carrie's voice.

"Did she say anything about taking me back?"

"Charlie, may I be frank with you?"

"Sure. You always have been."

"We've been friends for a very long time," she answered. "And as your friend, I'm telling you that you must look at things from Lottie's point of view. Don't just think about going back. You have to understand Lottie's feelings and why she asked you to leave."

Tears filled his eyes. "I've been trying to understand that. I just can't grasp it. We loved each other so much."

"It's very simple, Charlie. Lottie can't live with the way you drink."

He frowned. "You know what a terrible couple of years we've had, Carrie. I've been through so much – losing my farm, my dream. And

Hazel's problems, and not being able to find a job for so long. Drinking a little has been my way to handle it."

"Charlie, there's a question you have to ask yourself, and you have to be honest about it. What matters more to you – the liquor or your family?"

"There's no question about that. My family, of course." Carrie seemed to be saying just what Lottie told him, but her voice was gentler.

"Charlie, listen to me. Even if Lottie is overreacting, even if you think you don't have a problem, whether she's right or wrong, you have to *show her* that she matters more. If you can stop drinking for good, she may take you back."

He paused and felt a weight lift from his shoulders. "I see, Carrie. I didn't really understand before. This is the one issue on which she clings to her father's beliefs. It isn't just annoying to her; it matters deeply."

"Yes, yes. My sister loves you so much. To have sent you away was the hardest thing she's ever done, and she could only do it if she was convinced that your drinking was destroying the family." She heard him take several deep breaths.

"I'm such a fool," he said and laughed out loud. "I've given in to Lottie on many things, happily, willingly, because her judgment is wise. I thought I could hold on to this one thing, that she should give in to me for a change. But I sure picked the wrong thing to be stubborn about."

"Yes, you did, Charlie. Now there's a choice only you can make – Lottie or the bottle. Can you quit drinking? It's the only way you can win back her trust."

131

He inhaled deeply and cleared his throat. "Yes, I can and I will. She is everything to me. Without Lottie and my children I have nothing."

Carrie's voice cracked. "I love you both so much. It pains me to see your marriage destroyed. Just remember what you said, Charlie, that she's everything to you. And she feels the same way -- without you *she* has nothing. She does love you and needs you for the children sake, and to make her life complete. Do whatever it takes to stay sober, and you can get her and your family back."

She sniffled and laughed weakly. "Only one thing keeps you two from living happily ever after. You've dealt with so much. I know you can do this."

"Thank you, Carrie. You're a jewel. I'm going to do it."

"Call me any time, Charlie. Let me know how things are going."

"Are you going to Lillian's wedding in July? I'll see you then and give you a full report."

"Yes, we're planning to be there. I'll see you then."

Charlie went on the wagon and didn't have another drink for four months. On the train to Edmonton in July he told himself to be patient, but he couldn't wait to see the love in Lottie's eyes again.

When the school term ended, Lottie and the children, along with Hazel George and Abby, took the train to Edmonton. Hazel was eight months pregnant and ready to deliver her baby soon. George was thoughtful and took care of Abby so she could rest on the train trip.

Lillian and Robert met them and escorted them to the boarding house Lillian had found.

Hazel went into labor five days after they arrived in Edmonton. They didn't have time to find a midwife so Lottie delivered a healthy baby boy. George was ecstatic to have a son. They named him George

Lottie's Lot

Kenneth Hopf. He looked like his father. George was a hands-on dad and loved every minute of holding, bathing and caring for his son.

Lottie felt comfortable in the new house right away. It had worn furniture and old wallpaper but was cozy and comfortable and roomy enough for all of them. She was relieved not to be responsible for running everything and cooking all the meals. Living expenses were much lower here. Charlie sent money each month to help pay the bills and she was grateful for that. But it was still hard to make ends meet with five young children.

Lottie, Buddy, and Lois slept in one room, and Charlotte, Bethany, and Ruby were in the room next door. Hazel, George, and their two children had a bigger room downstairs. It seemed as if everything was finally settling down.

Edmonton was a booming, bustling frontier town that had been incorporated only six years earlier. It became the Provincial Capital later in the same year. Excitement and hope crackled in the air. Folks flocked from far and wide to take advantage of the Canadian government's offer of large homestead parcels.

The new town was beautiful too. In June the trees sprouted leaves, and blossoms appeared foretelling fruits and flowers. Warm days were followed by cool nights. The air was clear and the water in the North Saskatchewan River was pristine. Near the house was a big open field next to the river, where the girls played games with their new friends.

The Hastings family soon caught the hopeful spirit of their new environment. It felt like the time and place to erase the past and begin anew.

Lottie spent most of the summer making new school clothes for the girls. It was a long time since they'd had anything new. Beth, Ruby, and Lois had never worn anything but hand-me-downs. George got a job within a week with the telephone company.

Lottie sat on the front porch one June evening to drink in the fragrant scent of the lilacs in bloom and the lilies-of the-valley popping their ivory heads up to sing the praises of the warm weather. How quickly their lives had changed in the past year, she thought. My, my! So many changes – she'd hardly had time to catch her breath.

Her heart ached when she thought about her Charlie, especially when she remembered last Christmas and her painful decision to send him away. She wished he were sitting next to her, holding her hand and telling her how beautiful it was, as he had done when they were courting and through all the years of their marriage. Would they ever sit close together again, sleep in each other's arms again? She wanted that more than anything -- but only if he would stop leaning on alcohol for comfort. He could lean on her all he wanted. Wasn't she enough for him?

The one good thing that had happened in this tumultuous year was Lillian's falling in love with Robert. They were so happy, and no one deserved a happy future more than Lillian. She was the most dutiful of daughters – a truly good, sweet, and caring young woman without a mean bone in her body. The best of the bunch, Lottie admitted to herself, though she would never say it out loud. How wonderful that she had found someone who really loved and appreciated her.

When Lillian told Lottie that Charlie was coming to the wedding her heart leaped she couldn't wait to see him again and the hoped for a reconciliation. Carrie had confided about her long talks with Charlie and his claim that he's been sober for four months.

In the first week of July, Charlie arrived in Edmonton by train. Lottie and met him at the station with a rented horse and buggy. He beamed when he saw her and her heart pounded when he climbed into the driver's seat -- where he should be, Lottie thought. He kissed her cheek and continued grinning at her as he said "Giddy-up" to the horse. She smiled too, but held tightly to her reservations. He would have to prove himself that he was indeed sober and could stay sober.

When they got to the house the ecstatic children climbed all over him. "Papa! Pa! We missed you so much." He hugged and kissed each one. Beth grabbed a piece of his shirt with her hand and never let go until they sat down for supper. "Don't go away any more, Papa. Promise me!" she said, and she hugged him hard.

Lillian and Robert came over for supper that night. Hazel cooked her father's favorite chicken and dumplings dinner with a cherry pie. Everyone laughed as he told them stories of railroad mishaps and near misses. The girls cleaned up and later Charlie helped put them to bed. With cat-sharp eyes and ears, Lottie watched him and liked everything she saw. She felt herself falling in love with him all over again.

"Slow down, Lottie," she told herself. "Wait and see."

She needed a moment with Lillian. "Lil, come upstairs with me," Lottie asked her. In her bedroom, she patted the bed and invited Lillian to sit.

Lillian blushed and thought, "Oh my! Here it comes, the 'mother and daughter' talk." She already knew what to expect. Hazel had told her what a man and woman do on their wedding night, and she and Robert had talked about it too. They even planned something special but nothing she would share with her mother.

Lottie went to her jewelry box and brought out a small blue velvet pouch. She sat next to Lillian and said, "Do you have any questions for your mother?" as she fondled the pouch. Lillian cleared her throat, thinking, "I should ask her something," but she couldn't think of what to ask.

"Well, Mama, is there anything you think I should know?"

"Do you know about intercourse?"

"Yes." Lillian blushed.

"Do you know how a woman gets a baby inside her?"

"Yes." Lillian's face got redder.

"Do you know what I have in this pouch?"

"No." Lillian laughed nervously. "No, I don't."

Lottie opened it and took out a beautiful antique cameo.

"This is for you to wear on your wedding day, Sweetheart."

Lillian's eyes filled with tears. "Mama, it's the most beautiful thing I've ever seen."

"My mama gave it to me to wear when I married your father, and her mama gave it to her when she married her first husband. It's for a daughter who marries for love. So now, my darling, it's yours. Wear it with pride and give it to your daughter when the time comes."

Two days later, on a warm sunny Saturday morning on July 8, 1911, Charlie walked his firstborn daughter down the aisle of the St. James Methodist Church of Edmonton. Lillian wore her cameo on the bodice of the lovely white satin and lace wedding dress and veil that Lottie had made for her.

As Charlie started down the aisle with Lillian's arm entwined in his, he said, "Well, Baby Girl, I want to tell you how proud I am of the magnificent woman you have become."

"Thanks, Pa."

"I love you very much."

"I know, Papa. I love you, too."

"Do you know why the chicken crossed the road?"

"No. Why?"

"To find her rooster, of course. Isn't that why you came to Edmonton?"

"Oh, Papa!" Lillian giggled. They reached the end of the long aisle where Robert was waiting for her, his face aglow. Charlie kissed her cheek as he offered her hand to Robert. He whispered in her ear, "Be happy, Precious." He sat next to Lottie and held her hand. Tears were sneaking down his wife's cheeks. He squeezed that lovely hand and she squeezed back.

They had a big party in the church hall to celebrate the wedding. All of Robert's friends were there and Carrie and her family came. It was a festive time. But, best of all, Charlie didn't touch one drop of liquor.

During the party Charlie asked Lottie to go for a walk with him. The evening was perfect, with fragrant flower scents filling the warm gentle breeze, and a beautiful full moon. They walked through the church grounds, skirting around the cemetery.

"You look more beautiful tonight than ever in your life," he told her.

"Oh, I'm getting so old. You can't mean that."

"But I do." He studied her face. "You look just like you did on our wedding day."

"Well, you look as nice as I have ever seen you. No barnyard manure, mud, clay, or railroad soot. Just clean and very handsome."

He smiled and reached for her hand, "May I?"

"Yes," she said.

"Lottie, I want to come home, to come back to you and the children. I'm so lonely, I'm nothing without you."

"Charlie, you know I have to ask you. Are you still drinking?"

"Not a drop in nearly four months. Not since early March. I swear."

She walked on silently, wanting to believe him but afraid to be wrong. "How can I know you're telling me the truth?"

"You can ask Carrie. We've had a few talks."

"Yes she told me, and she believes you." She went on, "What about your job? We rely on the money you send us."

"I've applied to the Canadian Pacific and it looks pretty promising that they will hire me. I want to apply for a homestead up here and I'll find something to do until that comes through."

"Don't they have an age restriction?"

"No, not here in Canada. That's a lucky break."

They sat on a bench. "I have to admit I'm so happy to see you, Charlie."

"You've missed me too, haven't you? I knew you would!"

"Yes, I've missed you terribly. But we can't just rush into things. We have to be sure we can resolve our problems."

He put his arm around her shoulders. "Lillian and Robert are lucky. They're sure they'll be happy forever. I envy them."

"Yes. Young brides and grooms think love will solve all their problems." Lottie smiled.

"Love solves a lot," Charlie said. "And we had happy times for many years, didn't we?" She nodded, allowing her head to lean on his shoulder.

"Lottie, I want to tell you that I'm so sorry for the pain and heartache I've caused you," Charlie said, turning to face her. "I didn't realize how bad it was, and once I understood, I wanted to run to you and fall at your feet and beg your forgiveness. I was selfish and weak and I'm ashamed that I wasn't stronger for you."

"Oh, Charlie," she said and dabbed at her eyes with a handkerchief already soaked with her tears from the wedding. With a little laugh she added, "I've cried more this year than in all the years of my life before this. I hope I'm finished shedding tears for a while."

He handed her a clean handkerchief and leaned in to give her a soft, brief kiss.

The kiss was as surprisingly thrilling as their first one, in her parents' parlor in Cresco more than 20 years ago, but she remained cautious.

"I want to forgive you, Charlie," she said softly. "I hope you understand that I have to be careful. I don't want things to continue as they were."

He nodded. "They won't, Darling. I promise."

"I believe you're sober and sincere right now. But I think I need a little more time to be sure." As she said the words, she felt just the opposite. She wanted him to stay, never to leave again.

"Whatever you say, Lottie. I understand your doubt. I'll do whatever it takes to prove myself."

They sat in silence for a while. Finally Lottie spoke.

"How about this? Let's plan for you to move here permanently at Christmas. Meanwhile, you work on getting a transfer to the Canadian Pacific and I will look for something else you could do here until a homestead comes through. It takes a while to get one, you know. There are so many applications."

Suddenly he swung Lottie around and kissed her on the mouth, a sexy, juicy kiss like they had kissed so many times before. She felt the old warm stirrings. She wanted him back as much as he wanted her.

He peered into her eyes. "I love you, Lottie Hastings. I never stopped loving you and I want to be with you every day of my life for as long as I live."

"I love you too," she murmured. "Charlie, you know I want you more than anything and our children need you. Can you give me five more months to be sure?"

"I'll be here at Christmas – or sooner if I can manage it. I'll be counting the days."

They kissed again and Lottie put her hand on Charlie's chest. "We'd better get back to the party. I want to see Lillian before they leave."

Two days later, Charlie took the train back to Superior. He promised Lottie and the children that he'd be back for Christmas – for good.

In late August, an ecstatic Lillian and Robert announced that she was expecting. With Lottie's help, Lillian began, knitting baby sweaters with matching booties and bonnets.

Charlie sent enough money to pay the rent and Lottie was glad to receive it, but there wasn't enough for anything extra. She worked two days a week as a sales clerk at the Hudson Bay Company. They gave her a discount on anything she bought and she got fabric to make more clothes for everybody.

As soon as they arrived in Edmonton George joined a local Seventh Day Adventist Church, promising to tithe 10 percent of his income every month. The church used the money to support hospitals, sanitariums, clinics, and missionary work around the world. Members believed in the literal word of the Bible, and in spreading the word about Jesus Christ to help ensure others could enter God's kingdom after death.

George again begged Hazel to join the church, but she said only that she'd think about it. She had attended services a few times, but she didn't like what she saw or believe what they preached. Social distractions like movies, dancing, jewelry, and make-up were limited or forbidden. Those were some of the things Hazel liked most.

George's religion became the source of conflict between them. She resented the church's emphasis on a strict vegetarian diet, requiring her to cook special meals without meat for him. The Hastings family dinners consisted primarily of meat and potatoes, plus a vegetable and sometimes a dessert.

Hazel had trouble following some of George's other "rules." If she did or said something he didn't approve of he was critical and paternal. Her father had never treated her like this and even Lottie bit her tongue some of the time. Hazel was an adult now, and even though her husband was head of the family, she resented him telling her to take off her jewelry or stop dancing to a tune on the radio. Tension grew with every incident. When he was affectionate she wiggled away. When he wanted sex she made excuses.

Lottie was happy for one daughter and worried about the other. But her thoughts were focused on Christmas and Charlie's return. She hummed and smiled to herself while she worked. She felt like a bride-to-be and counted the days until he'd be hers once again.

CHAPTER 10

At 7:00 in the evening on September 11, the doorbell rang. Lottie answered the door and saw a man standing there in a telegraph company uniform. She sensed immediately that it was bad news. Good news came in letters. Bad news came in telegrams.

"Telegram for Mrs. Lottie Hastings," he said.

"I'm Lottie Hastings," she answered.

"Sign here, please," he said, and handed her a notebook to sign. She signed and handed the book back to him. He waited for a tip, but she ignored him and closed the door.

Lottie opened the telegram as Hazel came into the room. It was from Elmer Hastings. The telegram read: *"Been trying to locate you-stop-terrible accident-stop-Charlie dead-stop-call me-stop-4672 Green Bay-stop-Sadly Elmer."*

Lottie dropped the bit of paper as all the blood drained from her face. She sank into a stuffed chair. The children were still up except for George, Jr. who was sleeping peacefully in his cradle. They gathered around her. Hazel picked up the telegram from the floor and read it. The little kids clamored, "What does it say?" in one voice.

Choking back tears she said, "It... says... that... Papa's... dead."

Time stood still, as each person was suspended in an electrified moment that would change his or her life forever. Then pandemonium broke out. The children cried out questions all at once. "What! ... Where?... When?... How?... No! It can't be true." Some of the children were crying, others were trying to hug Lottie. Some stood motionless in shock.

Hazel didn't have any answers. "I don't know! Settle down. We have to call Uncle Elmer. He sent the telegram." She turned to Lottie, who looked helpless and shocked. She took her mother's hand and said more gently, "Maybe he knows what happened. I'll go to the drugstore to call him. They have a telephone there." Her voice was shaking in spite of her heroic attempt to appear calm.

George was taking a catnap and she shouted to wake him up. "George, come here -- I need you, *now!*"

George came into the room, stretching and grumpy. "What's wrong?"

Her voice sounded strange and distant to her as she choked on her words. "We just got a telegram. My father is dead." She pleaded for his support with her eyes and then went on. "Please take the kids into the kitchen and give them some cookies and milk, tell them a story... anything.... I need you to take over so I can help Mama decide what to do."

"Yes, yes. Oh my God! I'm so sorry, Sweetheart. I'll do whatever I can to help," George said, herding the girls and Buddy into the kitchen. Hazel knelt beside Lottie and took her hands. "Mama, what do you want me to do?"

Lottie's eyes were glazed over and she stared straight ahead. She couldn't find her voice to speak. Hazel was frightened. She had never seen her mother like this before.

She shook her. "Ma, tell me what to do!"

After a long silence, trance like and with angry tears in her voice, Lottie spoke. "My worst nightmare.... Oh, God! All these years I was so afraid something terrible would happen to him, working for that damned railroad." Hazel held her mother, crying along with her.

Finally they were spent. Hazel said, "I'll go and call Uncle Elmer."

"I'm going too." They put on coats and went out to find a pay phone.

First Hazel called Lillian and asked her to come over right away because there was an emergency. She didn't tell her what it was. The telephone seemed too cold and distant. She wanted to tell her sister in person.

Next Lottie called Elmer person-to-person collect. Elmer answered, "Oh, Lottie." He told her what had happened.

"It was September 4. Charlie was returning to Superior late that night. He was on top of a railroad car, ready to set the brakes, and he fell off and fractured his skull."

Lottie gasped and whispered, "Oh, sweet Jesus. Please. No, no no."

In a moment Elmer continued, "No one is sure why he fell -- whether the cars lunged or he heard a sound and turned around to check it out or what." His voice choked for a moment. "Somehow he lost his footing and fell and hit his head on the track."

He could hear Lottie and Hazel sobbing but knew he should finish the story. "Lottie, they rushed him to the hospital in Superior and they tried to operate on his brain, but he didn't make it. He died at 3:30 in the morning."

Elmer explained that the authorities had found his name and address in Charlie's wallet, so they called him and he went to identify him. "I didn't know where Charlie was boarding so I couldn't find any information about how to get in touch with you. Finally, I got hold of Carrie and she told me where you were." He paused to catch his breath.

As Lottie listened, tears ran down her cheeks. Most of his words didn't register. Elmer went on, "Thank God we finally found you.

144

Lottie's Lot

He's going to be buried in Superior at Greenwood Cemetery, a beautiful place with big pine trees. I'll ask the funeral home to hold off until you get here. Can you come right away?"

Lottie couldn't talk. She opened her mouth but nothing came out. She couldn't sort out her thoughts and feelings, let alone put them into words. She just couldn't comprehend what had happened. Charlie was … he was … gone! Oh, God, the terrible past tense of it all! *I must be having a nightmare. Let me wake up, please! How could this be true?*

What about his homecoming? They were going to be happy again, with all their problems behind them. Her hopes and dreams dissolved into a void. What was she going to do now? They — she — had a family to raise. How could she do it all by herself?

"We had plans, Elmer," she said in a choked voice. "Everything was going to be fine again. He was sober and he was coming back to me and the children."

"I'm so sorry, Lottie dear," Elmer said. Words seemed so empty.

"Elmer, please talk to Hazel. I can't think right now." She handed the telephone to Hazel. Elmer told her the story again.

Lottie said, "Ask him who is paying for the funeral."

Hazel asked and he told her, "He had $12 in his wallet; the funeral home used that and the Great Northern Railroad paid the balance. It cost $350 altogether."

Lottie took the phone back and said, "I'll get on the next train." She choked on her sobs.

"Wire me when you'll be arriving," Elmer told her. "Fanny and I will meet you in Superior."

145

"This must be hard for you too, Elmer," Lottie said, making an effort to pull herself together.

"It was really a shock. I still can't believe it. We were frantic trying to find you. Finally another railroad worker knew where Charlie was staying, and I went and packed up what few belongings he had. I have them in a box ready to send to you if you want them."

"Of course I do!" Lottie said. "But no need to send them. I'll get them when I'm there. Elmer, I have so many questions but I can't think right now. We can talk more later."

"Of course," he said.

Lottie continued, "I don't know what to do next. I just need some time to sort things out. I can't take it in … that Charlie is…is...." She sobbed, unable to finish her sentence. Hazel took the phone and talked to Elmer for a few minutes, then hung up and took Lottie home.

Lillian and Robert were at the house when they got back. George had already told them the news and Robert was trying to comfort Lillian. He was worried that the shock might affect the baby.

All the children were still up and clamoring for answers about what had happened. Hazel took them into the kitchen, quieted them, and told them what she knew. She put on the tea kettle. She nursed her hungry baby and sent the children off to bed. George then took charge of George Jr. and Hazel spent the rest of the night holding her mother on the ragged, worn sofa in the parlor. Lillian and Robert stayed. No one could sleep. Their lives had changed forever. They had no idea what I that meant.

By morning they decided that Lillian and Robert would move in to help George take care of the children while Hazel accompanied Lottie to Superior with George Jr. While they hurriedly packed Robert called the train station and sent a telegram to Elmer with their schedule. Lillian and Charlotte packed clothes and baby necessities. Charlotte and Beth made them a lunch of sandwiches, cookies, and fruit to take along.

Lottie's Lot

Black. They had to find black...a black dress, stockings, shoes, a hat or veil.... All black. They didn't have much that was black. A widow who lived next door had a couple of black dresses that would fit Lottie and Hazel. She had one black hat and a veil. Shoes weren't a problem but stockings were. They would have to buy some after they got to Superior.

Lottie watched the goings-on, letting others do the work for once. She spoke softly, as much to herself as to anyone listening. "I was always so afraid. Every time he left the house, I never knew if he would come home. I went to so many funerals of railroad widows and secretly gave thanks that it wasn't me. That job is so dangerous, so dangerous, and now it's happened to me. Oh dear God, what will I do without him?"

September days were still warm, but the nights could be cool. They wore coats to stay warm on the train at night. They had to buy tickets on the Great Northern line because Charlie had worked for the Northern Pacific. They couldn't afford a Pullman car and knew they'd be sitting upright in the coach for the 20-hour trip.

George went along to the station to buy the tickets, carry the suitcases, and settle them in their seats. He held his son on the way, nuzzling and kissing those smooth baby cheeks. He would miss him terribly. Little George smiled in response to his daddy's voice. He was the best thing that had ever happened to George, whose heart had dipped into a deep well of love he hadn't known existed in him.

Lottie sat against the window and watched the railroad workers preparing the train to leave. She wondered if any of them had known Charlie and whether they could tell her about him. She watched them work and tried to visualize Charlie in their place as he had worked so hard to support his family for all those years.

147

Maybe she hadn't appreciated him enough. Maybe she had been so caught up in her own problems raising the children that she hadn't comprehended or acknowledged his contributions to the family. Maybe they should have stayed in North Dakota on the farm. Maybe she shouldn't have insisted on everything being so perfect all the time. She chastised herself for neglecting him, judging him, criticizing his drinking, giving him the silent treatment…ultimately pushing him away. She had been so wrong and now… *now*…it was too late. She could never say she was sorry.

Elmer and Fanny had driven the three hours from Green Bay to meet them and had arranged hotel rooms in Superior. The funeral was set for 10 the next morning. Elmer drove them to the funeral parlor early so they could see Charlie before the casket was closed and sealed. As if in a dream Lottie approached the open casket with Hazel on one side and Elmer on the other. Fanny held the sleeping baby. When Lottie got close enough to see him her knees buckled and she collapsed. Hazel and Elmer caught her.

They got her to a chair and the funeral director brought her a glass of water. "Mama, are you OK?" Hazel scanned her face.

"I just need a moment," she said, embarrassed.

After a few minutes she stalwartly stood and went back to the coffin. Charlie was dressed in a black suit jacket with a white shirt and tie. She recognized it as the suit he'd worn for Lillian's wedding. He was scrubbed clean, eyes closed and hands folded across his chest. He was so still. She reached in and touched his cheek – he felt so cold! Giant tears cascaded down her cheeks. She put her hands over his and whispered, "I'm so sorry, Charlie… so sorry." She stood there for a long while with Hazel at her side.

And then she straightened to her full height and walked out of the room.

They got into Elmer's car and followed the funeral hearse on the long drive to Evergreen Cemetery. A minister none of them knew was standing next to a big empty hole in the ground with a mound of dirt to one side. When Lottie saw the hole her stoicism disappeared and she collapsed into Hazel's arms.

Lottie almost collapsed again when she saw the fresh mound of dirt heaped over her husband's coffin. The thought of never seeing him again, of never talking to him again, of never touching him again, left her with unbearable pain. It was so unbelievable. Her Charlie just couldn't spend eternity under that pile of dirt.

The rest was a blur for Lottie. She was completely numb.

After the burial Elmer invited them back to Green Bay for a few days. Lottie had so many unanswered questions and they needed to talk about insurance and other things. Gratefully, Lottie and Hazel accepted the invitation. They drove silently for the three hours, each lost in his or her own thoughts and grief. Baby George was a welcome distraction.

Fanny was a gracious hostess, sensitive and considerate. She prepared a big dinner and helped Hazel with the baby. They stayed for three days, asking questions and trying to make sense of this tragedy.

Charlie had life insurance through the Railroad Conductors Union. Elmer said he would help Lottie find out how to file a claim. Two weeks later, he sent her the paperwork and told her to file a claim for wrongful death and ask for $25,000 for her loss. She filled it out immediately and sent it in.

When they got back to Edmonton George met them at the train, overjoyed to see his wife and son. Hazel pulled away from his embrace. He took the baby and showered him with kisses. Little George didn't reject him.

With the funeral over, life settled back into a routine of sorts for the family. George pitched in with more rent money and Robert and Lillian came up with the difference. However, little was left over for food and many nights they just had bread, milk, and soup, or beans and rice for supper.

The girls crowded into one bedroom, leaving a room that Lottie could sublet. She used the money to buy food and other essentials. She insisted that the girls continue to go to school.

In November, 1911, Rebecca, Elmer and Charlie's mother, died. Elmer hadn't told his 85-year-old mother about Charlie's death two months earlier, fearing the bad news would be too much for her.

Lottie recalled how kindly Rebecca had received her as Charlie's bride, and how she always remembered the children on their birthdays and at Christmas, sending gifts or a card with a bright new dollar bill in it. She would miss this gracious old woman.

All of their parents were gone now. Lottie was now the oldest living person in her family.

Christmas of 1911 was dismal. No presents, not even fresh fruit. Lillian and Robert bought candy canes for everyone but no one rejoiced. Each one felt Charlie's absence and grieved in his or her own way. Lottie spent most of the day at church. Bethany walked along the riverbank pulling dry petals from the bushes she passed. She threw them, sprinkled with her tears, into the swirling water. Her entire body felt heavy and sad.

1912 began badly. Lillian had problems with her pregnancy. She started bleeding when she was seven months along. The doctor ordered bed rest and she complied. Early in January she went into labor, and on January 8 delivered a premature baby girl.

They named her Mary Jean after Robert's mother. But the infant had congenital heart problems and died three days later. Lillian was inconsolable. She'd lost her father just a few months ago and now her first child was dead too.

She sank into a deep depression. Luckily, Robert's claim for his homestead came through in February and Lillian was cheered a little when they went to survey their 160-acre parcel. She remembered many happy days on the homestead in North Dakota. Robert told her they would have many more children and gradually she felt better.

They planned to build a small cabin as soon as winter gave up its long grip on the frozen land. Lillian got some seed catalogues and Robert began sketching plans for the cabin.

Then suddenly Lillian woke in the middle of the night with severe pain in her abdomen. She cried out and Robert immediately woke up to see her bent in half, holding her stomach. He said, "I'm getting you to a hospital right away."

They used a horse and buggy, which they rented from the livery stable at the corner for transportation. Everyone would be asleep at this hour, so Robert ran down and harnessed a horse and buggy himself. He helped Lillian onto the seat and galloped toward the hospital. Suddenly one of the harness straps attaching the horse to the buggy came loose and the buggy toppled over, spilling Lillian and Robert onto the street.

A police officer saw the accident and came to the rescue. Robert explained that Lillian was in severe pain and needed to get to a hospital immediately. The officer called for the police trolley which soon arrived and speedily took them to the nearest hospital.

After cleaning up the cuts and bruises the hospital staff examined Lillian and determined she had appendicitis and needed an emergency operation. It took two hours to get the operating team into the hospital and ready to do the surgery. When they opened her up they found that her appendix had ruptured. They cleaned her out the best they could, but shook their heads, realizing that peritonitis -- a toxic infection -- was already ravaging her body.

Lottie sat by her daughter's bed day and night for four days, crying, praying, and holding her hand. Robert couldn't bear to see the love of his life suffering. He went out and got drunk. He blamed himself. *If only* he had harnessed the horse and buggy better, *if only* he had heard her earlier and gotten her to the hospital sooner, *if only...* *if only...*

Lillian died on April 3, 1912, and was buried beside her baby daughter in the Edmonton Cemetery. She was just 22 years old. The family didn't have money to buy a gravestone.

Robert got drunk after the funeral and stayed that way for the next six months.

Lottie's grief was so overwhelming that she couldn't function. Losing Lillian so closely after Charlie's death was more than a body could bear. Hazel was forced to put her own grief aside. Lottie didn't want to get out of bed, couldn't bear to think or to move. When Hazel forced her mother to get up she had to help dress and feed her.

Lottie spent her days staring out the window in the parlor until Hazel led her back to bed. The children talked in whispers, afraid they were losing their mother too.

Lottie had rarely allowed herself to indulge in feeling sad for very long. For all of her 41 years she had deliberately swept hurt and sadness, even anger, under the carpet. It had always worked for her in the past. "I'll think about it later when I have time," she would tell herself. "No time for tears now. Duty calls."

It didn't work this time. Lillian's death was the final straw. All of the losses from her past caught up with her and she was flooded with grief. She couldn't stop crying. She'd remained steadfast when she lost her mother and when her sister Cora died unexpectedly in childbirth. Both Charlie's father and her own had died, too.

But losing her husband, her baby granddaughter, and now her first-born daughter within a few months was just too much. Grief for all of her past losses overwhelmed her and weighed her down. A heaviness wrapped around her heart and weighed her down. She was immobilized.

Lottie's Lot

A voice kept repeating in her head: "This is too much. I can't bear it!"

She turned to God. Hourly she asked God why …why…WHY…he had brought her so much sorrow. She beseeched, "Lord why do you place such a heavy burden on this poor soul? How have I offended you?" She prayed, questioned, begged for help, and then prayed some more, quiet, secret, silent prayers. Then she waited for answers that never came. She felt as if she had fallen into a dark hole from which there was no escape. Not even her beloved son's presence could ease her grief. She spent hours alone in her bedroom, staring at the walls.

Buddy was almost four when Charlie died. He understood that his father was gone but thought he might be coming back. He was used to Charlie leaving for long periods of time so he didn't miss him much. Every time he came home he had to get to know him all over again. Sometimes he wondered why his Papa didn't love him enough to stay close to him.

He didn't like it when his parents argued. He would put a pillow over his head to shut out the loud voices. When his father was gone, he had his Mama to himself and she was calmer.

Lottie had stopped nursing him abruptly and he was confused and angry. He had a hard time trusting his Papa and now he wasn't sure if he could trust his Mama either. It seemed that both of his parents had abandoned him. The seeds were planted for a lifelong distrust of men and resentment against women.

The responsibility for keeping life relatively normal for the family fell to Hazel, in spite of her own tormented grief for her father and sister. She forced herself to put her own feelings aside and spent her time caring for her siblings, getting them off to school, cooking, cleaning, and washing clothes – all the things Lottie used to do.

George Jr. also took a back seat in those terrible first months. She didn't have the energy or emotional stamina to give him the mother's love he needed. She passed him to one of his aunts to feed, burp, change, and bathe. Feeling his mother growing distant, he bonded more with his father.

Tensions escalated between Hazel and George. Both were emotionally stretched to the limit with little reserve left to nurture their relationship. Hazel rarely if ever felt like having sex and showed no tenderness toward George. They disagreed about every little thing and minor matters took on monumental importance. While they tried to keep their arguments private, the whole family was aware of the hostility between them. Hazel became a shrew, making him the scapegoat for all her pent-up sadness and frustration.

The biggest issues were over money. With her family in dire financial straits they needed every penny they could get their hands on just to survive, and Hazel resented George's tithing to his church. George was unmovable on this issue. His faith was his anchor, the one place in his life where he found comfort and consistent support.

As she grew increasingly angry and critical of him, he became more cross and withdrawn. She seemed to nag him more on Saturdays, the day he went to church. "George, we need that money to buy food. How can you let your family go hungry and give money to that church?"

"Hazel, I've told you a hundred times. I made a promise -- a commitment -- and I have to keep it. My church is important to me even if it isn't to you. I just ask you to respect what I believe in and let me honor my promises."

"So your church means more to you than your own children. How does it feel to see your children go hungry?"

"I give you money for food. Not just for our kids but for your sisters and brother and mother too. I'm supporting everyone. Why don't you appreciate that?"

Lottie's Lot

"It isn't enough. We can't just eat potatoes and stale bread every day. We need milk and eggs and baby food, never mind vegetables and fruit...." She paused and flung her arms toward the ceiling. "If you gave me the money you give to your damn church we could eat better."

His face turned red and he said gruffly, "If you want more money then why don't you or your mother or Charlotte get a job?'

She opened her mouth to reply but he yelled, cutting her off. "I give you every penny I earn except for my tithe! I should be entitled to do what I want with at least a little of my own money. I'm working overtime to earn extra money for your family. You never thank me. You just nag and complain all the time. I'm getting tired of it. Sick and tired. Do you hear me? Lay off!"

"Oh, dry up!" she shouted back.

He stamped out the door and George Jr. started to cry. Hazel snatched up her baby and glared at the door. Then she walked over and kicked it so hard she broke her toe. The reality was that George didn't make enough money to support so many people, but Hazel had no idea how to solve their money problems just now.

Robert Hall was steeped in his own world of pain. When Lillian died a part of him died too. He couldn't bear life without her and tried to drown his feelings in liquor. The Hastings family nurtured and took care of him. Charlotte sometimes cleaned his room and brought him food. As soon as he sobered up and remembered his losses, he would go on a new binge. When he could no longer pay his rent he moved in with Lottie's family and slept on the chesterfield.

Out of desperation Hazel called her Uncle Elmer for help, wondering if there was any news about the insurance settlement stemming from Charlie's death.

Elmer told her there were problems with collecting from the railroad for a wrongful death because Charlie had lied on his application about his age and name. When the railroad's attorney reported this the court dismissed the claim against the railroad. Elmer said the union was going to appeal the claim but the prospects didn't look good.

He tried to sound encouraging. "Don't give up, Hazel. These things take time. The wheels of justice turn very slowly."

"We're having such a hard time," she complained, her voice wavering. "There's not enough money to buy food or clothes. We're behind in the rent and are about to get evicted." Through tears she said, "I'm sorry, Uncle Elmer. I just don't know what to do."

"I'll call the lawyers tomorrow and keep the pressure on. You've got to hang on. I'll keep sending what I can."

"Thank you! We are so grateful for that $50 you wired recently. It's kept the wolf from the door."

Hazel hung up, disillusioned. She leaned her head back against the wall of the phone booth and sobbed. At age 20 years she felt the weight of the world on her shoulders.

The family struggled along for the next few months, blessing Elmer for sending money to sustain them and supplement George's income.

Lottie slowly recovered and began to take back the family reins. Little by little she engaged with her daughters and Buddy. She resumed holding Buddy and rocking him until he wiggled away, tired of her smothering and afraid she would love him one minute and then push him away the next. She would comb and plait Lois's and Ruby's hair for school. And when Bethany had a part in a play at school she went to see her.

Before long she was in the kitchen making a supper dish or a dessert. And she occasionally joined the family at the dinner table. It

156

was a slow, gradual process, but she was healing and returning to her life.

Robert managed to stay sober for a month and went back to work driving trucks. He stayed with the family whenever he was in Edmonton. The younger girls called him Uncle Bob. He would get down on the floor and wrestle with them. Seeing Bob and a pile of kids tickling, laughing, and having fun gave Hazel, Lottie, and George some cheer.

Hazel and George continued to argue, often in front of the entire family. Hazel solicited support from Lottie and her sisters and sometimes they ganged up on George, giving Hazel a sense of righteousness. At other times Lottie sided with George.

"Hazel, sometimes you're too hard on George and too quick to criticize him." She was wary of Hazel's behavior after her own experience with Charlie. Maybe she had been too hard on Charlie when he was only trying to do his best.

"Ma, he's not listening to me. It makes me so mad." Despite her best efforts she couldn't stop belittling her husband. Her sharp tongue could cut to the quick.

"He's trying his best. He does what he says he'll do."

"Well, it isn't enough," Hazel said, with venom in her voice.

"You'd better calm down Young Lady. He's supporting this entire family. I don't know where we'd be without his help."

"Well, he married into this family and that's what I expect him to do."

"Maybe you should show him a little gratitude. You know you can catch a lot more flies with sugar than with vinegar."

157

Abby grew to dislike her stepfather. She thought he was picking on her mother and making her unhappy.

When a vacancy in the house became available Hazel insisted that George take the room.

"Hazel, why? I'm your husband. You can't throw me out of our bedroom," George moaned in frustration. "I've moved all your clothes into the room downstairs but you can go somewhere else if you'd like. I don't want you near me and I don't even want you in this house."

She slammed the bedroom door in his face and shocked he walked downstairs and into his new room.

Lottie returned to her job at the Hudson Bay Company so they weren't quite so dependent on George. For several months he continued to pay as many bills as he had been doing, but when Hazel hired on as a waitress at the Hudson Bay Company's lunch counter he paid only his own rent. Soon he moved to another boarding house.

George was devastated by Hazel's separation from him. It was clear that she didn't love him anymore; in fact he wasn't sure she ever had. He was confused, hurt, and at times furious with her.

His greatest fear was that Hazel would take his son away from him. While living in the same house he could still spend time with Georgie at meals and in the evenings. Now he could only see his son on Sundays.

CHAPTER 11

Hazel soon settled into her new waitressing job and her home life without George. She felt she had already lived a lifetime of hardship and tragedy. Why should she have to put up with so many problems? She just wanted a life that was more stable and peaceful and with George out of the picture she felt calmer. The endless fighting had taken its toll–she had a constant cold and had little patience with her children.

Sometimes at night, she cried for her father and her sister. The only time she gave George a thought was when he came to visit George Jr. on Sunday. His visits left her feeling empty and sad. Something was missing in her life. She longed for love and companionship, someone to hold and comfort her.

Six weeks after her separation from George, she struck up a friendship with a regular lunch customer, Roy Darden. Like her, he was lonely and seemed unhappy. He and his wife had lost a 1-year-old son, John, to influenza, last year. Overwhelmed by grief, they blamed each other and argued all the time. The burden of grief left his wife Mildred, inconsolable. Nothing Roy did or said comforted her. Finally, with no resolution in sight she left him and returned to her family in Ontario, taking their 5-year-old daughter, Dolly, with her.

159

In time he confided in Hazel, "I miss Dolly every minute of the day," he said, "but Mildred.... I don't miss the arguing." His eyes drifted, "I've lost so much."

Hazel nodded her head. "I know."

He patted his mouth carefully with his napkin. "Ah, but the single life isn't for me. I work as much as I can. Staying busy helps some but it isn't enough. The evenings are lonely. I miss having a family."

"Well, one thing I have is a family," Hazel replied, "a big one." She told him about her children, her mother, and siblings.

Everyone called Anthony Leroy Darden "Roy." He was 13 years older than Hazel, just as George was. At 5 feet 10 inches, he was taller than either her father or George. His eyes were bluer than the sky and little lines rippled next to them when he smiled. His balding head shone above his round face and strong chin reminded her of Charlie. He had straight white teeth that glistened when he smiled.

Hazel noticed that Roy constantly cleaned his fingernails. As an automobile mechanic, he couldn't avoid getting his hands covered with grease and dirt.

"That's the only bad thing about my job. I like to be clean."

They chatted casually for a month or so at the lunch counter; then, to Hazel's surprise, he asked her out for dinner. He was easy to talk to and she needed a shoulder to lean on. She agreed and two evenings he came to her house and they walked to a nice restaurant close to her home.

They had so much in common and found that they could talk easily and for hours. She revealed how difficult her life had been in Canada with the unexpected deaths of her father and sister, the poverty, and her conflicts and separation from her husband. Roy listened intently without comment.

Lottie's Lot

He told her about growing up on a big farm in Ontario, Canada with a big farming family, but being a farmer for the rest of his life didn't appeal to him. He loved working with his hands and had a natural knack for fixing mechanical things, farm machines, wagons, etc. The new automobiles intrigued him so he decided to learn more about them.

He went to a school in Toronto for 10 months to learn about servicing and repairing cars before he moved to Edmonton in 1903 with Mildred and his brother Ernest who was a physician. He had more education than anyone Hazel had ever met.

Roy was forward-thinking and believed that the horse and buggy would soon be replaced by automobiles, with every family owning one, and that a network of roads would crisscross the country, maybe even replacing the railroad system in time. His eyes lit up when he talked about such things. Hazel had never heard anyone speak that way about the future, passionate about things that seemed impossible. Listening to him seemed to lighten her own load.

Hazel wasn't surprised when Lottie pounced with questions after she returned from her dinner with Roy.

"Who was that, Hazel?" Lottie sternly queried.

"Someone I met at work." Hazel was evasive.

"Well, tell me about him."

Hazel told her what she knew about him.

"He's married?" Lottie was alarmed.

"Yes, but so am I."

"Well, that makes it doubly bad."

"Ma, I'm lonely. I like this man and want to know him better," Hazel pleaded.

"You made your bed, now you lie in it."

"You know I can't stand George."

"I don't care. He's your husband and the father of your child. God knows you need to make peace with George."

"Ma...please let me work this out for myself. I know you have your beliefs, but this is my life and you can't live it for me," Hazel said calmly but firmly.

"Listen to me, Hazel. Don't you remember when you met George? At the lunch counter? He was older than you, safe, clean, polite. You're repeating the same behavior. How do you know this man won't disappoint you, just as George did?"

"Ma, this is different."

"Oh? How?"

"I don't know. It just feels different. He's not like George. He helps me. I can talk to him about my problems. Anyway, he's only a friend."

Lottie looked her daughter in the eye for a long time then turned and walked away without another word. She hoped that Hazel and all of her children would find someone to love and marry, as she had done, but to begin a courtship in sin didn't bode well. However, Lottie knew that Hazel would do exactly as she wanted, no matter what her she said.

The next week when Roy invited her to dinner again, Hazel began to wonder whether this was just a friendship or a date? She borrowed the best clothes the sisters had between them and this time he came to call on her at the boarding house. She introduced him to Lottie, who was cool viewing him skeptically. She was puzzled by her daughter's attraction to older men.

Lottie's Lot

When Roy met Abby and George, Jr. they liked him immediately. He charmed them with his quick hands playing "Got your nose." When they collapsed in giggles he knew he was on the high road with them.

After dinner Roy and Hazel walked and talked. Hazel felt that she had known him for years, instead of just a few months. When he took her home he squeezed her hand and said he would see her soon. She felt something stirring in her body again. She leaned against the wall in her room and tried to sort out her feelings. It was very confusing. Was this love? She had never been in love before.

The following Sunday afternoon Roy knocked on the boarding house door unannounced with a bouquet of day lilies for Lottie, a candy bar for Abby, and a teddy bear for George Jr. This was the first bouquet anyone in the family had ever received and Lottie tried not to let on how much it delighted her. So she invited him to stay for Sunday dinner with the family.

He fit right in. He entertained the children with silly knock-knock jokes. Lottie couldn't help thinking of Charlie and of Robert when he and Lillian first met and married. Having a cheerful man in the house again seemed like old times. It lightened everyone's mood. Charlie would have liked this intelligent, charming young man.

Shortly after dinner George arrived to spend time with his son, as was his custom.

"George, I would like you to meet Roy Darden," Lottie said formally. They shook hands. George sensed something new in Hazel's demeanor and he was suspicious of this stranger.

Over the next month, Roy visited Hazel several times, taking her for walks and outings with her children. When he played with Abby and George Jr., Hazel could tell that he missed his own children. Watching her children grow fonder and fonder of him, she recognized that she had strong feelings for him too.

The more George saw of this interloper the more he feared losing Hazel and his son altogether. His family was the most important thing in his world and he hoped to reunite with them. Now he could see everything he loved slipping away – this willful young woman had all but destroyed his life.

He confronted Hazel. "I don't want my son or you around that man."

Hazel ignored him.

"Did you hear me?" he repeated. "I don't want Georgie around that man."

"You don't have a right to tell me who I can have as friends." Her sarcasm stung.

"I don't want Georgie around that Roy fellow. I mean it! He's still my son and I have a say about him."

"Don't tell me what to do. We're separated. Go whine to your church friends."

Angry now, he shook her by the shoulders. "I still have a say about my son."

She tried to pull away but he held her tighter. She slapped him across the face. He slapped her back. Shocked at what he had done, he let her go. He could see his hand print blazing on the side of her face. Furious and defeated, he stomped out of the house. He knew she would make him pay for this.

The next day she had a black eye. At dinner when Roy asked her what happened, she gave him a pleading look. "George did it." He was outraged. He reached across the table, took her hands in his, looked into her eyes, and said, "No woman deserves to be treated so badly."

She nodded and sniffled as he continued. "I've been thinking. Maybe we should leave Edmonton."

She gasped. "What?"

"I want to take you away from Edmonton, from George Hopf, from all the problems he causes you."

Hazel was flooded with mixed emotions. She had fallen in love with this man but never imagined they could be anything more than friends. She was afraid and excited at the same time. This is what she had secretly wanted to be rescued and to get George Hopf out of her life. She didn't know how to escape from the husband who was growing more demanding every time she saw him, and now Roy was offering her a way out and with him in the bargain. She held his hands tighter and tears started flowing down her cheeks.

"How?" She barely choked out the word.

"We can run away, take the kids, go somewhere where he can't find us."

"Where would we go?"

"I'm not sure right now, but we can figure it out."

"Oh my goodness." She began to cry more. He gave her his handkerchief.

"Roy, what about my family, my children, my mother, and sisters, and Buddy -- I can't just go and leave them behind, can I?"

"I know. When I fell in love with you I inherited a whole family. We'll take them too."

That got her attention. "When you what?" she whispered. "*When you what?*"

165

He smiled and moved across the table to sit next to her. He put his arms around her. Getting close to her ear he said softly, "When I fell in love with you, Hazel. I love you and want to be with you for the rest of my life." He turned her head around to face him and looked her deeply into the eyes. "I love you and hope that you love me too."

She held his gaze and then hugged him back. "I do."

Now she knew what love felt like. She hadn't dared to let herself hope that she and Roy could ever be together. Now he was offering her everything she had dreamed about. He was her hero, a guardian angel who would protect her from all the things she feared.

But there were so many obstacles. Both were married to others. And even though Lottie skeptically accepted him as Hazel's friend, she would never approve of her daughter living with a man who was not her husband. And she had her children to consider. Georgie loved his Papa.

Hazel's emotions were in turmoil and her thoughts conflicted. She felt vulnerable and out of control, something she rarely allowed to happen. She was mature beyond her years. She had learned to steel herself against disappointment, but at this moment she couldn't stifle her hopes.

Roy waited for her to take in his words. Then he kissed her on the cheek and said, "Let's go for a walk."

They walked and talked for a long time, discussing the pros and cons of running away together. When they stopped to sit on a park bench, he kissed her on the mouth several times. Hazel felt her heart pounding. Her knees were so weak she didn't think she could stand up.

A disapproving Lottie was waiting for her in the parlor when she opened the front door a little after midnight.

"Hazel, do you know what time it is?"

"No, Mama, I don't know what time it is and I don't care what time it is."

166

Lottie's Lot

Lottie saw her daughter's flushed face and heard the excitement in her voice. "Oh my goodness, Hazel. What have you been doing?"

"Ma, that's my busi…." She stopped. There was no need to antagonize her mother not now.

"Don't worry, Ma. We've just been walking and talking."

Lottie shook her head slowly. She had her doubts. But whatever was going on in Hazel's life, it was out of her hands now. Hazel was an adult.

Roy and Hazel discussed their plans at dinner the next night. They returned early to the boarding house. "Ma, we need to talk to you." They sat at the kitchen table and spoke in low voices so that no one else would hear. When they revealed their plan to Lottie, she couldn't take it all in and had to ask them to repeat it. She was surprised and overwhelmed.

As she realized they were serious a tiny smile formed. Her life in Canada had been an ongoing nightmare and she'd be glad to move away. But how could this possibly work?

"I need time to think about this," was all she said.

Over the next few days Lottie searched her heart and soul for the right answer. Her sense of right and wrong had guided so many of her decisions. But sometimes her judgment had led to unexpected heartache.

She still harbored sadness and regrets over Charlie over three and a half years after his death. If she had been kinder to him, more forgiving, would he still be here with her? The thought tortured her constantly, though she never spoke of it.

She had learned the hard way that believing what was right didn't always lead to the best solution. Or to happiness.

While she couldn't openly approve of Hazel's relationship with Roy, she knew that Hazel loved him and that he treated her well. Like any mother she wanted her daughter to be happy as she and Charlie had been for so many years. And, although she believed that marriage was sacred, she would be glad to see George and his arguments with Hazel out of their lives.

For the next few days Hazel waited for Lottie's answer. Whenever they passed in the hallway, she looked at her mother expectantly, asking with her eyes, "Have you decided?"

If her Ma wouldn't agree to their plan, she was not sure what to do – go away with Roy herself and perhaps never see any of her family again? Or stay with the mother and siblings she loved so much?

Each day Lottie grew more certain that she wanted to go, to take her whole family out of this country and away from the horrible memories of their time in Canada. She got down on her knees.

"Dear God," she prayed. "Guide me now. Let me know if this be the right thing to do.". Amen."

Three days later when Roy stopped by to see Hazel, she motioned for him to come into her bedroom. "Ma got down the suitcases and has begun to pack. She said she got a sign from God that this is the right thing to do."

Roy grinned, "That's my kind of God!

Lottie came in. "Yes," she said.

"Your relationship may be wrong in God's eyes but He seems to be telling me to follow my heart. I think we should leave, Roy. If you're willing to take responsibility for getting all of us away from here, I thank you and I will help in any way I can."

Lottie's Lot

Roy and Hazel both clasped Lottie in a tight embrace. Flustered, she stiffened and patted each of them on the back.

"Thank you, Ma!" Hazel whispered as loudly as she could. "Ma, I love you so much. Thank you."

They chose Detroit , Michigan as their destination, mostly because Roy was sure to get a good job in one of the city's new automobile factories. There would also be plenty of opportunities for the women to be hired as store clerks or waitresses.

Lottie, Hazel, and Roy decided to keep the plan a secret from the children until the last minute, so George wouldn't find out. Hazel feared he would stop her from taking little George away.

Lottie and Hazel began sorting things to take and what to leave behind in mid-March of 1915, telling the girls they were moving to another boarding house. Roy sold his prosperous automobile repair business he shared with his brother Ernest. Ernest decided to move to California.

Roy bought train tickets for everyone and they left on the night train to Toronto on the anniversary of Lillian's death. Although it had been three years her absence left a hole in the hearts of everyone in her family. Leaving Lillian and Mary Jean behind in the Canadian cemetery saddened Lottie but leaving Canada was almost a joy. She hoped and prayed that life would be better back in the United States.

Lottie had lost so much in the years she lived in Canada. She was profoundly changed. She realized how fragile and fleeting life could be. She vowed to appreciate her family more and cherish every day. You never knew what tomorrow could bring.

She turned 44 years old on April 7, 1915, on the train trip to Detroit. Hazel had brought cupcakes and managed to keep everyone quiet while she lit candles on them. Lottie was dozing in her seat as they silently made a circle around her. Then Charlotte's strong voice led them in singing "Happy Birthday." Lottie opened her eyes in confusion, then delight, as she saw the light of the candles and, even better, the glowing faces of her family.

"Thank you." Tears filled her eyes as she asked for help to blow out all the candles. The rest of the evening was filled with laughter, hugs, and songs, as the children's excitement grew about their new adventure. Everyone was happy except Beth, who hadn't been able to say goodbye to Arnold, her beau in Edmonton. Lottie hoped Beth would soon forget about Arnold. She was only 12, far too young to be getting serious about anyone.

They used fictitious names on the two-day train trip to Toronto. From there they took another train to Springford, Ontario, and stayed at Roy's family's farmhouse to rest up and plan the remainder of the journey. They would have to cross the border into the United States without filling out permits so that there would be no paper trail for George to follow.

After a week they decided to take a ferryboat from Sandwich, Ontario, close to Windsor, across the Detroit River to Detroit. They sent their belongings ahead by train and piled into a hay wagon at night. Roy's cousin drove them to the ferry crossing and they took the first boat in the morning. No one asked for boarding passes. This was a popular tourist vacation spot and many people crossed between Detroit and Canada daily.

When they were across the Detroit River Roy hired a horse and buggy big enough to hold everyone. They went to a cheap hotel and everyone slept well into the next day. They didn't know a soul in Detroit but they were so grateful to be in the United States again it didn't matter.

Elmer had finally helped to settle Charlie's insurance claim but for much less than the family had hoped for. The union settlement gave $2,500 to Lottie. If Charlie hadn't lied on his employment application it would have been for much more. But if he had told his true name and age he wouldn't have had the job.

Lottie was disappointed at the amount, but grateful to have anything. At least this sum would help the family get a new start in Detroit. The timing of the windfall was perfect. Thrifty as always, she put $1,500 in a bank account for emergencies and for her later years.

After they rested, Lottie, Hazel, and Roy looked in the newspaper for flats to let and found a ground floor flat with four bedrooms. They went to see it and found it was a big house divided into four units, two downstairs and two upstairs, with common electrical service and a coal furnace for heat in the winter included in the rent. It was close to schools and a streetcar ran just a block away. The rent was reasonable.

Each flat had either two or three bedrooms and was furnished with a living room suite, a dining room table and chairs, beds, and bureaus for clothes. The kitchen had an electric stove and oven, an icebox, cupboard, and some mismatched dishes, cups, glasses, silverware, pots and pans, and a table with two benches. Everything was shabby but sufficient to get by and set up housekeeping. They had lived with worse.

Hazel and Roy took a downstairs unit with two bedrooms. Lottie used some of the money from Charlie's railroad settlement and rented one of the upstairs flats with three bedrooms for herself, Charlotte, Bethany, Ruby, Lois, and Buddy.

It was an ideal arrangement. The families were close but separate. Thinking of Hazel and Roy living in sin by openly sharing a bedroom sent chills through Lottie. But she held her tongue and prayed that they would find a way to marry soon.

171

Within a week Roy found a job as a mechanic. Hazel stayed at home to take care of Abby, six and George Jr., four, and to help with her sisters and Buddy so that Lottie could work as a clerk at Kern's Department Store.

She felt responsible for her mother and siblings. She wanted to help them, and as long as Roy accepted her involvement with them, peace reigned in their home. He did accept her family but he wished they didn't have to live under the same roof. He liked his privacy and wanted more time alone with Hazel. It seemed that either Lottie or one of the Hastings children was always in their flat.

When he met Hazel he had found a young vulnerable woman who needed him. After she responded to his attention initially, and after she fell in love with him she appreciated his every word and gesture. He could do no wrong. She rarely differed with him and gave him full rein over her children. Abby became Abby Darden and she called Roy "Dad."

Hazel had never felt this way about any man before except for her father. Loving Roy was different from being with George. He loved her back. He made love to her. He was her rescuer, her knight in shining armor, her best friend. For the first time since childhood she felt safe and truly protected. They rarely argued and she was relieved to have him to help support her children.

Gradually Roy chafed under the presence of the large family. He became standoffish with her mother and siblings -- courteous and pleasant, but emotionally distant. He warmed up to Abby but not to George Jr.

At four Georgie didn't understand where they were and kept asking when his Papa was coming to see him. Hazel made excuses or ignored his questions. One day she told him that his Papa wasn't ever coming back. He didn't love him anymore and now he was a soldier fighting the bad Germans.

Lottie's Lot

Georgie started to cry. "I want Papa!" he sobbed over and over. Hazel slapped him and said, "Roy is your Papa now, your *new* Papa."

He said, "No he isn't. I don't want him to be my Papa."

"Yes he is, and it's time you call him Papa."

"No! I won't. Never!" He ran crying to his room.

Roy overheard the conversation and told Hazel she was too easy on the boy. She allowed him to punish Georgie with spankings and harsh words. To placate Roy she changed her son's name to Kenneth Leroy Darden, using Roy's middle name and dropping "George." They called the boy Kenny. He was confused for a while but in time adjusted to his new name.

Abby basked in being the favorite child. She always made sure that Kenny was blamed whenever she got into trouble.

Lottie soon came to enjoy life in Detroit. Hazel and Roy were happy. The children were in school. Lottie made enough money for rent, food, clothes, and occasional extras. She made herself a few new dresses and even wore some of her skirts above her ankles. In the evenings she was able to return to her routine of a long bath and 100 hairbrush strokes.

When she first saw a few silver strands in her auburn hair she considered them symbols of the fortitude it had taken to survive her struggles. Her face had a few frown lines but retained its handsome structure. She smiled into the mirror, and realized the young and lovely Lottie had made it so far.

"Forty-four," she thought. "My, my. Some days I still feel like I'm 20." Not the naive young girl who believed she could make life perfect, but an older, wiser, and more tolerant woman. She pondered what she would change if she had her life to live over again.

Her job made her feel part of the larger world – a mixed blessing. She hadn't realized how isolated they had been from American life. The Great War was raging in Europe, and American boys were fighting and dying every day. Lottie wanted to do her part.

Some of the other store clerks told her about the Sons and Daughters of Temperance. She attended some meetings of Detroit's active branch and felt supported and confirmed in her belief that alcohol was the root of all evil. The more she thought about it, deep in her heart she believed that Charlie would still be alive if he had never drank alcohol. She dedicated her energy to creating a country of teetotalers.

As the war grew worse in Europe she heard stories of debauchery and drinking among the troops. This was the cause she was looking for -- a way to combine two issues near and dear to her heart. So she volunteered to write letters to American soldiers. In 1916 she spent every evening handwriting copies of the same letter:

Detroit, Michigan

July 15, 1916

To a Soldier or Sailor Boy,

The Women's Christian Temperance Union is sending comfort to our "brave laddies." We know you are brave, or else you would not be where you are.

This message is for you! The Lord blesses thee and keeps thee. The Lord makes his face to shine upon thee and be gracious to thee. The Lord lift up his countenance upon thee and give thee peace.

A Mother

Enclosed with the letter was a pledge card which the soldier or sailor was asked to sign, date, and return to the address given. The pledge was:

174

Lottie's Lot

"I hereby solemnly promise, God helping me, to abstain from all distilled, fermented and malt liquors including wine, beer and cider, as a beverage and to employ all proper means to discourage the use of and traffic in the same."

She began going to church again. Roy had been raised Baptist so with his encouragement Hazel took Abby and Kenny to church. Lottie was happy when she could convince the girls and Buddy to go and occasionally they all went together. But with or without her children, she attended church every Sunday and a temperance group meeting during the week. She felt righteous doing her part to save the country, and maybe the world, from sin and degradation. Lottie and her teetotaler friends celebrated victoriously when the 18th Amendment passed in 1919, prohibiting the sale and drinking of alcoholic beverages.

Vivid scenes of his inebriation colored Lottie's happy memories of her life with Charlie. He would tell stupid jokes, his speech would be slurred, and a few times he fell. When he got this way she felt ashamed of him and remembered James' warning words, "He is a drunk and will break your heart."

Still, even though she hadn't been able to live with his drinking, when Lottie put herself in his place and relived Hazel's pregnancy and her own insistence in moving to Minneapolis, his job problems and disappointments, she felt guilty for rejecting him and responsible for his death.

Had her complaints about his drinking driven him to seek out the bottle even more? Should she have let him move to Edmonton with the rest of the family instead of making him stay in Superior? If she had, would he be alive today?

And why, just when he was overcoming his problem and they were planning to reunite. Why! Why did God take him away? She found it hard to ask God that question directly. Every time she started to say the words in her prayers a simmering anger rose in her heart. She finally admitted to herself that she was angry at God. She prayed to forgive him.

These thoughts haunted her when she permitted them, stirred her to overwhelming sorrow. She spent many late nights in her bedroom in tears. She may succeed in forgiving God, but she would never forgive herself.

CHAPTER 12

The older Kenny got the more he looked like his father. He was slender and shorter than his friends, his smile, eyes, gestures, and demeanor were all a carbon copy of George Hopf. Changing his name from George Jr. to Kenneth Leroy Darden hadn't erased the similarities.

Hazel never came to terms with this. The five years she spent with George Hopf were miserable for her, and she secretly resented this child who reminded her of him every time she looked at the boy.

Subconsciously she blamed him for the entire relationship and punished him for the sins of his father. If she hadn't married George her life might have turned out very differently. Sometimes when she looked at her son, powerful feelings of disgust and revulsion washed over her. She knew it was wrong but couldn't stop herself.

She felt guilty and tried to resist her hostile feelings, but she ended up hurting her son in little ways. She would give him a pinch or a punishment more severe than necessary for a childish prank, or she withheld comfort when he needed it. She rarely held or cuddled him as she did her daughter. Abby was her doll. She was cute, coy, and cunning enough to know how to get her mother's approval as well as her stepfather's.

Like Hazel, Roy unconsciously resented Kenny, though for different reasons. Because his own son had died he took out his grief and anger on this boy. Kenny was alive while John had died and his death had ruined Roy's marriage and changed his life.

177

Kenny was a typical little boy. Curious and always getting into things he wasn't supposed to, frequently triggering his mother's wrath. Smugly she would justify punishing him, thinking,

"He's a bad boy and needs to be taught a lesson."

Kenny was confused. He tried to please his mother but couldn't figure out what she wanted from him. He would watch Abby and do what she did and still get into trouble if he did the same thing. She would be praised and he would get punished. At first, when Roy punished Kenny the boy would look to his mother for protection but she always sided with Roy. He believed in spanking and Kenny got spanked often

Sometimes if Kenny was lucky he was ordered to stand in a corner facing a corner of the wall for ten minutes with his nose and toes touching the wall. If he was unlucky, he would get a spanking with a razor strop on his bare backside. "Keep up that crying, you Little Baby, and you'll get more of this strap," Roy would shout if Kenny let his tears show.

The little boy tried hard to stifle his pain. But he was more hurt inside. He never got over that pain. Later in life he realized he was angry at the unfairness of it all. When he turned to his mother for justice or comfort she denied it to him. He felt rejected and so the seeds were planted for mistrusting people for the rest of his life, especially his mother and consequently other women.

Back in Edmonton George Hopf stewed over Hazel's betrayal. Outraged that she had gone off with another man and had taken his only son away, he put all the blame on her, never reflecting that he might have had any responsibility for the breakup. After all he had done for her and her family, and this was how she repaid him. Seeing himself as a victim, at first he raged and wanted to kill both her and Roy. Then he considered suicide, but he couldn't do it. For weeks he was so despondent that he quit his job and moped around in his pajamas.

Lottie's Lot

Robert Hall rescued him. The former brothers-in-law talked for hours and Robert let George rant about getting even and getting his son back. The only trouble was he didn't know where Hazel was.

World War I was engulfing Europe, and Robert persuaded George to enlist. On July 13, 1915, both of them signed up for overseas duty with the Canadian Army. Now they had something to think about besides their losses and troubles with the Hastings family.

George spoke German, so the Army sent him to the front lines in France for active duty and trained him as a medic. In 1917 he was hospitalized four times for flu and myalgia, severe muscle pain in his hips and legs. Blood tests revealed a plus 3 Wassermann test, indicating that he had syphilis, probably in the secondary stage. He was shocked at the news. George told the doctors he had a small sore on his penis after an encounter with a prostitute when he was 18 and was treated with a mercury oxide ointment. The chancre had cleared up and he thought the disease was gone.

"I haven't even thought about it in 20 years," he said.

The Army doctors told him that the disease had lain dormant within him all these years and was now emerging again in the secondary stage. They ordered immediate treatment in a hospital in England.

As a practicing Seventh Day Adventist George didn't believe in taking drugs. The newest treatment for syphilis was a series of seven intravenous injections of Salverson 606, a mixture of mercury and arsenic, a combination of two strong poisons administered a week apart. This new concoction was lauded as the new "magic bullet" against syphilis. If untreated the disease could progress to a third stage affecting the nervous system, brain, heart, and other unforeseen body systems.

179

Syphilis was an epidemic during the late 18th and 19th centuries. Many men and women infected each other without realizing they had the disease or the consequences. Most went undiagnosed, but sexually transmitted diseases like syphilis and gonorrhea have left mutations for future generations in the form of both physical and mental disabilities.

With great trepidation George agreed to the treatments and underwent injections for seven weeks. The shots made him deathly ill and induced severe side effects -- chills, vomiting, diarrhea, abdominal pain, splitting headache, and depression. After the treatments George's Wassermann test still indicated a plus 3.

The Army doctor gave George the bad news, "Well, George, apparently this treatment didn't work for you. We can offer you a medical discharge and send you back to Canada if you like. But we strongly recommend that you repeat the Salverson treatment at the Army hospital in Calgary."

He gave it some thought and declined. He regretted the hellish treatment he had already endured and wasn't about to go through it again. After he signed a waiver stating that he refused further treatment, the Army discharged him on January 24, 1919.

All the time he was in France he fantasized about living a fairy tale *"happily ever after"* life with Hazel and George Jr. It kept him going. He found out that the Army was sending her a $25 check every month to General Delivery in Detroit, Michigan, to support his son. He wrote several letters to the same address but never got an answer.

He read that the Canadian government was giving free homestead land to returning veterans. On the ship carrying him from England back to Canada he wrote to request a second homestead. Shortly after his arrival, the Canadian government granted him a homestead in Peace River between Edmonton and Calgary.

When he saw the parcel he could clearly envision himself, Hazel, Georgie and Abby living an idyllic life in that beautiful spot, but first he needed to find Hazel and convince her to reconcile with him. His heart ached to see his son. He hoped she had come to her senses and would welcome him with open arms. Yet another part of his mind said, "She dumped you, Fool. Don't get your hopes up or you'll just be hurt all over again."

He knew she was in Detroit and would find her come hell or high water. He crossed the border from Windsor, Canada, on February 18. Instead of trying to find a needle in a haystack he went to the Police Department and reported his wife and son as missing persons. To validate his claim he showed them his receipts for the checks that Hazel had cashed from his Army paychecks.

A few days later the police located her. The family was living in a downstairs four-flat house. He got the address and watched the house for a few days and was happy to catch a glimpse of his son, now eight, as he left the house to walk to school. George's impulse was to run and embrace him but he resisted. He couldn't believe how much his Georgie had grown.

George needed a plan. As far as he knew, Hazel thought he was still in France or maybe Canada. As long as she thought he was far away she felt safe and wouldn't run. Maybe she would be calm enough to speak to him. He had to choose the right moment and approach her in a non-threatening way.

One morning as she swept the front steps, he watched Roy Darden came out of the house and kissed her before getting in his car and driving away. He longed to hold and kiss Hazel again. His heart sunk to see that she was still with that man. He felt a rage building and fought the urge to confront her. But reason prevailed and he turned and briskly walked away. He needed time to revise his plan.

His emotions soared and plunged like a roller coaster. He had powerful feelings of love and visions of a life with Hazel and his son.

Reality sunk in and shattered his fantasy. His hurt, pain at her rejection and unresolved ranger again bubbled to the surface.

Hiding behind a big shrub across the street he silently shouted the familiar questions inside his head: *How could she have abandoned me and taken my son away from me? How could she have left me for another man? How could she have betrayed me like she did?* Taking deep breaths, he forced himself to calm down, knowing that if he lost his temper they would never reconcile and she wouldn't go back to Canada with him.

One Sunday afternoon in March it all came to a head. He watched Roy, Hazel, Abby, and George, Jr. walk a few blocks to a moving picture house. He followed them in and sat behind them throughout the movie. Afterward he followed them out, and on the street he approached them from behind, "Hello, Hazel." He said casually.

He was wearing his Canadian Army uniform and smiled as they all turned to look at him. Hazel was stunned and took a few steps backward, Abby hid behind her, and Roy stared, unmoving.

Then he said, "Georgie, come to Papa," and knelt on one knee. Kenny had almost forgotten he'd ever been named George but he recognized his father immediately and ran, jumped into his arms, and hugged him around the neck.

"Papa, you did come back!" he said. "I knew you would. I prayed every night to see you again."

Roy recovered his composure and said, "What are you doing here?"

George stood, holding his son in his arms. "I came for my wife and son. You stole them away!"

A crowd began to gather around the group. George gritted his teeth, walked closer to Roy and growled. "You dirty dog! You stole my wife and kids. " His eyes flashed rage and through tight white lips he hissed, "I've got a mind to kill you." He advanced with his right hand in his pocket as if he had a gun, and pointed a finger at Roy.

Hazel begged, "No! No! Please don't hurt him."

Kenny was frightened. "No, Papa, don't do it!"

Roy raised his hands above his head. "I didn't steal them away. They came voluntarily. They wanted to get away from you."

George snarled, "I don't believe you. You're a thief and a liar. You abandoned your own wife and children and then stole mine. Killing is too good for you. I want my wife and son back."

Then, turning to Hazel, his voice softened. "Hazel, will you come with me now?"

Hazel began to weep. "George, please go away and leave us alone."

George pleaded. "Hazel, I love you. I want you to come back to Canada with me ... *now.*"

Georgie wiggled to be let down and went to his mother's side.

"No, I won't! Not now or ever." She sobbed. "Go away, I don't love you. Please leave us alone."

A police officer walked up quickly and asked what the ruckus was all about.

Righteously, Roy said, "Officer, this man threatened to shoot me in front of my wife and children."

The officer asked George if this was true. He laughed and turned his pockets inside out.

"Just a joke, Officer, to expose this coward." George explained the situation.

"This is a matter for the courts to decide," the officer said, standing between the two men. "Go home, all of you. Don't do anything foolish or you'll end up in jail."

"I haven't seen my son for almost four years," George complained. "I want to spend some time with him now, today. I've just come home from the War."

"He has to go to school tomorrow and all his schoolbooks and clothes are at my house. He can't go with you now," Hazel said, fearfully.

"I'll bring him back to your house later."

"Now, Sir," the policeman intervened. "We're grateful for your service, but you're upsetting the children. Get yourself a lawyer and work this out in court, like civilized folks. That will be best for everyone."

George backed off and reluctantly agreed, but only after Hazel promised to let him come and see Kenny the following Sunday.

"But call me first," she insisted.

They went off in opposite directions and the crowd dispersed, chatting about the little drama they'd witnessed on a Sunday afternoon.

After settling the kids down, Hazel knocked on the door of Lottie's flat. They sat at the kitchen table with a cup of tea. Hazel told her, "Ma, George is here."

"Where?" Lottie was surprised.

"Here in Detroit." Hazel told her about the incident.

"Oh my!" Lottie studied her daughter's face.

"What should I do, Ma? I'm scared." Her voice shook.

"What does he want?"

"He wants me to go back to Canada with him and he wants Georgie err... Kenny."

Lottie's Lot

Lottie searched for something to say to help Hazel. She hadn't expected George to find them. "And what did you tell him?"

"I told him I would never go back to him."

"Well, you did run out on him. He has every right to be mad at you. You were wrong when you took his son away with no forewarning. Somehow you should make this right now," Lottie told her. But that wasn't what Hazel wanted to hear.

George rented a flat a few blocks from Hazel's house and called to arrange a visit with his son. He called twice every day for the next five days but there was never any answer. Finally he went to the house and rang the doorbell. Hazel answered.

"Kenny isn't at home."

"Who's Kenny?"

"That's my son's name now."

"Well, where is he?" George said, feeling his anger ready to blow.

"Somewhere where you will never find him." Hazel refused to budge.

"Oh, Hazel. I know you still love me. I want my family back."

"No, George. I never will go back to you. I'm happy with Roy. For the first time in my life I'm happy. He's good to me and the kids. I love him and I'll never leave him for you or anyone else."

Despite her firmness, George continued to beg for another chance. He alternated between fiery anger at Hazel and Roy, and a tender dream of reconciling his family. He hired a lawyer and filed papers for a legal separation and for full custody of George Jr. Hazel countered by suing for divorce. The legal battle was on.

At the first hearing, in April 1919, George was granted visitation rights every other Sunday from 8 am. to 8 pm. He picked up his son the following Sunday morning at 8 . They went to a baseball game and had cotton candy, sodas, and hot dogs. Later they had dinner at a diner and George brought him back on time.

They visited every Sunday for the next several months and had wonderful times together.

In September Superior Court awarded George a divorce on the basis of mental and physical cruelty, and abandonment, but Hazel received full custody of Kenny with increased visitation for George.

The following November Hazel became pregnant with Roy's child. Now that Hazel was divorced. They applied for a marriage license in Detroit on December 19, 1920, on Abby's 12th birthday. Because he was still legally married Roy applied under a false name. The name he used was Leroy Darden and stated his place of birth as Hillsdale, Michigan. A minister in a small church married them on January 4.

Hazel's pregnancy finally made it clear to George that he would never win her back. But he still couldn't stand losing his son. In June, after school was out for the summer he decided to take Kenny back to Canada with him during the month they were granted together.

He didn't bother to make arrangements with Hazel. Every encounter ended up in an argument or with Hazel sabotaging his plans. So he simply stopped at the house one day while Hazel was out.

Abby answered the door. "What are you doing here?" she demanded, sounding just like her mother. Hazel had made her promise never to let George take Kenny out alone. "Stick to your brother like glue," Hazel said.

186

Lottie's Lot

"I came to take Kenny out."

"You can't take him if my mother isn't here," she said with all the snootiness she could muster. Kenny had heard the doorbell ring and came into the living room.

George said, "Hi, son! We're going on a little trip so go and pack some clothes, toys, and your toothbrush. Don't forget pajamas."

Kenny gave him a hug and said, "Yippee!" He ran off to pack.

Abby said loudly, emphasizing each word, hands on her hips, "I Told You -- You--Cannot –Take –Him--When –My--Mother's— Not--Home."

George ignored her. "Hurry up, Kenny. Do you need some help?"

"All right then I'm going too," Abby said indigently remembering her mother's directions to stick with Kenny no matter what. This was a big responsibility for a 12-year-old.

"Fine, come along then. Pack your clothes fast. We'll be gone for a while," said George. "Hurry up. I'm leaving in five minutes—no longer."

He went into Kenny's room and helped him pack. They put some clothes in a pillowcase and added some books and paper and pencils. They were taking Kenny's things out to the car when Abby came dashing out with her clothes in a burlap sack. She got into the back seat.

"Wait!" she said. "I want to leave my mother a note or she'll be worried."

"Hurry up!" George told her.

She ran back into the house and left Hazel a note.

Dear Mama,

Kenny and I are going away with George for a few days.

I will call you.

Love, Abby.

George started the car. Abby ran back and jumped in just as he took off. He crossed the new Ambassador Bridge and into Canada. They drove all day finally stopping at a hotel for the night in Kingston.

The next morning Abby asked, "Where are we going?"

He said, "To see Aunt Bethany." Beth was married and living in Millet, near Edmonton.

Abby said, "I don't believe you. Take us home right now."

"Shut up!" said George, losing patience with her.

"If you don't take us home I will call the police."

George pulled the car over to the side of the road. He turned toward the back seat and slapped her face, shook her by the shoulders, and shouted, "Listen, Missy, I don't like your attitude or tone of voice. Either you shut up and do as I say or I am going to let you out right here and you can get home on your own any way you can."

She scooted as far back in the seat as she could go. George restarted the car and they drove on. Abby sulked about her promise to her mother not to leave Kenny alone with George Hopf. She didn't want any part of this.

Nine-year-old Kenny was excited. He wasn't afraid of his Papa and he wanted to see his aunt again. This was a big adventure. His father had always been kind to him.

They drove for two more days, not stopping except for bathroom breaks, a snack and to get gasoline. George only took a few hours here and there for a nap and then got back on the road. Kenny and Abby entertained themselves counting horses, playing tic-cat-toe and hangman, and reading books. Whenever they started to quibble, George let them take turns sitting in the front seat next to him.

After three days, when they finally got to Beth's house in Millet, George was exhausted. He slept for a day and a half. The children were excited to see Beth and her baby, Terrance. She was expecting twins and had a big belly.

The Randall's lived in a small house near the livery stable in Edmonton that Arnold still helped his family run. Kenny and Abby had a good time playing with the baby, and Beth was thrilled to see her niece and nephew. George told Beth that he had Kenny for a month in the summer and that this was his time.

When Hazel returned home and found the note she was alarmed. She waited until dark and when they didn't call or come home she panicked and called the police. They told her to stay calm and wait a few days. After three days with no word she filed a missing persons report. The press picked up the story and the "INTERNATIONAL KIDNAPPING" of two children made the headlines of the Detroit Free Press.

Up in Millet Abby was worried about what her mother must be going through. Beth didn't have a telephone, so she got George to drive her into town and called Hazel.

"We're fine, Mama. We're at Aunt Bethany's."

"Oh my God," Hazel exclaimed, though she was relieved to hear from Abby. "You tell that son-of--a … tell George to get you two home immediately or I'll have him arrested for kidnapping!"

Abby repeated Hazel's order to George and he knew that Hazel meant what she said. She'd like to see him in prison. Realizing that he might never see his son again, and with a heavy heart, he

189

kissed Kenny goodbye, gave Abby money for food, and put them on the train with tickets to Detroit.

On August 10, 1921, Daniel Wayland Darden, a beautiful baby boy joined the family. He looked like his daddy with blond hair and blue eyes. Hazel and Roy were ecstatic about their new addition. Roy finally had a son to carry on his name. Kenny and Abby were happy too. The baby was like having a new toy.

However, their happiness was short-lived. Just five months later, Abby came home from school and found Roy leaning up against a tree in the front yard. He was as white as a ghost and breathless. He was too weak to walk up the steps to the front door. She ran to get her mother. "Ma, come quick. Roy's sick."

Hazel took one look at him and called an ambulance. As she climbed into the vehicle next to him she called to Abby, "Go get Gram and get Auntie Charlotte to take care of the baby."

"Yes, Mama," Abby said.

"Tell Gram we are going to Harper Hospital and to meet me there."

"OK, Mama." Shaking she went inside and called out to Lottie who was just getting home from work.

"Gram, Mama said you need to go to Harper's Hospital right away. Roy is really sick. An ambulance came and took him there."

Roy was rushed to the emergency room and diagnosed with heart failure. The hospital staff treated him aggressively.

Lottie took a taxi to the hospital and arrived within an hour. When she got the facts she called Charlotte, Lois, Ruby, and Buddy.

Ruby and Art Schultz, a plumber, had planned their wedding for the next day. They hurried to the hospital and Ruby tearfully said to her mother, "We can't get married at a time like this. We'll change our plans."

"I don't think that's a good idea," Lottie said. Hazel agreed.

Lottie's Lot

"All your plans have been made -- the church, the food, flowers, music, the reception hall, everything. You can't call everyone at his late moment and cancel it," Lottie said.

Hazel held Ruby by the shoulders and looked her directly in her eyes. "Roy would want you to go on and get married."

Ruby said, "But Roy was going to give me away."

"Well, maybe Art's father will do the honors."

"Are you sure? Roy's illness is more important."

Hazel hugged her sister. "You've always been left out, but not this time. Get married and have your special day. I won't be there but you know why. My heart will be with both of you. Go."

She went on, "Ma, go with her and help her get ready for her big day. There's nothing we can do here but wait."

Lottie went back to the flat she shared with Ruby. Another wedding without Charlie to walk his daughter down the aisle, she thought on the ride home. Charlotte had pressed Ruby's wedding gown and veil and laid them out on her bed. Lottie had made the dress, it had a Chantilly lace bodice and front panels all the way down the front inset in satin and a four-foot train. Her veil was a cloche with over 100 hand-sewn seed pearls and surrounded by netting.

Lottie knew that she had shortchanged Ruby, giving her much less attention than she'd given the other children. Making her wedding dress was one way to make up for that now.

She fixed some tea. "Come and sit down and relax, Ruby dear. I know this is hard for you. It's hard for all of us. Poor Roy is only 40 … so young. He may just have an infection and will be better soon."

191

"Let's hope so," Ruby added.

"I have something special for you," Lottie said with a smile. "I'm glad we have a few minutes alone."

"What is it?"

Lottie reached in her apron pocket and took out a small blue velvet pouch.

As she opened it she said, "This is a cameo brooch that my mother gave me when I married your father. She wore it when she married her first husband."

Ruby couldn't believe her eyes. "It's beautiful, Ma. So beautiful!"

"It's a family tradition," Lottie told her. "My grandmother wore it at her wedding. It's supposed to go to a daughter who marries for love."

"I think I've seen this before." Ruby was puzzled.

"You did. I gave it to Lillian and she wore it in her wedding. After she died Robert returned it to me to give to another daughter."

"Oh yes! I remember now."

"And you must give it to your daughter when she marries -- someone she loves, I hope."

Ruby reached across the table and squeezed her mother's hand. She had so seldom heard the kind and loving voice Lottie was using now.

As if reading Ruby's thoughts, Lottie said "It's the least I can do." They shared another precious moment of silence. Then Lottie stood and began tidying up the kitchen.

"Now I think we should get some sleep. We have a big day tomorrow." They finished their tea and went to bed.

Lottie's Lot

The wedding was lovely Ruby was a beautiful bride, but an air of anxiety and sadness permeated the day's events. Art and Ruby postponed their honeymoon they never took it.

With the best available medical care, Roy lingered for three days. He died on February 1 at 10 o'clock in the evening with Hazel and Lottie at his bedside.

The autopsy revealed an infection in the pericardium, the lining of his heart.

The doctors could not explanation the cause. They also found that he had atherosclerosis and his arteries were clogged. The doctors couldn't tell Hazel exactly what caused his death at such a young age.

Hazel was stunned and numb. She couldn't believe that she had lost her beloved Roy. What a cruel twist of fate. After years of struggle, she had finally found someone she loved and expected to grow old with him. Now at 29 she was a widow with three children.

At the request of Roy's family, Hazel had his body sent back to Springford, Ontario for burial. The family rented a car and drove three hours north to attend the funeral. Hazel wept uncontrollably at the grave site. She screamed "Roy! Roy! Don't leave me now."

She refused to leave and had to be physically carried to the car for the return to Detroit. "No! No! NO!" She sobbed all the way home.

When they got back to Detroit, Lottie moved in with Hazel and took over the mothering role of Hazel's children. She gave up her flat and brought Lois and Buddy, who were still in school, with her.

Hazel couldn't function. She quit nursing Danny and sat in the same chair in front of the living room window every day for six months, as if waiting for Roy to come home. She couldn't believe he was gone, gone forever.

Lottie knew Hazel's pain all too well, and her heart went out to her daughter. Hazel was even younger than Lottie had been when her beloved Charlie was suddenly snatched from her. She held and rocked Hazel for hours as she moaned or quietly wept. It felt natural to wrap her arms around her suffering daughter in a way that physical affection had never felt to her before. Hazel brought some of her difficulties on herself, Lottie knew, but hadn't she been punished enough?

She was in deep despair. The only man she had ever loved, the only one who had ever truly loved her, was gone. She wanted to die too, to be with him forever. She hated her life. She hated men. Every man she ever counted on had abandoned her: her father, George, and now Roy. She didn't trust them and she would never *never* let another man win her heart again. She bitterly vowed to reject any man who came too close to her heart. She couldn't face grieving like this again.

Lottie offered Hazel cups of tea, a hand to hold, and prayers to help her bear her sorrow, but Hazel wanted whiskey, to be alone with her private grief, and curses. It pained Lottie to see Hazel turn to alcohol for solace but this wasn't the time to chastise her.

At times when she had a lot to drink she lashed out in a rage. "GODDAMN GOD! How could a God who cares for us allow this? What did I do to deserve this? I hate my life." Hazel had nightmares and crying jags that went on for hours. She thought the booze would dull her intense sadness but it didn't. Nothing did.

"Mama, I want to die too. I want to go with Roy."

"No, Sweetheart, no, no, you don't," Lottie murmured, pressing Hazel's head against her breast and stroking her hair. "No, no, no, we need you, and your children need you."

Thoughts of her children only triggered more anger in Hazel. Not only did Hazel not want to raise her children alone, she didn't want to raise them at all. In fact, she had never even wanted these

194

children, especially the first two. Now Danny was all she had left of Roy. But instead of embracing Roy's baby, she couldn't bear to hold him or even to feed him. Just looking at him reminded her of Roy and renewed her profound grief.

CHAPTER 13

In the 17 years that the family had lived in Detroit the Hastings girls became women and Buddy became a man. School, work, relationships, marriages, children, loves, and losses framed their lives against a backdrop of tumultuous social change in America. The years from 1915 to 1932 marked a period in which many of the old social and behavioral constraints fell away.

The Hastings offspring adjusted easily to city life. In fact everyone loved it except Bethany. They all finished grammar school and Lottie pushed them to attend high school. She knew her daughters were as smart as any man she'd ever met. She also knew an education would give them more choices than she'd had for better jobs and more independence.

While living in Canada and dealing with the tragedies that had befallen them, Lottie and her children had been out of touch with the world events that were affecting and irreversibly changing society. But in Detroit they were aware of and often engaged in the momentous events of the day.

The Balkans War (1912-1913) in Europe set the stage for the Great War (later called World War I), which involved almost every country in Europe. President Woodrow Wilson of the United States tried to stay out of the war, but in 1917 German saboteurs attacked a munitions plant in Jersey City, New Jersey, and Wilson was forced to declare war on Germany. Thousands of American boys were sent to Europe to join the allies and fight against Germany.

Sigmund Freud published **Introduction to Psychoanalysis** in 1917 opening the door for people to look inward to examine their individual reactions to events and problems. In 1918 the world was seized by an influenza pandemic that killed nearly 20 million people, half a million in the United States alone. Lottie took all precautions to protect her family.

After almost 70 years of dedicated hard work, sacrifice, and demonstrations to persuade women, men, and political leaders that women should have the right to vote, the required three-quarters of the states ratified the 19th amendment to the United States Constitution in 1920.

After the victory for suffrage, women found ways to unite their voices to wield political clout. Some focused on giving their sisters a say-so in their personal lives -- about reproduction, marriage, work, and holding office. Other women were adamant about the evils of drinking alcohol, insisting that drinking ruined lives and families, and led the temperance movement to ban the manufacture, transportation, and sale of alcoholic beverages.

Charlotte became active in the women's suffrage movement in 1918. Besides supporting the vote for women, she worked to give women the right to manage their own finances and to file lawsuits. She dreamed of the day women would have the right to fair wages and benefits equal to what men got and the legal right to control their own reproduction.

The Hastings women held many dinner table discussions about the events of the world. One Sunday afternoon in 1921, after finishing a family chicken dinner in Hazel's flat the women were enjoying a cup of tea before washing the dishes.

"I went to a very interesting meeting for the new Margaret Sanger clinic last week," Charlotte said.

"Who's Margaret Sanger?" Lois asked. She was 15 and in high school.

197

"Lois, don't you ever read the newspapers?" Charlotte asked. "You must become more informed about your world."

"All right, Charlotte, I will. But who's Margaret Singer?"

"It's *Sanger,* not Singer. She's the leader of the family planning movement. She's going to bring birth control to all women, so we can choose *when* and *if* we will have a child."

Lottie frowned. "Humph... They'll be the day. God's the one who makes plans for bringing children into the world." At her church and at temperance union meetings she had heard that family planning was a dangerous idea.

"Ma!" Hazel and Charlotte shouted simultaneously. "You've got to join the 19th century."

Hazel spoke up. "I guess it was God's plan for Gus Stover to violate me so I could have a child out of wedlock when I was only 16." Lottie flushed at the reminder of the circumstances that had brought her first grandchild into the world.

"Hush, Hazel." Lottie looked around to be sure Abigail, now 13, wasn't at the table. "We can't understand God's ways. And we wouldn't have our Abby if ... [in a whisper] that hadn't happened."

Charlotte added, "Hazel, that's not really what family planning means. We do need to figure out how to protect women against violations like what happened to you, but it's a different topic."

Charlotte turned to Lottie. "Anyway, Ma, how can you be so close-minded? Don't you remember ragging at Pa because you were having another baby that you didn't want? You know, we heard those whispered arguments that ended with you in tears and Pa drinking."

"I remember how sick you were and tired all the time," Hazel added.

"Be honest, Ma. If you'd had another choice you wouldn't have had so many kids, would you?" Charlotte asked.

Lottie's Lot

Lois piped up, "I don't want a lot of kids."

Ruby said, "Me neither!"

Lottie pondered and sipped her tea. "Well, you have a point there. We tried everything we knew to do and a few wild things the Grange women suggested to prevent pregnancies."

She grinned and they waited. "One woman said I should put half of a hollowed orange or lemon inside to..." She laughed out loud in embarrassment and her daughters snickered.

"I never got desperate enough to try that one."

"Ma, that's the way the diaphragm works! Only they're made of rubber," Charlotte explained. "Margaret Sanger is distributing those in all the family planning clinics across the country. We're going to have one here in Detroit soon."

Hazel peered closely at her mother. "Ma, tell the truth. If you had had a place to go to get one of those diaphragm things or some good information on birth control, would you have gone?"

"Well …now that you put it that way. Yes! I believe I would have gone for help if it was available." Lottie knew she would have run at top speed to a family planning clinic but she wasn't sure she liked this Margaret Sanger. She didn't approve of women making speeches and shouting in public. And Margaret Sanger had been arrested – she must have done something wrong.

Lottie felt victorious in 1919 when the 18th Amendment was ratified, prohibiting the sale and drinking of alcoholic beverages. She was still a teetotaler, although all her children drank. On the few occasions when she went to a bar or a nice restaurant she always ordered a Boulder Dam, ice water.

Her children just wanted to "have fun." The whole concept of "having fun" was foreign to Lottie. Duty was her guiding rule. Responsibility came before anything else.

"We have responsibilities, Ma," Charlotte or Ruby would say when Lottie began to expound on the topic. "We have jobs. We pay our way and help you with our money. Mama, we're not on the farm any more. It's different now."

She couldn't refute that argument. They did pay their own way, and as they married and had children they took good care of their families.

Her children naturally took on city ways and the values of these permissive times. She lost many battles with her daughters and Bud over their indulgences – in alcohol, tobacco, staying out late, dancing to raucous music played by colored musicians, wearing immodest clothes, swearing, and probably having sexual relations. She often felt exasperated and out of touch.

Smoking cigarettes was the fashionable thing to do and Lottie knew her children smoked, though they never did it in front of her. Nonetheless, she hated the practice. It was a tool of the devil, and it looked cheap. She was sure it must be unhealthy.

Bud and the girls hated confrontations with Lottie so they did what they wanted to do behind her back, making excuses to go outside or for a ride when they wanted a cigarette. They tried to keep other parts of their lives secret as well. Telling the truth to Lottie was pointless. She stubbornly held to her strong opinions on almost everything. Out of respect they listened to her rants, but they knew she didn't listen to them with an open mind.

One day when she found cigarettes in Charlotte's pocketbook, she confronted her. "What are these?"

Charlotte's face turned red. She knew Lottie's stand on smoking,

"They're cigarettes, Ma. You know what they are."

Lottie's Lot

"Do you smoke?"

"Yes, I do."

"Well, you shouldn't. I don't want you to smoke."

"I know that but, Mama, everyone my age smokes. It's the thing to do." Charlotte shrugged.

"That's no excuse. Have some backbone and stand up for what's right."

Charlotte didn't respond.

"And what are you wearing? You cannot go out in public wearing a skirt that shows your knees. That's indecent, Charlotte. You should know better."

"Kern's Department Store sells these clothes, Ma. You must have lots of customers who dress like this and bob their hair."

"Maybe so but I think it's indecent to show so much of your legs.

"Oh, Ma. If everybody's doing it, it can't be indecent."

Lottie shook her head repeatedly. "I thought I had taught you better than that."

"Why can't you see things from my point of view sometimes? I'm just fitting into the world I live in."

As Charlotte walked out the room, Lottie made one last stab. "Some things are just wrong."

In 1915, when they had first arrived in Detroit, all the children had enrolled in school except Charlotte. Lottie encouraged her to complete high school but she quit school after finishing the 10th grade when she was 16. She wanted a job so she could buy herself a few pretty things and help Lottie with household expenses.

Charlotte was the prettiest and most sophisticated of all the girls. She took Beth, Ruby, Lois, and even Lottie s to women's rights rallies a few times. She marched in protest parades and wrote letters for the movement.

She invited Hazel to join her but Roy didn't approve so Hazel stayed home though in her heart she supported her sister's favorite causes.

In 1917 Charlotte moved into a flat with two girlfriends. She continued to give Lottie money every week. By that time Beth was taking care of a neighbor's children after school to help out financially and Hazel often contributed groceries.

Lottie had expected Charlotte to live at home until she married but Charlotte assured her that many young women were living '*on their own*' now. "I can take care of myself, Ma. I'll be with my friends all the time."

How had she managed to produce such willful children? Lottie wondered. Some of her Temperance union friends said their daughters chose to live alone too.

"But why?" she asked and the other mothers were as baffled as she.

"Oh, their independence. Women's rights. All of that," one woman answered.

"I don't like it either, but I've been to my daughter's apartment and she's fixed it up nice," another said. "There are four girls in the same building and they have dinner together and check on each other. If they're making their own money and paying their own rent I don't see how we can stop them."

Lottie decided to get her own place too in a different house from the one she had shared with Hazel and Roy and their children. She found a smaller flat on Bagg Street for herself, Lois, Ruby, and

Lottie's Lot

Bud. Each day she walked to the streetcar stop on the nearest corner to get her ride to work at Kern's.

In 1920 Charlotte and her women friends danced in the streets to celebrate ratification of the 19th Amendment. "Ma! Hazel! Lois! Everybody! It passed," she exulted when she next saw her family. "We can vote!" Lottie couldn't help grinning at Charlotte's joy and they all joined in a little dance of celebration.

"Oh, my," Lottie said, sitting down and catching her breath. "Well, all I can say is, women have been doing as much hard work as men and making as many decisions as men, so I don't know why we shouldn't vote."

"Oh Ma, I love you!" Charlotte exclaimed.

All the Hastings women registered to vote as Democrats. They rejoiced over the long overdue recognition of a right that moved them one step up the ladder toward equality with men.

At her job as a telephone operator for the Pennsylvania Bank Charlotte fell in love with her boss, Sam, who was married. Throughout their two-year affair he promised to leave his wife and marry her.

When she missed two periods Charlotte remembered Margaret Sanger's warning that diaphragms were effective *most* of the time, not foolproof. And there were a few times when Sam had been in such a hurry she hadn't had time to insert the diaphragm.

Upon hearing that Charlotte was pregnant Sam glared at her with hard eyes. "It's time for our association to come to an end," was all he said. She was devastated and didn't know what to do. Telling Lottie was the last thing she would do, so she turned to her big sister Hazel who was sympathetic but couldn't offer any help.

203

The thought of having an illegitimate child terrified her; she had seen what Hazel and the family had been through. She wasn't going to go through the same thing. She couldn't support a child and didn't want to move in with her family again. The thought of what Lottie would say sent chills down her back.

She got names of three people who might be able to help her end the pregnancy. Abortion was illegal and people who performed it were very secretive and careful. If they got caught, they could be arrested and put in jail for several years, even life. After making some calls she finally got one of them to agree to do the procedure.

She was instructed to go to a downtown hotel at 9 P.M. and ask for the key to a certain room. Then she was to go to that room and wait. She had to bring $75 in cash. Lois went with her.

An hour after they got there a man and woman showed up. They were upset that Lois was there but backed down when Charlotte refused to pay them if they didn't allow her sister to stay.

They worked quickly. "Get undressed," the woman ordered while putting a rubber sheet on the mattress. The man opened a packet of silver instruments and placed them on a nightstand that he moved to the end of the bed. Then he left.

When Charlotte was ready the woman asked her to lie on the bed and put her heels together, letting her knees fall apart; then she draped a sheet across her knees. She put towels under Charlotte's buttocks and gave her shot of whiskey and a piece of leather to bite on.

Lois stood near her sister's head and held her hand. Charlotte was sweating. Lois was trembling. They were both scared and didn't know what to expect. The man came back to the room and sat at the end of the bed between Charlotte's legs. He told her she would feel pressure and then would begin bleeding, heavier than a normal menstrual period. He said she might pass some clots and would probably continue to bleed for another week or ten days. Then it would be over and she would resume her normal periods.

Lottie's Lot

He asked if she was ready and when she said, "Yes," he inserted the instrument in her vagina and she stiffened against the pain. She bit the leather but tiny screams escaped from her throat.

Lois shouted, "Stop -- you're hurting her!" They ignored her. Charlotte squirmed.

"Stay still," the man ordered. "You could hurt yourself." She sobbed.

"That's it." He withdrew the instrument, wiped off the bright red blood with a towel, and wrapped it in the flannel. The woman put some towels against Charlotte's vagina and told Lois to hold them there firmly for an hour. They told Charlotte to stay in the hotel room all night until she got her strength back, and they left her some orange juice to drink.

"If she has any problems," they told Lois, "take her to her regular doctor. Tell him she might be having a miscarriage." Lois nodded. The woman held Lois' arm tightly.

"Listen. This is important. *Don't* tell them she had an abortion. Do you understand? Under no circumstances can you tell anyone about what we did here."

Lois nodded again, more frightened than before.

After they left Charlotte kept bleeding. Lois didn't know a person could have so much blood inside. She kept putting clean towels under Charlotte to catch the blood and around 3 am. it seemed to taper off. Charlotte fell asleep in the bed and Lois stayed close by in a chair, trying to keep an eye on her sister but occasionally dozing off.

By morning Charlotte wasn't bleeding as much. She got dressed and they took a streetcar home to her apartment. She stayed in bed for the next three days. She cried and cried, feeling betrayed and abandoned by her lover. She didn't know where her life was headed. Her worst fear was that Lottie would find out what she had done. Her sisters swore to keep the secret and Lottie never found out.

Charlotte found another job within two weeks. She was so pretty that men were immediately attracted to her but she had learned her lesson the hard way. She rebuffed passes from her new boss and other men. She didn't date at all for a long time. She didn't trust men. In fact she thought she hated them.

A few years later she met Clarence Keller,, a toolmaker with a good job who was four years younger than she. After an eight-month courtship, they married in 1926. When she didn't get pregnant again she worried that the abortion might have damaged her and that she would never be able to have children, but finally in 1932 she gave birth to a son. One child was all she wanted. She faithfully used her diaphragm after that.

Ruby was 11 when the family moved to Detroit. She went to school through the 10th grade. Lottie helped her to get a job as a sales clerk at Kern's Department Store. Her pay was $6.50 a week. She gave half of her pay to Lottie and kept the rest for herself.

One advantage of working for Kern's was that employees got a discount of 20 percent on purchases. Ruby found an elegant ivory-colored silk blouse with long sleeves and ruffles around the neck. She had never owned anything so beautiful. She put it on layaway and paid 50 cents a week until it was hers. It took her three months to pay for it and take it home.

Everyone admired the blouse. One evening when Ruby wasn't home, Lois borrowed the blouse without permission and wore it to a party. She accidentally spilled red wine on it. She was horrified, knowing how much this blouse meant to her sister. At first she hid it, thinking she could wash out the stain and Ruby would never have to know. That didn't work so she took it to a dry cleaner. They couldn't get out the wine stain either.

Lottie's Lot

Ruby looked everywhere for her blouse. Lois finally had to confess and showed Ruby the damaged blouse. Ruby was livid.

"How dare you wear my blouse without asking me first?" She slapped Lois across the face so hard Lois fell down.

Surprised and hurt, Lois protested, "I told you I'm sorry! I will pay for it." She got up and pushed Ruby. Ruby pushed her back.

"I hate you!"

"I hate you too!"

Charlotte came in stopped the fight and hugged and comforted Ruby. Lois ran out of the bedroom, in tears. Ruby never forgave Lois to her dying day.

Art and Ruby's first child, Michael, was frail and she had trouble nursing him. At a family gathering at Cranberry Lake in cold and windy February Ruby spent the whole time huddled near the potbelly stove, holding and rocking the baby Michael, who was sick with a cold and cough. He died two weeks later. She grieved profoundly and even though Lottie tried to console her with soft words Ruby's grief was deep and painful.

A few years later Ruby later had a daughter and later another son. Joyce was a robust, energetic girl who ruled the roost -- demanding what she wanted until she got her way. Ruby always gave in to her. Ruby believed that, since her mother hadn't loved her, she must not be worthy of love or kindness. Lottie and Charlotte tried to show their love but couldn't always override Ruby's entrenched ideas about herself.

Lois was the only one of Lottie's children to finish high school. She graduated from Central High School in Detroit in 1924. She was pretty, fun-loving, and popular. During her senior year she went steady with Richard Gully, and they talked of getting married. But Lottie wouldn't hear of one of her children marrying a Catholic.

"Ma, what's wrong with Catholics?" Charlotte asked.

"They're all slaves of the Pope." She glared.

"You and Pa had different religions when you got married."

"Oh Lois. There's not much difference between Baptists and Methodists, as you would know if you would go to church. You would also know that Catholics are a cult that worships statues. They are not true Christians."

Two months later, when Lois realized she was pregnant, Lottie had to change her tune. Lois threatened to get an abortion if Lottie meddled with her plans to marry Richard. Lottie backed off and attended their quiet wedding ceremony. Six months later Lois gave birth to a baby boy and five years later had another son.

CHAPTER 14

When Bethany Hastings met Arnold Randall she was 12 and he was 23. Bethany had a natural, wholesome beauty, long, curly, strawberry blonde hair, with a clear rosy complexion, smiling blue eyes, and a cheerful personality. At 12 she was already 5-feet-5-inches tall with budding breasts, and rapidly maturing into a lovely young woman.

Her nickname was "Cherrie" to match her way of seeing the world. Her glass was always half full. More often than not she could tactfully turn trouble into something positive. She was kind and cooperative, always ready to pitch in and help with chores unfinished by her sisters.

Lottie looked at her with wonder. This daughter rarely got upset or talked back. She took everything in stride. She reminded Lottie of her sister Carrie -- kind, insightful, a good listener, blessed with the natural wisdom to see a solution to any problem in a new way.

Arnold Randall's family ran a livery stable in Millet just outside Edmonton while they waited for their homestead grants to be issued. Arnold was one of four sons who worked renting out horses and buggies.

The first time Arnold saw Beth he fell head over heels and flirted with her every chance he had. At first Lottie ignored him but she became alarmed when she caught Beth giggling and flirting back.

"Don't make goggle eyes at that young man, Bethany. He's much too old for you," Lottie warned her.

"Don't worry, Mama. But he is cute, don't you think?" Beth teased her mother.

"No, he is *not* cute. He's downright homely," Lottie replied indignantly.

Lottie didn't like Arnold Randall. He stared at the ground when he talked and constantly fidgeted. On occasion she suspected that he had been drinking. He was **not** the kind of man she wanted for her daughter.

But his persistent flirting flattered Beth. "I'd like to take a buggy ride with you," he whispered. "Just the two of us." She smiled and blushed. On one occasion when he was helping her up the step into the buggy seat he pulled her off balance and she fell into his arms. He squeezed her tight and nuzzled her hair before he released her.

Lottie was furious. "Unhand that child right now!" she demanded.

Arnold feigned surprise. "Sorry, Ma'am, the step must be slippery."

Lottie scowled. "It didn't feel slippery to me."

After a few months, Beth began to sneak out at night to meet Arnold. They went for walks and rides and he boldly kissed her a few times. Their secret courtship was cut short, however, when the family moved to Detroit. Lottie was relieved that her daughter was now out of Arnold's reach.

In Detroit Lottie watched over her daughters with eagle-sharp eyes, suspicious of every man who showed interest in any of them. As their only parent, she had her hands full with four daughters growing into puberty and young womanhood. Hazel's unfortunate pregnancy made her even more vigilant. Oh how she missed Charlie now! She needed him to help her raise these girls and find suitable husbands for them.

One day in their third year in Detroit, while Lottie was changing the sheets in Beth's room, the mattress slid over to reveal a stack of letters. As she picked them up, her heart sank to see Arnold Randall's return address. She opened one, then another and another, and found with shock that they were full of endearments like "Sweetie" and "My Darling" and "I miss you." Lottie's hands shook as she read them and realized that Beth, her sweet girl, was still enthralled with this disgusting oaf. She sat on the side of the bed to calm herself and sort out her options.

Her first instinct was to confront Beth and demand that she stop writing to or even thinking about Arnold Randall. But how could she be sure Beth would comply? Lottie had learned that laying down the law did not always work – it hadn't worked with Charlie or Hazel.

Maybe a softer approach would produce better results with Beth. This was a serious matter and she must handle it correctly or Beth might just rebel and leave – much as the young Lottie had done when her father forbade her to marry Charlie. But Lottie had been almost 18 and earning income from her sewing business. At 15 Beth was too young to leave home, especially with a do-nothing like Arnold. If Lottie could convince her to stay in school and bide her time surely she would find a much better prospect.

Lottie tucked the letters back under the mattress. She decided not to reveal that she knew what was going on. She would take a more positive tack and encourage Beth to make new friends by joining a youth group at church and going on outings with them. She could invite the boy across the street over for dinner on a Sunday or ask Charlotte to take Beth on double dates to the moving pictures or picnics at Belle Isle. She prayed that it wasn't too late.

That night at dinner Lottie said, "At the store today, there was a delightful young couple shopping for furniture. I showed them a selection of bureaus and they told me they would be getting married in the fall. They seemed so happy."

The girls kept eating and Buddy stretched his legs to kick Ruby under the table.

"Ouch. Stop it, Buddy," Ruby said.

"Ruby be quiet. Mother is talking," He rolled his eyes and grinned.

Lottie ignored them. "Anyway, they told me they had met at church when they were 10 years old. They had been friends for more than half their lives. The girl said she didn't like him at first but she kept noticing that he was an honest young man who was always courteous and took good care of his mother, and he was a devout Christian."

"Aw, Ma. You meet the nicest people at Kern's," Lois said with a giggle.

Lottie gave her a withering look, "The point is she grew to love him after she knew him well and after she was mature enough to appreciate the qualities that made him a good man. And that is what I want for all of you girls – a good, upright, God-fearing man who has strong Christian values."

The girls nodded, eager to get to the apple pie they could smell from the kitchen.

"I'm sure Hazel would agree with me that life is hard enough for women without getting into a bad marriage."

Hazel spoke up. "Oh Ma, I think the important thing is to fall in love with someone. Just look how happy I am with Roy compared to George."

"Well, Hazel, I'm glad you're happy. You're fortunate," her mother replied. "But, Girls, just think about what happened to Hazel. She didn't know George well and they found out after they had married and had a child that they were incompatible on some important matters."

212

Lottie's Lot

She looked around at the fresh faces at her table – four daughters from 12 to 19. Beth seemed absorbed in mopping up the gravy on her plate with a biscuit. Lottie had to make these girls understand the potential horrors of choosing the wrong man she had to protect them from the heartache of a bad marriage.

She set down her fork. "There are many situations that are much worse than Hazel's. A girl may think she loves someone because he is charming or handsome or buys her nice things or says he loves her. But many a girl has found out later that this man drinks or beats her and their children. There are other men who never give their wives any money to spend but they have plenty to spend on their floozy girlfriends or on whiskey. If you marry a bad man who doesn't take care of you, you're stuck with him. If you leave him, how will you support yourself and your children?"

"Hazel got a job and that's how she met Roy," Charlotte said.

"But that job paid almost nothing," Hazel responded. "I couldn't live on that money with two kids to support if I didn't have Ma. The only jobs women can get pay pennies. I bet a man who does Ma's job at the store probably gets paid about ten times more than she does."

Lottie nodded in agreement, impressed that Hazel had learned some life lessons. "That's why I want each of you to get a good education so that you can get better work, like being a teacher or a nurse. At least you can meet a better class of man."

The girls were getting restless. She kept watching for a reaction from Beth.

Finally Lottie said, "Hazel, would you serve the pie? Now listen, girls. The most important thing–and that is all I am going to say–is to find a man of good character. Find someone who is honest, sober, doesn't gamble, and doesn't hide his money. Find a man who goes to church. Even if you don't love him at first you can learn to love him and you'll have a good, decent life."

As her children grew, Lottie found the challenges of being the only parent increasingly difficult. Parenthood often presented her with complicated situations she would never have imagined; her childhood beliefs about right and wrong and perfect behavior didn't prepare her for real life as clearly as she had expected when she was a girl. The hardest thing was to consider her children s wishes and listen to them patiently, even while inwardly screaming to tell them why they were wrong. It would be so simple if they would just listen to her and follow her rules.

Bethany puzzled her. She was always good and rarely in trouble. Lottie thought that Beth was the last one who would defy her or bring trouble. But Arnold's letters had made Beth her number one concern. Now Lottie had to do everything in her power to see that Beth forgot about Arnold Randall.

She didn't realize that it was too late. Beth was not about to forget Arnold. In some ways he replaced her father. Charlie had been her hero -- easy to talk to, fun to be around, always listening to her and never dismissing her questions or concerns.

From the time she could walk until he died when she was 8, she had followed her Papa all over the farm. He often swept her up onto his saddle and took her for a horse ride through the fields. She followed him as he tended the crops and explained to her everything he was doing. She seldom understood what he said but she loved hearing him talk to her. He was comical, even when he was drinking and never mean. She loved him so much.

After they moved to Canada, leaving Charlie to work in Superior, Wisconsin, she missed him terribly. When he died she suffered deeply. In her heart she blamed Lottie who was always complaining and nagging him about his drinking. Beth hated listening to their fights. She would put a pillow over her head to shut out their voices.

214

Lottie's Lot

The sudden unexpected move to Detroit left Beth depressed and angry. No one asked her if she wanted to move. She felt she didn't count and her mother didn't realize how unhappy she was. Her cheery personality changed to gloomy.

Hazel didn't have time for her. Charlotte was caught up in her new job and new friends and didn't notice that Beth was sad. No one did. City life held no attraction for Beth. She loved being close to nature and working in the outdoors. Arnold's letters to her awakened Beth's memories of her childhood in North Dakota -- the happiest time of her life. For solace she spent long hours sitting on a bench in the park and having imaginary talks with Charlie. Her Pa was still her best confidante.

"Papa, Arnie writes me letters and he tells me he loves me. He is nice to me and he doesn't have any other girlfriends. I think he loves me almost as much as you did."

That sounded right so Beth added, "I feel so alone, Pa. There has been an empty place in my heart ever since you went away. I need someone to fill it." She blew her nose and brushed a few tears away.

"I wish you had met Arnie, Pa. I think you would like him. You could have had a drink together." She smiled to herself.

She lived to hear from Arnold and rushing home from school to go through the mail before Lottie got home. Getting a letter from him was the only thing that made her feel good. She wrote him long letters back, telling him how unhappy she was and how much she missed him. He wrote that he couldn't live without her. She savored every word. Over three years, each letter was like a new log on the fire of their love. It grew steadily stronger. Finally she wrote him a short note:

"Arnie, please come and get me."

One humid summer afternoon in 1918 Lottie came home from work and found Arnold Randall sitting in her parlor. Beth was sitting beside him looking star-struck and stroking his hand. Lottie was caught off guard for a moment. Then she stood straighter and stared formidably.

"What are you doing here?" she demanded when she got her voice back. Her back was up and she was prepared to fight for her cub's life. The time for subtle hints and patient understanding had passed.

He stood and timidly held out his hand. Looking Lottie in the eye he cleared his throat and said bravely, "Howdy, Ma'am. Good afternoon."

"What are you doing here?" she repeated.

"I came to ask Beth to marry me."

Lottie ignored his hand and took a few steps toward him. "No! No! No! She's just a child and she isn't going to marry anyone now." She took a few menacing steps forward and he took one step backward. Lowering her voice almost to a whisper, with her teeth bared, she went on. "She is only 15 and I still make decisions for her."

Beth, almost as tall as Lottie, stood next to Arnold and started to speak. Lottie grabbed her by the arm and yanked her toward the door and out of the room.

"Go to your room, Young Lady right now!"

After Beth headed upstairs she turned back to Arnold.

"Mr. Randall, why don't you find someone your own age? Your interest in my daughter borders on criminal."

"I'm sorry, Mrs. Hastings. I tried. I fell in love with Beth the first time I laid eyes on her, and I can't get her out of my mind. I want her to be my wife and to have my children."

"It is *not* going to happen." She put all the strength she could find in her voice.

216

Lottie's Lot

"She wants to marry me." Arnold wasn't giving up.

"She's too young and immature to know what she wants. And she can't make such a decision herself." Lottie snapped back. She kept her eyes on this country bumpkin as he shuffled uncomfortably from one foot to the other.

To Lottie's surprise Beth came back into the room carrying a tray with a pot of tea and three cups, along with bowls of sugar and cream. She set it on the coffee table and sat down. Lottie glared at her.

"How about a cup of tea, Mama?" Beth asked sweetly. "Let's all calm down and be civil to each other."

"I thought I told you to go to your room."

"Yes, you did. But I have something to say."

Lottie raised her eyebrows. "Don't defy me, Bethany. I am still your mother and I know what's best for you. This is the time for your education, not for this foolishness."

Silence reigned momentarily but it seemed like a year. Beth stalled, hoping Lottie would calm down a little.

"Please sit down, Mama, and have a cup of tea. Let's talk this over quietly." Beth straightened the napkins on the tray and struggled to appear composed. Then she folded her hands in her lap and looked Lottie directly in the eyes, cleared her throat, and softly said, "Mama, I asked Arnold to come and get me. I want to marry him."

Lottie was speechless and Beth continued.

"Here's your tea -- just the way you like it." She handed Lottie the cup and saucer. Her hands were shaking but her voice was firm. Lottie set her cup on the table without taking a sip.

Beth poured a cup for herself and one for Arnold. Lottie watched this composed young woman, straight in posture, sure in her actions, barely revealing any emotion. Ah, she was so much like a young Lottie. Charlie would be so proud of her. Would he take Beth's side in this or hers? she wondered.

Arnold sat down, grateful for the warm beverage and something to do with his hands.

"Bethany." Lottie took a deep breath. She would give reason one more try. "Bethie," she said more softly. "You should be going out with boys your own age. You have your whole life ahead of you."

Her voice rising, she went on. "Look at this man! He's almost twice your age! He's losing his hair and his teeth are bad. He looks like a scarecrow. You deserve someone better than this uncouth fool. And he drinks too much. Look at what drinking did to your father. Do you want the same thing for yourself?"

Arnold squirmed and stared at his shoes.

Beth lowered her voice to a whisper. "Mama, I love him. I have for a long time from before we left Canada. I've talked with other boys and gone for walks with them and none of them appealed to me at all. They are like children. They just make me miss Arnie more. You don't know him. He's kind and caring."

Beth fell to her knees in front of her mother and reached for Lottie's hands. She pleaded, "Mama, *please!* I love you and I love him. I don't want to hurt you but I am going to marry him with or without your approval."

Lottie jumped up. "No! I forbid it." Beth stood up and looked her mother in the eyes. Tears streaming down her cheeks, she announced in a breaking voice, "When he goes, I am leaving with him."

"**No, you are not!**" Lottie walked to the door and opened it.

"Goodbye, Arnold. Don't come back."

218

Lottie's Lot

Arnold looked from Beth to Lottie and back to Beth. He hugged her, kissed a tear away, and walked out the door.

Emphatically, Lottie said, "That's the end of it. Now Beth, go to your room. You may come down when you are ready to apologize to me. And I forbid you to ever see or write or communicate in any way with that man ever again."

Without another word Beth went upstairs to her room and began packing. At midnight while Lottie was sleeping, she crept downstairs. She went out the back door. Arnold was waiting for her in his car.

Lottie tossed and turned all night. She had an unsettling dream of a nest of baby doves and a mother dove who couldn't keep them all in the nest. One would fall out and the mother would swoop down to rescue it. The smallest one kept stretching her wings and the frightened mother cried, "No, no, no, no. You are too small." The little bird jumped off the edge and Lottie woke up reaching out a hand to try to reach the baby dove.

The first thing Lottie saw the next morning a note on the kitchen table and she knew before picking it up what had happened.

> *Dear Mama, I wish things had turned out differently. I told you that I was leaving – now I am gone. I still want your love for me and I am sorry for any hurt I have caused you. I will always love you.*
>
> *Your daughter, Bethany*

Lottie sat in a kitchen chair and closed her eyes and folded her hands over the top of her head, defeated and exhausted. Another daughter lost. Why? Why hadn't she seen this coming? Beth was always so good she escaped Lottie's close scrutiny. Now it was too

Nancy O'Connor

late. She blamed herself. She feared for Beth but it was out of her hands now. All she could do was pray for her, and she would pray hard. Charlie, damn you! Where are you when I need you most?

She resisted dwelling on her own rebellion when she defied her father and eloped with Charlie. History was repeating itself. Why can't children learn from their parents mistakes? She wondered, I guess they must learn their own lessons. In her heart she thought this relationship would come to a bad end for her sweet Bethany.

The other children were afraid to talk about Bethany in front of their mother although they all knew what had happened. A few days later, after her initial grief lifted a little, Lottie realized she must protect her other daughters from a similar fate.

At dinner, she said, "Now, we all miss Beth, and I want each of you to pray that no harm will come to her. You certainly may write to her and let her know we care. She is still your sister and part of this family."

They murmured, "Yes, Mama."

Lottie continued. "You see, I'm afraid for Beth. She doesn't know Arnold well enough. Not only is he too old for her but he drinks, I've seen that." She paused to butter a roll.

"Now, all of you know how much your father and I loved each other. We were fortunate and we were very happy. We had some ..." She choked up a bit and took a moment to compose herself. "Your father and I were working out our problems because he was a good man who cared about all of us. But you can't always trust those feelings of being in love especially when you're young. And 15 is too young."

She paused again. There was one more thing she must make clear, as difficult as it was to talk about with her children. She cleared her throat nervously. "You see, Girls, there are men and boys who will tell you anything if they think it will help them get close to you -- to kiss you and ... well, touch you. Ruby and Lois, I know you don't understand what I mean but you will."

220

Buddy mimicked an exaggerated noisy kiss. Lois saw him and laughed.

"Lois, you will be grown up before long, so please pay attention. They will say they love you. They'll promise you a beautiful home and wonderful things and swear to stay with you forever. Sometimes they'll promise to marry you. But after they get what they want they will disappear and the sweet words will come to an end."

Charlotte, 19, looked at her plate, pushing bites of green beans and corn around.

"All I'm saying is-be careful. It's better to wait and take some time to find out if he's being truthful. Look for a good man. He's worth waiting for."

In the fall, Charlotte received a letter from Beth saying that she and Arnold had been married at his mother's home in Millet. Lottie looked at the letter and touched Beth's neat handwriting with her fingertips.

"Oh, daughter," she thought. "I hope you will prove me wrong."

Abandoning any of her children, no matter what they did, was out of the question. She had accepted Hazel's relationships with George and Roy; she had accepted her children's lack of interest in church; she must learn to accept Bethany's new life and the pain of not seeing her for months or years at a time. She took out a pen and a sheet of her best stationery and wrote:

Dear Bethany,

Congratulations on your marriage.

As you know, I believe you are too young for this step, but I pray the Lord will bless your union   and that your life with Arnold will be happy.

Please understand that, no matter what happens, you are still my daughter and I care deeply about what happens to you. I pray for you every night.

I hope you will write me soon and tell me about your life. I'll be sending a wedding gift shortly.

She paused for a moment and then signed the note:

I love you.

Mother

Beth cried when she got Lottie's letter. She read it over and over, so grateful for Lottie's gesture of reconciliation. She sent a brief, sincere thank-you note when she received a large package of pillow cases and hand towels with flowers embroidered on the edges by Lottie.

In early March Lottie received another letter from Canada:

Dear Mama,

I have wonderful news. I'm going to have a baby and would love to have you here to help me through the delivery and first few weeks of learning how to be a good mother. The baby is due in October, about the 15th.

We are still living in Edmonton but Arnold is building us a house on our new homestead in Saskatchewan near Kitscoty, a small village just over the Alberta border. We were granted 600 acres. His family all got land nearby so I won't be all alone here.

The Canadian Pacific train stops at Kitscoty. So it will be easy for you to visit after we move into our new home I love you, Mama, and miss you and everyone. Please tell them I send my love and they are always welcome to visit.

Lottie's Lot

I am happy with Arnold. He treats me like a queen and gets me anything I want.

Please say you will come, Mama.

Bethany

Through tears, Lottie read the letter to the children and they encouraged her to go to Beth in October. She got a leave of absence from Kern's and took the train to Canada. She spent five weeks there, arriving just before Terrance was born. He weighed almost 10 pounds, making a difficult delivery for Beth. Lottie felt very much needed as she taught her daughter to nurse the infant and he guzzled all the breast milk she could produce.

Lottie made peace with Arnold and met his family. She was fond of Addie, Arnold's mother, a tough farm woman who had moved from North Carolina with six of her children to take up Canadian a homestead. The Randall's pitched in and helped each other build their homes. Lottie was comforted to know Beth had a close new family to look after and protect her.

Lottie and her daughters wrote to Beth often and visited over the next few years. Though still young she was a responsible mother and wife.

Beth was thrilled when they moved into their new home on their homestead in 1922. It was a basic 800-square-foot house, a single story with two bedrooms, a kitchen, and a front room that doubled as a dining room. It had a mudroom and porch that wrapped around three sides of the house. There was no indoor plumbing, electricity, or telephone.

Five years later Beth had had five pregnancies and four living children–two boys and two girls. She had given birth to twin boys who died—one at 9 months and one at 11 months, and she grieved for a long time.

Beth loved her babies and wrote stories about each one to her family in Detroit. She sang to them, played with them, fed them, rocked them, and worried about them when they got sick. But as much as she loved her children she was exhausted. She didn't say anything to Lottie and her sisters but she dreaded the idea of another child.

Beth had figured out that her children had been conceived about halfway between her periods so she tried to keep Arnold at arm's length during the middle of the month. But when he was drunk he didn't listen—he wanted sex now and he couldn't always pull his penis out before he released his semen. Bethany vaguely remembered overhearing arguments between her parents about pregnancy, and now she thought she understood why her mother was so tired and so often angry at Charlie.

In the summer of 1929 she got pregnant again and was frantic and angry about it. She didn't want another child. She had almost died when Lynn, her youngest son was born. The house was too small now with four children. She couldn't think of where to fit another. More important, Arnold was drinking more and more and their home was no place for a new baby. Keeping up with the children she had now and the farm used all her energy and wore her out.

When she knew she was pregnant again Beth was furious at Arnold. She told him that she would not have another baby, no matter what. She went to see a doctor in Lloydminster, a larger town than Kitscoty, and told him she didn't want any more children.

"I don't understand," the grey haired man responded from behind his desk.

"There's a history in my family of eclampsia. It happened to my mother twice and to my grandmother. And you know my last pregnancy two years ago was dangerous for me. "

"Well, Mrs. Randall, you've had five successful pregnancies with no untoward problems. There's every reason to believe this will be successful too.

"But I'm so tired. I feel worn out all the time. I've already lost two babies. I don't have the strength to go through this again. I know that pregnancy is dangerous for me, doctor."

He shifted in his chair. "Now Mrs. Randall. Women have been undergoing the tribulation of childbirth for a long time. You look like a strong young woman and if you have faith the Lord will see you through this." He nodded his head and looked at the door.

But Beth was not ready to leave. She tried to look him in the eye but he was fiddling with papers on his desk. She spoke a little more loudly. "I would like to have the operation where you take out my womb so I cannot get pregnant again."

"Oh, no. No, no, no. I'm sorry but a hysterectomy is completely out of the question for a healthy young married woman."

Despite the impatience and annoyance in his voice, Beth made one more try. In a whisper she asked, "Then can you please help me stop this baby?"

The doctor's face grew dark and he spat out his words. "That is an outrageous suggestion. It is against the laws of man *and* the laws of God. I have never been a part of it and I never will."

She began to cry softly and the doctor resumed his paternal role. "Now, Beth. I'm sure everything will be fine. You'll soon realize your foolishness."

Despondent on the ride home, she stared at Arnold's rough hands on the car's steering wheel. She would be happy if those hands never touched her again. There must be some way that she could gain more control of her own life. She wracked her brain to think of anything, anyone, who could help. She remembered Sophia Gilman, the local midwife, who knew something about ending a pregnancy. It had been a whispered topic of conversation at a quilting bee almost a year ago. She must talk to Sophia.

She got her chance just after Thanksgiving at another quilting bee. They were trying to finish several Christmas projects but Beth's mind wasn't on the quilts. When Sophia went outside to the privy, Beth stood on the icy porch and waited for her to come back.

"My goodness, Beth, aren't you freezing out here?" Sophia asked as she approached the house.

"Sophia, remember a few months ago, you were talking about, uh, when someone is expecting and she doesn't want to have the baby. You remember, don't you?"

"Yes, of course, Beth. It's called termination or abortion." Beth nodded, gathering her courage to share her secret. Sophia waited, then spoke softly, "Beth, do you know someone who wants to end a pregnancy? Is it you?"

She nodded. Sophia didn't seem particularly shocked. She gently lifted Beth's chin. "All right Dear. I can help you. Now let's get inside where it's warm."

On Christmas Day in 1929 Beth's kitchen was cozy and inviting, radiating a warm glow and a symphony of wonderful smells. For a week the children had been helping Beth make Christmas cookies and cakes and decorate them with green, red, and white frosting. She placed a plateful of them on the table.

They made caramel popcorn balls dyed with red, yellow, and green food coloring and hung them on the lovely spruce tree on Christmas Eve. They sang Christmas carols while adding paper chains and tinsels to the tree. Two-year-old Lynn peeked out the window looking for Santa Claus.

Lottie's Lot

On Christmas morning, the children were delighted with their gifts. Terrance had reached the magic age of 10 and received his very own stallion -- a spirited two-year-old that Arnold had bought from a neighboring ranch. He named him Kelso after a horse in a book he had read. It was love at first sight for Terrance.

Arnold's sister Pauline, her husband Bill, and their three boys arrived at noon for a family Christmas dinner. The two families' farms adjoined and the houses were only five miles apart. Pauline had become like a new sister to Beth. While the children and men were outdoors playing, the women put the finishing touches on the meal.

Beth asked, "Can we sit down for a minute, Pauline? I want to talk to you about something."

After a moment Beth sighed and said, "I am thinking about not having this baby."

"What?" Pauline asked, aghast. "How?"

"You know Sophia Gilman? Well," she quickly went on, "remember when she visited relatives in Germany last year and she brought back an instrument that doctors use to open and clean the uterus when a woman doesn't want to have a child or has a miscarriage. Sophia used it herself and got rid of her pregnancy with no problems. She loaned it to someone else who solved her problem too."

Pauline looked troubled. "Beth, why don't you want your baby?"

"Too many …too close. I'm so tired all the time I don't have the energy to raise another child now, and this house is too small for another child."

Pauline worried about the possibility of an infection, bleeding, or something else going wrong during the procedure. "If you have problems you're too far away from a hospital to get help in time. We don't even have a doctor close by."

"I'll be fine. Arnold is going to help. He agrees with me that we have enough children." Pauline was silent. Beth reached for her hand and looked her in the eyes, "Pauline, I know Arnold is your brother, but the truth is that he is drinking more and more and I don't want to bring any more children into a home with drinking problems.

My dad drank too much, though he was a wonderful man. My parents had so many arguments over his drinking and her unwanted pregnancies. And now I'm in the same situation. My mother saw this in Arnie and she tried to warn me. Sometimes I wish I had listened to her." Her voice trailed off with a melancholy tone.

"How far along are you?" Pauline asked.

"About four months," Beth replied. "I'll have to do it soon or it will be too late. It's already late but I wanted to wait until after Christmas."

Pauline's nodded her head. "I understand. My parents had the same problem. That's why Ma left my Pa and brought all of us out west."

"Pauline, you're like a sister to me. I want to ask you something important."

"Of course, what is it?"

"If anything goes wrong… happens to me…will you see that my kids are taken care of?"

Pauline choked back tears. "Oh Beth! Don't even talk that way."

"Please, Pauline. I need to know."

" Of course I will. I just wish there was another way."

Lottie's Lot

Beth squeezed Pauline's hands, and shook her head. "I wish there was another way too. But there isn't."

"When are you going to do it?" Pauline asked.

"In a couple of days," Beth said. "Don't worry – I'll be fine. I'm young and strong." Beth smiled and shrugged off the dread that crept into her heart when she thought about what she planned to do.

The phone woke Lottie from a deep sleep on the night of December 27. She heard a man's voice that kept saying, "Pauline … Beth … Arnold … died … so sorry … Kitscoty." Lottie could make no sense of the muddled message at first and then gradually realized the caller was Bill McClean, Beth and Arnold's brother-in-law.

"What?" she asked over and over. "What are you saying?" All too soon she realized Bill was saying, "Beth is dead."

Lottie shook her head to try to clear it. "No. She can't be dead. I just talked to her on Christmas. She sounded fine."

"Ma'am, I think you need to call your other daughters and make arrangements to come to Kitscoty. We will pick you up at the train station."

"Where is Beth now?" Lottie was stalling for time to get some clarity through the fog of her mind.

"The provincial coroner took her body to Lloydminster to do an autopsy and determine the cause of death."

"NO! No" Lottie–startled awake now dropped the phone and screamed.

Lottie and Charlotte took the first train the next day to Kitscoty. The McCleans met them at the station and took them back to Addie Randall's house where they were invited to stay until the funeral. In the morning she fixed them a big farm breakfast and, over steeping mugs of hot coffee, Pauline haltingly told them the story as she knew it. Lottie felt numb all over.

Pauline blew her nose and then took another sip of her coffee. "We had a wonderful Christmas dinner, everyone was laughing and the children played with their new toys. We went home about 7 after washing all the dishes and cleaning up. Then about midnight two days later there was a terrible pounding on our front door. Bill and I went to check it and there was Terrance -- cold, shivering, and sobbing with his new horse tied to the porch post."

Lottie and Charlotte were holding hands and listening with rapt attention.

"Go on."

"He told us that Arnie said we should call a doctor and come over right away. He said something awful had happened to his mother. My blood ran cold and my heart stopped. I knew that Beth was gone." Pauline's voice broke and after a long pause she made herself go on.

"I called ol' Doc Giddings and he said he'd be there as soon as he could. We all piled into Bill's car and drove so fast the road slid under us.

"When we got there Arnie had put Beth on the chesterfield and he was sitting beside her limp body holding her hand, his eyes glazed as if he wasn't all there. I could see that Beth was gone, she looked so white and limp." Pauline choked on her words for a moment. "I looked in the bedroom and the mattress and towels were soaked with blood."

From deep in Lottie's soul came a wail that sounded like a wounded animal. Charlotte cradled her in her arms, and they sobbed together. Pauline and Addie joined them. They loved Beth as one of their own.

Lottie's Lot

After a little while, they guided Lottie to the sofa and helped her lie down. They took off her shoes and put an afghan over her. Pauline had a pill that would help Lottie sleep, and at the others' insistence she swallowed it with some water.

Pauline went on to tell Charlotte that the law required an autopsy. They were waiting for the results.

"What do you think happened?" Charlotte asked. "Did Arnold kill her?"

"Oh, no, no. Not that," Pauline replied. "Charlotte, Bethie was pregnant again. And she said she didn't want to risk another dangerous pregnancy. You know that having Lynn almost killed her."

Charlotte nodded silently, pinning Pauline with her eyes.

"She tried to end the pregnancy. One of our neighbors, a midwife, had an instrument, and assured Beth it would be all right. Arnold was helping her. Something just went wrong."

"How do you know all this, Pauline?"

"Beth told me on Christmas what she was planning to do. I tried to talk her out of it, but her mind was made up. She was already more than four months pregnant."

Now it was Charlotte's turn to moan from deep in her heart. "Oh Bethie, poor Bethie. My baby sister! Why didn't you tell me? I could have helped."

Lottie slept most of the day, and when she awoke she could only moan and cry. Her grief was raw and inconsolable. There were no words that would take this pain away.

Charlotte debated telling Lottie exactly how Beth had died and decided her mother should know. Lottie turned pale at the news and almost fainted. "But why?" she asked almost soundlessly. In her heart she knew. She had felt the same desperation with several of her pregnancies. She knew exactly how Beth felt and she wept over her daughter's pain at making such a terrible decision. Shocked at the dangerous solution her daughter had attempted she felt an even deeper ache in her heart. Was there no safe and reasonable way for a woman to have control over her own body?

A few days later, the autopsy Beth's body stated the cause of death was a self-induced abortion. It was illegal, but there were no inquiries into whether others had helped her. Her body was released for burial and she was buried the next day in the cemetery at Kitscoty.

Charlotte returned to Detroit and her job but Lottie stayed on for a few more days. Something had to be decided about Beth's children.

Arnold got drunk and stayed that way for a long, long time. The family decided to farm out the children until he could care for them again. Lottie volunteered to take the girls back to Detroit with her. Lynn would go to live with Pauline and Bill. Terrance would go back and forth between Pauline and Bill's place and his own, where he could help his father with the chores on the farm. Addie moved into the farmhouse to take care of Arnold and Terrance.

Almost two years would pass before Beth's daughters would be reunited with their father and brothers.

CHAPTER 15

Within a week Beth's little girls were standing in the small train station at Kitscoty with their grandmother Lottie and Beth's trunk containing her childhood mementos, her wedding dress, family photos, and other treasures. Lottie promised to return the trunk to Merle when she was grown up. The little group watched the Canadian Pacific train arrive in a storm of smoke with whistles blowing and horns blasting.

Addie, Bill and Pauline, and Terrance hugged the girl's goodbye and Lottie led them to seats on the train. Arnold was embarrassingly absent. As they pulled out of the station, the children waved and pressed their small faces against the window, and watching their family fade and disappear.

The girls were upset and scared. They didn't know this Grandma Lottie, whom they had seen only a few times. Merle was the oldest daughter and felt responsible for her little sister and brothers. She knew and loved her other grandmother, Addie, and felt safe with her and their uncles and aunts in Kitscoty. She wanted to stay with them and with her father and brothers but no one would listen to her. And where was Papa now? Did he know they were going away?

No one had told her that all the adults had decided to distribute the children until Arnold could pull himself together. And that Lottie had volunteered to take care of her and Lorraine until Arnold could get a grip on his life again. She didn't know that Arnold was sitting on the chesterfield at home, staring at the floor, moving only to take a swig from his whiskey bottle.

233

She only knew that Lottie was taking her and Lorraine away. She remembered hearing stories of Lottie's family living in a tent when her mother was a child, and she worried that they were going to live in a tent now, too.

Lorraine didn't understand what had happened in her family during the past week. She repeatedly cried, "I want my mommy." When she was told that her Mama had gone to live with God in Heaven she said, "I don't want her to be with God. I want her to be here with me!"

Lorraine didn't understand that her Mama wasn't coming back to take care of her. Beth always told the children when she was going to town or to visit Aunt Pauline, when she would be home and she hadn't told Lorraine she was going anywhere this time. She hadn't even given her a goodbye hug and kiss like she always did. Now her Mommy had mysteriously disappeared and the grown-ups were crying all the time. Now they were taking her and Merle away. She was very confused and scared. Nothing would console her. She cried the entire way to Minneapolis.

Merle, on the other hand, knew her mother was dead. She had seen the body herself. Growing up on a farm, she was used to seeing dead animals and she had helped her Pa bury or burn their bodies. She remembered when the family's little dog, Skippy, was hit by a tractor and killed. Arnold dug a big hole and buried him and then everyone said something nice about him and put flowers on top of the dirt mound.

At first, Merle had kept expecting Skippy to come bounding around the corner, even though she *knew* he was dead. But soon she stopped expecting him and after a while she only thought about him occasionally. She wondered if she would forget about her mother too. She still kept expecting to wake up from a bad dream and find Bethany at the stove fixing porridge for breakfast and asking her to set the table.

The girls stared out the train window, wondering where they were going to end up. Lorraine sat on Lottie's lap sucking her thumb and
234

whimpering. Merle was silent. She prayed that this really was just a bad dream and she would wake up soon. Please God! Let this be only a terrible dream. She brought her hands together closed her eyes and bowed her head. *Please God...Please God...* she said silently over and over.

During a three-hour layover in Toronto they grew restless sitting on a long, hard bench. Donuts and hot chocolate temporarily soothed their small aching hearts. Lottie didn't say much to them but she held their hands when they walked around the station. She bought them each a coloring book and crayons and a big lollipop. Finally they got on another train.

Merle was engrossed in watching the passing scenery and the flurry of activity at each station. She liked to watch the people. Some families were welcoming someone home and others were saying goodbye to someone leaving. The goodbyes made her sad, and tears would surge up and flood her eyes. She blinked and turned her head away to hide them from Lottie, who had told her to be a big girl and not cry. She just couldn't help it.

When she thought about her Mama, her stomach ached. She felt so sad she and afraid that she wanted to run away, as fast and as far as she could go. She couldn't erase the picture in her mind of her mother lying on the chesterfield – so still and silent, eyes closed, head turned at a strange angle, and with drool trickling from her mouth. At that second, she knew her mother was dead.

In shock she shook her gently, "Mama, Mama. Wake up!" She touched her hand and it was stiff and cold. She sat there frozen and scared. It was the last time she'd seen her mother and the frightful memory was frozen in her mind.

Her life had changed so fast. She was full of questions. When she asked where they were going and why Lottie told her, "Hush now. Don't worry. Everything will be fine." Merle wasn't fooled. She felt like her feet couldn't find the ground and she knew everything would *not* be fine.

A few times she saw tears glistening on Lottie's cheeks and she wondered if grown-ups were supposed to be "big girls," too. She didn't bring up the subject, fearful of displeasing her grandmother and being scolded. Very quickly she realized that Grandma Lottie wouldn't comfort her or answer her questions.

It was January and the train was chilly. They bundled up against the winter cold, even though their car had a potbelly stove stoked up to keep them warm. They sat away from the choking smoke it cast out. Lottie stated out of the window, holding Lorraine on her lap, occasionally wiping a tear from her cheek and blowing her nose. Merle entertained herself by coloring and tried to distract Lorraine playing with the dolls they got for Christmas.

"You're a pretty girl, Lorraine, and such a good girl too," said Merle, holding her doll in front of her face. "I love you."

Lorraine held her doll up and, crying, she said, "Mama, I miss you. Please come back."

Merle hesitated. "I wish I could be there right now. I'd give you a big hug and lots of kisses."

"Mommy, don't be gone. Mommy, where are you?" She threw her doll on the floor and huddled against Lottie.

"I want my mama." Lottie frowned at Merle.

Lorraine sobbed, "I want my Mama to hold me."

Merle's doll answered, "You know I love you. Be a good girl and make me proud. Now let Merle give you a big hug and then go to sleep. Good night, Lorraine."

Lottie's Lot

Merle put her doll down and hugged her sister tight. Lottie embraced both girls, holding each one in her arms as tears rolled down her cheeks.

"Good girl, Merle. I know you love your sister and want to help her." She patted both of them, "Close your eyes and try to sleep. We have a long ride ahead of us."

When they arrived in Minneapolis, Carrie met them at the train station. Dear, dear Carrie -- always there when Lottie needed her. Lottie fell apart when they were alone and Carrie held and comforted her.

Carrie's house was spacious and warm. Uncle Bill was a successful banker and had prospered in the 1920s. The adults were talking about something called "Black Friday." Merle heard them say something about a stock market collapse last year. Uncle Bill was smart, they said he'd seen the crash coming and had taken most of his money out of stocks before October 1929, so he wasn't suffering like a lot of other people were.

Aunt Carrie and Uncle Bill were friendly and kind. They fed the children hot chocolate with little marshmallows floating on top and special tuna fish sandwiches with the crust cut off. They had olives and pickles and a selection of cookies left over from Christmas and stored in a pretty tin. Thinking about Christmas made Merle even sadder. It had been a wonderful Christmas until a few days later.

After they ate the girls soaked in a bubble bath in a bathtub built right inside the house. Then they were tucked into a big soft bed with lots of covers. It was the first time Merle had really slept since that dreadful night when her mother had died. She slept soundly at first, and then had a nightmare about Beth lying on the couch not moving her head or answering her when Merle talked to her. In her dream Merle shook her gently then Beth opened her eyes then slid away.

Then just as Merle was reached out for her Beth flew away from her in a flowing white nightgown, eyes closed. Merle tried to go after her but couldn't reach her and woke with a startle, feeling cold and alone. She woke up crying, "Mama... Mama...I'm coming ...wait for me..." She would relive the night of December 27 in her nightmares many, many times to come. Always a variation on the same dream.

Lottie and Carrie heard her crying and went to comfort her. "I can't find my mama," Merle cried.

Carrie cradled the child in her arms. "I know, sweetheart. It must hurt so much. I know you miss your mama. I missed my Mama for very long time after she died."

"Did your Mama die too?"

"Yes but I was already grown up. No matter how old you are you always miss your mama when she dies. She was your grandma's mother too. We are sisters just like you and Lorraine." Carrie put her arm around Lottie's waist and hugged her.

"Why did she have to die?" Merle whimpered.

"I don't know, Sweetheart. No one knows. *Why* is a question with no answers. We must just accept that she is gone and won't come back."

"I want her to come back. I want things to be like they were before." Merle leaned against Carrie's soft, warm body.

"I know you do. We all do. But even if she can't come back like she was, she will never die in your heart. You will always carry her here." Carrie tapped Merle's little chest. "She will live forever in your memories of her."

"But I can't see her or touch her."

"That's true but you have photos of her and you can still talk to her and draw her pictures. Can you do that?"

"Yes, I guess I can." Merle sniffled and she almost smiled.

Lottie's Lot

Carrie put the child back under the covers. "Close your eyes now and tell your mama how much you love her as you fall asleep."

She kissed Merle on the forehead and turned off the light. Lottie followed her out the door. "Where did you learn to be so loving and smart?"

"From you, big sister and from Mama." She hugged Lottie and they walked back to Lottie's room arm in arm. "Lottie dearest, I don't know where you get the strength to cope with all the tragic losses you've had. You have just lost another daughter -- how your heart must ache."

They went into Lottie's room and as they sat on the side of the bed, Lottie fell into Carrie's arms and surrendered to deep belly-wrenching sobs until she was spent. She wanted to talk, but crying and talking at the same time was close to impossible. If she could talk to anyone it was Carrie. Finally emotionally drained, Carrie took off her shoes, slid her under the covers and tip-toed out of the room.

As much as Lottie tried to sweep away thoughts of Bethany's desperation, wouldn't go away. The images intruded of her daughter hemorrhaging and being in pain and fearful invaded her thoughts with dreadful images day and night ever since she'd received the phone call. Throughout the week's events, one nightmare followed another, and on the train trip with Beth's daughters, they remained, no matter how hard she tried to stop them. Sweeping her emotions under the carpet had worked for her in the past, at least until Lillian died.

She shuddered as she remembered those dark days when she had fallen apart and lost herself after Charlie's and Lillian's deaths. During those pain-filled days, time stood still. She fought against sinking into that disabling depression again.

Talking helped but Beth's death was too fresh, too sudden, and too unbelievable to even begin to deal with. She knew it was going to take a long time for her to heal and even longer for these two little girls. She was determined to stay strong to help them in any way she could.

Dear God, how can so much pain come into one person's life? She wondered. She had buried her parents, her grandchild, her husband, her sister, and now three of her own children. She trusted that God would make it clear in His own time. Her faith was her fortification.

She turned her thoughts to her new little charges, Beth's daughters. She was 58 years old and hadn't taken care of small children for a long time. Bud, her "baby," had turned 22 in October. Lottie knew that she had to be strong for her granddaughters. It was her way of pitching in and helping in this terrible crisis.

Lottie and the girls stayed in Minneapolis for a week. Carrie was her rock and always helped Lottie to get clarity and to heal. They talked and talked. Lottie was soothed by Carrie's calm voice and sage advice.

By the time they got on the train to Detroit the girls were seasoned travelers. Their eight-hour trip went smoothly. When they arrived at 3:30 in the afternoon, Charlotte, Lois, Chuck, and Buddy were waiting to meet them. Chuck brought his pick-up truck and he and Buddy loaded up their valises and boxes, along with Beth' trunk.

There were hugs all around and so many questions. Lottie put them off in front of the girls. There would be plenty of time later to tell them what she knew.

The girls were awestruck by the noise and activity of the city. They had been raised in the country and it was a shock to see so many houses so close together and car after car speeding up and down in every direction.

Merle was bewildered when they arrived at her Aunt Ruby's house and unloaded Lorraine's things but not hers. She had never been separated from her little sister and felt she had to protect her in this new place. Lorraine was a shy child, timid and quiet, and Merle could see that she was frightened.

When Lorraine went into the house, boisterous Joyce greeted her with a big hug Lorraine quickly ran back to Merle. Inside the house, there were so many people, so much noise. Merle could see that many of the women had been crying, but they wiped their eyes and gave her and Lorraine big hugs and smiles. Merle tried to get their names straight but she was too tired. Lorraine hid behind her, holding her coat with one fist and wiping her own eyes with the other.

Aunt Ruby had fixed a lunch of potato salad and ham sandwiches with some sliced apples and milk and cookies. Merle was so hungry that she ate a big plateful. She urged Lorraine to eat. The strangers stared at everything they did, every bite they put in their mouths, every time they held hands or looked around the room. These new adults smiled at them a lot, patted them on the head, and pinched their cheeks.

As Lottie put on her coat to leave, Merle said, "Am I staying here with my sister?"

Lottie answered, "Aunt Ruby and Uncle Art don't have room for both of you. You're coming with me for now." She smiled and tried to sound reassuring, "Lorraine and Joyce are both almost six years old and they can play together." Clarence and Charlotte were living with them too. Charlotte had Paul her son three and she stayed at home and took care of the children while Ruby worked.

"I could sleep on the sofa or even the floor. I want to stay with Lorraine," she protested.

Ruby said, "I will take good care of your sister. And you can come and visit her whenever you want to."

Lottie understood the child's concern. She said, "Merle, these arrangements are just temporary until we figure out where you girls will be staying. Everything happened so fast. We need time to sort things out." As they went out to the car Lottie took her hand and told her, "You'll be fine with me for now. Come along, now – we're all tired after such a long trip."

Defeated, Merle put her fingers in her ears as they drove away so she couldn't hear Lorraine crying and calling her name. She hoped they would be reunited soon. She knew her mother would want her to look after her little sister.

The next stop was Dan Steele's house, where Lottie lived. "I take care of Mr. Steele's house for him, and my room is in the back. There's a room right next to mine for you."

When they got there Bud unloaded their suitcases and Beth's trunk.

Lottie told her to call the man Grandpa Steele. It was an old house full of furniture that was much older and prettier than the things in Merle's house in Kitscoty. There was a big round oak dining room table with beautiful wide carved legs and six ornate chairs. In the middle of the table was a candy dish full of mints. The first thing Lottie told Merle was never to take a candy without permission, because Grandpa Steele wouldn't approve. Merle had not even met the man and she was already a little afraid of him.

"You are a guest in this house and must act accordingly," Lottie told her. Merle had no idea what that meant but she would find out over the next two years.

Lottie took Merle by the hand and showed her to the bedroom she would have all to herself. To Merle, the house was huge. In truth it was a three-bedroom bungalow in a nice neighborhood. Merle's bedroom had a mahogany double bed with a big fluffy white eyelet bedspread. That night after eating a bowl of tomato soup and a peanut butter sandwich she went right to bed.

Lottie's Lot

As tired as she was Merle couldn't fall asleep. She lay in the dark studying the beautiful carved pineapple posts on the end of her bed. The headboard matched. Looking around, she saw a tall dresser with a mirror in a frame that matched the bedposts and a vanity table with a big mirror. The same beautiful pineapples at the top of the mirror frame. Finally she drifted off to sleep to dream about the forbidden candy dish – she stood before it desperately wanting a piece but not knowing how to get what she wanted and needed.

An hour later Lottie peeked into the room, then tiptoed in and pulled the covers up over the sleeping child. She rested her hand on Merle's forehead for a moment, then sighed and quietly went out, leaving the door open a few inches.

In her room she stretched out on the bed, not even taking time to undress. Exhausted, she fell into a fitful sleep and dreamed of her precious Bethany when she was a baby the happiest and best-natured of all her children. From infancy on, Beth had been caring, selfless, compassionate, and always willing to help. Cheerie was a good name for her.

At 3:30 in the morning, Lottie woke up in a cold sweat. Shivering, she went to the bathroom, put on a nightgown, and decided to look into Beth's trunk. She pored over her daughter's treasures, setting aside the wedding dress and photos to see what was underneath. A corn husk doll Charlie had made for Beth on their North Dakota homestead triggered soft tears. Wearing a little dress that matched one she had made for Beth, it brought back memories of their happiest days on the homestead, before all the losses began. She remembered Beth toddling after Charlie all over the farm and managed a smile.

The Saturday after Lottie and the girls arrived in Detroit the entire family got together at Dan Steele's house. Abby picked up Danny at military school and arrived a little after noon. The women brought food and the men brought Canadian Club. While all the adults drank highballs, Lottie stuck with her favorite glass of ice water.

The gathering was a memorial for Bethany. After everyone arrived and settled down they expressed their feelings about Beth, their good-natured, compassionate sister. They were sad and curious about what had caused her sudden and untimely death. They asked Lottie what happened and she told them what she knew. The children were sent out to play while the adults talked, cried, and tried to understand why their sister had died so young and healthy.

Merle came in the house to go to the bathroom. She had never seen a house with a bathroom inside until their stop in Minneapolis to visit Aunt Carrie. She liked to go into these fancy bathrooms and watch the toilets flush and the water run in the sink.

When she came out she hid behind the bathroom door and listened to the adults talking. She heard snippets of the conversation. "Pregnant... instrument from Germany... bled to death.... Arnold couldn't stop it... no doctor close... no telephone... Arnold's drinking, lost." Merle didn't understand everything she heard but now she had an idea of how the grown-ups saw the situation.

It was so hard to think of her mother suffering, bleeding, and dying. She knew her Papa was suffering and sad too. She missed them both so much. She missed the farm, the animals, her own bed, her toys, Beth's stove, and the smell of food cooking. She missed her mother's good night kisses, her soapy clean smell, her big smile. She missed her brothers, cousins, grandmother, and the rest of her family.

These new relatives tried to be kind to her but she didn't know them and they didn't know her. From the tears and sobs she heard in the room she knew they had loved her mother. But how could they know her mother like she did when they had only seen her once or twice in all of Merle's life? How could they love Beth the way her own child did?

Lottie's Lot

She desperately wanted her life to be just like it was before Christmas, only a few short weeks ago. Now she knew things would never be the same, and this made her saddest of all.

Merle's new home was a strange one. Grandma Lottie and Grandpa Steele talked to each other like they were married – discussing every detail of the household and sometimes arguing but Lottie slept in her own bedroom so Merle thought they must not be married. One day, as Lottie was putting their lunch on the table, she dared to ask, "Grandma Lottie is Grandpa Steele your husband?"

"Oh, no, no, child. He's my employer." Lottie saw the curiosity on the child's face and added, "But he did ask me to marry him."

"He did? Why didn't you? Don't you love him?"

"Love him? Oh heavens, no. The only man I ever loved was your grandfather, Charlie Hastings. I'll bet your mother told you a lot about her Pa." Lottie sat down and took a bite of her sandwich.

"Yes, she did. She said he was really funny and he let her ride horses and she loved him a lot. And when he died she really missed him."

"Oh my, yes. We all missed him. I still miss him and he's been gone for more than 17 years. I miss him every single day." Lottie smiled at Merle, as if seeing her for the first time.

The child took a few bites, and emboldened by Lottie's smile, asked, "But then why are you here at Grandpa Steele's house."

Lottie dabbed at her mouth with her napkin. "You see, I was working at a big store and for a while I was selling neckties in the men's department. And Mr. Steele was a regular customer and a good friend of my boss. Everybody called him Ol' Man Steele. He ... liked

245

me and he took me out to dinner a few times. I was much younger and prettier then. Of course, Mr. Steele was much older…"

She poured Merle another glass of milk.

"So, when Mr. Steele wanted to marry me, I just couldn't. I will always be married to my Charlie. So I told Ol' Man Steele I would be his housekeeper. And since all my children were grown and he had plenty of room I would live at his house."

Merle thought a minute. "Grandma, I think Grandpa Steele loves *you.*"

"Well, I don't know about that. Come on, we have to get supper ready." And Lottie closed up again, like a flower that could only bloom for a few minutes. She continued to answer most of Merle's questions with a "Hush, Child."

Dan Steele was a wealthy bachelor with several rental houses. His home was full of antiques that he had inherited from his family. He appreciated the finer things in life. But he was as tight with a dollar as Scrooge and held his purse close to his chest.

Lottie had to account for every penny she spent on groceries and household expenses. All of her adult life she had been in control of the money and most other family decisions and she resented his tight reins. She didn't like being accountable to someone else, not one bit. They frequently fought about money and other control issues. She had her ways of getting even, though: She would buy extra groceries with his money, and when her daughters came to visit she secretly loaded them up with food from his kitchen.

While he was only 16 years older than Lottie, he looked and acted much older. She had never been physically attracted to him. He was tall and lanky and so thin you could see his ribs. At 74 he looked 94. His teeth were bad and when he talked or smiled you could just see his lower teeth. His shoulders were stooped and when he walked he sometimes used a cane to help him keep his balance.

Lottie's Lot

One day as he pulled his car up to the curb in front of the house, he saw Lois leaving with a bag full of his groceries. He jumped out of the car and said, "Aha! I finally caught you!"

Lois was embarrassed but Lottie boomed from the doorway, "I gave them to her. They don't have any food at home."

"I give you money to buy food for us, not to feed your children. They can work and buy their own food!" His face turned red as he shouted, "Take that food back into my house right now!"

Lois turned back toward the house.

Lottie said, "No. Take it home. Go! Now! I'll handle this." Then, as Lois left, she adopted her firmest tone of voice: "Dan, I work for you for practically nothing. If I want to give my daughter a few things to eat when she needs them I will. I don't care if you like it or not."

He smoldered. "This isn't the first time you've given food to them, is it?"

"No. It isn't. We have plenty. How do you expect me to see my children going hungry when we have more than enough?"

"When I hired you and took you in, I didn't take all your kids in too."

"Well, I didn't stop being their mother when I came to work for you. I think it's time for me to leave. I'm going to pack now." She slammed the door and retreated into her bedroom.

An hour later he knocked on her door and apologized.

Dan Steele and Lottie developed a pattern of fighting, separating, and then reuniting. There would be an incident, they would argue, she would leave. He would cool off, get lonely, and call or find her and beg her to come back. She would promise not to take advantage of him with no intention of keeping her promise. He would agree to be more generous with no intention of keeping his word.

Steele had never had any children but he was fascinated with Lottie's 8-year-old granddaughter, who she had insisted must live with them. Merle listened to his stories for hours and he took her for long walks. He even got her a kitten the first Christmas she was there but made her promise to keep it in her room or outdoors. He wasn't willing to risk little claws damaging his valuable antiques.

During the years that Merle and Lorraine were in Detroit, Lottie left Dan Steele about 12 times. Merle had heard her parents argue a few times, but never with the rage and bitterness of these arguments. Mostly she felt sorry for Dan, because she heard the terrible comments the Hastings sisters made about him behind his back. They called him Scrooge and King Midas. Merle knew, even at her tender age, that Lottie and her daughters were taking advantage of him.

Whenever Lottie left Steele, Merle missed school because they would go stay with one of her aunts in another part of the city and she couldn't get around on a bus or streetcar by herself.

She wanted to see Lorraine more often. It was a full day to take the bus to Ruby's house. Grandpa Steele refused to put in a telephone, saying it was too expensive. So the only way Merle could talk to Lorraine was when they visited Lois and used her telephone, or if she could get Lottie to go to a pay phone and call.

Lottie kept in touch with Addie and Arnold by letters and telephone calls. For months, he continued drinking constantly and not taking care of the livery, the crops, or the animals. Terrance, Bill, Wayne, and Ben filled in with the chores and the winter repairing of farm equipment. The women saw to it that he ate, stayed warm, changed clothes, and took occasional baths. They cleaned the house, did laundry, and cooked. His mother stayed at his house for several months, and little Lynn, 3, and Terrance, 10, were shuffled between relatives.

248

Lottie's Lot

Bill had replaced the mattress on Arnold's bed with a new one. He burned the old one, soaked in Beth's blood, out behind the barn. But Arnold couldn't bring himself to sleep in his bedroom, even with the new mattress. An empty bed without his precious Beth was just too painful to contemplate. He slept on the chesterfield instead -- when he slept at all. He dreaded the nightmares that woke him, his body soaked in sweat and pictures of Beth's last moments replaying endlessly in his mind. When he was sober he was convinced he had caused his wife's death and he wanted to die too.

Terrance tried to be the man of the family. He did as many of the chores as he could, taught his little brother to ride a horse, and took him camping and fishing. Late at night in the girls' old bedroom Terrance often lay awake and remembered all the things he could about his mother. Only in the darkness when his father and brother were asleep could he cry.

Addie and Terrance looked forward to the monthly telephone calls from Lottie and the girls. For the first six months Arnold couldn't speak to them; he would become too overcome with emotion.

Gradually he realized that his brothers were doing his work on top of their own and that Terrance was too young to be taking on the burdens he had assumed. He began to work when he was sober, and the sober periods lasted longer and longer. Soon, when the girls called, he was telling them he loved them and he wanted them to come home soon.

It took over two years for Arnold to pull himself together, get sober, and accept the responsibilities of being a father.

CHAPTER 16

Lottie was a smothering mother hen with her only son. Throughout Buddy's childhood she defended and protected him against all situations and conflicts.

She nursed him until he was 4 years old and weaned him only after Charlie died. Charlie worked away from home for most of Buddy's life so he barely knew his father. His early memories were hearing his parents arguing over "the drink." He vaguely remembered a Christmas morning when his parents were angry over him.

From the beginning Lottie poured her love into Buddy. He looked just like her. He was the treasured son that she and Charlie had always wanted. She had almost lost him before he was born, but thanks to her devotion and tender care he lived and thrived. She adored him, sheltered, and overprotected him. She spoiled him by indulging his every wish and would not tolerate any criticism. In her eyes he could do no wrong.

The girls doted on their baby brother, but as he got older they watched Lottie let Buddy get away with things they had been punished for. She never blamed him, even when the problem was clearly his fault.

"Hey, Ma, Buddy broke your mixing bowl, Lois reported one morning when Buddy was six. He had carelessly swept his arm across the kitchen table and run out of the room when the bowl hit the floor.

Lottie replied, "He's still a baby."

"I got spanked when I broke a glass," Lois complained.

"Never mind." Lottie told her, "Don't pick on your brother."

Lottie set out to make Buddy into the perfect little man – perfect for her.

Lottie's Lot

She made his clothes. He had several sets of knickers with matching jackets and caps and was always well dressed. She scolded him gently when he got dirty or spilled food on his clothes, and forbade him to tussle or play with other boys his age. As he grew older she monitored what he wore and him on his clothes and supervised his every activity.

She wanted to be close to Buddy all the time. From the time he could walk, she held his hand, and was always at his side to protect him from unseen dangers. She constantly questioned him. "What are you thinking? Why do you want to do that? What shall we do now?" Lottie was a completely different mother to Buddy than she was to the girls, and sometimes she treated him more as a friend than a son.

She wanted him to be what Charlie was at his best. And though she was not conscious of it, she was trying to get from him what she had gotten from Charlie at the beginning of their relationship and early marriage – unconditional love and adoration. He needed to be perfect, and never let her down or disappoint her. Her Buddy would give her the emotional validation she wanted.

Buddy was clever and learned that his mother would be happy as long as he *seemed* to be doing what she wanted. If she said no to a request from him, he would turn it around and make her think it was her idea.

"Ma, Billy asked me to have dinner at his house Friday and spend the night," Nine-year-old Buddy pleaded putting on his face with the smile his mother liked best. Early on he became a master manipulator. Lottie gave in afraid he would turn away and reject her.

"There's no point in that, Buddy. I don't know those people and you're too young to stay away from home."

"All right, Mama. I'll tell him what you said. And he'll have to tell his mother that I can't show her that new blue shirt you made for me. She says you're the best sewer she ever saw." He turned to walk away.

"Oh, Buddy, what a sweet boy you are. The word is 'seamstress,' not 'sew-er.'"

"Thanks, Ma. Seamstress."

She began to melt a bit. "Is Billy a new friend? Do I know him?"

"Yes, you met him at church a few weeks ago. Remember, he had on that brown leather cap you liked?"

Lottie couldn't quite remember but she said, "Oh yes. He goes to our church then?"

"Yes Ma'am and we were going to practice for the church Bible drill for next month."

He looked so adorable with his beautiful blue eyes that were just like Charlie's. "All right then, Buddy. If they go to our church I'm sure they're fine people. I'll call and speak with his mother and if everything sounds all right you can go."

Buddy whistled as he walked toward Billy's house Friday after dropping his schoolbooks off at home. He remembered to take his Bible. After dinner, they went into Billy's room and practiced – not looking up Bible verses as fast as possible, but forming spitballs and throwing them at Billy's sisters and the windows of the house next door.

Buddy's rebellious adolescence hit Lottie like a bomb. By 14 he was drinking and smoking with friends, at first behind Lottie's back but soon not bothering to hide it at all. He was tired of her meddling in every aspect of his life and got a thrill out of defying and disappointing her. When he came home late she easily recognized the signs of drunkenness. She was beside herself with hurt and rage. She knew he was slipping away from her control.

"You've been drinking!" she shouted.

"Now, Ma. Don't get your bloomers in a knot!" He snickered.

"Bud, you know how much I hate drinking."

"Yeah! I know. But Mama, you're an old stick in the mud," he grinned at her agitation.

"Don't talk to me like that." She felt more hurt than angry.

"I'm going to bed, old lady. G'night!" He stomped up the stairs to his bedroom and slammed the door to irritate her more.

She sat alone in the dark chilly parlor for another hour, simmering down. She was wounded and confused. Thinking, "I never talked to my parents like that. Where did I go wrong? I gave him everything … *everything* … and look at the way he talks to me."

Slipping to her knees, she put her hands together and held them in front of her lips. "Dear God, please help me to understand and do the right thing with Buddy and my other children. I am your poor servant and beg your guidance to be the best mother I can be. Help me. Show me the right direction. Amen."

She found her Bible, opened it and turned to Psalm 119. "The Lord is my comfort in my affliction." She felt better after seeking divine guidance.

As Buddy's adolescent rebellion escalated they began to argue, a little at first then a lot. She had survived her daughters' adolescence but this was entirely different. Buddy insulted her, defied her, and seemed to relish hurting her. She felt helpless as felt him slipping away. She was glad at least that he stayed in school until he was almost 17. Then a crisis brought everything to a head.

One evening in late August 1924 there was a knock on the front door. Lottie was surprised to see a policeman standing on the porch and shocked to hear him ask, "Is this the residence of Charles Hastings?"

"He's dead," she managed to whisper.

"Excuse me, Ma'am. I mean Charles Hastings Junior."

Gaining control, Lottie said, "Oh, you mean Buddy. Yes, he lives here. Why?"

"Is he here, Ma'am? I would like to talk to him."

"No. He isn't here. Is there a problem?"

"Well, there may be but I just need to talk to him."

"Can you tell me what the problem is?" Her defensive maternal instinct kicked in. She stood a little straighter and pinned the officer with her eyes.

"It has to do with bootlegging, Ma'am. He has been identified as a person conducting illegal transport and sale of alcoholic beverages."

"Officer, we are not a drinking family. This can't be true." She clutched her throat.

"When will he be here, Ma'am?"

"I don't know."

The officer handed her a slip of paper. "Please ask him to call me when he returns. It's important. Here's is my name and telephone number."

Shaken, she took the paper and closed the door.

Hazel and her children were having dinner with Lottie, when Hazel heard the knock and came to see who was at the door.

"What was that all about?" she asked.

"It was a policeman looking for Buddy."

Lottie's Lot

"What for?"

"Something about bootlegging, he said."

Kenny was at her side. He snickered.

Lottie pounced on him. "Do you know anything about this, Young Man?"

He backed off. By 13 he had learned that "ratting" on someone could get you in big trouble. "No…I don't know anything."

Hazel grabbed him by the ear and pinched it hard until he yelled in pain, "Stop it, Ma."

"Tell us what you know," she twisted his ear harder.

"OK, OK. But I don't want anyone to know who told."

Hazel let go of his ear. "Talk."

"Bud and Chuck Gully are going to Canada and bringing back five-gallon jugs of hooch and selling it to a speakeasy on Grand River."

"How do you know this?"

"I went with them a few times to be the lookout. It was fun!"

Lottie threw her arms in the air and screamed, "Mercy me! Mercy me! What has this world come to? MERCY ME!" She shook her arms over her head.

Hazel said, "Ma, settle down. We'll get to the bottom of this."

Kenny said, "Everyone is doing it. It's no big deal and a good way to make a ton of money … fast."

"That's enough out of you, Young Man. Wait for me in the kitchen. I'll deal with you later." Hazel glared at Kenny and he left, grateful to be out of the battle zone. Just as he left the front door opened and Buddy came in. Kenny hunkered down behind the kitchen door and listened. When Abby joined him he held his index finger to his lips. "Shhhh."

Lottie flew at her son in a rage. "How could you do this and bring shame on this family?"

Buddy backed away. "Do what?"

"Bootleg alcohol! *How could you?!* You know how I feel about drinking alcohol. And breaking the law on top of it!! Do you want to kill me?" Lottie screamed at him.

He opened the door and backed out, closing it in her face. He turned and ran down the steps and didn't come home that night. The police didn't pursue him.

The next week Buddy quit high school and moved in with Lois and Chuck Gully. He got a job at Ford Motor Company as a janitor and within six months he had moved up to an assembly line position making better money. Before long he was trained as a machinist because he was a quick learner and good at working with his hands.

Buddy was in teenage heaven. Finally he had freedom and was out from under Lottie's scrutiny. He could do as he wanted, go where and when he wanted, with no one to answer to. He could drink and smoke all he wanted -- away from her suffocating surveillance.

Buddy and Kenny hung out at Cranberry Lake along with Dave White, Roger Berry, and Chuck Gully. Caught up in the bootleg lifestyle of the Roaring Twenties they all made booze runs during Prohibition. If they'd been caught they would surely have gone to prison, but to them it was a great adventure and a lucrative money-making scheme.

Lottie was devastated by Buddy's leaving and mourned as if it were a death. Hazel was coming out of her fog and a year after Roy's death she was able to take back the reins of caring for her family. She continued to drink every day but was not as flagrant about it as Buddy

256

had been. Now Lottie's nest was empty. No one needed her any more. Dreading the day this would happen, she clung to Buddy as long as she could.

With Hazel caring for her own children again, Lottie moved into her own flat and found a good job at Hudson's Department Store.

After Roy's death in 1921, Hazel had vowed never to give her heart to a man again. But after being financially supported by George Hopf and then Roy Darden, she found it difficult to pay her own way with three children to raise.

Two years before he died, Roy had met a man about his age named Charles Cleveland Fredericks. C.C., an amateur inventor, convinced Roy to take part in a joint venture to market a car turn signal he'd invented. C.C. needed Roy to speak with his contacts in the automobile industry to sell this apparatus to car manufacturers. They started the Arrow Signal Indicator Company in 1920 and renamed it Auto Indicator Company the next year. Headquarters was at Hazel's address on Bragg Street.

In addition to being an inventor, C.C. Fredericks was a super salesman and a fast talker – if truth be told, a con man -- and he managed to con his way into Hazel's life. After Roy died, he started coming around frequently, offering to help Hazel in any way he could. She had never thought of him except as a business colleague of Roy's.

Lottie didn't like or trust him. There was just something about him that sent chills up her spine. He was a big man, over 6 feet 4 inches tall, with a paunch, a double chin, big puffy hands, and a balding head. He had large liver-colored lips and a habit of licking them often. He was meticulously clean, always well groomed, and wore expensive clothes with suspenders to hold up his trousers.

He was introverted and liked time to himself. When Lottie or any of her children tried to engage him in a conversation about his work or sports he was courteous but withdrawn. They accepted him because Hazel did.

C.C. had a cottage at Cranberry Lake, near Rochester, Michigan. As the children and grandchildren grew up they loved spending weekends there, picnicking, fishing, swimming, and diving.

Kenny learned to swim the 100 yards from the dock to a raft with a diving board in the lake in front of C.C.'s cottage. He practiced diving from the board and C.C. complimented him and encouraged him to use his natural talent and enter competitions. He won several medals for his diving. He was approached by an Olympics diving coach about training for regional competition but Hazel refused to let him go.

In March 1923 Hazel went back to work part-time as a sales clerk at Kern's Department Store. Hazel arranged for a neighbor to take care of Danny while she was at work. Kenny and Abby were both in school. C.C. continued to hang around Hazel and her children, offering to babysit, fix things, shop, and even cook dinner- ingratiating himself as much as he could. When Hazel thanked him he told her, "I know you need time to get over Roy. I'm very fond of you. I'm a patient man. Take as long as you need." He added, "I loved Roy too and I know what a terrible loss his death has been for you."

When Hazel suffered a sudden attack of appendicitis everyone panicked, remembering what had happened to Lillian. She got to the hospital in time and emergency surgery removed her appendix before it ruptured. She was in the hospital for 10 days.

Lottie stopped by Hazel's place on her way home from work to cook supper for Abby, Kenny, and Danny while Hazel was in the hospital.

C.C. kindly offered to move in temporarily to help care for the family. Lottie wasn't happy and Abby protested, "We don't need him. I can take care of things. I'm 15 and know how to do everything."

Lottie's Lot

She thought C.C. was pulling the wool over her mother's eyes, though she wasn't sure what it was about. But Hazel appreciated having an adult supervising her children while she was away, and he helped her pay the bills.

C.C.'s temporary move-in turned out to be permanent. He never moved out. After Hazel recovered from her surgery she went back to work and put Danny in a nursery school. C.C. made himself indispensable to her. His work hours were more flexible. Most days he picked Danny up from nursery school and took care of him until Hazel got home. He started dinner so Hazel could rest after being on her feet all day.

Lottie disapproved of the arrangement. She invited Hazel for lunch at Hudson's to tell her so.

"What are you doing, Hazel? Letting that man live with you is a big mistake."

"Ma, he's a big help and pays the rent. I can't make it on my own. He's kind and thoughtful and doesn't bother me about, you know, having relations. He never touches me."

"Really? That doesn't seem normal."

"Normal or not, its fine with me. I don't want any of that nonsense anyway."

"Well, are you going to marry him?"

"I don't know." Hazel added, "He did ask me."

"Then you'd better do it, relations or not. You are setting a terrible example for your children. Not to mention you're just living in sin....again"

"Oh Ma, you are so far behind the times."

Lottie scoffed. "Humph. Don't tell me...."

Hazel cut her off. "All right I'll think about it." She kissed her mother on the cheek, paid the bill, and left.

Hazel didn't love C.C. and he didn't want sex, so his presence in her life was uncomplicated. God forbid she have another child. C.C. was easy to have around. He never complained about her drinking. He just wanted to help and he pitched in and did things without being asked. He brought her surprise gifts – nice jewelry and clothes. And he was good with the children – or so she thought.

Little did she know that C.C. was compulsively attracted to little children younger than 5 or 6, even infants. Every chance he got he played with Danny's penis and taught the boy to touch his. For months, he molested Danny every afternoon before Kenny got home after school while Hazel was working.

One day, when Danny was four he went crying to Hazel, telling her that C.C. had hurt him in his private parts.

"What?" Hazel quizzed "What did he do?"

"He sucked my pee-pee in the bathroom." Hazel turned scarlet and slapped Danny's face. "Don't lie to me, you little brat!" Danny started to cry but Hazel grew more furious. "Where did you learn such things?"

One weekend in August, C.C. and Hazel went to Niagara Falls, while Lottie looked after the children. On Saturday night as she was tucking Danny into bed, pulling the covers up to his chin, he looked his grandmother intently in the eyes and whispered, "C.C. touched my pee-pee."

Lottie pulled back, startled, and looked at the boy in confusion. She had never heard of such a thing. Why would a grown man want to touch a child that way?

"Oh, Danny, you must have had a bad dream."

"I'm scared. He might get me in the night." She could tell from his voice that he was really frightened.

"Honey, just close your eyes, and ask Baby Jesus to protect you and keep you from being afraid. Everything is OK."

"No. No. I'm scared." She patted him on the head, uncertain how to comfort him any further or put such strange thoughts out of his mind.

"Well, I'll tell you what. I'll sit here with you till you fall asleep." And she watched the little boy close his eyes tightly, then gradually relax into sleep.

She put the incident out of her mind as she did so often when something painful came up that she didn't know how to handle.

When Hazel and C.C. returned on Monday, they grinned and announced, "Guess what! We got married." Abby glared at them and left the room. Lottie's first reaction was a hearty "Congratulations!" She was relieved they'd made it legal. But the look on Hazel's face made one thing clear – she didn't love C.C.

The marriage didn't make them a happy family. Danny had frequent nightmares and started to wet the bed. Hazel made him wash his own sheets by hand as a punishment. When he misbehaved she would spank him with a belt after C.C. refused to. After his mother hurt him Danny went to C.C. for comfort because he had no one else to turn to. C.C. held him and whispered reassurances. The solace added to the child's confusion. He didn't like what C.C made him do when they were alone but other times C.C. was kind and gave him special favors, like an ice cream cone, a secret Baby Ruth candy bar, or a cinnamon roll. He taught Danny to keep secrets.

By six Danny was rebellious. He deliberately disobeyed his mother and anyone else in authority. He avoided C.C. as much as he could.

He became such a behavior problem at school and at home that Hazel couldn't handle him. The more she punished him the worse he got. It never crossed her mind that Danny's misbehavior might be related to C.C. molestation of him.

By the time he was eight, Hazel couldn't take any more so she put Danny in a military school. Emotionally and physically abandoned by his mother, he never trusted women again. Hazel put thoughts of Danny out of her mind and decided to let the school make him grow up right. Any questions about C.C. from Lottie or her other children were handled with a "mind your own business" and a shot of Canadian Club.

C.C. was cagy. He chose children who were too young to tell what had happened, or to make them believable. He made sure Hazel continued to depend on his financial support and other help.

He had a ripe pasture of little children to harvest from her large family with all those sisters having babies. For years, C.C. hid his true nature like a panther in the dark, carefully choosing the right moment to pounce on the newest toddler from Lottie's lot.

Abby, always rebellious, asserted herself by defiantly changing her name to Shirley when she was 15. She'd always hated "Abigail" and didn't like "Abby" either. She knew she had been named for her great-grandmother, Abigail Young Walker, but she'd never met Abbie, so being her namesake didn't mean much. Abigail was an old-fashioned name to her, while *Shirley* sounded sophisticated and glamorous.

When she announced her name change, she threatened everyone with death if they ever called her Abby again. When they forgot she ignored whoever spoke to her until she had them trained. The new name suited her well. Soon she really became Shirley.

She quit school and started working at J.L. Hudson's Department Store part time as a stock girl when she was 16. She gave Hazel money every week. With what was left she and her best friend, Sally, spent their 22-cents-an-hour wages on fancy underwear, shoes, purses, and jewelry. On occasion, she pinched something she

262

especially wanted. She would put fancy panties on and wear them home

Shirley loved her mother -- to the extent that she could love anyone besides herself. After Roy's death, her heart broke to see her beloved mother in so much pain. Roy was the only man Hazel had ever loved, and he was the best man Shirley had ever known and she missed him too. She knew their lives would never be the same. But after C.C. moved in, the distance grew between her and Hazel, who seemed to prefer this new man over her own daughter. She moved into a boarding house closer to her job.

During the Depression, C.C. and Hazel tried to run a dry-cleaning business, but as the times got worse few people had enough money to get their clothes dry-cleaned. They were forced to close their business in 1931. At that point, they didn't have enough money to rent an apartment so they stayed in hotels. They stayed in one place for a few weeks, then skipped out on the rent and left in the middle of the night or by the back door. C.C. usually had the next place lined up before they left. Kenny quit school and did odd jobs to help put food on the table.

They couldn't afford to pay the tuition for Danny's military school so he moved back in with them. Shirley stayed at a boarding house and continued to work for Hudson's until she was laid off in August of 1932.

CHAPTER 17

The Hastings family was like a flock of migratory birds: They all flew together as if guided by some unseen force. The end of 1931 heralded another big change for them.

The Great Depression took its toll on each of them in one way or another. As businesses closed, hundreds of thousands of people lost their jobs. Everyone was struggling to stay alive and meet their basic needs for food and shelter. Family members joined together to survive and share expenses. Charlotte and Clarence moved in with Ruby and Art. Buddy moved in with Lois and Chuck to share food and shelter.

Clarence and Bud were holding on to their Ford factory jobs as machinists in spite of massive layoffs. Art was a self-employed plumber. Chuck was out of work. Lois needed extra food to produce enough breast milk for her son David born in 1930. They were often hungry. Bud paid the rent and a few of their bills but not much was left over for food.

C.C. couldn't find work. Hazel didn't have a job. Kenny got a job as a milkman, delivering milk to houses and apartments. Shirley moved back with Hazel and did odd jobs.

Lottie lived with Ol' man Steele but worried about her children. Everyone shared what little food they had with friends and family but many suppers consisted of potatoes, rice, macaroni with cheese, and a little meat when they could afford it, along with whatever Lottie could pilfer from Dan Steele.

It seemed like a good time to look for greener pastures.

The family gathered at Hazel's apartment for a modest potluck Thanksgiving dinner in 1931. Lottie had managed to bring a couple of large roasting chickens from Dan Steele's house but there was no turkey that year. Hazel, C.C., and Shirley promised them a big announcement.

Lottie had her own announcement.

"Arnold called from Canada a few days ago and he's ready for the girls to come home. I know they want to go, too."

Merle cheered and danced around the room. She hugged Lorraine so tight that the little girl coughed to catch her breath. "Yea! We're going home," she cheered.

"Someone has to go with them. It's a long trip," Hazel said.

Shirley said, "I'll go if Arnold pays my way."

"He will," Lottie assured her.

Hazel said, "Good. Now that that's settled, I want to talk about something else. We've been thinking about moving to California."

The news was met with a stunned silence, but after a few minutes they all started asking questions all at the same time. "Where?" "Why?" "How?"

"Quiet down and let me tell you." Hazel continued, "You all remember Roy's brother Ernest, the doctor he was in business with in Edmonton? Well, he and his wife Ethel moved to Los Angeles after he closed the business in Canada. He's stayed in touch with me."

Smiling, she went on, "He always raves about the weather. He told us that flowers bloom on Christmas Day there. Can you imagine! I'm sick and tired of winters here. I hate shoveling snow, slush, icy walkways, freezing my ass off for months."

Shivering, she hugged herself. "Warm weather year around sounds like paradise!"

Lottie was dumbfounded for a moment but soon chipped in. "I would love to live in warm weather for a change. It would do these old bones good." She had arthritis and at times her joints hurt when she moved or walked. She believed the wet and cold wet weather caused her aches and pains.

"It sounds wonderful to me! Sunshine in winter. Great!" Lois said.

Hazel went on, "Ernest also says there are jobs out there. C.C. is going in March to check it out."

Shirley said, "I want to go! There's nothing for me here." Laughing, she added, "Maybe I could be a movie star!" She pranced around the room, one hand on her hip and the other behind her head, her chin to the heavens. She struck a movie star pose, "I could be discovered just walking down the street!"

Everyone laughed and clapped while she strutted around the dining room.

"The new Clara Bow!" Buddy cheered her on.

Lottie chimed in, "Well, I'm ready to get away from you-know-who for good. If I have to move across the country to do it that will be fine." Her constant bickering with Dan Steele was taking a toll on her health and moods.

Kenny was skeptical. "I just met a girl I like. I don't want to leave right now."

Danny said, "I want to go. I think it's a swell idea."

Hazel told them, "It's *just* an idea at this stage. Let's see what C.C. finds and then we'll decide. I just wanted to let you all know what we are thinking of doing."

On March 1, 1932, C.C. took the train to Los Angeles. He found the town booming with opportunities for jobs and a better life, great weather, and the dazzling Pacific Ocean. He called Hazel to give her the good news and they decided to make the big move.

Lottie's Lot

Hazel, Lottie, and Shirley made plans to leave as soon as Danny was out of school. They packed up most of their belongings and shipped them by freight. With hope in their hearts they boarded the train to Chicago and then transferred from Chicago, to Los Angles. It was a great three-day trip, full of hope and laughter. They never looked back.

A few months later Chuck and Lois packed up and drove across the country with Buddy and their two little boys. They rented a small house in Compton. Chuck and Bud both found work within a month.

Some family members stayed behind in Detroit. Art had an established business, and he and Ruby weren't interested in moving. Kenny and his new wife, Dorothy Burke, had a baby girl in 1933 and she didn't want to leave her family. They settled into their life in Detroit.

Charlotte was torn. She wanted to be close to Lottie but she decided to stay in Detroit to be near Ruby, her favorite sister. Clarence thought his job was secure until he got laid off in 1936. So after much soul searching and discussion they moved to North Hollywood, and he got a job right away. They bought a house, enrolled their son, Paul, in school, and put down roots.

When the first Hastings group got to California, they had little money. Everyone pitched in to find work of any kind. Hazel and Shirley found waitressing jobs, and C.C. looked for sales work. Danny was enrolled in school for the fall term.

C.C. found a small two-bedroom apartment on Grace Place with a large living room and a big window overlooking colorful flower beds across the street. The rent was only $30 a month. The unfurnished upstairs flat had a stove and a refrigerator, so they slept on blankets on the floor for over a month.

267

Gradually, they were able to furnish the apartment with used furniture a sofa , beds, a used dining room table and chairs, and kitchen appliances, dishes etc. from the Salvation Army store.

Lottie shared one of the two bedrooms with Shirley, while Danny slept on the sofa bed in the living room. Hazel and C.C. had twin beds in the other bedroom.

Lottie felt at loose ends. She wasn't used to staying at home all day with nothing to do. Keeping the apartment neat and clean didn't fill her time. She longed for a place of her own, but didn't have the means to pay rent. Hazel's bad moods and drinking bothered her, and she instinctively disliked C.C. The situation was less than ideal.

To escape she took long walks in the neighborhood. The weather was balmy almost all year-round, and her legs and hips felt better here. Walking invigorated her. Sunny days and friendly people elevated her mood. One day on her walk, she saw a small HELP WANTED sign in the office window at the Grace Methodist Church a few blocks from the apartment. She opened the office door and peeked inside. A trim, clean-shaven young man was sitting at a desk piled high with papers.

When she tapped on the door he stood up and welcomed her, "Come in. I'm Reverend Walker. Hello."

"Oh, my, my," she said as she stepped inside. "My maiden name was Walker. I'm Lottie Hastings now." She held out her hand and gave him a big smile. "Do you have any Walker relatives from Iowa? Cresco, Iowa?"

"Not that I know of." He gestured toward a chair and she sat. "It's a common name."

"I saw the sign in your window," she said, noticing several heaps of books and papers on the floor, in two other chairs, as well as on each corner of the desk.

Lottie's Lot

"Yes, I just put it there. You can see that I'm way behind in my paperwork. There don't seem to be enough hours in the day to get everything done."

"I know how you feel. I raised seven children," she said. "What kind of help are you looking for?"

"I need help to get organized, someone to answer the phone and take messages, file papers, keep up the membership files, send out occasional letters, prepare the weekly bulletin. It sounds like a lot but once it's organized it will be less hectic." He smiled.

"I can do all those things. My daughter Charlotte showed me how to type a little. But I don't want to work full time. I'm 63 years old, and I live with my daughter's family. She needs my help with the apartment. But I have some spare time."

"That's fine. I was thinking of asking someone to work 20 to 25 hours a week." He liked this straightforward, confident woman. God had surely sent this angel to rescue him from the overwhelming burden of paperwork.

"Are you interested?"

Lottie had already made up her mind but she asked one more question. "How much will you be paying?"

"Churches don't have much money. How about $1.25 per hour paid weekly to start?"

She thought a moment and then nodded. "Okay! Let's give it a try. When do you want me to start?" she said with her nicest smile.

"How about now?" he grinned. She removed the sign from the window and set her purse on the floor. She followed the tall, graceful young man as he showed her around the church and explained the organization of the office.

With a little trepidation she sat down in the office again she frowned.

"Before I start Rev. Walker, there is something I think I should tell you. I hope it isn't a problem."

"What's that, Mrs. Hastings?"

"I'm a Baptist."

He nodded, unfazed.

"My mother was a Methodist," she continued, "and so was my late husband, Charlie, and all his family and they were wonderful people. But I still consider myself a Baptist."

He smiled. "I don't think that's a problem. I'm glad to know you're a devoted Christian."

"Oh yes, you can be sure of that. And please call me Lottie."

They agreed she would work from 11 am. to 4 pm. Monday through Friday to begin with. After he bade her goodbye, he leaned against the door, raised his eyes to the heavens, and said, "Thank you, Lord."

Lottie walked home with a spring in her step. She looked up to heaven and said, "Thank you, Lord!" She was grateful that she had someone new to take care of.

Exploring all that was available to do in California was an adventure. The wondrous Pacific Ocean had long stretches of sandy beaches, piers with clam chowder restaurants, and charming shops. At Long Beach the pier had an amusement park with a merry-go-round, a Ferris Wheel and other rides. There were also movie studios to visit, free tickets to radio shows, horse races, fishing, boat trips, and more. Something for everyone.

Lottie and her daughters loved going to the movies, which they called *talking pictures*. They got to know the names of favorite movie stars and were intrigued by the bold women portrayed by actresses like Katherine Hepburn, Bette Davis, and Joan Crawford.

Lottie's Lot

They admired the handsome Clark Gable and the dashing Errol Flynn. Lottie's favorite was Henry Fonda, because he seemed like a strong, honest man – he reminded her of Charlie.

"Just think," Shirley said when they talked about movies. "They're made just a few miles from here. Those stars live just down the road in Beverly Hills and Malibu! We're living so close to those glamorous, famous people."

On weekends, C.C. often drove the family along the ocean. They enjoyed walking on the piers at Hermosa Beach or Manhattan Beach. Sometimes he would park the car to let the younger ones play in the water, while Lottie and Hazel sat on beach chairs and watched the youngsters. C.C. would saunter along the Santa Monica boardwalk by himself.

Hazel bought Lottie a pair of sunglasses and teased her, "Ma, take off your stockings! You're at the beach!"

Lottie conceded and dug her bare toes into the sand.

"It feels good," she admitted. "So warm and good."

"If you would wear a bathing suit you could get a tan," Hazel said as she took off her sack dress and spread a blanket on the sand.

"I wouldn't be caught dead in one of those naughty things! They're shameful."

"Oh Ma! Don't be so old fashioned."

"Look at all that skin showing. Shameful, I say."

"You know, Ma, you could use some more fashionable clothes."

'My clothes are fine. Lots of wear in them yet. I paid good money for them at Kern's and Hudson's."

"But they're out of style."

"I'm too old to care about style. If I need anything new, I'll make it myself." Hazel rolled over and dozed off in the sun.

Lottie wanted to see the footprints of Mary Pickford and Douglas Fairbanks at Grauman's Chinese Theater in Hollywood. As they were driving down Hollywood Boulevard, they saw people walking and running around in the middle of a side street. Huge lights were shining from poles taller than the houses, and one man was sitting on a moving chair almost that high.

"Oh," Shirley gasped, "they're making a movie! Stop the car!" She jumped out and ran toward the activity. When a young man holding a clipboard stopped her, she smiled and giggled and briefly touched his arm, and before long he let her go closer to the filming. After several minutes she ran back to the car. "It's Jimmy Stewart! I saw him, right there in person. Oh, my gosh, he smiled at me!"

Hazel was almost as excited and even Lottie was impressed by their brush with stardom. Shirley occasionally saw celebrities at her job as a cigarette girl at the Santa Anita racetrack. She dressed in a sexy, skimpy outfit with a perky hat, black tights, and a tiny skirt to show off her petite figure. With her wares -- cigarettes, cigars, chewing gum, candy -- in a box strapped in front of her, she soon discovered that flirting increased her tips. In no time she mastered the technique of winking and smiling sweetly while holding out her hand.

One of her frequent customers was a young single man with a new Buick roadster, fashionable suits, and a wad of money. Hal Sloane was handsome and charming, fun, spontaneous, and impulsive. They began dating.

Lottie didn't approve of their relationship because Hal Sloane was Jewish. But when Shirley announced that she was pregnant she looked the other way. Better to be married than to have an illegitimate child like Hazel did. They got married in July 1933.

The marriage only lasted six months. Hal didn't work much and when he did, he gambled most of the money away. After the divorce

Lottie's Lot

Shirley moved back into Grace Place. C.C. paid for her prenatal care and the delivery with the condition that she name the baby after him. She resented the bribe but had no choice so she named the baby boy Edward Frederick Sloan, and called him Freddie. He was born on her brother Kenny's birthday.

Ever competitive, Shirley had been envious that her younger brother had a child before she did. But Kenny had a girl so she felt victorious when she had a *boy*. She proudly took a photo of him, naked with legs straddled and his little penis displayed for the entire world to see, and sent it to Kenny with a handwritten note: "I got one of these! Better luck next time!"

Shirley wasn't interested in nursing her baby and loaded up on bottles and formula. A week after he was born she got dressed up, fixed her hair, put on make-up, and went out to a bar with her girlfriends.

"Thanks for taking care of the baby, Mama." She gave Hazel a peck on the cheek as she breezed out the door. "I need to get out -- it's stifling in here.

Hazel cared for the infant while Shirley worked and played. In fact, she left her child with her mother almost all the time and later moved into her own apartment. At 25, she hated being tied down. She preferred to go out with friends and explore the Hollywood nightlife. She always had at least one man in her life.

Hazel remembered how much she had missed of her adolescence with a baby to care for at the age of 16. She sympathized with Shirley and understood her need for fun. Having another infant who needed her gave her new purpose. She bonded with little Freddie right away. Lottie liked having the baby around and shared in his care when she wasn't working.

Except for Freddie's presence, Hazel was depressed most of the time and felt that she had been dealt a bad hand for her life. She indulged in self-pity for the losses she had suffered. Bitter and cynical, she drank to drown her sorrows. With lowered inhibitions, she took everything she hated about her life out on C.C. He knew that she just wanted to pick a fight and defending himself was pointless. That fueled her rage even more and she berated him for not standing up to her.

"What's the matter with you, you coward?" she snarled. "Why don't you stand up like a real man and defend yourself? "He ignored her and retreated to the bedroom, which made her even madder. He knew that the next day she would forget what she had said or done. Letting her rant was a small price to pay for keeping her dependent on him so he could pursue his obsession.

He occasionally treated the family to dinner at a nice restaurant, but more often he volunteered to babysit while the others went nightclubbing, which they often did to celebrate birthdays and anniversaries.

Lottie's distrust and disapproval of C.C. hadn't changed but she couldn't put her finger on what made her so doubtful of his sincerity. He seemed sneaky and dishonest, and she wasn't the only one who thought so. None of the other adults warmed up to him, Danny openly hated him, and both he and Shirley avoided him as much as possible. Everyone wondered why Hazel kept him around at all but they tolerated him nevertheless, for Hazel's sake. He seemed oblivious to the tension and ignored it.

One afternoon when they were alone in the apartment, Lottie broached the subject. "Hazel, why do you stay with C.C?"

"Oh! Here we go again." Hazel clicked her tongue and opened her arms wide, palms up. "Mama, I've told you a hundred times. He's good to me and to the children. He supports us and doesn't ask for anything in return."

"He's strange. I don't trust him."

"Well, he stays out of your way. Why can't you just accept him and let it go at that?" Hazel lit a cigarette.

"I don't think he's good for you." Lottie knew she was losing this discussion again.

"It's my life and my choice...so just back off." Hazel poured herself a stiff drink.

"I wish you wouldn't drink so much," Lottie murmured under her breath.

"I heard that." Hazel turned to face her, eyes blazing. "Mama, I'm a grown woman. And you can't tell me what to do any more."

"I know. It's your life. But I also know what's right and what's wrong." Lottie went into her bedroom and closed the door.

Hazel knew that C.C. worshiped her and that she could manipulate him to get anything she really wanted. He was generous to her when he had money. She also knew that he would be crushed if she kicked him out. She depended on him for her survival so she put up with him. Still she felt trapped, afraid to let go of the security he provided. When her resentment boiled over she treated him with scorn and contempt.

Canadian Club had become Hazel's best friend. Her children were seldom around; her sisters were busy with their lives; her mother criticized her and she missed having someone to love her and hold her like Roy had done. The bottle was the one reliable comfort in her life.

One night in December 1936, all the adults went to a nightclub to celebrate Shirley's 28th birthday. C.C. didn't want to go so he volunteered to watch Maggie, Shirley's best friend Alice's three-year-old daughter. He waved them off with a big smile. Alice had put

Maggie in Hazel's bed and was confident she was sleeping before she left. She thanked C.C. with a grateful smile.

A half hour after they left C.C. went into the bedroom, got undressed, lay down next to Maggie, and gently rubbed her belly. He lifted her nightgown, rubbed her belly again, then her legs and her pubic area. Maggie stirred and tried to move away from him. He put the little girl's hand on his erect penis and, with his own hand on top of hers, showed her how to squeeze it and rub it back and forth. He started to breathe heavily and she woke up and tried to pull her hand away. He held it tightly in place, shushed her, and rubbed his puffy finger between her legs. She squirmed and began to whimper.

He whispered, "Quiet now. Be a good girl," but she soon broke into tears and called out "Mommy!" in her loudest voice.

Suddenly the door burst open and Lottie was framed in the doorway. Expecting to see only the child, she felt a lightning bolt of shock when she saw C.C naked and lying next to the child. She was speechless. Equally shaken, he jumped up, grabbed his dressing gown, and headed for the bathroom.

Lottie froze momentarily, then grabbed the little girl and took her into her bedroom. She held and rocked the half-awake child in her arms and sang a lullaby in her ear.

Hush, little baby, don't say a word;
Mama's going to buy you a mockingbird.
If that mockingbird won't sing,
Mama's going to buy you a diamond ring.

She couldn't remember any other words and sang the same verse over and over. When Maggie whimpered, Lottie whispered, "It's just a bad dream. You're safe now." She comforted Maggie until she went back to sleep.

C.C. didn't show his face. She heard him go out the front door and heard his car start.

Lottie's Lot

Lottie trembled as she sat in the kitchen and drank a cup of hot tea, trying to sort out what had happened. She had suspected there was something strange about C.C.'s interest in children but she had never heard of a grown man touching children in that way. Then like a bolt of lightning she remembered what Danny had told her about C.C. years ago. Oh my God! She tried to calm herself and comprehend what she had discovered.

The group got home about 1 am, laughing, drunk, and holding on to each other to remain steady. Alice went to get her daughter and was surprised to find her in another bed. She asked, "Where's C.C.?"

In the steadiest voice she could muster, Lottie said, "He had to go out, so I took over. She's a little angel."

Alice picked up the sleeping child and smiled, "Thank you for taking care of her."

"Glad to help." Lottie breathed a sigh of relief.

She realized Hazel and Shirley were too drunk to grasp the magnitude of what had happened. She would tell Hazel tomorrow morning when she was sober.

The rest of the night, Lottie tossed and turned, stewing about how to tell Hazel. Her suspicions about C.C. were validated. Finally she had proof that C.C. was a fraud and worse. *So* much worse!

"Dear God, how could you let such monsters roam the earth?" she asked. "Do you condone such disgusting evil?"

Looking for the truth and to soothe her soul, she pulled her Bible from her bureau drawer. She found what she was looking for in Psalm 10:

He sitteth in the lurking places of the villages: in the secret places doth he murder the innocent...

He lieth in wait secretly as a lion in his den: he lieth in wait to catch the poor: he doth catch the poor, when he draweth him into his net.

Those poor helpless children, she thought. C.C. catches them in his net and takes them to secret places and he murders their souls, Lottie thought. Verse 14 gave her the strength to do what she had to do next:

Break thou the arm of the wicked and the evil man: seek out his wickedness till thou find none.

The Lord needed her to help destroy this evil and she would give it all of her strength. Like a great warrior, she would use every weapon she had and break him. She vowed to help God protect the poor little children by exposing C.C.

Lottie got up at dawn, brewed a bigger than usual pot of coffee, and settled down to collect her thoughts. Hazel was quicker to anger these days and Lottie needed her to listen. She hoped Hazel didn't have a hangover from the party last night.

Hazel staggered into the kitchen at about nine. Her hair was disheveled. She yawned, pulling her bathrobe around her. Lottie was ready.

"Sit down. I poured your coffee."

"Thanks, Ma." She took a sip of the steaming brew.

"We need to talk," Lottie said, a slight quiver in her voice.

"About what? Hey, do you know where C.C. is?"

"Something happened last night, Hazel. Something terrible. I need you to understand what I saw."

"What happened?"

"I caught C.C. doing things to that little girl. Bad, dirty things." Lottie exhaled. It was finally out.

"*What?!* What are you talking about?" Hazel snapped awake.

"I heard the child cry out and I went into your bedroom to see what was going on. I opened the door very quietly and what I saw shocked the daylights out of me."

"What did you see?"

"C.C. was buck naked and lying next to the child, and he was touching her private parts. He had his hand between her legs."

She struggled to maintain control but was determined to tell it all.

"I couldn't believe my eyes, and I couldn't say a word. I was flabbergasted. When he saw me he jumped up and dashed into the bathroom. I got Maggie and took her into my bedroom and calmed her down until she finally she went back to sleep. Meanwhile I heard C.C. run down the stairs and start his car."

Shaken, Hazel said, "Dear God. This can't be true. Maybe you were mistaken."

"Hazel, I know what I saw. He didn't come back last night, did he?"

"No."

"I don't think he will be coming back. He knows he got caught. Finally!"

"What do you mean 'finally'?"

"I've told you before that I thought he's strange. So does everyone else in the family. I couldn't pinpoint the problem until now."

Hazel sighed painfully. "Oh my God! What if she tells her mother?"

Lottie said, "I don't think she will. She's not quite three and doesn't have the words to describe it. I told her it was a dream, and I think she believed me. She finally went back to sleep."

"I hope you're right." Hazel's hand shook as she lit a cigarette and Lottie filled her coffee cup.

"Remember when Danny told you C.C. was touching him? I guess we should have believed him. That's probably why Danny became such a handful."

"I didn't believe him. I'd never heard of a grown man touching a child like that."

"Last night I remembered something I did wrong too. When you and C.C. went to Niagara Falls to get married Danny told me that he was afraid of C.C. for the same reason, and I just ignored what he said. I didn't believe it either."

Hazel stared at Lottie, letting it all sink in.

"This is a nightmare. I can't believe it."

"Believe it. I know what I saw."

"I can't believe C.C. would hurt a child. He's such a gentle person."

"Sometimes people fool us. We believe what we want to believe and don't see what is right in front of us," Lottie said.

"Maybe this explains why Danny has always hated him so. If it's true then I'm a terrible mother." Hazel stared straight ahead, her eyes glazed.

"No, no. You just didn't pay attention because you didn't know what to do." Lottie's heart went out to her wounded, confused daughter.

Hazel lit another cigarette and walked to the sink to keep the smoke away from Lottie. She frowned. "Ma, why would C.C. do something like that with you here?"

Lottie's Lot

"He thought I went out with you. There was so much commotion when you all left and Alice put Maggie to sleep in your bed. I was already in bed in the other room with the door closed. I wouldn't have been the wiser if I hadn't heard her crying."

"Oh, Ma, this is too terrible! I can't believe it. What am I going to do?"

"I don't know about you but I'm going to call the police," Lottie declared.

"No. Please don't do that now. They would have to talk to the kid's parents. Let's sort this out first."

Lottie nodded, "Okay. But I am going to report him."

"I need some time alone. I'm just stunned right now," Hazel said and went into her bedroom.

It had been a tough night. Lottie took a short nap before going to her job at the church. As horrible as this was, maybe they had gotten rid of C.C. at last. At least Hazel had listened to her without getting angry. That was a small victory.

C.C. didn't call or show his face for over three weeks. Christmas passed without him and Hazel stayed home on New Year's Eve.

Then early one afternoon in January there was a knock on the door. A young man in a uniform from Atlantic Avenue Flower Shop held out a large rectangular box for Hazel. In the box were two dozen red roses. The note said, "I want to come home. Love, C.C." The phone rang an hour later and C.C. asked to come over and tell his side of the story. She agreed.

He told Hazel that it was all a mistake. He was getting into his pajamas and the little girl started to cry because she had a stomachache and he was comforting her Lottie burst into the room in

281

a rage and accused him of all kinds of awful things. He knew she wouldn't listen or believe him so he left.

Hazel was skeptical, but he knew exactly what would persuade her and he came prepared. He offered her a ring with five diamonds forming a band and set in 18-karat white gold. To her own surprise, Hazel was past her outrage and glad to see him. She was easily seduced by his offering and with a little more persuasion she agreed to let him come back.

When Lottie got home from work, she saw C.C. and screamed, "Hazel, what is he doing here?"

"He came to tell me his side of the story. Ma, it was just a misunderstanding."

Lottie fumed. "Hazel, you know I'm right. I *know* what I saw."

"Will you just listen to C.C.? He can explain everything."

"How dare you question me!" Lottie's face grew redder. Hazel hadn't seen her mother this angry since Gus Stover's violation. "I'm through listening to his lies and I'm through watching you believe his lies," Lottie shouted. "You will do anything to keep him so you don't have to support yourself. Don't you have any pride or self-respect?"

"Ma, please listen to his side of the story."

Lottie spat out the words. "He's lying. I don't need to hear it."

She glared at Hazel and Hazel stared back, then Hazel turned her eyes away.

"This is it, Hazel. Either he goes or I go." Hazel didn't look at her. Knowing she had lost, Lottie stormed into her bedroom and slammed the door.

From work the next day she called Charlotte, Lois, and Buddy, and asked them to help her find her a place to live on her own. She stayed away from the apartment as long as she could that night, eating dinner at a café. Then she went straight into her bedroom and started packing her things. The next afternoon Charlotte called and told her she had found a cute two-bedroom bungalow about a mile from Hazel. "It's furnished and it's only $45 a month including utilities. That's a good deal, Ma."

Lottie received Charlie's railroad pension of about $30 a month, so Lois, Charlotte, and Buddy each agreed to contribute $5 to make up the difference in the rent. Her wages from the church would cover food and other expenses.

The girls moved her into her new house the following Saturday. Hazel begged her to stay, but Lottie refused to talk to her. Hazel was secretly grateful not to be living in the middle of the tension between C. C. and her mother any more. C.C. was relieved, too, but still fearful that Lottie could cause him trouble. He would just stick to his story.

When Freddie was about three Hazel wanted to try something else in her life so she took a course on selling real estate. But when she showed a house and the prospective buyers walked away, she felt rejected and resentful and gave it up.

In 1937 she met a man who wanted to sell his cabin in Silverado Canyon in Orange County, a three-hour drive from Los Angeles through miles after mile of orange groves.

The cabin was small, with two bedrooms and a great stone fireplace in the center between the kitchen and living room. It was on a year-round creek, with a stone fence surrounding the big lot and a bridge across the creek just 50 yards from the property line. Hazel loved the place, and the man sold it to them for just $100 and said they could pay for it over two years with no interest.

The timing was perfect, as Lottie had just moved out and Hazel wasn't sure she trusted C.C. one hundred percent. She felt at peace in the canyon so she and Freddie moved there in the spring. C.C. stayed at Grace Place during the week and went to the canyon on weekends.

Hazel and Freddie shared one bedroom, while C.C. claimed the other bedroom for himself. He always kept the door locked. Even Hazel was forbidden to go into his room. He said he was working on inventions and nothing must be moved or disturbed in his room. He didn't ask for much for himself, so everyone respected his privacy.

It soon became a gathering place for family members. Shirley and her boyfriends visited often as did Charlotte and Lois and their families.

CHAPTER 18

Lottie's Lot

Living alone for the first time took some adjustments for Lottie. With no one else to talk to, she didn't know what to do with herself in her free time. She played solitaire and knitted squares for afghans while listening to the radio. But she was often restless and lonely.

Buddy had a telephone installed and came to visit her once a week, and she called Lois or Charlotte almost every night. On weekdays, she took a short bus ride to her work at the church.

Weekends were the worst. She began going to the Methodist Church where she worked and found it to be similar to her Baptist Church. Reverend Walker always gave her a secret wink when he saw her. She liked his sermons and the way he interpreted the Bible, with a little liberal twist. It opened her mind to other ways of seeing things and ways to think about the scriptures.

She agonized over the problem with C.C. She had to do something to protect the children but she wasn't sure what course to take.

She desperately needed someone she could talk to. She finally decided to confide in Reverend Walker. She had come to respect and trust him and his counsel. He was kindhearted and always took time to counsel a member of his flock.

The next Wednesday afternoon, when the office was quiet, she asked for a few minutes of his time for a "personal matter." He invited her to sit in one of the worn leather chairs across from the window. He took the chair next to hers.

She started timidly. "I found out something awful and I don't know what to do about it." Her voice was quivering but she cleared her throat, mustered her courage and continued. "I had a terrible fight with my daughter over it."

"What happened?" he asked.

"It's embarrassing." She hesitated. "Her husband, uh, uh … he does things to little children."

"What kinds of things, Lottie?"

"Dirty things," she whispered.

"Dirty things?" His calm voice helped Lottie feel more comfortable.

"I always thought he was a little strange. I tried to warn Hazel, that's my daughter. But she never would believe me."

"What did he do, Lottie?" He looked at her steadily, kindly encouraging her to go on.

Lottie rubbed her forehead with her fingertips and took a deep breath. "This is hard for me to say."

"It's all right, my dear. Just tell me in your own words," he said gently.

"About five or six weeks ago, just before Christmas, I was at home while my daughter Hazel went out with friends. He didn't know I was there. One of her friends left her three-year-old child at the apartment sleeping because C.C. had agreed to watch her. About midnight I heard the child crying and opened the bedroom door to see what was wrong and … I saw him buck naked lying next to her and touching the child …" she lowered her head and whispered, "between her legs." Lottie let out all her breath and looked pleadingly at Walker.

"Oh dear Lottie. I'm so sorry." He patted her hand briefly.

"I don't know what to do. I'm beside myself." To her dismay, tears formed in her eyes and she could feel the deluge just ready to break. She sat up straight. "Confound it!" I don't want to cry. I 'm so mad I could spit."

"Where is this man now?"

"That's the problem. I told my daughter about it and she believed me. He left for a few weeks. But he came crawling back. He told her a crazy story and gave her a diamond ring. He told her I was seeing things and had jumped to the wrong conclusion. And she believed him. So now it's my story against his. He supports her so she won't kick him out."

"And you?" Reverend Walker handed her a tissue. She wiped her eyes and blew her nose.

"I was so angry. I felt betrayed so I moved out and got my own place. I hate not being able to talk to her. She's my daughter and I love her but I'm still so mad that she took him back and doesn't believe me."

"What do you want to do, Lottie?"

She looked directly at him for the first time since she had begun her story. "I don't know what I can do," she hesitated. "But I do know for sure that I don't want him to ever harm another little child."

"All right, let's think about how you could do that."

"Good." She sat up straighter and glanced at the trees through the window. It was a lovely day and she was feeling better. She was glad that she had gotten it off her chest and talked to the Reverend. She felt like a burden she had been carrying all alone had lifted. "I've prayed about it and I still don't know what to do, Reverend. I can't tell my other children."

"What he did is a crime as well as a terrible sin. Have you reported him to the police?"

"No. I told Hazel I was going to call the police and she asked me to wait. Then when he came back and told her I was seeing things I thought it would be his word against mine. So I haven't called yet, but I want to."

"I have an idea, Lottie," Reverend Walker said. She looked at him hopefully. "A member of our church is a retired police detective and has worked with similar cases. Would you like to talk to him and see what he advises? It wouldn't be an official report, just a discussion, and it wouldn't go beyond the two of you. I'm sure he'd be willing to help."

"Yes! That sounds like a good idea. Will you set up a meeting with him? I would like you to be there too if you have time." She felt like she was making progress.

"I'll call him today and see when he can come over."

Detective Goodwin met with Lottie and Reverend Walker in the rectory office the following Tuesday afternoon. He was in his early 60s, balding and stout. He sensed her anxiety and smiled encouragingly as Lottie told her story. He listened without saying a word, head lowered and fingers pressed together forming a pyramid. When she finished he took a few minutes to digest what he heard her say.

Finally he spoke slowly, "Mrs. Hastings, I know you're very upset by what you saw. Unfortunately this happens much more often than I can tell you. And I'm afraid there's not much you can do."

Lottie frowned as he continued. "I'm going to be honest with you. You can report it and the police will take your report and then it will get filed in some obscure filing cabinet, never to be seen again. If you were really insistent and got the child's mother to press charges they might send a patrolman to question the gentleman, Fredericks, is that his name? He will tell his story and will tell the patrolman that you never liked him and were trying to get him in trouble. He might call you a senile old woman, though I can tell he would be very wrong." His smile was gentle and open.

"The officer would write another report and it would get filed away and that would be the end of it. Meanwhile you would have stirred up the child's parents and who knows what hard feelings would result. I don't want to discourage you but this is the unfortunate reality."

Lottie listened with increasing helplessness. She took a deep breath, "Then you are telling me that there is nothing I can do?"

"I'm telling you that nothing will be done even if you do report this crime. I wish it were different but I think you should know the reality."

"Then how can we protect the children from monsters like this?" Her voice rose in frustration.

"The best thing is to never leave children alone with him and that way you remove the opportunity for him to molest a child. When a child is violated in that way the police term is molesting or molestation. It's important to keep the children away from him. Can you do that?" He smiled again.

"Yes, I can do that, and I will. I wish I could do more." She offered him her hand. "Thank you so much for talking to me."

He shook her hand. "Thank you for caring about the children. Maybe someday we will be able to prosecute this crime and have laws with teeth to stop this but that may be a long time coming." He said his goodbyes and left.

On the bus ride home, Lottie fumed to think about how little the police cared about children being harmed like this. But she would do what she could. That night as she ate her dinner alone in her house she decided to tell Charlotte, Lois, and Shirley what happened. They all had children and at least she could protect her own family. She called each one and invited them for lunch on Saturday afternoon to celebrate her new apartment.

She made her famous tomato stuffed with tuna salad, iced tea, and a lemon meringue pie. They had left their children at home at her request, and they had a lovely visit. Each one brought her a small house-warming gift and she was pleased that she had trained them well. She opened her gifts with excitement -- a set of homemade hot pads from Lois, a new teapot from Charlotte, and bag of multicolored yarn from Shirley with a hint of how much she would welcome an afghan for her bed. Everyone laughed. Lottie liked nothing better than making afghans.

"Now I have something serious to talk to you about," Lottie announced as they finished their pie. Her serious tone was familiar to them. Lois gave Charlotte a "here it comes" look.

"It's about C.C.," Lottie began. "You have all asked why Hazel isn't here today and wondered why I moved out on my own. You also know I don't like C.C. very much. Something about him always bothered me but I couldn't put my finger on what it was. Now I know."

She took a sip of tea. They looked at her curiously now. This was different from Lottie's usual "serious talks" – she didn't seem to be scolding any of them.

"The night of Shirley's birthday party I saw C.C. … touching little Maggie Hogan. It's called molesting." The women gasped in unison and continued listening in rapt silence. "He thought I had gone out too but I felt sick and was in bed in my room. About 11, I heard the child cry out so I opened door to the other bedroom."

She closed her eyes and took a deep breath. "He was lying in bed next to her stark naked and touching her in her private parts between her legs. When he saw me, he jumped up and dashed into the bathroom, got dressed and left in a hurry in the middle of the night." Every time she told this story she felt a little more comfortable and more confirming of what she'd seen.

She paused and looked at each of them, registering the shock on all three faces. No one said a word. "Well? Say something."

"Does Hazel know?" Charlotte asked.

"I told her the next day. She was very upset. She had no problem believing me."

"Is that when C.C. was gone for three or four weeks? I thought he was away on 'business,' whatever his business is," Lois asked.

"Yes, and then he came back." Lottie explained how C.C. had persuaded Hazel to take him back and not to believe Lottie. "That's when I called all of you to help me move out."

"Oh, Mama how awful for you," Charlotte said, reaching across the table to squeeze her Lottie's hand. She was impressed with her mother's calmness. "Why didn't you tell us sooner? This is a terrible thing to keep to yourself."

"It has been hard to live with. I didn't know what to do or whether telling you would betray Hazel somehow. It's been keeping me awake at night. Last week I talked to Reverend Walker and a parishioner of his who was a police detective. I feel better now."

"You called the police, Ma?" Lois asked.

"I *wanted* to report it to the police, but this retired detective told me when I met with him that it wouldn't do any good. I want to protect the children. His advice was never leave the children alone with C.C. So I'm telling you now because you all have children. You must be sure that you never–*never* leave your children alone with him, under any circumstances. And be sure your friends don't either.

"The detective said right now it's really the only thing we can do to protect the kiddies. The police won't take it seriously and Hazel won't leave C.C. because she depends on him. So we have no other choice. Please promise me."

291

They nodded; they would look out for their own and each other's kids. Lois's boys were 16 and 11, too old to interest C.C. Charlotte's son Paul was 9 and Shirley's son Freddie was 7.

Shirley gritted her teeth and stood up. "I want to kill that son of a bitch." She hit the wall with her open hand. "Now I wonder if he did the same thing to Danny, like Danny said. My mama didn't believe him either."

Charlotte asked, "What if we all confront Hazel together?"

Lois laughed wryly. "You know Hazel. She'll just get mad at us. Nothing will change."

"What if we all confront C.C.? Tell him we are going to call the police?" Charlotte asked.

Lottie shook her head. "He has made up his version of the story and the detective told me it will be my story against his and it won't go any farther. He probably knows this already."

Charlotte nodded. "And you know what a good talker he is. He can sell ice to Eskimos, and he can make anybody believe whatever he tells them."

"Ma," Lois asked. "We all have boys. Maggie's a girl. Maybe he only likes girls."

The other three started to speak at once but yielded to Lottie. "Remember Danny," she said then she told them what Danny told her and that he was afraid of C.C. and what he had done to him. They sat in stunned silence for a few minutes then Shirley pounded the table.

We should've believed the children. They don't make up stories like that. I wonder if he has molested Freddie. He lived with them for so long off and on. Oh! Dear GOD! Ma didn't protect Danny and I didn't protect my Freddie.

Lottie refilled the iced tea glasses and served each of them another sliver of pie. They ate in silence while this startling news sunk in and thought about their predicament.

Lottie's Lot

"Maybe we need a man to scare him," Lois said. "Chuck would enjoy beating C.C. up. He never liked him. I'll bet Clarence would join in, wouldn't he, Charlotte?"

"I'm sure he would, but that may not be the best thing."

"Why not ?" Shirley asked. "He deserves a good beating."

"It could backfire. He might press charges against our men and we would still have no way to prove anything against C.C."

Lottie spoke up. "I don't want to encourage the men to take that kind of action, for Hazel's sake. It could create a terrible breach between her and the rest of us. I don't intend to tell Buddy anything. Whether you girls tell your husbands is up to you but be sure they don't do anything rash."

All summer and fall the women kept an eye on C.C. and made sure no children were left alone with him. When he offered to take a group of youngsters to a movie, they made sure one of them or their husbands went along as well. Lottie stayed away from Hazel's apartment and the Silverado Canyon cabin.

On Thanksgiving, the family gathered for dinner at Charlotte's home. Everyone was there. C.C. came with Hazel and Danny. Lottie, Buddy, Lois, Chuck, and their boys came, and Shirley brought Freddie and her latest boyfriend, Johnny Jacobs. It was the first time Lottie and Hazel had been in the same room since January. When Hazel sat next to Lottie on the couch, Lottie said, "I'd better go help Charlotte," and got up and went into the kitchen.

Hazel followed her. Just outside the kitchen she said, "It's good to see you, Mama."

Lottie looked her in the eyes. "Is it?"

293

Hazel swirled the ice around in her drink. "Mama, this has gone on long enough. Let's call a truce even if it's just for this day. After all we are celebrating the things we're thankful for."

"Whatever you say," Lottie said and began to set the table, but she purposefully avoided Hazel for the rest of the day. It hurt her to be so angry with Hazel after all they'd been through together. Lottie wanted to forgive her daughter but she couldn't do it yet. Not only had Hazel dismissed what she had told her about C.C. but Lottie felt that Hazel, by her denial and ignorance, was allowing C.C. to continue molesting children.

The dinner was abundant and festive. Before the day was done everyone was laughing and enjoying the get-together. The beer and whiskey flowed and they put on happy faces in spite of the obvious tension between Hazel and Lottie.

Shirley tried to start a sing-along but no one joined in, so she sang several songs herself, complete with gestures and chitchat to the "audience" until she noticed no one was paying attention except her new boyfriend Johnny who clapped and smiled.

C.C. watched his mother-in-law and sisters-in-law bustle through the day, serving food and laughing cheerfully. He had zeroed in on their pattern of never leaving kids alone with him. He realized Lottie must have warned them. So what? He thought. These women had no power to harm him.

But protecting the children wasn't enough for Lottie. She wanted C.C. to get the punishment he deserved. The anger she had kept bottled up inside surfaced. She visualized the image of him lying next to that little girl. She ached to strike another blow against him. She wanted to beat him to a pulp, but that was unrealistic. In her entire life she had never been so angry.

She watched for her chance. Finally he got up to go to the bathroom and she followed and waited for him outside the door. When he stepped out he almost tripped over her.

She grabbed his shirt and pushed him against the wall. She bared her teeth and said, "I know what you did to that little girl and you know I know. I made a police report so they are on to you. You …will …*never…ever…* touch … another …child. If you do, I will *personally* see that you go to jail for a very long time." She whispered huskily, *"DO YOU UNDERSTAND ME?"*

"Let go of me, old woman," he said, struggling to control the fear in his voice. He shook free from her grip and straightened his shirt and tie. He pushed her aside and putting a big smile on his face he went back to the living room as if nothing had happened and sat next to Hazel and taking her hand in his.

Behind his outwardly calm mask, he was making a plan.

CHAPTER 19

Lottie was cooking breakfast on December 8, 1941, looking out her kitchen window at a sunlit stretch of green grass and listening to the news on the radio. The announcer was describing yesterday's attack by the Japanese on U.S. Army Air Corps bases in Hawaii. All the talk at church yesterday and in the neighborhood had been about war.

Families had huddled around the radio trying to comprehend the horrific news of the vicious attack and the implications for the United States. President Roosevelt would have no other choice but to declare war on Japan, everyone said. People in California and the West Coast felt especially vulnerable, fearing that the next attacks would hit them first.

Men were angry, women were worried, and children were frightened.

It was almost 10:30 when Buddy slouched into the room.

"Hey, Ma," he mumbled as he poured himself a cup of coffee. At 34, he seemed no closer to finding his way in life than he had at 18. He was a talented mechanic and machinist but his belligerent attitude often got him fired. As far as Lottie could tell he spent the rest of his time drinking and chasing cheap women. He stayed with her whenever he was out of work.

"Good morning," she replied brightly, grateful for his greeting however clumsy. "Have some eggs and toast?"

He grunted as she set a plate filled with food in front of him. She sat down with a cup of coffee to keep him company. She had eaten her own breakfast hours ago.

"See what a beautiful day it is," she offered. "I can't believe it's less than three weeks till Christmas. I still can't get used to all this sunshine for the Holidays, even after being here almost 10 years. The poinsettias and tea roses are in bloom and so beautiful."

"Hmmm." He scratched his armpit under his open shirt. His hair fell over his eyes and Lottie was sure he had worn the same pair of pants all week.

"I ironed your clean pants and put them in your closet with your shirts."

He mumbled. "Thanks, Ma." After the news of the attack came yesterday he and some buddies had gone out drinking. The bars were filled with angry men fueling their blood lust and building up each other's courage to fight the enemy. Buddy was hung over today.

"It's a nice day for a walk," she said to engage him in a conversation.

That produced another "hmm." It was hard to know what to say to Buddy. She had long ago given up trying to influence his behavior. They were two people who lived in the same world without having much in common. This wasn't the way she had envisioned her relationship with her son. He grew increasingly distant and remote, even as she tried to reawaken their former closeness. She was constantly disappointed, trying one thing after the other to squeeze a little warmth from him.

She felt much closer to her daughters. All she knew to do was to keep being the best mother she could to Buddy and pray that someday he would realize how much she loved him.

There was a slight pause on the radio and then a serious voice announced: "Ladies and gentlemen, please stand by for the President of the United States." Lottie turned up the volume and together they sat attentively in front of the radio. They heard Franklin Roosevelt's familiar voice declaring yesterday's attack on Hawaii "…a day that will live in infamy." Lottie made a mental note to look that word up when she got to work. The president went on to say that the Japanese attack had been an act of war and that the United States had no other choice than to declare war in return and aggressively fight the enemy. He spoke for only a few minutes but his message was direct and clear. Everyone knew that Congress would declare war that day. He tried to ask people to remain calm when he said, "There is nothing to fear but fear itself."

"Oh no," Lottie gasped. "I have been praying it wouldn't come to this." Buddy sat straighter in his chair and looked Lottie directly in her eyes. "Ma, I've got to go," he said in a firmer voice than she expected in his condition. He strode out of the room with a new purpose in his step, as if he had suddenly sobered up.

"Buddy," she called. "Buddy, where are you going? You didn't finish your breakfast."

She heard him rattling around in his bedroom then he came back into the kitchen, hair combed and dressed in the clean clothes she had ironed for him. He grabbed his coffee cup, and pecked her on the cheek. He said nothing as he jumped into his car but she knew where he was going. He came back hours later a little drunk, and told her he and his friends had enlisted in the Army Air Corps and would be leaving in 10 days after completing tests.

She sank into a chair, feeling that her legs wouldn't hold her up any longer. "But, Buddy. It's so dangerous."

He knelt beside her chair and took her hand and in his. In a rare tender moment of compassion he gently explained, "I just have to do it, Ma. I would be a yellow coward if I didn't. You don't want that, do you? Besides, I couldn't live with myself." He kissed the tears that were sliding down her cheeks. "It's going to be all right, Ma. I'll come home again. I promise!" She sat in the chair for a long time after he left, feeling numb and cold with fear.

Lottie's Lot

That night she prayed, "Dear God, don't take my boy away from me. Be merciful and take me first. I can't bear to lose another child. Amen."

The first time she saw him in his uniform with his hair trimmed and his tie in a perfect knot under his starched collar, she brimmed with pride to see the man she had long hoped her son would become. And then he was gone.

Every night she prayed for his safety and quick return. "Dear Lord, keep Buddy safe and let him come back to me whole." It became her daily mantra.

She wrote to him almost every day and sent him care packages filled with his favorite sugar cookies, toothpaste, and shaving cream, cigarettes, and candy bars when she could find them. She got a letter from him every few weeks. She knew he was a bombardier stationed in England; he was on a crew that flew over enemy territory, dropping bombs all over Europe. Germany, Belgium, Poland, Russia, Italy–it didn't matter; he was in a strange place a million miles away from her doing dangerous duty.

Fear for him welled up whenever she passed his room or stared at his empty chair at the table. She offered doubly intense prayers, holding God responsible for Buddy's safety.

Lottie followed the war news in the newspaper and on the radio, wanting to know what was happening and at the same time afraid to learn. Even the movies didn't offer escape; the newsreels showed entire towns destroyed by bombs dropped by the Allies. She hated knowing that her Buddy was killing innocent people. The news reported on "dog fights"-battles in the air between German and U.S. planes, and she trembled in dread that Buddy's plane had been shot down in an explosion of flames.

The entire nation was caught up in the war effort and all eligible young men were drafted. Her grandson Danny was drafted in April 1942 and Lottie added his name to her prayers. Of course, she assured God, she wanted all the American boys to be safe and she wanted America to win the war. But those were less important to her than bringing her son and grandson back home without injury as soon as possible.

In May, Lottie was surprised to get a call from Freddie inviting her to a performance of "Peter Pan" at his school; he was playing one of the lost boys. Shirley picked her up and brought her a corsage with a fresh orchid of the palest lavender. It looked beautiful against her light green dress. She settled into her seat beside Shirley and as the lights went down she saw Shirley's boyfriend Johnny sitting on Shirley's other side. Next to him was Hazel, who was wearing the same corsage.

Johnny took the group to Foster's Freeze for ice cream sundaes after the play. Shirley and Hazel praised Freddie's performance and Lottie added, "You really were the best one, Freddie. You should have played Peter Pan." Hazel caught her eye and smiled and Lottie smiled back.

In the ice cream parlor, their relationship began to thaw and soon Hazel and Lottie were chatting on the phone regularly. Lottie stopped by Hazel's apartment after work at the church one day and it became her regular practice to stop in a couple of times a week when she confirmed that C.C. wouldn't be there. Their close relationship was reestablished, but there were some things they couldn't discuss.

Lottie ranted on and on about her worries over Buddy whenever she visited her daughters. They were worried about him too but sometimes grew impatient with her tirades, especially Hazel.

"Ma, my son is in the war, too," she chided during a visit from Lottie in November 1942. "Don't you think I'm just as worried and scared as you are?"

Lottie's Lot

Hazel was distraught about Danny. Over the years she had resented him, hated him, and loved him, felt guilty about ignoring him. But now her feelings were clear. He was her son and she was terrified that he might be hurt or killed. To calm her fears she turned to her best friend the Canadian Club bottle.

"Well, of course you're worried, Hazel. But Danny's been to military school. Maybe he knows how to protect himself. I'm praying for him too. It's just that Buddy is so ..."

"Spoiled?"

When she saw the hurt look on her mother's face she apologized. "I know, Ma. I'm scared to death for both of them."

"I think the Lord wants us to do our best to support our boys," Lottie said. "I'm going to help the Red Cross when I'm not working. Why don't you come down with me tomorrow? We can make bandages and write letters and whatever they need."

"No. I can't. I'm not feeling so well." It was 2 o'clock in the afternoon and Hazel was still wearing her dressing gown.

Lottie peered at her and frowned. "Now that you mention it, you don't look quite right. Do you have a fever?" Lottie placed her palm on her daughter's forehead. "Do you have the flu?"

"I don't know what it is, Ma. I just don't have any energy and my stomach hurts a lot. It feels like it's getting bigger – but I'm sure as hell not pregnant," she said bitterly.

"I thought you were going to go to the doctor."

"I did and he said it's probably just the change of life and not to worry. You know I'm 50. He told me to take better care of myself."

Lottie frowned. "Did he tell you to drink more whiskey?"

"No," she snapped sarcastically. "But I *am* drinking more orange juice. See?" She poured some juice into her whiskey glass.

"Hazel ..."

"Don't start, Ma. I know what you're going to say."

"No, you don't. I was going to say, if you aren't feeling any better you should go back to the doctor or see another doctor."

"You're right," Hazel sighed. "C.C. made an appointment with a new doctor for tomorrow. We'll see what he has to say."

"Good. Ask him to do some tests," Lottie said. "I'm worried about you, daughter."

The next day as she prepared for her appointment, Hazel was shocked at what she saw in the mirror. Her grooming habits had become lazy, and today was the first time she had put on makeup or set her hair in several weeks.

"God, I look a hundred years old," she muttered to herself. What would the doctor think?

C.C. was putting on his tie and jacket, which he had laid out on his twin bed. "You look so tired, dear. I'm worried about you. As soon as you're ready I'll help you out to the car."

Dr. Harper's office was in a sleek new building on Wilshire Boulevard. Hazel seldom saw this part of Los Angeles. She had carefully chosen one of her nicer dresses and a diamond brooch C.C. had given her so she wouldn't look out of place among the well-dressed people getting out of their large shiny cars in the parking lot.

"You call me as soon as you get home, Hazel," Lottie told her on the phone. "I can get the bus and come right over."

In the examination room the doctor felt her belly and looked closely into her eyes. He asked about her bowel and bladder habits – were there any changes? He asked about her periods – had those changed? He also wanted to know how many children she had and their ages.

302

"They're grown. The oldest is 34. My youngest is serving overseas. He's just 20."

"Well, I'll bet you're proud."

When he asked if she found intercourse painful she stammered and finally said, "Sometimes." She didn't want to explain about her marriage with C.C.

"We need to do a pelvic examination," he said and called a nurse into the room. The nurse helped Hazel place her feet in the stirrups at the end of the table and Hazel lay back with her knees spread, embarrassed and afraid.

The doctor inserted a vaginal speculum and looked inside her with a light, then slid his fingers inside her and felt all around. Her embarrassment quickly gave way to pain.

"I'm sorry, Mrs. Fredericks, I don't mean to hurt you. But I do feel some swelling in here." He continued poking around. "I'm going to take a tiny bit of tissue from your cervix. Now you'll feel a little pinch," he said just as she felt it and let an "ouch" escape.

"There, we're done," the doctor said. "You can get dressed."

She dressed and waited, sitting on the edge of the cold steel examination table, her feet not quite touching the floor. She felt like a child waiting to be picked up from school.

The doctor came back in. "There are several possibilities and I don't want to alarm you," he said. "I did feel something odd on one of your ovaries but before we jump to any conclusions I am going to order some blood tests. You can get them done at the lab on the ground floor before you leave today. And we'll make an appointment for next week."

"Do I have a tumor?"

"I suspect so but it may just be benign, nothing to worry about. Let's get the results before we choose a course of treatment. I'll be able to give you more answers then."

She nodded. She didn't know much more than she had when she came in.

"Uhmm, I do need to ask one thing, Mrs. Fredericks, and I hope you won't be offended but we want the examination to be complete. Have you ever had a disease of the pelvic area, such as syphilis or gonorrhea?"

She felt the blood drain from her face. What kind of question was this?

"No, of course not. I'm not that kind of woman."

"I know, ma'am. I'm sure you aren't. But sometimes a person is exposed through contact with another who may not even know he is infected."

"Contact? Oh you mean ..."

"Yes, sexual contact. How long have you been married?"

Why does he want to know that? Hazel wondered. Then she realized he was suggesting C.C. could have given her the disease. But they had never ...

"Uhmm, about eight years. But I was married before."

"I see," the doctor said. "You could have been exposed many years ago and that could be the reason for the symptoms you have now. We'll know more after the tests are done."

On the drive home, she told C.C. that the doctor had taken some tissue from her insides and she had some blood tests. She didn't mention the tumor or the doctor's other suggestion to him or to Lottie when she phoned her later.

While she waited for the results, one thought played over and over in her mind: a venereal disease! What a strange thing for him to mention! Hazel thought those were diseases of sailors and prostitutes and people who slept around. She had only been intimate with two men in her life – George Hopf and Roy Darden – oh yeah, and that bastard Gus Stover.

George was so religious and so careful about everything he ate or touched. How could he have had such a disease? And Roy had been married and faithful until he met Hazel, as far as she knew. Still he was so perfect for her, never cheated on her; surely such an ugly disease couldn't have been a part of him.

Hazel worried and wondered. Ignoring the beautiful spring weather, she sat on the apartment porch and drank and smoked while she brooded. Maybe it was just a mistake or a wrong guess by the doctor. Or maybe life was dealing her another bad hand.

She asked Charlotte to drive her to the next appointment and told Lottie, "I really want you to come with me, Ma." She didn't know how she would tell them if she did have syphilis or gonorrhea but she wanted them near.

Dr. Harper invited her into his office, saying he didn't need to examine her today. "Can my mother and my sister come in with me?" Hazel asked.

"Of course, if you would like them to."

They sat in his spacious office with its glass tables and blond furniture and a view out the picture window of rows of identical palm trees. "Please take a seat." He studied some papers on his desk. Then he looked up and spoke in a serious tone. "I'm afraid we've found something that could be bad. I want you to see a specialist, a gynecologist, who knows more about these things than I do."

"A gyn...?" None of the women understood his words.

"The results of the tests showed some cancerous cells."

"Cancer!" Hazel felt the blood rush to her face. She felt faint and dizzy.

"I'm sorry," the doctor said. "It appears that you have cancer in your female organs." He quickly explained the anatomy of the female reproductive system with a plastic model on his desk and a drawing he gave her to keep and study when she felt calmer. He couldn't be sure just where the cancer was located but probably in her ovaries.

Hazel was in with shock. Charlotte held her sister's hand while Lottie put a handkerchief over her own mouth to stifle her cries.

"Mrs. Fredericks, I've spoken to the specialist, Dr. Rogers, and sent him your records." He handed her a card. "He can tell you more including what treatments are available. He worked you into his schedule and can see you at 3 this afternoon. He's just upstairs. I recommend you see him today."

He rose and the women knew he was finished with them. They walked silently out of his office, holding onto each other.

"Thank you, doctor," Lottie said as they left.

After examining Hazel and the test results Dr. Rogers met with the three women in his office. He told them he thought Hazel had a lemon-sized tumor on her right ovary and a smaller one on the left ovary.

"The only way to know exactly where the cancer is located and the extent of it is to operate. We can remove the organs but I must advise you that by this point it's possible the cancerous cells have spread to the uterus and liver and other organs. If that's the case surgery would only speed up the inevitable."

He said gently," Would you like to set a time for surgery?"

"No. I need to think about this. I can't take it in. I don't understand." She reached for a cigarette but decided against it. She needed a drink.

"I understand but it's important to act quickly. At this time our choices are limited."

"At this time?" Charlotte asked. "Do you mean if you had found it earlier, it would have been easier to cure?"

"In a sense, yes. You see, most women only have an examination of their reproductive systems when they are expecting a baby. But if they had regular pelvic exams even after they've stopped having children, we could see problems such as tumors much earlier. Without the exam we don't know anything until you start having pain and discomfort in your belly. And sometimes by that time ...."

"Are there any other choices besides surgery, doctor?" Lottie asked.

"We can give her pain medication to keep her comfortable."

"Are you telling us that she is going to die?" Charlotte couldn't breathe. That dreaded and hateful word!

"I'm afraid that's the likely outcome when the cancer is this far advanced," he avoided Hazel's eyes.

"How much time does she have?" Charlotte had to ask.

"It's hard to tell exactly. But ovarian cancer – if that proves to be what she has -- goes fast and spreads quickly to other organs. So I would say it's a matter of months."

The three women drove home in near silence except for stares and sniffles. They had no words to express how they were feeling. Even Lottie couldn't find anything to say in the face of the shocking news. How could she stand losing another child?

CHAPTER 20

Hazel decided to keep her news a secret from the rest of the family until after Christmas. She didn't want to spoil the holiday for everyone. She told C.C. she was fine just a little tired. In the new year Lottie visited frequently when C.C. was at work or out of town, and they discussed the decisions Hazel had to make.

Hazel saw Dr. Rogers in March 1944 and told him she had decided to have the surgery. He scheduled it for the following week. Then she asked, "Do you think this was caused by a venereal disease, doctor? If I had one, I never knew it."

"Your blood tests showed syphilitic cells. I'd say you've had syphilis for about 30 years."

Thirty years! 1913? George Hopf!

"But how can that be? I was never sick. My ex-husband never said anything about it."

Dr. Rogers nodded. "That is the problem with syphilis. You may not even know you have it. For women a sore – what we call a chancre -- may be up inside of them. A man would have a chancre on his penis but get treatment and think he was healed. But you're never really healed. The bacteria linger in the body dormant; then the disease can return with vengeance years later. If he had it he might not have known it himself."

"Maybe that's what happened to George," she said.

"Yes it could be. The symptoms are like a mild flu so you wouldn't even suspect it was anything else without getting a vaginal examination. Women can pass it on to their children."

"Oh my God!" He waited a moment for her to absorb the information.

"Once the bacteria are in a woman's body she can pass them on to her fetus. We don't know all the answers yet but there is a lot of research going on right now. Did you have any children with this ex-husband?"

"Yes, we had a son, Kenny. And I had another son with my second husband. What about him? Could he have been infected too? We were married after I divorced George." She shook nervously, afraid to hear the answers.

"Him too. It can affect any children or spouses you have after exposure. Did either of your sons have skin sores or rashes when they were young?"

"No." Hazel kept shaking her head, as if to make the bad news go away.

"What about soft teeth? Seizures? Slow development?"

She shook her head no.

"Those are some of the identified symptoms for congenital syphilis. But your sons could have other problems later in life with the liver, bones, or skin, or even in their thinking – really any system in the body."

Hazel was overwhelmed by so much information. It was more than she could take in. "My daughter would be OK, wouldn't she?" she asked. "She was born before I met George."

"If you're sure that this George is the one who infected you then your daughter wouldn't have any risk. But I believe you should warn your two sons and your husband and urge them to be tested."

He rose from his desk and held out his hand. "I'll see you next week for surgery. Good luck."

Hazel returned to the waiting room and where C.C. was waiting and followed her out. As they drove home she explained what the doctor had said about syphilis, trying to be calm and objective the way Dr. Rogers had been. But that was impossible. She slammed her hand hard on the car's dashboard. "Goddamn George Hopf!" she cried out. "He did this. He gave me syphilis but he didn't tell me and now it's killing me. He is still hurting me after all these years!"

C.C. reached a hand over and patted her on the arm. She wasn't finished screaming.

"I thought George Hopf was long in the past but he's come back to have one last laugh. I wonder where that son of a bitch is now." She threw her cigarette out the window and lit another one. "I hope he died a long and painful death."

Neither Hazel nor her son Kenny had heard from George since the divorce. The ex-husband who had been so adamant about seeing his son had moved away and lost touch with him before he reached his teens.

"How can I tell Kenny and Danny? What should I tell them? I hate George Hopf! I want him to know what he's done!"

"The boys haven't been sick or had any problems that the doctor talked about, have they?" C.C. asked. "They're probably fine. But you do whatever you think is best."

Hazel felt a rare wave of affection for C.C. He knew she didn't love him but he was always helpful and supportive. She was grateful for his kindness since she had been sick. He knew much more than she did about the world and she tended to take his advice on many things.

"I'll bet you're right, C.C. Besides, they can't get the kind of cancer I got – they're men! I just want to find George Hopf – and kill him."

C.C. smiled. "All right, Hazel. If that's what you want I'll look for him."

Lottie's Lot

That night she woke up suddenly about 3 am. She got out of bed quietly, not waking C.C. in the other bed or Freddie in the other room, and walked into the living room and looked out the window. The world was silent and still. She was surprised at the brightness of the stars.

She remembered something; both the boys had had soft teeth and needed dentures in their teens. How could she have forgotten that when the doctor asked? But how could soft teeth have anything to do with syphilis? she asked herself. There was no need to disturb the boys with this news.

C.C. hired a private detective to look for George Hopf. The detective looked in Detroit where the family had last seen him, in Pittsburgh where he was born, and in Edmonton, Canada, where they had lived when they were married. He checked military discharge records and police records across the United States and Canada but found no trace of a George Hopf. They told Hazel that he seemed to have disappeared off the face of the earth.

Dr. Rogers removed Hazel's ovaries, cervix, and uterus. After the surgery he said, "With luck we may have gotten all of the cancer. We'll hope for the best."

Hazel had several good months after she recovered from surgery and told herself the cancer was gone. She spent a couple of summer months in Silverado Canyon with Freddie, enjoying the cooler temperatures and the tranquility. But early in 1945 the abdominal pain and fatigue returned, this time twice as bad as before. The doctor confirmed that the cancer was back and there was nothing to do except to medicate her for pain.

C.C. cut back on his work hours and stayed home with her most of the time. Hazel depended on him to help her get comfortable in bed, bring her meals, and give her medication. He let her drink as much as she wanted, knowing it helped her bear the pain.

Lottie, Shirley, Charlotte, and Lois agreed to take turns, each staying two days and nights in the apartment's second bedroom. They prepared meals, bathed Hazel, read to her, and took care of any other needs. They agreed to declare a truce with C.C. and to put Hazel's needs first. It was a small space and they needed to make it a peaceful place for Hazel.

Lottie took Freddie, home with her. He moved into Buddy's old room. Lottie saw that the boy ate properly and got to school on time, and took him to church. She tried to teach him right from wrong and good manners. His presence helped take her mind off Buddy and Hazel for a little while each day. He had a key and let himself in after school when Lottie was on duty at Hazel's. One of his aunts would come by to make dinner and spend the night and get him off to school the next day. He often asked about his grandma Hazel and visited her a few times.

Shirley, sometimes took Freddie to a movie or to the beach, but was happy to let her grandmother handle his day-to-day care, leaving her free to go out at night to parties and nightclubs, just as she had let Hazel take care of him when he was small. She gave Lottie money from her waitressing jobs whenever she had some extra.

By 1944, Freddie was a well-behaved 10-year-old. He always combed his hair just so and was careful not to get food or dirt on his clothes. He did whatever his mother, grandmother, or great-grandmother told him to do – in fact, what any adult told him to do. Lottie frequently remarked, "You're such a good boy, Freddie."

Shirley couldn't understand why her son was so precise about his dress and his manners. He never seemed to enjoy the things other kids liked. She hadn't seen him laugh or look happy since he was a toddler.

One Sunday in late June 1944 she decided to take Freddie and his cousins, Paul and David, for an outing at Silverado Canyon. "Come on, boys. The creek is waiting!" she shouted as they piled into the car with their swimming and fishing gear.

"Gosh, Aunt Shirl, you're the fastest driver I ever saw," Charlotte's son Paul said as they zipped past one car after another on the two-lane road. She shouted "Slowpoke!" at each car they passed. Freddie chewed his fingernails to the quick as he watched the orange groves speed past on either side of the curving road. He hoped they would make it to the cabin and back alive.

They got to the cabin in record time – barely two hours. Paul and David, Lois's son, scrambled out of the car and ran for the creek, jumping in with loud whoops. Freddie went into the house to change into his swim trunks.

"Come on, Freddie. I'll race you," his mother shouted, peeling off her shorts and shirt to reveal a tight dark green swimsuit underneath. She skipped and ran ahead, trying to get Freddie to chase her or catch her. He let her win. She splashed her way down the creek and watched him step gingerly into the water. This is why she was happy to let Hazel and Lottie raise Freddie. She didn't want to deal with a kid's moods and problems. This kid didn't even know how to play.

The three boys caught tadpoles and salamanders. Shirley paddled around in the deepest part of the creek, which was only about 4 feet deep, and frequently stood up and stretched her arms and legs. She wondered if there was anyone around who could see how good she looked.

They grilled hamburgers and ate them with a potato salad Charlotte had sent along, wiping their greasy hands on their clothes as often as on napkins. When they were done with the burgers she ordered, "Go get the watermelon, David," as she sipped more Canadian Club from her coffee cup. At the edge of the creek 14-year-old David bent down and lifted the green watermelon out of the water. She cut slices for them from the sweet red center.

"No wading for half an hour!" Shirley shouted after they ate. David and Paul chased each other through the trees, and Freddie cleared the table and put the leftover food into boxes, which he placed in the car trunk.

"Thanks, hon," she said to her son as she poured another drink and closed her eyes.

After dozing for a few minutes she went into the cabin to wash her hands. Searching for soap she opened a cabinet and saw several bottles of whiskey at the back. She found a stepstool and got two of the bottles down. The next cabinet revealed a set of sturdy clear glasses. "I can use those," she said to herself. She found an empty box and put the glasses and bottles in it.

She continued searching. Soon the box held a coffeepot, some bars of soap, and a half-empty box of cereal. She headed for Hazel's bedroom. There she looked in the dresser drawers and the closet but found only a yellow dress with a stain on it.

"Freddie," she called, looking around. "Did you leave any clothes or toys here?"

He got down on the floor and looked under one of the beds, pulling out a baseball bat and some toy six-guns.

"Just these," he said.

"In the box," she gestured. "Then help me with this."

They moved the dresser away from the wall, and to her surprise Shirley saw something taped to the back of the dresser.

"Mama, you sly dog," she said, and pulled the package away. Inside, wrapped in several layers of newspaper she found an ordinary wristwatch and an old, thin wedding ring. She looked at them and felt some stirring of recognition. This was Hazel's wedding ring from Roy Darden and a watch he had bought her!

314

"Oh, Mama, why couldn't you hide something worth some money?" She threw the pieces into the box.

She found Freddie sitting in the front room.

"Don't you ever play?" she asked him before seeing him wipe tears from his eyes.

"Hey, what's the matter, baby?" she asked as she sat beside him.

He was staring at the locked door to C.C.'s room and she looked too.

"There's a padlock on it. Did you leave something in there?"

He shook his head.

"Then what is it?"

"Shirl, why am I named Frederick?" he asked, taking her totally by surprise.

"My God, kid, you think of the weirdest things. Oh, I don't remember. It's a good name."

"Am I named after Grandpa C.C.? His last name is Fredericks."

She gasped at the sudden memory. "Well. Yes, in fact you are."

"Is he my father?"

"No! Good God, Freddie. Where would you get an idea like that?"

He frowned at her, clearly not satisfied with her answers.

Shirley said, "All right, I'll tell you. When I was expecting you I was broke. Your father, that louse, was long gone and I had to move in with Ma and C.C. He agreed to pay my medical bills on one condition: If I had a boy I had to name him Frederick. I had no choice so I agreed."

Freddie looked at the floor.

"Look, son, if you don't like that name, change it. That's what I did. I told you, didn't I, that I was named Abigail after a grandmother I never met? So when I was 15…"

"I hate him," he whispered, interrupting her tale.
"What?"

"I hate Grandpa C.C."

Her blood went cold as Lottie's story about C.C. flashed into her mind.

"Freddie, did C.C. ever … I've heard some things, that C.C. may have … touched some children. Did he ever do anything strange or scary to you?"

Freddie was silent, still looking down.

"Now look, Freddie, if he did it isn't your fault. You're not in trouble but I need to know."

She could barely hear him as he answered. "He used to make me get in the bed with him, and then he would take off my clothes and he would take off his and…"

"Oh my God!" she shrieked, not letting him finish his story. "He did it to you, didn't he? That son of a bitch! Come on, Freddie. We need to go see Gram."

She ran toward the car. Freddie stared at his mother. Did she want to know what happened or not? Why did she ask him if she wasn't going to hear the whole answer?

"Paul! David!" She yelled for the boys and they came out of the creek.

"What is it, Shirl?" David asked.

"Quick, get in the car. We've got to go."

"What's the big hurry?" Paul asked.

Lottie's Lot

"Come on, come on. Hurry up. Don't ask questions." She threw them some towels. "Wrap up in these. Come on. We have to hurry. Get all your things and get in the car....now."

As soon as they were all in the car, she floored the gas pedal and zoomed down the mountain road, one sharp curve after another. The boys bounced against each other in the back seat and gaped wide-eyed as she swooped around cars and barely missed hitting two of them head-on in the left lane.

"Shirl, slow down!" David yelled but Shirley acted like she'd forgotten they were there. She smoked one cigarette after another, swearing at the traffic all the way back to town, and passing every car that loomed in front of her.

When she pulled up at Paul's house Charlotte came out to greet them. "Did you have fun?" she asked the boys with a big smile as David and Paul jumped out of the car, shivering in the cool night air.

Shirley called out from the driver's seat, "Gotta go." And she sped away.

"Gram!" Shirley shouted as she entered the apartment, dragging Freddie behind her. "Gram, he did it to Freddie!"

"Whatever are you shouting about, Shirley?" Lottie asked, wiping her hands on her apron as she emerged from the kitchen.

"C.C. He got Freddie. Oh I hate him, I'm going to murder him."

Lottie sat down and looked at Freddie. "Oh no." She had an urge to hug him but he was too big for that sort of nonsense.

"Freddie, I just took some peanut butter cookies out of the oven," she said. "Why don't you go in the kitchen and see if they've cooled down enough to eat?" He did as she told him. "Pour yourself a big glass of milk, Honey," she called after him.

317

"Now Shirley, calm down," she said. "Tell me what you're talking about."

Shirley told her the story. "I have to do something, Gram. I was … I was afraid to ask him all these years but he finally told me. What do I do now?"

"First of all, you can try being a better mother to your son."

"Yes, yes, I know I'm no good as a mother. That's why I need you and Ma."

"But you *are* his mother. He needs you," Lottie said. "Let him talk about it if he wants do. Don't make him feel it was his fault."

"I already told him that. He knows he's not in trouble."

"Shirley, it took me a long time to learn how to be a good mother and I still have a lot to learn. Try to remember, this is his pain, not just yours."

"It needs to be C.C.'s pain." She started to light a cigarette, then remembered where she was. One of Lottie's no-nos.

Lottie wasn't sure what to do either. "All right," she said. "Don't do anything tonight. Let's talk about it tomorrow."

"OK. But I'm coming by tomorrow morning and we're going to figure this out."

"Why don't you stay and have supper with us? I think that would mean a lot to Freddie."

"Yeah, the poor kid. I'd love to stay but I promised to meet some friends." She stood and gathered her things. "Tell Freddie goodbye for me, will you?" And she ran across the lawn to her car as if she couldn't get away fast enough.

Lottie joined Freddie in the kitchen, where he had eaten two cookies. Then he sat at the table to wait for her.

"Where's Shirl?" he asked.

"Oh, she had to go," Lottie replied. "But she said to tell you she enjoyed the outing. She hopes you had a good time."

"Hmmm."

"I know life hasn't been easy for you, Freddie." She patted his hand. "It hasn't been easy for any of us." Lottie wanted to say the right thing to her great-grandson but wasn't sure what that was. "Help me set the table," she said. He obeyed and they ate dinner in silence.

The next morning Shirley made her usual boisterous entrance. Freddie had gone to school, and Lottie was cleaning up after breakfast. She poured Shirley a cup of coffee and stared pointedly at the cigarette Shirley took out of her purse. She put it back.

"I've decided, Gram. I'm going to call the police."

"That won't help. You have no evidence."

"Sure I do. Freddie will tell them what happened." Her eyes burned with eagerness.

"Freddie will be scared and they won't believe him," Lottie cautioned. "They'll think he is just saying something you told him to say. They'll say, why didn't he come forward before? And do you really want to put your son through a police interrogation?"

"I'll make them listen. They'll believe me when they see how upset I am."

Lottie shook her head. "It isn't enough. But there's one thing I can do."

They drove to Hazel's and sat beside her bed and talked about things of no consequence – movies Shirley had seen, a new outfit she'd bought, the latest news from Buddy. It was Lottie's turn to stay the night.

Nancy O'Connor

Hazel said softly, "Oh, here. I want to show you." She was fairly lucid today. "Hand me that letter," she said, and Shirley handed her a paper that been folded and unfolded many times.

Danny had sent a photo of himself in front of a fancy stone building.

"That's a church in France. He's going to all the French towns and chasing the Germans out."

"Well, Hazel, I guess our boys are winning the war," Lottie said proudly. "I've lost count of the bombing missions Buddy has been on. All I want to know is when they're coming back."

Shirley asked more questions about her brother and Lottie excused herself. She stopped in the bathroom and took a deep breath.

In the kitchen C.C. was fussing with dishes and food. "Oh hello," he said as he saw Lottie enter. "Just making my girl some lunch."

She nodded. "Would you step outside with me for just a moment, C.C.?"

"What? Well, I guess so." He followed her out of the apartment and down the stairs to the first landing.

"We had an interesting talk with Freddie yesterday," Lottie began.

"Oh, how is the boy? Hazel misses having him around. I hope he'll come and visit soon."

"I'm sure he'll visit Hazel soon." She waited a beat. "He told us everything."

"What?" and in a moment his expression changed from composed to guarded. He lowered his voice and spoke with slow deliberateness. "When are you going to shut up about that nonsense, you old fool? You don't know anything. You think anyone is going to believe you and that scaredy-cat boy?"

"Yes, they will. Very soon. Shirley's already called the police."

320

"That little tart! Hah! You couldn't find a worse witness. She doesn't know anything about her own son." His voice was threatening but controlled. He straightened to his full imposing height and took a step toward her and looked down. Lottie didn't budge. She noticed that his hands were sweaty and making fists and his face was flushed.

She in turn stood at her full 5 foot 8 inches and looked up into his eyes. "There is one thing that I know for certain, C.C. Sin will always catch up with you. Not always how we expect it, but someday in some way you'll pay. I hope you pay on this earth, but if not here then I know you'll have an eternity to burn in hell. I hope the devil has a special room with extra-large flames for you."

C.C. snickered. Then he walked past her, brushing her shoulder, and went back into the apartment. "You and your fire and brimstone thinking, old lady. *Leave me alone.*"

Back in the kitchen he leaned on the counter and took several deep breaths to calm his racing heart.

CHAPTER 21

After spending two nights at Hazel's Lottie returned home feeling sad and exhausted. She realized that her precious daughter was slipping away from this life and it broke her heart. She did all she could do to keep Hazel comfortable, at the same time struggling to suppress her feelings of grief in front of Hazel. Watching her suffer was almost unbearable.

After confronting C.C. on the stairs, Lottie held her tongue inside the apartment. He went out for several hours each day, and when he was at home he walked past Lottie as if she weren't there. She moved into Hazel's bedroom and slept in the C.C.'s bed next to her daughter. He didn't object. Lottie knew he was depressed about Hazel too, but that didn't excuse what he had done. She kept her rage under control. Hazel didn't need anything to add to her misery in her last days.

At 73, Lottie didn't sleep well most nights, even at home. She woke several times to go to the bathroom, and then stayed awake worrying about her problems. At home sometimes she napped for a couple of hours. She was always tired. She couldn't stop her worrying about Hazel, and she was still caring for Freddie. She felt like she was on an emotional roller coaster, sad one moment, afraid the next and angry when C.C showed his face.

She decided to have a good talk with Reverend Walker. Even though she no longer worked at the church, they had remained good friends. She trusted him. He always took time to listen to her and she respected his counsel and guidance. His comforting words restored her self-confidence, especially when her faith was faltering. She called and set a time to visit with him.

"How is Hazel doing, Lottie?" he asked as they settled into their familiar comfortable chairs. He knew her family members intimately and never forgot a name.

"Oh, Reverend, it's awful. I just spent the last two nights there and she's in so much pain. We give her more opiates and then she can hardly wake up."

"I'm so sorry to hear that. I can see the toll it's taking on you."

"Yes, I'm very tired –what with worrying about Buddy, and taking care of Freddie, and Hazel's illness. It's too much for an old lady."

"Oh Lottie, you'll never get old." He gave her a big warm smile. She smirked.

"I'm already old! But the problem I told you about when I started working here – it's come up again."

"You mean Hazel's husband? Has he molested someone else?"

"It's Freddie. He told his mother that C.C. had touched him when he was little."

"I'm so sorry. The Lord has given you many heavy burdens. And He will help you to carry them. What can I do to help?"

"I'm not sure what to do next. Shirley is furious and wants to hurt him."

"That won't solve the problem. Will it?"

"No, I don't think so either. I've talked to my daughters and they believe me."

"Have you prayed for divine guidance?"

"Yes, I pray all the time. And I appreciate your prayers too."

"Then let's pray together now."

They closed their eyes and Walker began a prayer that mentioned all of Lottie's troubles. "Our Father, help your loyal servant, Lottie. Make her heart easier, and hold her in Your mighty hand and comfort her through these dark times. Give her the strength and wisdom to do Your will. In Your name we pray. Amen."

His words and his understanding and support moved her to tears. Sometimes she felt so alone. With him she felt safe being vulnerable and crying. It seemed to lighten her burden even for a little while. He reassured her that it was all right to be sad and not to have all the answers.

"May I ask one more thing?" she wiped her eyes. He nodded.

"I know Hazel doesn't have much time left – maybe just a few days. She's already lived a year longer than they predicted. My greatest wish is that she could see her boys one more time. I've written to Kenny and he's on his way. But I don't know what to do about Danny. Do you know if the Army would let him come home because his mother is dying?"

He nodded and jotted a note. "Yes, Lottie, I think the Red Cross can intervene to get him home. I'll look into it today and let you know."

She thanked him again for his friendship and help. She went home with a lighter step and headed for the kitchen to bake cookies. When Freddie came home she said, "I've got fresh cookies. And if you can guess what kind they are, I'll let you eat some before dinner."

Freddie smiled at the idea and sniffed around. He headed to the kitchen and took in a deep whiff. "Oh, Gram, they're peanut butter. my favorite!"

"Well, I can't fool you. Here you are." She placed a plate with four warm cookies and a glass of cold milk on the table. "We can treat ourselves now and then, can't we?" With a wink and a grin she helped herself to a cookie.

She wanted to give Freddie some of the sweetness and fun he had missed out on. The boy seemed so serious, so sad. He touched her heart in a way most of her grandchildren never had. Maybe I'm getting softhearted in my old age, she told herself with a smile.

Lottie found ways to show Freddie her love without hugging or saying the words. She struggled to figure out how to tell him she knew about C.C.'s abuse and that he shouldn't think it was his fault. One night at dinner she said, "Freddie. I know you told your mother about the bad things that C.C. did. It was brave of you to tell her."

"Shirl got mad."

"But not at you. Oh no, she was mad at C.C. and I am too. He's a bad man."

"But Nan Nan loves him, I think. I mean she's married to him. Does she know he's bad?"

"Well, it's difficult to explain. Sometimes people care for somebody even though they're bad or they need that person in some way even if they don't always love them. Do you understand?"

Freddie looked puzzled. "No, not really."

"Well, you will when you grow up. But right now, with your Nan Nan is so sick, we can't really do anything about it and we don't want to upset her."

"I know. We must be very nice," he played with his fork. "She's going to die, isn't she?"

"Yes, I'm afraid she is, and pretty soon. We're all very sad. You can go see her whenever you want, and I, Shirl or someone will be with you. You don't ever have to be alone with C.C."

Freddie nodded. "I'm not afraid of him anymore. I think he only hurts little kids."

"I think you're right. You're a smart boy, Freddie, and you're brave." She hesitated. "But if you ever want to tell me anything more about what he did when he bothered you or made you do things you didn't want to do, or if you remember something you had forgotten, you can tell me. I know it wasn't your fault."

"Thank you, Gram."

Lottie prayed for Hazel that night as she did every night. "Lord God my savior! Please don't let her suffer any more." She had never dreamed she would ever pray for a child of hers to die. But humbly, and with a tiny bit of guilt, she pleaded, "If you have to take her, please spare her from any more pain. Let her soul rest in peace." She continued to pray each night for Buddy to come home safe and for Danny, too.

That night she added, "And please help me be a good Gram to Freddie. Lighten his heart so he can be a happy child. And give me guidance about C.C."

Lottie gave Freddie a camera for his birthday. He had fun taking pictures of her and other family members. He showed her one that a friend took of him at school.

"Oh, that's nice. We should have taken more pictures of you when you were smaller."

Freddie looked at her and opened his mouth.

"Gram, I just remembered something."
"What, Dear? Did you forget to bring your school books home?"

"No, no, that's not it. I remembered that C.C. took pictures of me."

Lottie's stomach did a flip flop.

"When did he take your picture, Freddie?" she asked gently.

"You know, when he ... you know."

"Oh." She couldn't think why C.C. would want pictures of the children he used. But there was much she didn't know about C.C. Or about this insane attraction he had to children. Did it have a name? The detective said it was "more common that anyone knows." If she could find out something more, maybe she could take some real action against him. She went to the library and looked in the card catalog under "molesting" and "children, molestation" and similar terms. There were no books under those topics, and she was too embarrassed to ask the librarian for help. Apparently this was something no one talked about or wrote about.

The next day she asked Charlotte, Lois, and Shirley to come by for coffee. When she told them what Freddie had said about pictures, they exchanged a look.

Shirley jumped to her feet and clenched her fists. She declared, "Goddamn son of a bitch. He's dead! He's a dead man."

"Shirl, calm down," Charlotte said, annoyed. "Just give me a minute." To Lottie, she spoke calmly. "Ma, I've heard that people like C.C. sometimes take pictures of children, so they can, uh, look at them later. Did Freddie say anything else? What kind of pictures?"

"Was he naked?" Shirley asked.

"What? Oh my heavens. I don't know. He didn't say what kind of pictures. I didn't ask him. I didn't know ...."

"I know, Ma. It's all right," Charlotte said, and drained her coffee cup. "Well, I think it's time we broke into that locked room at Silverado Canyon. I don't know why I didn't think of this before. Clarence and I can drive up on Saturday. Who's going with me?"

Shirley grabbed her arm. "Oh no, no, no, no. We're not waiting! I'm going today. Are you coming with me, Aunt Charlotte?"

"You're not going without me," Lottie said.

"Ma, are you sure?"

"Damn right I'm sure," she said, her eyes widening when she heard herself curse.

"OK, let's go."

They scrambled into their jackets and Lottie washed the coffee cups.

"Gram, come on!" Shirley tapped her foot and grabbed the doorknob.

"Just one moment, Young Lady. I have to take care of your son."

Shirley rolled her eyes, then flung herself on the couch as Lottie knocked on the door of the next apartment. She asked her neighbor to look in on Freddie when he got back from school. "There's meatloaf in the refrigerator. Just see that he gets supper. I'll be back this evening."

It was Lois's turn to stay with Hazel, so the three of them were free to go. They got into Charlotte's car and headed north. She drove purposefully but kept to the speed limit.

"Charlotte, let me drive!" Shirley said. "We'll never get there at this rate."

"We *will* get there at this rate, Shirley," Charlotte said. "Paul told me how you drove when you took the boys to the cabin. I don't think my son will be riding with you anymore. Or my mother."

Shirley pouted as they drove through the orange groves, listening to the war news on the radio. Lottie decided to broach the subject of Shirley's drinking.

"I worry about how much you drink."

"What?" Shirley was shocked to be chastised by her grandmother.

"It's time you grew up and settled down. You act like an immature teenager going out every night, drinking and who knows what else. You have a son that needs you."

"I don't have a drinking problem. I just like to have fun...and...I don't think it's any of your business."

Lottie's Lot

"It is when I have the responsibility of raising him. He needs you and wants you to be a mother to him." Shirley slouched and looked out the window. She knew Lottie was right but didn't want to give up being a playgirl.

Lottie was on a roll.

"You're following in the footsteps of your mother, drinking too much. You need to get control of your life … the sooner the better."

No one had had the courage to confront Shirley so directly before but Lottie had nothing more to lose and taking care of Freddie, as much as she cared for the boy was an extra burden right now.

"Okay. I'll go to Alcoholics Anonymous. Does that make you happy?"

"Good. Tomorrow then. Is that a promise?"

"Yes." Shirley sniped.

Charlotte grinned as she looked in the rear view mirror. Good for you, Ma, she thought. It's about time someone told her off.

They got to the cabin about noon, and Charlotte took a hand ax out of the car trunk. They went inside quickly and she broke off the padlock. With another hit, the doorknob broke off too. She pushed the door open.

The room was neat and tidy with a bed, a night table, a small dresser, and a tall cedar wardrobe. Charlotte opened the wardrobe and looked at the shelves that filled one side of it.

"Wow, this looks like an expensive camera," Charlotte said. "Made in Germany, before the war no doubt." She took out a tripod and several lenses. "He's got a lot of film in here and…" She noticed a door on the other side of the room and opened it to see a small windowless room with a sink. "Ah, he's got a darkroom in here. So he can develop all this film himself."

Shirley was yanking dresser drawers open. "There's nothing in here but some underwear and old clothes," she said in disgust.

Lottie went to the big wardrobe. On the inside of the door against the wall, a hook held a wrinkled suit on a hanger.

"I guess he took most of his clothes back to Grace Place," she said, as she pulled back a curtain that covered half the wardrobe. "Oh my heavens!" she said. "Look at this. These aren't *his* clothes."

Behind the curtain were two clothes rods, one about three feet below the other. They were covered with tiny clothes pinned to hangers – little dresses and suits, shirts, children's shorts, and pinafores in different colors. She reached for a couple of the outfits – a cowboy suit with its own little metal gun, a princess dress, a ballerina costume, a fake leather pilot's jacket.

Shirley grabbed more of the clothes and threw them on the floor. "These are cheap junk," she said. "But I guess kids wouldn't know the difference."

"Shirley, don't mess everything up. You know we might find some evidence that could be important," Lottie warned her and rehanging the clothes.

Charlotte was on her hands and knees on the floor, reaching under the bed. She pulled out a long flat box and set it on the bed. A leather clasp held it closed. "He's got four or five of these boxes under here."

They gathered around as she opened the box. All three gasped mouths opened and their hands flew to shield their eyes from the graphic scenes before them. There were stacks of photographs of children – some in regular clothes, some in costumes, some naked in suggestive poses.

Shirley yanked one stack of the photos out of the box. "Oh my God, it's Freddie," she cried, pawing through them. "He was about 5 years old here. God, here he is wearing that cowboy costume." Suddenly she screamed and started to tear the pictures in half.

"Let me see, Shirl," Charlotte said and grabbed them. They both pulled at the pictures.

"No, no, no, no, no, NO!" Shirley howled. "Nobody can see these. My baby, my boy! Oh my poor boy!" Her grip loosened and Charlotte looked at the pictures. There was Freddie in his underwear. In three pictures the boy was naked.

Shirley reached for the photos again but Charlotte held on. "It's horrible, Shirley, but you can't destroy them. We need them. We can show them to the police!" Shirley moaned again, sounding like a dying animal, and frantically flailed her arms toward the boxes of pictures. Lottie and Charlotte stood in front of the bed to keep her from seizing any more photos.

"Now, Honey, just calm...."

"Shut up, Gram! Don't tell me to calm down!" Her eyes wildly looked about for something to vent her anger on. She snatched up a dresser drawer, and banged it against the wall until it broke into pieces. She grabbed at the camera but Charlotte seized it. "Shirley, don't break the camera. It's evidence."

Shirley collapsed, exhausted, and sat panting on the floor.

As she caught her breath, Charlotte continued opening the boxes. There were more photographs, all neatly organized in small stacks held together by rubber bands. She picked up several stacks and leafed through them. "There are duplicates in here, four and five copies sometimes. I wonder if he was selling these photos to other men like him. Maybe that's where he got his money. Christ, there must be hundreds of pictures here, dozens of children."

She pulled out one stack and slid the pictures under a pillow. Lottie started to open her mouth but Charlotte shook her head and Lottie said nothing.

When she opened the third larger fastened box, she gasped, "Oh, Jesus. Oh sweet Jesus!"

"What is it, Charlotte? Who is it?" Lottie asked.

"It's magazines." She was turning pages and muttering. "This is so sick. That sick son-of-a-bitch…. That goddamn creep."

Shirley stood up and glanced at the magazine. "My God, I can't take it," she cried, and headed for the kitchen. She had brought along a quart of whiskey and poured herself a large drink.

Lottie picked up a magazine.

"Don't, Ma. I don't want you to see." Charlotte tried to take the magazine from her.

"I have to see, Charlotte. I have to know."

Lottie opened the magazine and saw pictures of children, even babies. They were all naked. Some had their legs spread apart; some were bending over and showing their bottoms. There was page after page of these pictures, some black and white, some in color. She felt ill but she kept turning pages. Suddenly she dropped the magazine as she crumpled onto the bed. She wept, holding her head in her hands.

"The devil incarnate! Satan right here among us, with our own children! My Lord Jesus! I didn't understand how horrible! Oh dear God, how could you let this happen to these innocent children?"

Charlotte picked up the magazine her mother had dropped. The open page showed men – naked, with their legs and genitals visible, but no faces showing. They were holding children on their laps, sometimes with their hands on the child's crotch. The next page had a close-up of a man's erect penis, with a little hand wrapped around it. Beside it was a shot of a pair tiny of pink lips kissing the penis.

Lottie's Lot

"Dear God, forgive me, forgive me," Lottie was moaning, rocking forward and backward as she sat on the bed.

"You have nothing to be forgiven for, Mama. Nobody knew how evil it was. You're the one who's tried to stop it."

Lottie let her daughter hold her. "Thank you, Charlotte, but I'll never forgive myself for not doing something sooner." She kept her eyes closed so she couldn't see any more of the horrible pictures. Charlotte quickly put everything back in the boxes and closed them.

"What's under the pillow, Charlotte?"

Charlotte pulled out a stack of photos. "Don't tell Shirl, not now. And don't tell Hazel." It was Danny – a series of grainy photos of him in clothes that Lottie vaguely remembered from his childhood. In other pictures he had on a shirt but no pants.

Lottie groaned, "If only we had understood when Danny told us. We could have saved so many children. Why didn't we believe him?"

"I know, Ma. But we didn't know about such things. It was too hard to believe."

They closed the bedroom door and went out to the porch. They sat for a moment, Lottie taking the only remaining outdoor chair. "Come out here, Shirl," she said in her old authoritarian voice. Without an argument for once, Shirley joined them a tall glass of whiskey in her hand.

Lottie looked disgusted but held her tongue.

Charlotte asked, "Ma, are you all right?"

"I'm fine, Dear. I'm a tough old bird, you know. I've been through every kind of death and horror in my life and I can take it. But this was truly beyond my imagination."

"Maybe we should take you to a doctor," Charlotte replied, checking Lottie's pulse and watching her breathing carefully.

"No, we're going to Brown's Store so we can call the police. Finally we have something they can use. Some hard evidence."

At the little store, a few minutes up the road, Lottie first called Detective Goodwin. "We found it, Detective. We've got evidence. Horrible pictures and magazines. Oh they're straight from the devil."

"Pictures of children? Naked? Men and children together?" he asked.

"Yes," she replied. "All of those."

"Good. I mean, I'm sorry you had to see that, but this is good evidence. Mrs. Hastings, here's the number for the Orange County sheriff. You call and tell them and they'll come out and look."

Lottie rummaged through her purse for a pen and wrote the number down. "All right, I'll call them right now. Is it enough? Can they arrest C.C.?"

"I would think so. Do you know any of the children in the pictures?"

"I saw my grandson and my great-grandson. I didn't look at all of them."

"I understand. This is a very important find. You've done a courageous thing, Mrs. Hastings. I admire your persistence and your bravery."

She thanked him and hung up. Then she called the Sheriff's office.

Charlotte roamed the store and picked up bread, mayonnaise, mustard, cheese, and baloney. She got three apples and a large box of cookies. "I'm starving," she told Shirley as she put the items on the counter. Shirley added two bottles of Canadian Club to the booty.

They got more change from the cashier. Charlotte asked Shirley to take the groceries to the car. "Don't open *anything* till we get back to the house." She put dimes in the phone and called Lois to tell her what they had found. Then she called Clarence and asked him to take Paul to Lottie's place and stay with Freddie until they got home.

Back at the house, they gathered in the kitchen. Charlotte and Shirley poured themselves drinks and Lottie made sandwiches.

"Oh for heaven's sake, you two," Lottie said. "Alcohol is not the answer to anything."

"Gram, we *need* a drink. You want one?" Shirley said.

Lottie scowled at her. They dug into the food hungrily. Lottie drank water from the faucet.

"The stupid police won't do anything," Shirley muttered, her mouth full.

"Yes, they will," Lottie said. "We have evidence now that we didn't have before, Detective Goodwin told me. This proves he made those children do things."

Lottie was relieved and energized, realizing the enormity of the find.

"How could he get kids to pose to get their pictures taken like this?" Shirley asked.

"Shirl, you know that no kid would willingly pose for pictures like that," Charlotte said, "He had to seduce them somehow. Maybe promise them candy, a toy or something they wanted. Hopefully the police can find some of them and get them to testify. This is great evidence! It will really nail him"

"My, my I didn't realize I was so hungry," Lottie said, as she finished her sandwich.

Munching on a cookie, Charlotte said, "I wonder why he left all that stuff here."

"He probably thought he could come get it later," Shirley said. "You know, he could be on his way up here now."

"Bite your tongue, Girl," Lottie said. "C.C. never quite believed we could really hurt him. He sees us as a bunch of silly, weak women, especially me. Then when Hazel got sick, his mind was on her and so was ours. He never dreamed anyone would go in his precious room."

"Well," Charlotte said, finishing off her drink. "If the police won't do anything, I vote for letting the guys kill him. Chuck and Clarence would do it, too."

"I wish Buddy and Danny and Kenny were here to help," Lottie added.

At 4:30, two Sheriff's deputies pulled up to the cabin and identified themselves. "What's happened here?" they asked.

Lottie told the story and the men listened attentively.

"Thank you, Ma'am," one said and they went into the bedroom and looked around.

Shirley leaned against the kitchen door and waited for the deputies to come out of the bedroom. She fixed her eyes on one and walked up to stand close to him. "I'm so upset, officer. You see, I found my son's photos in there. You've got to catch this bastard and throw away the key." She touched his arm. "My poor, poor boy."

"I can understand why you're upset, ma'am," the man replied, quickly looking her up and down. "We've never seen anything like this. I mean, I've heard of it but I've never seen it. It's hard to believe. I'm sure we can find some fingerprints."

The other deputies asked, "Do you ladies know where this man is today?"

"Yes, at their apartment on Grace Place in Los Angeles. He's there now," Charlotte said.

Lottie's Lot

"Thank you. We'll send another car to pick up the evidence and photograph the scene, and we'll call the LAPD. They'll send someone to arrest him."

"But..." Lottie objected. "My daughter. She's in the apartment and she's very ill. She's dying. I don't want her to know. I can't let you upset her."

The men looked at each other. "We'll explain that to LAPD. I'm sure they can get him to come outside."

As they drove away, Charlotte roared with laughter. "Shirley, you are incorrigible. Flirting with that young cop at a time like this."

"I'm just a passionate person. I can't help it. I wanted to make him see how bad this is."

"You're shameless is what you are." She shook her head with a grin. "Oh, I'd better call Lois when we leave."

At the Grace Place apartment, Lois hung up the telephone in the living room, stunned. Charlotte sounded so excited, like all of this with C.C. was going to come to an end. She couldn't wait to tell Chuck and quickly dialed her home number. C.C. Was listening in the hallway and heard Lois talking. He stood very still and listened.

"They opened the door to his room and found terrible things. The Orange County Sheriff deputies came, and they said they're going to send someone to arrest him," she whispered. "I can't talk now. I'll be home late."

C.C.'s inner alarm sounded in full force. He went into his bedroom, closed the door, and took two suitcases out of the closet. He quickly packed his best suits, shirts, ties, underwear, shoes, an envelope full of cash, the box of photos he had hidden at the back of the closet, and his mailing list of customers.

He sat on the bed beside Hazel and watched her as she slept deeply. He smoothed her hair and kissed her on the forehead and said, "Sorry, Babe. I can't stick around for the end."

He put his overcoat over his arm, picked up the suitcases, and quickly ran down the stairs. Lois was drinking coffee in the kitchen. She saw his back as he quickly passed by. She didn't see the suitcases. She heard the new Hudson car start. He must be going to the drugstore for something they need, she thought.

After heating some soup and eating a bowl full, she went back into Hazel's room. Something didn't look right. C.C.'s closet door was open and the closet was empty.

At 6 o'clock that evening, three squad cars pulled up in front of the apartment building. The Los Angeles cops walked quietly up the stairs and stationed themselves at all the exits to the building. A plainclothes detective knocked on the apartment door.

"Good evening, ma'am," he said calmly. "Is Mr. C.C. Fredericks at home?"

"No," Lois said in a tiny voice.

"I'm sorry?"

"No, he isn't here. He left about an hour ago."

"Did he say where he was going?"

"No."

The detective peered past Lois but could see no activity in the apartment. He showed her his badge. "Ma'am, we're here on police business. Do you mind if we come in?"

She opened the door wider and six policemen quickly entered. The detective spoke to someone else who ran downstairs to one of the cars and got on the radio.

"We need to look around, Ma'am," an officer in a uniform said.

"All right. But my sister is in that room and she's very ill."

"We'll be as quiet as we can."

They quickly looked through the apartment, checking all the windows and opening all the doors. They pushed the clothes aside in the closets and shone flashlights in the corners. An officer walked quietly through Hazel's bedroom, noticing the empty closet.

He stepped out. "Why is that closet empty?" he asked Lois.

"It's C.C.'s closet. He packed his suitcases and took everything with him."

"When was this?"

"About 5 o'clock, I think."

"I'm sorry but we have to go in there and check more carefully and take some pictures."

"Just be quiet."

She followed them in and sat on Hazel's bed, ready to distract her if she woke up. The men opened drawers, looked under the beds, and stripped the sheets off C.C.'s bed. They took photos of his half of the bedroom.

The noise and brightness of the camera flash caused Hazel to stir. "What is it? What's going on?"

Lois held her hand. "It's nothing. Go back to sleep."

Hazel tried to look across the room but her eyes were blurry. "Are there people here?"

"It's just Chuck. He's helping C.C. with something. I told them not to wake you up."

"With what?" Hazel asked, then her eyes closed and she was asleep again.

339

After the sheriff's deputies had collected all the evidence from C.C.'s room at Silverado Canyon and taken down the women's names and addresses, the cabin was quiet again, and the sky was dark.

Charlotte gathered up the remaining groceries and their other belongings. "Guess it's time to head back home."

They locked the door and drove off watching the cabin recede as they pulled away.

Lottie looked over at Charlotte behind the wheel and saw a smile. Charlotte turned to her, "We did it, Ma. We nailed him."

Shirley shouted "Yea!!" Then she started singing, "Ding Dong, the witch is dead! Which old witch? The C.C. son-of-a-bitch!"

They breathed sighs of relief as they drove home, gradually relaxing and letting themselves laugh and cheer.

"Oh, I can't wait to tell Rev. Walker. I'll call him first thing tomorrow," Lottie said.

"Let me tell Freddie," Shirley said as they pulled into town.

"Are you going to tell him about the pictures?"

"Not right away. It depends on what the police do."

"Good," Charlotte said. "Now you're thinking like a mother."

The three-hour drive through the dark relaxed and soothed them as they realized what they had done. Lottie dozed off from exhaustion and Shirley from whiskey.

They awoke as the car turned onto Grace Place.

"One thing we know for sure," Charlotte said as she parked in front of Hazel's building.

"What's that, honey?" Lottie asked.

"There's no C.C. in that apartment. Not anymore!"

Lottie's Lot

They cheered again as they got out of the car and grinned at each other as they walked up the stairs. It was almost midnight.

"Ssshh," Lottie said. "Don't wake Hazel up."

They knocked lightly on the door and Lois opened it. They saw her red eyes and shaking hands.

"What is it, Lois?" Lottie said. "What's wrong?"

CHAPTER 22

Lottie, Charlotte and Shirley followed Lois into the parlor. Chuck was sitting on the sofa, head in his hands. Lois couldn't stop crying.

"What's wrong?" Lottie demanded alarmed. "Where's Hazel? Is she all right?"

"Yes, Hazel's all right, Ma. She's in bed. It's C.C.... he's gone," Lois whispered.

Shirley said, "The police took him, right!"

"No, he left before the police got here."

"*WHAT*!" Lottie, Shirley, and Charlotte shouted in unison.

Hazel heard the commotion and called from her room, "Why are you all here so late?" Her voice was foggy. "What's going on?"

Charlotte went into her room, kissed her cheek, and lied. "We went to a party and wanted to stop by and see how you are. How do you feel?"

"Little better I think, but the pain in my back is ferocious. It never seems to go away," she said and rolled over on her side. "Where's C.C.?" she asked.

Charlotte said, "Here let me give you a back rub. That will make it feel better."

Lois said, "He had to go to a late meeting. He should be back soon."

Hazel spotted Lottie. "Ma, are you OK? This is late for you to be up."

"I'm just a little tired," Lottie answered. "I'm going to sleep in the other bedroom. Do you need another pain pill?"

"I'd rather have a shot of Canadian Club," Hazel grinned, "but I'll settle for a pain pill."

Lottie gave her one and kissed her on the cheek "Get some sleep now Baby Girl." Hazel smiled her Mama hadn't called her that for a long, long time. They closed her bedroom door and quietly went into the kitchen.

In whispered tones they grilled Lois about C.C.'s leaving. Exactly what happened? How did he suspect? She confessed that she had called Chuck to tell him the good news, and C.C. had probably overheard the conversation. "He left about half an hour later without saying a word, and he seemed to be in a hurry."

They were so tired, deflated, and depressed that they couldn't express anger at Lois for her carelessness. Shirley and Charlotte just left with nothing more to say. "We'll talk tomorrow, Ma," Charlotte said, kissing her good night. Lottie was totally exhausted and fell into bed with her clothes on.

The next morning Lottie called Detective Goodwin and told him everything.

"But we have evidence now," she added, trying to cheer herself up.

"Good," he said. "But you don't have him."

"Well, can the police pick him up? We know the car he's in."

"It's worth a try. Do you have the registration and license for the car?" he asked.

"I don't know. I'll look for the papers. He bought it for Hazel but no one asked to see the paperwork."

"Call me back when you find it. I especially need the license plate numbers and the make, model, color, and year of the car."

Hazel kept her important papers in a fireproof box, which Lottie quietly took from the bedroom closet and carried into the kitchen. She looked through everything inside. There was no car title. She sat in despair. How could that rotten, despicable man get away? Every minute that passed meant that he was farther away.

She called Goodwin back with the bad news. She described the car as a 1941 blue Hudson sedan with two doors. He said he would do what he could.

Charlotte came by and they talked a little. "They'll get him, Ma," She kept saying.

"Maybe they won't. They may never get him," Lottie replied.

They drank coffee in silence. There was nothing more to say. They didn't see Shirley for several days. She didn't even call Freddie. Lottie wondered if she had kept her word and gone to an AA meeting and stopped drinking. She had her doubts.

In fact, C.C. had bought the car under the phony name "William Hough" and given a false address in Alberta, Canada, for the title. When he left Los Angeles he drove straight north through the night, stopping in Washington state to swap license plates in a motel parking lot. He crossed the border into Canada at Vancouver, showing William Hough's I.D. Once he was safely in Canada, he changed his name and disappeared into the Canadian population. The family never heard from him again.

Lottie took the defeat hard. She wanted so much for C.C. to pay for his sins, and more important, to be kept away from children. She lay awake at night wondering, what if I had acted differently, would he be in a jail cell by now? Maybe she should have reported it to the police sooner, or maybe she had been too bold in letting him know she was out to get him. She went over and over every detail several times, playing out different outcomes in her head.

344

She decided to have another talk with Reverend Walker. He always had some wisdom that restored her to sanity. Even if he couldn't solve the problem, he gave her comfort and often a different perspective. She took the bus to his office the next afternoon.

He greeted her with a genuine smile. "Lottie, it is always a pleasure to see one of my favorite people." They sat in their usual chairs. She knew he was busy but had made time for her.

"What's going on?"

She related the events of the past few days and told him what they had found at Silverado Canyon and that C. C. had slipped away.

"Oh, Reverend. The pictures were so horrible. I never imagined such things. And the magazines…" she began to shake. "The devil is among us, Reverend. I've seen the proof."

"Lottie, you showed great courage in facing this evil. You did everything you could."

"That's what Detective Goodwin said. But she was disappointed that they couldn't catch C.C. The police were so good they came to the apartment ready to arrest him, but it was too late. He had already left."

"If it were me I'd head for Canada without missing a beat," the Reverend said grimly. "He would be harder to find there."

"I'm so afraid he'll just keep finding other children to harm. I feel so helpless." Lottie wrung her handkerchief into a ball.

"Lottie, I'm going to tell you something you may not want to hear."

"What?"

"It's in God's hands now. You've done a remarkable job of uncovering his heinous activities. You have found evidence. You've bravely confronted this man with little thought of harm to yourself."

She nodded. "Yes, but it wasn't enough."

"Yes it *was* enough. You did everything humanly possible to bring him to justice. Now you must fall back on your faith. Let Go and Let GOD!" He held her hand and peered into her eyes. "Look at me. We don't have to personally punish every affront or sin we witness. *"Vengeance is mine; I will repay, saith the Lord!'* You know that verse, don't you?"

She nodded again. She knew he was right but it was hard to forgive herself.

"Lottie, you have a dying daughter. Your focus should be on her now. Help her to clean up her life, make amends where she can, and die in peace so she can enter the gates of Heaven." She teared up.

"You're right, Reverend. You always are. Nothing matters now but Hazel. But…"

"But nothing, Lottie. Forgive yourself if you need to. You've done nothing wrong. I'm sure God is happy with you and proud of you. Remember….*let go and let God*!"

She stood up to leave and he stood too. He held her hand in both of his. "If Hazel would like to speak to me privately I will gladly visit her. Please let her know I stand ready if she calls me to her side."

Lottie was blowing her nose as she left his office. She managed to mumble, "Thank you."

Hazel knew she was dying. After the surgery she remained hopeful until the pain came back. As it got increasingly worse she began to face reality and come to terms with her impending death. She didn't want to die in a convalescent hospital; she wanted to be at home. Her doctor advised the family to give her pain medicine, as needed to stay as comfortable possible. But don't give her too much, he said. "After all we don't want her to become addicted to pain killers."

When Shirley heard this she hit the ceiling. "Who in the hell cares if you become addicted to anything if you're dying? What an ass! We'll give her anything she wants or needs to be as comfortable and pain-free as possible."

The family shifted its focus to Hazel. They reaffirmed that someone would always be with her day and night. With C.C. gone they had to do extra duty and they did it willingly, never complaining. When Hazel was awake she frequently called for C.C. and asked where he was. The women made excuses and told her that he was at the market or the drugstore.

Finally they told her that his patent attorney had called him to go to Washington, D.C., to demonstrate the prototype of his mixer to the patent board. He tried to reschedule the meeting, but the federal agency had made that impossible. It was his most important invention so he had to go.

"Why hasn't he called?"

"He called last night, Honey," Lottie said. "You were sound asleep and he didn't want to wake you. He'll call back." Lottie hated lying to her daughter, but Hazel's peace of mind mattered more than the sin of lying. They could never tell Hazel that C.C. had left for good.

Lottie moved into C.C.'s bed to be there at night if Hazel woke in pain or needed something. Lois took Freddie to her house and drove him to school every day with her boys.

In the summer Shirley had bought folding lawn chairs and with help Hazel could maneuver the stairs and sit outside to get a little sunshine and enjoy a summer day. But by early October she could no longer go up and down the stairs. She told them that she wanted to see her sons again before she died. By November 3 she didn't want to get out of bed.

Kenny flew out from Detroit after a call from Lottie. With Rev. Walker's intervention, the Red Cross got an emergency pass for Danny to come home and see his dying mother. Hazel cut back on her pain medication for a few days. She wanted to be more lucid for the boys. Seeing them lifted her spirits.

When Kenny arrived he was shocked to see how much weight his mother had lost. "Mom, I hate not being here with you when you're so sick. I just couldn't get time off from work any sooner."

"I understand, Son. You have to live your own life, not mine. You have five children to support. That's a lot of responsibility. You have to do what's best for them."

"What are the doctors telling you?"

"The news isn't good. They took out all my female parts, but there were still some cancer cells. Now it's spread to the liver and stomach and I don't know where all. I can't eat much now, just sometimes drink a little soup.

"Are you in a lot of pain?"

"Yes, but the pills help ease it some," she said stoically, swallowing a pill with water.

"Oh God Mom!" He held his head in his hands. "I feel so helpless, so confused. Is there anything I can do? I don't know what to do."

"There is one thing I'd like you to do for me," she said, trying to make it easier for him.

"What? Anything!"

"I would like to see my new grandchild before I die."

"You will, you will!" Ken promised. "Dot or I will bring the baby for you to see as soon as possible."

"Son, one more thing. Don't worry about me. I'm proud of you and I love you."

Lottie's Lot

"I love you, too, Mom. I don't want to lose you," he said, swallowing hard to stop the tears. She had a hard time focusing and her words were slurred. The pill was taking over.

"Kenny, there's something I need to tell you about your father," she said, her words fading. She fell asleep before she could tell him about George Hopf and his syphilis.

Danny flew in the next day and immediately went to his mother's apartment.

"Danny!" she exclaimed. "You look so handsome, just like your father. He would have been so proud of you." Lottie, looking up at the tall handsome, young man standing next to her, nodded with a proud smile.

"Sit down," Hazel said. "Tell me about your job in the Navy. What does a Sea-bee do?"

He started to tell her and she dozed off before he finished the first sentence.

Lottie guided him into the kitchen, where he saw Ken and gave him a salute.

"Hey Brother. It's good to see you." She poured coffee for both of them and told them the doctors said Hazel probably had only a few more days to live. Seeing her boys again was a great joy and her final wish.

The boys stayed in the second bedroom and talked to Hazel as much as possible over the next few days. "My boys!" she said whenever she woke up and saw them. "I'm so proud of my boys." Then she would drift off. "Your father ... he gave it to me ... I'm sorry, so sorry," she murmured a few times, but they had no idea what she meant.

A few days later Lottie was sitting at her bedside holding her hand. Hazel opened her eyes and said, "Mama, is that you?"

"Yes, Sweetheart, it's me. I'm right here."

"I don't have much longer, Mama." Lottie started to object but Hazel went on. "Have I told you how much I love you? You stuck by me even when we didn't see eye to eye. Thank you, Mama."

"Well, you stuck by me, too. That's what families do. They help each other and love each other, no matter what." Lottie asked, "Do you want a pill now?"

"Not yet. I want to talk, just you and me. We may not have another chance." She tried to sit up and Lottie put some pillows behind her. With an exhausted sigh, Hazel began, "Ma, I know you didn't like me living with Roy and not being married legally, but I believe in God's eyes he knew we belonged together. He just took him away too soon. Maybe that was his way to punish us."

"Now, Hazel, don't fret over the past."

"I know you don't like C.C., wherever he is. But he was always kind and good to me and to my children. I don't believe I would have made it this far without him. So please make peace with him for my sake."

Lottie swallowed hard and cleared her throat. "I'll try, Honey … for your sake."

Hazel closed her eyes and Lottie thought she was drifting off to sleep. But she began to speak again.

"Mama, I know how hard your life has been -- much, much worse than mine and you were strong and determined all the way. If you hadn't stood by me when that man …raped me. You stood by me and treated little Abby so well I know it cost you a lot. I don't know what would have become of me without you."

"There was no question. That man wronged you so much and you were still a child…."

350

Lottie's Lot

Hazel was speaking again. "I've been weak compared to you. Drinking -- a crutch -- got me through some painful times. You hated it but I was too weak to stop. Compared to you, I'm a coward."

"Now, Hazel you did the best you could. You had some very hard things to deal with."

"I never lost a child. You've lost three, now four. I don't know how anyone can survive that -- and you loved Pa so much and lost him too early." She took a few breaths. "I lost one person I loved and it did me in. Your losses just made you stronger."

Lottie bit her lip and fought to hold back her tears listening to Hazel's words. She was astonished that Hazel could find the strength to tell her these things and that Hazel had such an understanding of their lives. The full impact of losing this precious child whose life had shaped hers in so many ways hit her hard, and she began to cry silently.

"I think I'll take that pain pill now," Hazel whispered. "Just wanted to tell you how much I admire you and love you. And thank you for being my mother all these years."

Lottie couldn't speak and could barely see for the tears filling her eyes, but she gave Hazel the pill and helped her lie down again.

Finally she found her voice. "I'm so glad you're my daughter, my dearest daughter. Your father always said you and I were made with the same cookie cutter, stubborn, strong-willed, and smart. That's what he loved about us but he also found it hard to take the pair of us sometimes." She smoothed her daughter's hair, stroked her face with tender fingertips.

"Oh, Hazel. I hope and pray we will be together again in a better place, where all our troubles will be gone. I love you, Hazel. I have always loved you."

Hazel had dozed off by then and Lottie held onto her hand for several minutes. When she felt she had cried all the tears possible, she lay down on the next bed.

Hazel didn't wake to consciousness again. Shirley, Kenny, Danny, and Lottie were all at her side when she died peacefully about 7 pm. the next evening. As she let go of life, peace showed on her face. All the pain of so many years was finally gone. Lottie glanced at the calendar. It was November, 10 1944.

Lottie called Reverend Walker and asked him to conduct a funeral service. Kenny, Danny, Clarence, Buddy, Chuck, and Johnny Jacobs were pallbearers. Shirley and Lottie arranged for her burial in Forest Lawn Cemetery. After the burial service in the Forest Lawn chapel. They all went back to Grace Place. Relatives and neighbors brought food and drinks

Shirley was already drunk. Freddie avoided her. She tried to hug him tearfully saying, "I miss my Mama so much." He didn't like to be around her when she had been drinking.

Lottie was worn out and grief stricken. She just wanted to lie down and sleep until the ache in her heart subsided. It had been a long and painful year. She sat on the couch. Freddie sat beside her, holding her hand and understanding her silence.

"I'm hungry, Gram," He finally whispered.

"Go get something to eat," she finally told him, "and visit with your cousins." He headed for the kitchen.

Kenny took Freddie's place beside Lottie. "She didn't get to see her new grandchild. I promised she would, but he wasn't been born yet." he said, his voice choking.

"That's all right, Son," Lottie said. "Your promise made her feel better."

He took a gulp from his drink. "Hey, where is C.C.? I didn't want to ask Mom, and everybody else just shook their heads like I wasn't supposed to ask."

She started crying. "He left … he left before we could have him arrested."

"For what?"

Lottie said, "It's a long story and a dreadful one. I don't feel like talking about it today." She lapsed back into an exhausted silence. Everyone was drinking and smoking and she couldn't tolerate it. She asked Reverend Walker to drive her home.

Shirley had overheard Kenny asking about C.C. and she told him, "Shut up and mind your own business. She just buried her daughter for Christ's sake." She said, her voice slurred. Her lifelong anger and resentment at Kenny was bubbling to the surface.

"I'm not trying to pry, just understand. After all, he was my father. At least my stepfather," Ken answered defensively. "Yours also. He was pretty good to us and to Ma too."

"He wasn't my father. And I am only your *half*-sister, you know." Shirley spit the words at him.

"What? **What!**" Kenny was stunned.

After drinking for several hours her inhibitions were down. She no longer had to be quiet and polite for Hazel's or Lottie's sake. "*Your* father was that bastard George Hopf. He was so mean to us, Mama left him and ran away with Roy Darden."

"When? I don't remember that."

"When we lived in Canada. She met Roy and they ran away together from George Hopf and went to Detroit. You were only four. Then later George kidnapped us, you and me, when you were eight and I was twelve. You must remember that, you idiot."

He stared and she went on. "I stayed by your side like Mama told me to, and we finally got home. He took us to Canada, remember? We visited Aunt Bethie. Don't you remember that stupid?"

"I sort of remember and I had a good time. I didn't know it was a kidnapping. He didn't hurt us," Kenny said, trying to process this new information. "Are you telling me that all three of us had different fathers?"

"Yes," Shirley said belligerently. "Yes. I am."

"Who is *your* father, then?" Ken asked.

"None of your goddamned business."

"Why is our last name Darden? Did Roy adopt us?"

"No," Shirley said spitefully. Charlotte overheard the ruckus and sat next to Shirley patting her on the arm attempting to calm her down. Shirley brushed her away.

"Why not?" Ken asked, more curious than disturbed.

"He wanted to but couldn't. Mama just changed our names. It was easier for them if their children had the same names as they did."

"But they were married, weren't they? Why didn't Roy legally adopt us?"

"Because they were both still married to different people, that's why!" Shirley lashed out enjoying watching Kenny scrim. "Look Mama left George and he joined the Canadian Army and went to the war. When he got out, we were in Detroit, so he tracked us down and said he was going to take you away. He hoped Mama would go back to him, but she loved Roy and would never leave him. That's when Mama finally divorced your father and she got custody of you. Then she got pregnant with Danny, so she and Roy went to a minister and got married. But he used a different name."

"Oh, Jesus. This is too much." He finished his drink and got another one. Shirley followed him to the kitchen bar.

354

"All right, why did Roy use a fake name?" He swallowed the new drink in one gulp and poured another. Shirley grinned at him with glee, loving to see her brother confused.

"Roy never got divorced from his wife in Canada. They couldn't use their full legal names or they could have been charged with bigamy if anyone reported them. Roy's real name was Anthony Leroy Darden, but on the marriage certificate he just put Leroy Darden."

Ken stared at her, trying to comprehend all she had said.

"You have more questions, little brother?" she said sarcastically enjoying his discomfort.

"I'm trying to remember," he said and paused. "I kind of remember George Hopf coming to see me and … Yes, he did say he was my father. But Mama told me he was lying. She always said Roy was my father and yours and Danny's too."

"He did sire Danny. But not you and me." Shirley laughed at him.

"Mama was good at keeping secrets, that's for sure. Why didn't she tell me the truth?" Kenny asked, confused at who he could trust.

"Because it might make you hate her." Shirley paused and then said, "Maybe she thought you would want to live with your father and she wanted you to stay with us. I don't know her reasons. I can't answer for her, and now that she's gone, she can't tell you either."

"Well then," he asked, "What is my *real* name?"

"George Kenneth Hopf."

"Was she ever married to my father?"

"Yes. They were legally married. But Roy Darden was the only man she ever loved."

Ken's confusion turned to anger. He wasn't sure whom to be angry at–Shirley? Or His mother? George? Roy? But Shirley was in front of him now taunting him…she knew this all the time and never told him…why not?

Shirley was in her element, loving the chaos she had created and not caring that the rest of the family was listening to her.

"Here's another news flash, loser. Your father had syphilis and he gave it to her and that's why she got cancer and died so young. It's all your fault."

This last revelation was like a punch in his gut. Kenny slumped into the nearest chair. "Where is my father now?"

"I have no idea," Shirley smirked. Charlotte tried to stop Shirley again but she pushed her away.

Ken focused on her viciousness. "Thanks, *Abigail*," said Ken, his resentment flaring. "You bitch. You've known this all these years and *now* you choose to tell me – at our mother's funeral!"

She flew at him in a rage, but was held back by Charlotte and Clarence. He slapped her hard across her face. She reeled backwards and glared at him with all the hatred she had harbored in her heart from the time he was born.

He turned to Clarence and Charlotte. "I want to get the hell out of here."

He took a minute to hug Danny goodbye. His brother was flying out again that night, back to the action in the Pacific. The drinks he'd had shielded him from completely absorbing the shocking facts he had just learned, but his mind was whirling with mixed emotions -- grief, anger, betrayal, and confusion. Charlotte and Clarence drove him to their house to spend the night.

The next day Charlotte took him to visit Lottie before his plane left for Detroit. Lottie fixed them lunch and she and Charlotte told him everything they knew about C.C. Ken was horrified. Then he remembered.

"You know, when C.C. first moved in with us, he used to walk around naked when Mom wasn't at home. I thought it was strange. But he never touched me. At least that I can remember. But I was only eight."

He asked them about his father, and Lottie and Charlotte told him what they remembered. Most of it was positive. They were grateful for how hard George had worked to support his family as well as Lottie and all her children after Charlie died. They told him how Hazel fought with him over almost everything.

Lottie apologized to Kenny. "We couldn't tell you because Hazel swore us to secrecy. I'm so sorry Shirley told you the way she did. Hazel wouldn't have wanted that. I'm sure she didn't realize how much hiding the truth would hurt you."

"Ma kept saying she wanted to tell me something about my father, but she never finished a few days ago. I didn't think much about it. I never dreamed …"

Then they told him about the escape to Detroit and how Roy and Hazel schemed to abandon George.

"Yes, he did come to see you in Detroit," Charlotte said. "He fought hard to get custody of you and then to have visitation rights. Your Dad won the divorce but he lost custody of you. He loved you very much and after that defeat in court he was heartbroken. "

"Hazel made it hell for him to visit you and after he took you to Canada and he had to send you back. He just disappeared. We never heard from him again."

Ken felt depressed and small as he heard these facts. How could he not have known about this, about his own father? How could he not have remembered?

"Your Ma kept it from you as much as possible," Lottie said. "She thought it was best if you thought Roy was your father. She thought you would forget about George."

"I did–until my bitch sister decided to ruin my life."

"Now, Kenny," Lottie patted his arm. "You have to forgive your mother. She had a lot of problems and she tried to do what she thought was best. We all make mistakes."

He stared at her. He was a long way from forgiving.

"And...syphilis?" He told them what Shirley had said.

Lottie and Charlotte looked at each other.

"I think Shirley made that up," Charlotte said. "Hazel didn't talk to us about it." Charlotte didn't think Kenny could take the truth about having inherited syphilis after all he had heard.

Kenny left Los Angeles in despair, feeling betrayed and duped. Had everyone whispered about him and laughed about him behind his back all these years? Was he the only one who didn't know?

And how many other lies had Hazel told him over the years? He felt horribly betrayed. Who could he trust, if he couldn't trust his own mother?

CHAPTER 23

Lottie's Lot

Early on a Sunday morning in mid-June a knock on the door woke Lottie. She looked at the new electric clock on her nightstand. "My goodness, its only 5 o'clock," she said to herself. The knocking continued, a little louder. She put on her dressing gown and made her way to the front room and looked out the window. The sun wasn't even up yet. The knock came again.

Lottie opened the door, and when she saw who was there she grabbed the back of a chair to keep from fainting.

"Oh, my good Lord. Can this be true?" She was shaking as the handsome soldier put his arms around her.

"Hi, Ma, I'm home," Buddy said with a big grin. "Sorry it's so early."

"Buddy, my Buddy, I've been looking for you every day since the war in Europe ended on May 8th."

She held him for a long time in the doorway until he said softly, "Let's go inside, Ma."

"Oh yes, come on in. Am I dreaming? Is it really you?" They sat on the sofa and she kept touching his hands and his face to convince herself he was real.

He set down two large duffel bags and took off his overcoat. She could see several medals on his uniform.

"Are you all right? Have you been wounded? Is that why you're here?"

"Yes, I'm fine, Ma. No wounds."

"Well, is the war over?"

"No, it isn't over completely over yet," he smiled. "The war in Europe is over but we're still fighting the Japs."

She began to calm down and suddenly her face broke into a smile so big it was almost painful. She closed her eyes. "Thank you, dear Lord. Thank you for bringing my boy home unharmed."

She stared lovingly at Buddy as if in one hour she could erase more than three years of suffering and worrying about him. He looked a little older, wearier.

"Oh, tell me everything. Why didn't you let me know you were coming? I could have made you something special and called your sisters. What are all these medals for? Are you sure you're OK? You look very skinny. What are you going to do now? You could go to college on that G.I. bill, you know, and maybe be an engineer or something."

He laughed. "Slow down, Ma. Don't call everybody yet. How about some breakfast first?"

"Oh my goodness, I'm so silly. You must be hungry. How did you get here? On a boat or an airplane? What do you want to eat?" She went into the kitchen and was still chattering as she put pots and pans on the stove and got eggs, bacon, and butter from the icebox.

Buddy followed her as she began to cook. He sat at his old place at the table. "Oh, I should make coffee first." She heard a match strike and turned to see him light a cigarette. Today he could smoke all he wanted in her house.

They heard a sound in the hallway. Freddie stumbled into the kitchen in his pajamas, rubbing his eyes. "What's going on?"

"Freddie, I'm sorry we woke you up," Lottie said. "Look who's here!"

The boy squinted his eyes. "It's your Uncle Buddy. He's home from the war. Look at him, all his medals. He's a hero. We must thank the Lord for keeping him safe."

Lottie's Lot

Freddie nodded and Buddy extended his hand uncertainly.

"Oh, you're Shirley's boy. Wow, you're a lot bigger."

"Yep." Freddie ran back to his room to get his glasses, he needed them to read. He came back and standing tall he saluted his Uncle Bud. "Welcome home Soldier." Mimicking something he'd seen at the movie theater. Lottie and Bud laughed and Bud saluted back. Then grabbed Freddie and gave him a big hug.

Lottie poured her son a cup of coffee and noticed his hands shaking while he drank it. She kept talking, not wanting to uncover any worries. "I hope you like bacon and eggs. You used to, I'm sure you still do. What did you have to eat over there? I bet the food is different. Is it really strange? I'll get it on the table as soon as I can." Then she stopped and just stared at him with a big smile.

Buddy winked at Freddie. "I think your Gram is happy to see me."

"She talks about you all the time." Freddie laughed.

"Now, don't bother him, Freddie. He's tired. He just fought a whole war. Go get ready for school."

When Freddie went upstairs, Lottie whispered. "Buddy, did you get the news about Hazel's death?"

"Yes, Ma. Gee, I'm really sorry. I'm sorry I didn't get home in time to see her before….." He said sincerely, "Are you all right?"

"Well, I go to church almost every day and that helps me. Freddie goes with me on Sundays. Charlotte will come by to pick us up. Do you want to go with me today?" She hoped he would say yes. "Boy, won't you be a surprise when Charlotte sees you?"

Around eight, Charlotte walked into the house and saw the duffel bags on the living room floor. Just as she called, "Ma, what's going on?" Buddy jumped out from behind the kitchen door and gave her a big hug. She squealed and hopped up and down. "Let me look at you. Oh my God! You look great! A little tired maybe, but *great!*"

She gave him a big kiss on the cheek. "We have to have a party to celebrate my baby brother coming home as a war hero."

Lottie and Charlotte called Lois and Shirley with the good news. The entire family was thrilled to have Buddy back home and everyone wanted to see him as soon as possible. They planned a party at Charlotte's house the following Saturday afternoon. Everyone brought food and drinks.

Shirley brought Johnny Jacobs. Lois and Chuck invited friends and they celebrated until almost dawn. Lottie went home early after the booze began to flow like the fountain at Belle Isle. After she left, Charlotte had a sudden thought. "I'm going to call Ruby and tell her Buddy's back," she told Clarence. She waited until the noise died down and placed the call with Buddy at her side. Ruby was thrilled to hear from them. She sent Buddy a long-distance hug.

"Hey,Sis! How's everything?"

Ruby said she missed them all so much especially at holidays and wished they could be together again. Charlotte got a brainstorm.

"You know, next April is Ma's 75th birthday. Let's plan a surprise party for her. We've got almost a whole year to plan something great. Will you come, Ruby? That will really be a special surprise for her."

"I will try my best. Let me talk it over with Art. It would be fantastic if the whole family can come. Maybe over Easter break for the kids."

"Fabulous! Call me back when you decide and we will make plans."

Ruby called back the next week and said Art could use his vacation time and they would drive out for the birthday party.

Lottie's Lot

Danny came home in November, 1945 after Victory with Japan Day. Shirley married Johnny Jacobs and Freddie went to live with them when he was 14.

Buddy stayed with Lottie off and on, but the relationship was filled with problems. It worked out for a while, but Bud was usually drinking. He was sweet and caring toward Lottie and his sisters when he was sober, but when he drank he became belligerent, hateful, and had a mouth that could level a tall building. A few times he cut Lottie to the quick, swearing, calling her names, and insulting her. His erratic behavior frightened her and broke her heart.

Lottie was always on pins and needles not knowing what to expect from him next. Sometimes he would be friendly and talk to her and even fix things around the house. Then with no warning he would throw his dinner plate against the wall and yell at her, "When are you going to learn to cook? How can you expect me to eat this slop?"

Sometimes he would come home late at night stumbling over the furniture and swearing loudly as he staggered to his bedroom. At times he wet the bed as he slept off his drunken binge. Many times he had blackouts and the next day had no idea what he had said or done the night before.

One day Bud looked her in the eye and said bitterly and without hesitation, "Well, when you die it won't be a great loss. You've outlived your usefulness. You are no comfort to yourself or anyone else, you're a burden to everybody, especially me. I've had more than my share of you. But in many ways I will be relieved when you are gone. You smothering old witch, no ... I mean bitch."

If she cried at his cruel words he would pound on the wall and tell her to go to her room. "Alligator tears. Remember alligator tears?" He said sarcastically, "Don't you remember when I was a little kid and cried because I was scared or hurt, you said my tears were just alligator tears. So now who's got alligator tears? Huh!"

She spent many nights barricaded in her room crying and trembling in fear. She asked herself. "How did this happen? Was I such a terrible mother? God! Why have you forsaken me again?" She blamed herself. I must have done something wrong in raising him, she thought.

Many nights she lay awake listening for what Buddy might do next.

Buddy had come home, like so many veterans, with "shell shock." Adjusting to civilian life was difficult. He woke up with nightmares, thinking he was still in combat. Many nights he would wake up screaming and making rat-a-tat-tat gun-firing sounds. Or call out names and warnings to "Take cover! Get them! Jerry's on the left side of our plane! Dive, quick!"

He was sick and desperately needed help. In his sober moments he knew he was in trouble. He tried to get help at the Veterans Administration, but all they could do was to give him pills. He took them and still drank, compounding his problems.

The only thing Lottie knew to do was to pray harder, but even repeating her favorite Psalms didn't bring her solace now or bring about any changes in her son.

She regularly attended Rev. Walker's Methodist church. It helped her to reconnect with her values in changing times both in society and in her own family. He had so much common sense as well as wisdom that she always left church feeling more hopeful and more in control of her own destiny.

She had been obsessed with preventing C.C. Fredericks from molesting other children, but she was powerless over the way Buddy treated her now.

She kept reminding herself of Rev. Walker's wise words: "Lottie, *Let Go and Let God!* He will take care of it." But God didn't seem to change her son's behavior. Buddy, her dearest child, had become a monster who terrified her at times.

She hesitated to tell her daughters about the extent of his abuse. Finally in desperation she confided to Charlotte about what was going on. The following weekend Clarence and Chuck came over and moved Buddy into a rooming house away from Lottie.

Danny Darden came home with shell shock too. After finishing boot camp in 1942, Dan was on a train heading back to Los Angeles when he met a beautiful young woman named Gladys Sanmark.

For Dan it was love at first sight. Like many young people during the war they married quickly after just a few dates without knowing each other well. They were both 21 years old. Dan went back to his assignment in the Navy and Gladys went to work. In July, 1943 their first child, Thomas Leroy Darden, was born. Dan was overseas at the time and he was overjoyed by the news that he was a father.

The young couple wrote passionate love letters about how much they missed each other and how they wished the war would end so they could be together all the time. Dan got a 30-day leave in the summer of 1944, and Gladys became pregnant again. Linda Jane was born May 9, 1945, while Dan was overseas. When Gladys told Lottie that they had chosen her name in honor of Lottie Jane, she was delighted. This was the only child or grandchild named after her.

When Dan came home for good in November, 1945, he found himself with a ready-made family -- a wife who was still a stranger to him in many ways and two children.

Adjusting to civilian life was also difficult. Like so many others in the Hastings family, he drank to disguise his feelings of incompetence as a husband and father. When Gladys miscarried her third pregnancy, grief hit him hard. He was still grieving for the death of his mother and everything he did seemed to be wrong. He grew to hate himself for his self-defined weakness.

Like Buddy, Dan experienced nightmares about combat. One night he was strangling Gladys in his sleep until her screaming woke him. The VA could offer only pills, which, combined with alcohol, made his problems worse. He got fired from a sequence of jobs. To pay for his booze he took items from home and sold them for his drink money. He sometimes took Linda and Tommy Lee to bars with him. Gladys was furious. She was working to support the family and he couldn't hold a job. Finally he quit looking. After a year she had her fill. She was afraid that he would seriously harm her or the children, so she threw him out.

Danny had lost so much. He'd lost his buddies in the war, which he never talked about even though he often woke up at night screaming or in a cold sweat reliving the repressed trauma. He had lost his mother, his infant son, and his wife and children. He had lost more than one job. He didn't understand why he couldn't cope with normal life. All he could do was drown his feelings in booze. He kept a poem folded in his wallet and when he felt especially bad he took it out and read it.

The Price

I fought like hell for what I thought was right.

I've marched to the band and felt mighty proud,

Because I was one of the fighting crowd,

And now I'm back in this land of ours.

And will be in my civies in a few short hours.

But somehow or other it all seems bare,

And I feel like hell when people stare,

Lottie's Lot

For some are thinking of loved ones lost,

And others of how much we're going to cost.

Lottie prayed for Danny, too. His aunts and his sister didn't understand what he was going through or know how to help him. If only Buddy and Danny could talk, maybe they could help each other, Lottie thought. But the two young veterans seldom saw each other, and when they did, alcohol dominated their meetings.

CHAPTER 24

Charlotte, Lois, Shirley, Gladys were all excited about the birthday party they were planning for Lottie in April of 1946. Rev. Walker let them use the church hall for a cost of $20 to cover utilities. They hired a caterer for the food. Some Buddy's friends had a small band volunteered to play. They got busy learning some old songs from Lottie's youth, like "Alice Blue Gown," "In the Gloaming," "Goodbye, Sweetheart, Goodbye," "Annie Laurie," "Will You Love Me Then as Now?" and "O Solo Mio."

Lois created an album of pictures of Lottie with her children, grandchildren, and great-grandchildren. She worked diligently and contacted everyone in the family for photos to include.

Shirley sewed her grandmother a new fashionable dress with a matching coat jacket in maroon with pink velvet collar and cuffs. Shirley was almost as good a seamstress as her Gram. She could study an expensive garment in a fancy department store, buy the fabric, and go home and make it for a fraction of the store price. As a result she always looked like she had just walked off Wilshire Boulevard in Beverly Hills. When she had shoes, gloves, and a hat to match, she looked like a movie star.

Charlotte coordinated all the details, including flowers. She asked Ruby to bring and wear her cameo brooch for the party. She had invitations made and sent them to everyone in the family, to church members, neighbors, and friends. She made sure everyone knew it was a surprise and she asked people to be ready to share memories of Lottie. Then she prepared a special present for her mother. Gladys,

Lottie's Lot

Lois, Buddy, and Charlotte decorated the hall with crepe paper garlands and mementos of her life.

Charlotte called Lottie the week before her birthday and invited her out to dinner to celebrate. She said Lois and Buddy would be joining them. Lottie was pleased that her children had remembered her birthday. Shirley dropped by early in the day and presented Lottie with the new dress, which fit her perfectly. She brought new dress shoes and a pocketbook to match. While Lottie was marveling over the outfit, Lois knocked on the door.

"Your hairdresser is here, Ma'am," she called and she fixed Lottie's hair and put a little powder and lip rouge on her cheeks and lips. The birthday girl looked in the mirror and smiled, "Oh my! I wish my Charlie could see me now."

Buddy came by an hour later, clean-shaven, nicely dressed, and sober. "Ma, I've never seen you look more beautiful," he exclaimed. She blushed as he extended his elbow. "May I be your escort, Madam?"

He helped her out to the car. They met at the Brown Derby Restaurant. No one ordered a drink. She was impressed and surprised. They ordered a light entree knowing they had food at the church hall. She had a lovely time. They asked her to tell them stories of their childhood pranks and she had a lot to tell. They laughed at each other's antics.

When it was time to leave Lottie excused herself and said she would meet them at the exit. They had left a generous tip, and as she discreetly passed by the table on her way out she deftly and quickly scooped up the tip and tucked it in her bosom. A few extra dollars was always welcomed. And after all it *was* her birthday.

369

On what Lottie thought, was the ride home, Clarence swung by the Methodist Church, saying he had some papers to drop off. Reverend Walker came out to the car and asked them to come into the hall for a minute while he locked up.

"My! My! Lottie, you look absolutely radiant. Come in."

She followed him in and the others followed her. As soon as she was inside the hall, he flipped on the lights and everyone shouted, ***"HAPPY BIRTHDAY!"***

Clarence and Danny were standing behind Lottie in case she fainted, which she almost did. Reverend Walker gave her the biggest hug she ever remembered getting. Tears ran down her cheeks as she looked around and saw so many familiar faces all beaming at her. She was utterly speechless.

Then she saw Ruby and her family and she really began to cry. Ruby embraced her mother and the cameo brooch Lottie had given her on her wedding day pressed against Lottie's cheek. Lottie kissed the brooch. "I can see that you're taking good care of it," she said. She held Ruby at arm's length. "I can't believe my eyes." Then she hugged Art and said, "Thank you so much for coming and bringing my Ruby and Joyce and Lawrence." She hugged the children, then again looked around at everyone, completely overwhelmed.

She was even more flabbergasted to see two tall young women she didn't recognize, until they introduced themselves as Merle and Lorraine.

Everyone was there except Kenny and his family. He was tied up with union business in Detroit and he wasn't really eager for another confrontation with his sister. He sent a lovely bouquet of flowers and a note congratulating Lottie on her 75th birthday. The band started playing softly. Buddy approached her bowed and said, "May I have this dance?" She took his arm as he glided her across the floor. Everyone clapped as the dance ended. Charlotte got Lottie a chair. Lois took pictures of everything. Chuck brought her a glass of apple juice.

Lottie's Lot

She was so flushed that Charlotte was afraid she would have a heart attack. But she was in seventh heaven and had no plans to let anything bad happen. She wanted the chance to say hello to everyone and thank them for coming.

It was a magical evening for Lottie. She danced with Buddy and Chuck and Clarence and several grandsons. On the dance floor she whispered, "Dear Jesus, if this is a sin please forgive me, but I don't believe you would think this is a sin. I wish I had danced sooner. This is fun"

The food was wonderful. She looked at the photo album and laughed and cried and loved all the pictures.

Then it was time for the birthday cake. The four-layer cake had candles arranged to make the numbers 7 and 5. She made a wish and blew out the candles with the help of a few grandchildren.

While the caterers sliced and served the cake Charlotte said, "Ma, we have something special for you." She went to Lottie with both hands behind her. "Guess which one." Lottie chose one, and Charlotte said "No." She chose the other and Charlotte said, "No! Try again."

The game felt familiar to Lottie but she couldn't quite remember why. She chose yet again and Charlotte handed her a big box wrapped in pink paper and a blue ribbon. With all of her lot of offspring watching, Lottie pulled off the ribbon, saving it for future use, and then tore the paper with abandon, getting a big laugh from everyone. Inside was a smaller box.

She lifted the lid and saw a lovely velvet bag with a drawstring. In it was her precious cameo, the one her children had given her on her birthday in North Dakota, more than 40 years ago. She reached for Charlotte's hand and tears streamed down her cheeks. Then she saw the handwritten note in blue ink in beautiful handwriting. She began reading it out loud.

"Mother. Six letters that spell the sweetest word I ever heard. In all the world there is no other that means as much as that word – M.O.T.H.E.R!

"We all love you and appreciate all that you have sacrificed for us, taught us, and how you stood by us through thick and thin. You are the best mother in the world."

It was signed by Charlotte, Ruby, Lois, Buddy, and the husbands. Danny and Shirley signed, "Best Gram!" and Freddie added, "My favorite Gram ever." Lottie fought back tears of joy.

Charlotte pinned the cameo on the front of Lottie's lovely new dress. Everyone clapped and stood in line to hug her. Lottie had learned to appreciate a good hug and gave them more freely, even if it had taken her 75 years to get the hang of it.

Then it was time to open the rest of her gifts. She sat in a chair in the center of the room and the grandchildren piled them all around her. She had never in all of her life seen so many gifts. Charlotte sat next to her and as Lottie carefully removed each ribbon Charlotte gathered them into a colorful bouquet. She got a new flannel nightgown, face cream, White Shoulders cologne (her favorite), a pretty pair of pearl earrings, and so much more.

Slowly she stood up and raised the bouquet of ribbons above her head. She looked around the room and said, "Every thread that makes up these beautiful ribbons is a thread from my life, and the gifts you gave me tonight are glorified by the connections between us and have made my life complete. Our lives are interwoven as these ribbons are, and together they make a beautiful garland.

"Thank you all for this most wonderful day in my life and for all the threads -- some more colorful than others -- that have made up the bouquet of my life.

Lottie's Lot

"Now this old lady is tired and wants to go home to bed. The band can play music for you young folks. Thanks to all of you for coming."

Clarence, David, and Paul loaded her gifts in Clarence's car and he drove her home. She was still so excited that she couldn't sleep. When she got up to go to the bathroom and looked at the clock it said 4:15 and she hadn't slept a wink. She smiled non-stop for the next week, reliving snippets of wonderful memories from that enchanting evening. Then she sat down and wrote a personal thank you note to everyone who was there.

Lottie spent the next several days reflecting on her life. The 18-year-old girl who had left Cresco on a train with Charlie in her pink taffeta dress and had gone on her long journey to get married. Every detail was still vivid in her mind. She recalled the young girl's proud bearing, her meticulous attention to detail, her belief in perfection. Lottie smiled indulgently, as if the girl were one of her own grandchildren; naively full of the dreams and hopes that young people had.

Meticulousness. That quality had stayed with Lottie as a young wife and mother. But after a few years, she had had to let it go most of the time, when it no longer served her. With so many children and so many unexpected turns of events, it wasn't possible to watch every detail. She could forgive herself for letting go of unimportant niceties.

Perfection. She chuckled. Oh, what a young fool she had been to believe that simply following the rules was all that was necessary. The rules didn't always apply and sometimes you had to make up new rules or variations – her father had never understood that, but Lottie had learned it from her children.

Life was much harder than she'd expected. There was always a struggle for money, for time to herself. Always demands to accommodate everyone's needs. The struggle didn't lead to perfection; it only led to the next day's struggle. That was the only reward for staying in the fight. And she'd stayed in it and given it her best, no matter how hard it got.

Pride. She had pride today. Quite a different kind of pride than what she'd started with but a much better kind. She was proud of her life and her family. Despite all their imperfections, failures, problems, and her disappointments in them, her children and grandchildren loved her. After the party on her 75th she was sure of that. Most of them had grown up to be hard-working, decent, good people. They had served their country, loved their families, educated their children, and paid tribute to her. Even Buddy and Danny, even Shirley -- those whose problems she couldn't fix -- loved her. And she loved them.

What she had learned was that pride and perfection weren't so important. It was family and love that mattered. Charlie had known that from the beginning, but it had taken her 75 years to learn. At least she understood it now. And even though her heart still ached when she thought of Charlie, her first baby boy, her infant granddaughter Mary Jane, and her dear daughters Lillian, Bethany, and Hazel, her pain at losing them was cushioned by her love for them. What a joy to have known them.

In 1953 Clarence was offered a good job as a machinist for a new company in Sonoma, a little north of San Francisco. He and Charlotte loved the cool wine-growing country and decided to move. Charlotte convinced Lottie to move too. She felt closest to Charlotte, the most dependable of her daughters, and she wanted her to be near her. They found a small two-bedroom cottage for Lottie only a few blocks from the home they rented.

Lottie lived almost another 11 years, knitting afghans and socks for everyone in her family, playing solitaire, and receiving frequent visits from them. She enjoyed watching television in the evenings, though she couldn't always understand the jokes people were laughing at on TV. She still found it company and entertaining.

Lottie's Lot

Lois, Shirley, and Gladys and their families came up from Los Angeles to see her several times a year, She received an occasional visit from Ruby or from Kenny's wife, Dorothy, and their children, who still lived in Detroit. She missed Rev. Walker deeply but found a church near her, which she attended regularly until her legs could no longer make the walk.

For Lottie's 83rd birthday in 1954 Charlotte invited her for dinner and asked Lois, Shirley, and Gladys to come. Lottie had been feeling in poor health for a while now and was frailer than ever before. But she had a few surprises of her own in mind for this birthday party.

She went through her jewelry box and selected some treasures from her life to present personally to members of her family. She found some salvaged paper and ribbon and wrapped the cameo brooch she had received and treasured so many years ago for Charlotte. She wrapped up her engagement and wedding rings as a grateful gift for Lois in thanks for her loyalty and love over the years.

Freddie was in the U.S. Army and so were Paul and David. She gave Shirley the railroad watch she had bought for Charlie the first year they were married and asked her to present it to Freddie. She felt closer to this great-grandchild than to any of her grandchildren, and knew he would cherish it and perhaps one day pass it on to his son. She gave Shirley the pearl earrings she got at her 75th birthday party. They looked pretty on her dainty earlobes.

It was a lovely dinner and they told stories about Lottie in her younger days. After she went home she reminisced about again about the 17-year-old girl who was so proud of her sewing and was so much in love with the charming young railroad man who came through town.

She remembered the many things that had transpired in her long life, some sad, some truly tragic, and many happy. All of them helped her to grow into the old woman she was today. Overall she was pleased with the decisions and choices she had made.

Her biggest regret was that she didn't have enough time with her beloved Charlie. He had been gone for almost 50 years and her heart still ached for him at times. And she felt sorrow that she hadn't cherished every day they had together instead of taking them for granted.

If she had it to do over again she wouldn't change much, but she would have been more tolerant with Charlie, more understanding of his side and loved him more. She hoped to join him soon and that thought brought a smile to her face and a flutter to her heart.

Every day she tried to focus on what she was grateful for and sometimes it was just winning at solitaire. But mostly it was for all the loved ones who had touched her life.

She never saw Buddy again, but remembered him in her prayers every night and asked God to keep protecting her boy as he had done during the war. The last she heard of him he was living on skid row in Los Angeles drinking every day.

She took care with her appearance up to her last day. She remained strong-willed and opinionated– some said stubborn – about the things that mattered to her the most.

She died peacefully in her sleep in March 1956, just a month before her 85th birthday.

At her funeral the minister read an appropriate passage:

"Adieu, poor toil worn mother;

There are no more days of pain for you.

Undying vigor and everlasting usefulness

Is your inheritance."

All of her living children and grandchildren attended her funeral service, even Buddy and Danny. She had chosen to be cremated and they put her ashes in a lovely crypt in Santa Rosa, California, with these words on the vault:

Lottie Jane Walker Hastings
1871-1956
Lived a good life
May she finally rest in peace.

The End

Time Line of the life of Lottie Jane Walker-Hastings

Born in Cresco Iowa 4/7/1871 ---Died 3/6/ 1956 Sonoma California at 84 years.

Her parents were James M. Walker who was born in Louisville, Kentucky 7/24/1828 He was 42 years old when Lottie was born. Her mother was Abigail Young born in Malone, Franklin County, New York 5/21/1842 she was 29 when Lottie was born. Her parents were Simon and Charlotte Young who moved to McGregor, Iowa when Abbie was 14 years old in 1856. Both of Lottie's parents had been married previously and both were widowed.

SIBLINGS: Half-brother on her mother's side Delbert Woodworth, Stepsister & Brother on fathers side Mary Walker-Fisk and William Walker. Full siblings Cora Walker-Jennings, Estella

Lottie's Lot

Walker-Patterson, Born 1874, Carrie (Mable) Walker-Lord, and Lee Walker.

MARRIAGE: Married Charles Ira Hastings, date unknown, place about 1887 or 1888 when she was 17 or 18 years old. He was born at Fort Jackson, New York. In May 1867 his parents were Ira Hastings and Rebecca Converse. He had two brothers Elmer Xerces and Loren.

Charles worked for Railroads for most of his career and the couple moved a lot. All of their children were born in different places except for Ruby and Lois who were both born in Denbeigh North Dakota. He was died on September 4, 1911 in Superior Wisconsin while working for the Great Northern Rail Road of a fractured skull. He was working as a brakeman and fell from a boxcar. The "accident" happened at 1:00AM. She was living in Edmonton Alberta Canada at the time of his death.

CHILDREN:

Lillian was born in 1889. Married Robert Goulding Hall in Edmonton, Alberta Canada June 28, 1911. She had one baby daughter who died in January of 1912 and she died of complications of ruptured appendixes on April 3, 1912 and is buried in the city cemetery in Edmonton, Alberta, Canada. She was 23 years old.

Iris Hazel was born in Perry Iowa March 31, 1892. She died in Los Angeles California November 11, 1947 from ovarian cancer. Hazel had 3 children Abigail Charlotte (Changed her name to Shirley) born 12/19/1908 in Denbeigh, North Dakota. George Kenneth Hopf April 5, 1911 in Edmonton, Alberta Canada. (She later changed his name to Kenneth Leroy Vardon), and Daniel Wayland Vardon born. 2/01/1922. At 30 years she was widowed with 3 children. She married

George Fredrick Hopf in 1910, divorced in Detroit in 1920. Married Anthony Leroy Vardon in 1920, Anthony Leroy Vardon, called Roy, died from heart failure on August 10, 1921 and Charles Cleveland Fredericks. (Name Vardon changed to Dardon in this book).

Baby Boy Hastings was born August 7, 1896. Died as an infant from Eclampsia and died August 11, 1896 in Milwaukee and is buried in Wisconsin.

Charlotte R. was born on March 13, 1899 in Milwaukee Wisconsin. She died in Sonoma California in 1984 at age at 85 years. She married Clarence Koehler in 1926 at age 27 and had one son Paul.

Bethany L. was born February 28, 1903. Iron Mountain, Michigan. She married Arnold Randall in Edmonton Alberta Canada about 1920 She had 5 pregnancies in a short time including twins both died before I year old. She died December 27, 1929 at age 26 from a self-inflicted abortion. She left 4 small children behind.

Ruby Ellen was born August 3, 1904 in Denbeigh, North Dakota. She married Arthur Scheue in 1922 and had three children. The oldest son Michael, died in infancy. She had two other children Joyce and Lawrence. She died in 1991 at age 87 at Midland, Michigan

Lois Kermett was born March 9, 1906 in Denbeigh, North Dakota. In 1925 she married Charles Joseph Goulette. She had two sons. She died February 28, 1986 at age 80.

Charles Junior "Bud" was born October 2, 1908 in Minneapolis, Minnesota. He married briefly and died in Los Angeles California in 1976 on skid row of alcoholism.

Deaths & Losses
1896-----Her infant son died after living 4 days in August 7, 1896.
1898-----Her mother died in May of 1898 at age 56. Lottie was 27.
1902-----Her sister Cora died in 1902.

1909-----Her father died in 1909. Lottie was 38.

1911-----Her husband Charles Ira died suddenly from a Rail Road accident on September 4, 1911 when she was 40 years old.

1911-----Her mother-in-law died November, 1911 two months after her son died.

1912-----Granddaughter Mary Jane Hall died in January in Alberta Canada, daughter of Lillian.

1912-----Her oldest daughter Lillian died April 3, 1912 from Appendicitis in Alberta, Canada when Lottie was 40 years old (just five days before her 41 birthday).

1929----- Her daughter Bethany died at age 26 December 27, 1929 when Lottie was 58.

1947-----Her daughter Iris Hazel died November 1947, Lottie was 76.

1956----Lottie Died March 1, at 84 years in Sonoma, California.

Her father was a strict Baptist and her Mother was a Methodist who converted to the Baptist Church after she married James Walker.

Moved:
1888--- 1893 Perry Iowa

1893---Milwaukee, Minnesota

1902---Iron Mountain, Michigan

1904---Denbeigh, North Dakota

1908---Minneapolis, Minnesota

1911---Edmonton, Alberta, Canada

Nancy O'Connor

1915---Detroit, Michigan

1930---Los Ángeles, California

1951---Sonoma, California

ACKNOWLEDGMENTS

About 10 years ago my cousin Linda and I began the quest to learn more about our family history. We talked to relatives, spouses, cousins, researched genealogy records, copied photos for old family albums asked for stories and visited places where our relatives, lived, and died. I Learned so much.

We were a good team and had fun meeting distant cousins, their families and got more stories. We had a few family reunions so our children and grandchildren could meet. I was astonished by some of the stories and happy about others. Initially, I started looking into both sides of my family but no one on my mothers side was interested so I focused on my father's side. Lottie was my father's grandmother. When most of his family moved to California in the early 1930's he stayed behind in Detroit, Michigan so growing up I didn't know that side if my family until we moved to California in 1942 for three years then we moved back to Detroit.

Lottie's Lot

Later after I married I moved to Tucson in 1955, then to Los Angeles in 1958 once again I had the opportunity to connect with aunts and cousins. In 1955 my mother and I visited Lottie and Charlotte in Sonoma just a few months before Lottie died at almost 85.

I want to thank my cousins Linda, Tom, Eddie, Paul, Lawrence, Joyce and David for their contributions. Also Carol Sowell for her collaboration, Nancy Buchannan for her editing and Zorodesigns.com for the cover art. And my heartfelt gratitude to the numerous people who read the manuscript and gave me feedback.